Aidan Redding
Against the
Universes

Forever Falls
Hydrogen Sleets
Drinking Heavy Water
Sticky Supersaturation
No More Lonesome Blue Rings

Michael Warren Lucas

Tilted
Windmill
Press

Copyright Information

Author's Note

The two short stories at the end of this volume are the first Montague Portal tales: Aidan Redding's introduction and the very first Portal tale ever. *No More Lonesome Blue Rings* takes place decades before Redding's birth, but people tell me it must be in this omnibus so here it is.

These were written independently over several years, so minor edits have been made to ensure a consistent, bingeable read.

Redding is not done with me.

My beloved Patronizers (https://patronizeMWL.com) who send me money every month for no good reason: thank you all. A handful of exceptional folks don't merely support me. They shovel money at me. The least I can do is list these grand and glorious folks—Kate Ebneter, Stefan Johnson, Jeff Marraccini, Eirik Øverby, and Phillip Vuchetich—in the ebook and print versions of everything.

For Liz.

Contents

Forever Falls

1

Most universes don't get an official name, only a number, but for obvious reasons everyone called this place Freefall.

This universe also had the messiest corpse I'd ever seen.

Devin Gupper, experimental mathematician and metallurgist, looked like he'd lost an argument with an orbital mass driver. His remnants lay crushed against the steel surface of the Debris Shield. Broken bones jabbed through his torn flesh. Blood dries normally in Freefall, but his uniform was still drenched.

I breathed through my mouth and demanded my stomach still itself. *You will not throw up. You are Aidan Redding, security third and the toughest damn woman in this universe. You volunteered to come out here, and you will* not *throw up.* I insisted that I believed myself, but I felt pretty sure I was lying on all counts.

Security Second Ella Forecourt knelt beside the body, her thin face thoughtful as she studied the wreck of Gupper's body. "I can't say for sure—we need to get him down to Medical and get a proper autopsy." Ella had to raise her voice above her normal papery rasp to be heard above the constant rustle of wind. "But this doesn't look like a beating." The dinner-platter helmet perched on her head made her gaunt frame look even thinner.

"What then?" I really didn't want to take another breath. There's something extra horrible about the smell of a totally broken body, how everything that belongs inside you gets mixed into this gut-stabbing stench. I'd seen bodies before—you couldn't spend your first year out of college working security for the Montague Corporation, exploring and exploiting alien universes with different natural laws, without someone having a heart attack or getting assaulted by antimatter-propelled chipmunks or discovering that the grass would eat your face on alternate Tuesdays.

But Devin Gupper's death was the most spectacular and messy yet.

Forecourt looked up at me. "I'd say he fell."

I couldn't help it. I looked up.

The Debris Shield is a steel awning, about ten meters across and a hundred long, mounted in a long notch hacked in the jagged green-and-gray granite cliff. It reflected the endless sunlight with a brilliant silver shine you could probably see for kilometers. So long as I confined my gaze to the riveted and dent-pocked surface beneath my magnetic boots, I could pretend the steel deck was in a normal facility.

Looking up shattered that illusion.

The cliff goes up forever. No, it doesn't *look* like it goes on forever. It really does. A stone horizon splits the sky and circles around left and right. The sky glares the red of a volcanic sunset.

The whole universe hung sideways. The only solid surface was this vertical cliff, with the Montague facility clinging to its face like a desperate ant.

Fall off the edge and you'll never hit bottom.

Humans couldn't live here. Life couldn't even evolve here. The Portal's mathematical transformations changed us so we could survive, but the only living things in this whole universe were the ones we had brought with us.

Montague engineers hadn't built anything above the Debris Shield. That was the point of the Shield, to protect the facility from intermittent falling pebbles. If a rock came free directly over us, a hundred feet up or a hundred kilometers, it would eventually ping off the Debris Shield instead of my skull. Or anyone else's. The sloping surface encouraged everything to bounce away from the facility below.

I never feared heights on Earth. But this looming, lifeless infinity gnawed at my soul. My magnetic boots and hemp safety line seemed inadequate against forever.

Gupper had disappeared seventeen hours ago. And he reappeared, just now, atop the Debris Shield. Had he climbed the cliff? What for?

"Redding!"

I jerked my attention back. After two months of inspecting cargo and airing the uniform, volunteering to climb onto the Debris Shield had sounded good. Apparently I wasn't up for it yet.

Forecourt looked at me, head cocked. "The sooner you take the pix, the sooner we can get under cover."

Freefall didn't faze Forecourt at all. *Okay, Redding you're second toughest woman here. Still, get your act together!*

I fumbled for the optical camera dangling from my neck. We both wore broad helmets and heavy padded impact suits, but a pebble at terminal velocity would still leave a mark.

Back on Earth, sousveillance cameras would have caught Gupper's impact in life-definition video. If I'd needed actual photos, I would have used optic implants to suck in everything and sort out the good shots later. Digital cameras didn't work on Freefall, let alone implants, and this camera only had thirty sheets of light-sensitive paper. I needed to capture Gupper from every angle in thirty shots, without touching his body and without letting my shadow cross the image, all with equipment three centuries obsolete.

Freefall doesn't have a sun. It has many, a column of giant fuzzy orbs of fuming amber majestically plunging from the top of infinity to the very bottom, out in the middle of the hazy red sky. The red sky behind me, and below. So long as I didn't stand where Gupper and I made a perpendicular line from the cliff, the yellow-red orbs shed enough light for the optical paper to work.

Peering through the tiny glass viewfinder, I framed Gupper's black hair and a shoulder. The camera felt clunky in my gloved hands. At a press of the lever, the camera whirred to release a piece of plastic-coated paper no wider than my hand.

I set the exposed paper on the deck to dry, mindful not to touch the surface where the photograph would appear, and moved on to the next angle.

My magnetic boots clanked at each step. I got halfway around Gupper and had to circle back around to avoid dragging the safety line through the pool of coppery blood drying on the deck.

I'd joined Montague to see the universes, all the universes, not move shattered bodies.

Frame fractured flesh. Click. Whirr.

Thirty pictures isn't enough to really document a death scene, but I split them as best I could. Despite the breeze, when I finished sweat covered my face. My stomach had seethed itself into a turgid knot, but I kept my gorge down even with intermittent surges of bile at the back of my throat.

"Good," Forecourt said as I clicked the last photo, studying the images coalescing on the exposed films. "I can see why Montague put you on camera duty, you have a real eye for this. Now help me get him in the bag and down to Medical, and we'll see if we can figure out how he died."

I'm proud to say all three of us made it off the Debris Shield and behind safety rails before my lunch broke free.

2

Doctor Cleese took one look at Gupper's shattered remains and declared that he'd fallen. He took a few test samples, stuffed my death scene photos into Gupper's medical file, and sent Forecourt and I on our way. I hadn't gotten any blood on myself, but after stripping out of the impact armor I grabbed a quick shower in the locker room just to steam the stench from my sinuses. I came back to my locker, where I'd left my Montague uniform folded on a bench, and found a slip of paper on my khakis. *Find out why Gupper went up there – Forecourt.*

Forecourt supervised Facility security. I guess she had something more important to do than investigate the first accidental death on Freefall since the construction crew dug us into the cliff. I'd met every one of the one hundred and nine—eight people at the Freefall base, and vaguely remembered Gupper as the one of the maniacs who worked in the Diffusion lab, dangling from a zeppelin out in the haze. But a few of the Diffusion folks worked here.

And at least the Diffusion folks were less obsessed than the neutronium miners.

I slipped into my khakis, fastened the brass buckles on my boots, checked that my radio and taser were firmly clipped to my belt, and set out.

Where Medical and Security were buried inside the granite, the Diffusion lab clung to the outside of the cliff, supported steel girders driven a yard deep into the stone and high-tension cables strung up to the next layer of girders. At orientation they told me that the whole facility looked like an old North American pre-conquest cliff-dweller city. Better still, three of the Diffusion lab's walls were clear glass—no, not plasteel, but actual, old-fashioned, so-called "shatterproof" glass. I'd been through here on my orientation tour and never felt the need to return.

The lab was normally quietly busy, the only sounds the occasional power tool or mathematical discussion. Now four people stood in a tight knot amidst lab tables and sample bins and dangling spotlights and tools. Stacked notebooks and binders filled the spaces where computers would sit in a lab on Earth, and shelves of thick paper books lined the inner wall. Computers didn't work on Freefall.

Voices hoarse with grief cut off when I swung the door open.

News traveled faster than I did.

Haider Takamoto, mathematician and director of the Diffusion Lab, turned to face me and visibly steeled his round features. "Da?"

"Hello," I said. "I'm Aidan Redding, from Security. I know this is a hard time, but I need to ask you some questions about Devin Gupper."

"What was he doing up there?" a tiny woman said. Her name danced on the tip of my tongue, but the text over her shirt pocket reminded me.

"Miss Pouter, I was hoping you could help me find out," I said. "He worked with you fairly often."

"About half the time," Takamoto said. "Always the hope to stay here more, but his experiments drag him out to the Hindenbarge, da?"

That Ukraine Union accent can't *be real. Can it?* "What exactly were his duties, Doctor Takamoto?"

Takamoto turned to the other woman in the room.

I knew Doctor Cedar. You couldn't help noticing her. Redheads had become increasingly rare over the centuries, but some fluke of genetic chance had given Cedar copper-bright hair and a frame a handspan too tall for any other woman. A thousand years past, she would have manned the pikes just like the Irishmen around her and dared anyone to argue.

People called her Paddy. But not to her face.

"We were working on titanium," Cedar said, her voice tight. "Building models, floating them out into the diffusion zone, seeing if we could make a strong, stable, diffuse titanium."

"Don't we mostly diffuse steel?" I asked.

She nodded. Tears glistened in her green—*green*—eyes, but the set of her jaw would have cracked anyone else's bones. "Diffuse steel is profitable, but diffuse titanium would have been twenty-eight times so."

"You could have done it," said the fourth person, perched on his padded stool.

Cedar turned to glare at him, anger seeping through every word. "You told him it was stupid at every turn, Marcus."

Marcus shrugged his bony shoulders. "Male bonding." He ran his fingers through his curly Mediterranean hair. "You know. Just.. bullshit." His voice grew soft. "But he knew his stuff, or he wouldna been here. You two woulda whupped it. I had a hundred on next month in the pool."

The Montague Corporation's ridiculous return on investment meant they paid the best salaries in the world, and they were choosy on who they took on board. I had no doubt of Gupper's professional abilities.

Just his climbing ones.

Cedar shuddered, fighting back passions roused by Marcus' ambush of support.

Takamoto reached her side half a heartbeat later. "Is okay to cry." He put a solicitous hand on her shoulder. "Devin deserves a tear."

Cedar's chest shook for a moment, then she turned away from us, letting Takamoto's hand fall.

Takamoto's face flickered through worry, irritation, and distress. His eyes followed Cedar.

I knew the look. He had hopes, hopes involving Cedar and himself. With her unique look Cedar had probably caught the eyes of every man in Freefall, and kept half of them.

"I know it's hard," I said, "but I have to ask. Do any of you know why Gupper went above the debris shield?"

"He wouldn't have," Marcus said. "Not a chance in hell."

"Why?" I said.

"He hated it here," Pouter said, his hands idly twisting a circular slide rule. "Said he wanted solid ground underfoot."

I wished she hadn't said that. For a second I felt the emptiness beneath me. Yes, the facility had half a dozen more levels beneath me. The complex had roots sunk deep into the granite behind me. But for the space of a breath, the endless plummet sucked at my feet.

"We have our own floaters," Pouter continued. "If he ever wanted to go above the shield, he'd check one out and fly up."

"Was he—" Marcus coughed. "Was he wearing climbing gear?"

I thought back. Blood had soaked his clothes, but they'd looked like the usual Montague-issued khakis and loose-fitting shirt. His shoes had been the slip-on gum-soled corporate issue as well. You had to work security or construction to get boots. And the construction guys didn't get the bronze buckles. "No."

Cedar turned to face me. "If Devin got it in his fool head to climb above the shield, he'd have worn armor. He'd have the boots, the ropes, the gloves, the grappling hook gun. Devin liked the toys."

I frowned. "When did you see him last?"

Takamoto said "Yesterday. End of day." A sun, huge and fuzzy, loomed outside, its red light pouring through the tinted window. It had inched down in the few minutes I stood there. Even if that sun set, another hung right above it to take its place. Like so many other universes, our clock was a mutually agreeable fiction.

I peered around the room, trying to look past the work surfaces and drafting tables and hanging metal-working gear. "You said you had floaters?"

"He would not have," Takamoto said. "No."

"Devin didn't even like the zeppelin," Cedar said. "If he wanted something from above the shield, he would have had someone else float up and get it."

"And he had—" I glanced at my watch. "Eighteen hours to find someone to do that."

Cedar's face twisted.

I resisted the urge to pounce. "Excuse me, Doctor?"

Cedar looked like she tasted something bad.

Pouter peered up at Cedar. "Well, out with it!" She flung her hands in the air. "It's not like we don't all know."

Takamoto's eyes grew as round as his face.

"Know what?" said Marcus.

Pouter glanced between the two men. "All right then. The smart ones knew." She snorted. "Everyone with an innie."

"I saw Devin this morning," Cedar said. "Before breakfast."

I carefully didn't notice Cedar's rising blush. Researchers get touchy about those things. "So, about ten hours ago then."

"He said he needed to check some samples here." Cedar's voice sounded quieter than ever. "We were going out to the Hindenbarge today. Devin said he'd meet me in the mess hall."

"Did he?" I asked.

Cedar shook her head.

"You should have said," Takamoto said, forcing a smile over his stormy expression.

"It's not your business," Cedar said. "It's not anybody's business."

It's my business, I didn't say. I can be tactful.

"I did payroll at my desk this morning," Takamoto said. "Was due at noon. Paperwork, always paperwork. He never show up."

"If he had snuck in and flown up," Pouter said, "we would have seen him."

"The floaters have been here all day," Marcus said.

The floor of the Diffusion Lab felt tenuous enough. I wanted to walk back into the nice stable granite.

"I better check these floaters," I said.

3

The Diffusion Lab felt uncomfortable enough, with its glass walls suspended over the infinite void. I did not want to go outside it, into the open air.

But I'd wanted to see the universes. When the job tells you to walk through a door, you walk through it.

Doctor Takamoto led me around a freestanding cabinet to a door where the glass wall met smooth polished green-flecked granite. The glass door swung open at a touch, letting the warm sirocco flow around us as we stepped out onto the steel mesh walkway.

My eyes blinked in the sudden light. This side of the Diffusion lab stuck out further east than any other level of the Freefall facility. The warm wind rising through the walkway smelled of a dusty desert that hadn't seen rain for centuries and never expected to see it again. I instinctively grabbed the steel pipe rail separating the walkway from the long drop all around us.

I kept my eyes on Takamoto.

"Is impressive, nyet?" Takamoto said, raising a hand. "Is closest we get to Forever Falls. Without flying, of course."

You have to speak well to work for Montague. That accent has *to be deliberate. Doesn't it?*

Takamoto's arm pointed up. I had looked straight up earlier today. I intended to never do it again. But I made myself raise my head and follow his arm to look at the waterfall.

The waterfall tumbled from infinitely far overhead, coursing down the granite, splashing and spraying as it bounced between worn crannies of stone. The steaming red light sparkled off the spray, glittering gems that dissolved into the air. You couldn't help but look up, trying to trace its origin, and wind up peering into the infinite sky.

We were close enough to the waterfall to hear water surge and gush as it poured between the rocks. My hands ached to reach for the water, even though it fell meters beyond my reach. The air's parched dryness made the torrent feel like a taunt.

I'd heard the reverse physicists arguing about the waterfall over dinner more than once. The flowing water should have dissolved into spray, and then into vapor, within a few kilometers of wherever it started. The fact that it didn't meant that they didn't understand Freefall's physical laws as well as they thought they did.

Montague researchers had taken zeppelins up almost forty kilometers and down another forty, where the hazy air made the facility invisible and the electromagnetic interference made radio communication almost impossible. The waterfall ran all the way. As far as we could tell, the waterfall ran forever.

I traced the waterfall down, seeing it skip and splash from eternity to a point where it felt I should be able to touch it, and then receding again back down into forever—

—and I stared into the abyss.

It's one thing to look up and see the cliff face recede into eternity. You can look to left and right and see the cliff marching on and on. But most of us, when we look down, have that little monkey part of the brain that starts shrieking *There's no ground.*

There. Is. No. Ground.

The cliff face descends forever.

The only thing beneath the metal walkway was burnt amber sky.

For a split second, my mind tried to convince itself that I was sideways, lying on the ground. But that didn't work either. The cliff was too flat, the pull of gravity too strong.

One wrong step and I'd fall. Into the sky.

My stomach knotted again, and my hands clamped around the railing. My pulse hammered in my ears even as my breath froze solid.

Takamoto said something.

I tried to swallow, and couldn't.

The breeze flowed past me, rising. No, it wasn't rising. My gut plummeted, we were all falling—

Something seized me and shook.

I jerked.

Takamoto had his arm around my bicep. "Redding!" His Ukraine accent made my name almost unintelligible.

I met Takamoto's eyes. Sweat soaked the back of my shirt and my armpits, and tension strained my every muscle. My head quivered on my neck. The warm breeze suddenly felt cool over my face.

On my first day in Freefall, Pete from HR took me to the observation deck at the edge of the dirigible hangar and let me have a good look. This second look hadn't been any better.

"I am sorry." The accent faded. He sounded almost gentle. "You learn to ignore it. We do, at least." His lips twitched downward. A touch of bitterness leaked back into his voice when he added "Most of us."

I drew a shaky breath. "It's okay." Had Takamoto truly forgotten what most of us felt looking down the cliff? Or had his disappointment over Cedar and Gupper led him to minor cruelty?

"This way," he said, holding a hand along the walkway.

The metal balcony circled the Diffusion lab. I clutched the steel pipe rail as we turned the corner and started along the long way. The Debris Shield loomed floors above us like an awning, but offered no shade whatsoever from the horizontal suns.

"I come out here at lunch," Takamoto said. "This morning, breakfast. Sit on edge, let my feet dangle over, watch water fall. Peaceful." He chuckled. "Lost a shoe once. Supply clerk most upset. Had to insist I was *very* sure shoe not lost in quarters."

I kept my eyes on his back.

The floaters were at the far side of the balcony, on a wide launch platform. Each had a battery pack and two meter-wide fans, one pointed back, the other up. You would wear a flight suit and a self-packing parasail, letting the one fan blow you up and the other push you forward. It wouldn't work on Earth, but on Freefall, floaters were the easiest way to maneuver around the cliff. You stood on the platform, tugged the parasail trigger, and let the fans carry you away.

The Diffusion lab had two floater racks. Both floaters had a locking plastic strap with a date tag around its frame, tying it to the launch platform. Someone could take a floater any time they needed, but then a Transit flunky would replace the tag. Without computers, and with radio spotty at more than a couple kilometers, the facility relied on these kinds of tricks to keep track of equipment use.

Nobody had used the one floater for a week, the other for three days.

Takamoto glanced at me, then at the floaters, and shook his head. "However he got up there," Takamoto said, "it wasn't with our floaters."

I glanced at the window. The glass reflected my silhouette, surrounded by the glare of the falling suns. Inside that room were three people who insisted that Gupper would not have climbed above the shield.

I'd have to check the rest of the floaters, but I was beginning to think they were right.

Gupper would have only gotten up above the Debris Shield if someone had taken him there.

If I planned to meet a new lover for breakfast, I wouldn't have gone climbing or floating.

That meant someone must have taken Gupper up there.

Someone knew how he died. I could only think of one reason for them to keep silent.

Gupper hadn't fallen.

He'd been pushed.

4

Gupper had last been seen around seven AM. His body had appeared on the Debris Shield at half past four. Nine and a half hours. I spent another hour gathering and checking facts before rapping on Security Second Forecourt's door. My feet hurt and my eyes ached in their sockets. I'd been up early to start a long day, and if Forecourt granted my request it promised to be longer.

"Come in."

Forecourt's granite-walled office barely fit her, the raw granite desk, and two uncomfortably rickety office chairs. When adding a cubic inch means carving it out of granite, every space is as small as possible. Air tainted with machine oil whispered through a narrow ceiling vent. Two pole lamps in the corners shed light, which reflected off the unpolished green and gray ceiling. Every time I came here, I fought the urge to shade my eyes against the glare.

"Redding." Forecourt put her blue pencil down next to the paper on her desk. Earth ran on computers, but those of us in Montague grew accustomed to places where computers didn't work. "Report."

I stood straight and clasped my hands behind my back. "I've talked to Gupper's team, Surveillance, and Transit."

Forecourt's eyes bore into the point just between and above my eyebrows. "And?" Quiet background music would have smothered her soft voice.

"Something doesn't make sense, ma'am."

"Do tell."

"Gupper's team insists that he wouldn't have climbed up. He hated leaving the building. And he wasn't wearing climbing gear."

"But he was up there."

"I've checked with Transit. All the floaters are accounted for."

Forecourt leaned back in her chair. "So he must have climbed."

"I spoke with both daytime operators. Neither saw anything."

"The cameras don't have perfect coverage." The Montague Corporation's total border paranoia policy was somewhat relaxed in lifeless universes. "And we can't record."

"But there's cameras pointing straight down all three ladders above the Shield. And the daily reporting keeps the camera crew mostly alert."

"What about the overnight crew?" Forecourt asked.

"Gupper was seen by a member of his team before breakfast today." I shifted my feet. It had already been a long day.

She raised a thin finger to tap her lips. "Indeed. And why didn't this person say so earlier?"

"Doctor Cedar felt that the way she saw him was none of our business." I gave a thin smile.

"I see. And were you able to corroborate her story?"

"One of the canteen crew, McDevitt, reported seeing him this morn. Gupper grabbed a coffee on his way to the lab. He was whistling."

"And the canteen crew didn't report him?"

"McDevitt didn't realize who it was until I showed him a photo. Not those photos, ma'am."

Forecourt arched an eyebrow. "I assumed not *those* photos, Redding. The ones you took this morning didn't show Gupper's face except as an imprint in the back of his skull."

I fought the blush that threatened to creep up the back of my neck. I'd learned to control my attitude when I wanted something, but Forecourt could snark at her subordinates all she wanted. "Yes, ma'am."

"So," Forecourt said. "He wouldn't have climbed up, he wasn't dressed to climb, and he didn't take a floater. Do you think he hitched a ride on a zeppelin, and it detoured so he could jump out?"

"The last people who saw him reported he was happy," I said. "He wouldn't have jumped."

Forecourt snorted. "Are you saying—you are, aren't you? You think he was—" The corner of her mouth quirked. "—*pushed*?"

"Ma'am."

"Okay then." The smile came out of hiding. Forecourt leaned forward, put her elbows on her desk, and steepled her fingers. "What do you want to do about it?"

I took a deep breath. "A zeppelin arrived this morning and left an hour later. If anyone on the flight in had seen anything, the passengers would have said something. But six people, counting the pilot, flew back. And nobody's been back since."

"So you want to meet the next zeppelin and talk to any of those six who come back, then catch the flight out the next day."

"No, ma'am. I want a zeppelin to the Hindenbarge now."

The snort became a laugh. "A special?"

"Ma'am, those people might come back by ones and twos all week long. If I have to talk to them one at a time it will take days. I'll have to wait until there's a morning none of them come back, and catch the zeppelin then."

"I could send word with the next zeppelin. Tell them to come back the next morning."

My spine twitched with added tension. "The longer I wait, the longer they have to get a story together."

"And you're going to interrogate them," Forecourt said. "Oh, that's right, your degree is Criminal Justice, isn't it? Do they still do the virtual interrogation thing?"

"Virtual and role-play." *Oh, that sounds* great, *Redding. Now tell her you dressed up in a cowboy hat to play Thugs and Natives with the neighborhood kids.*

"Well, then, you have it all sorted out, don't you? Well, we have spare zeppelins, and those pilots just hang around picking their toenails. You can carry some messages for me while you go. Wear your metal-free uniform."

I felt a surge of victory, then Forecourt said "Tell me, Redding. Have you ever been to the Hindenbarge?"

"No, ma'am."

"They have their own security detail out there. And Security Second Lundbaugh is not as warm and fuzzy as I am." Forecourt's smile evaporated. "You will *not* make us look bad."

I fought back a grin. "Yes, ma'am." I'd grab my best uniform and pull out my fancy etiquette.

"That means," Forecourt said, "no puking your guts out over the rail. Again."

5

Freefall had large zeppelins, even huge ones for cargo and large numbers of crew, but the four-passenger was the smallest we had. Woven wicker and bamboo formed the walls. Thin foam pads covered in blue cotton were tied to the wicker seats to provide a small amount of protection. The zeppelin had round portholes almost large enough to stick my head through, but the wicker covers were pulled tight, leaving the gondola lit only with the sunlight that seeped between the weave.

I'd lost lunch and missed dinner, so my stomach threatened to implode my abdomen any time now. A kind word to the canteen staff got me a box dinner, fried chicken with an extra serving of roasted potatoes and slaw. Normally I wouldn't touch anything that greasy and heavy, but I felt ready to eat a camel if anyone had one handy. Duffel bag in one hand, boxed dinner in the other, I ducked my head to get through the hatch and discovered Takamoto and Cedar, sitting side by side in the front of the gondola, facing the rear door.

"What are you doing here?" I blurted.

I shouldn't have been surprised. When you don't have wireless networks, when you don't have implants or datalinks, when you don't even have computers, the fastest communication you have is gossip. And we got by on raw gossip for hundreds of thousands of years.

Takamoto said, "Someone has to tell the rest of the team about Devin."

"We heard about the emergency zeppelin," Cedar said. "It had space, and—well, telling Kirk and George and Lyssa won't get any easier tomorrow."

I should have told Forecourt I wanted a private zeppelin. Getting information out of this morning's passengers would be difficult enough without the Diffusion team so upset. With my luck, though, Forecourt would have told me to take a floater. *Just fly straight into the sun, you can't miss it.*

I shifted my way through the hatch. The floor hardly gave at all underfoot. I tried not to think about what would—or, more precisely, wouldn't—be beneath us once we took off, and tried to make myself comfortable in one of the remaining chairs. The bottom felt comfortable, but the back only came up to the bottom of my shoulder blades. A rack of glass eye goggles with silk straps hung on one wall. The cozy space smelled of bamboo and wood polish, with a growing note of fried chicken that my stomach threatened to lunge at. "No cargo?" I said.

"We have clean uniforms on the Hindenbarge," Takamoto said.

So, Doctor, you do know the word 'the.' "They let you have the weight?"

Cedar said, "They have cargo steel out there. Thirty pounds of personal effects for each of us isn't a big deal. And that's Facility pounds, not Hindenbarge pounds."

An older man with a mustache you could sweep floors with stuck his head in the hatchway. "You Miss Redding?"

"Yes."

His lip curled. "Good. Welcome aboard the *Tahiti Sunset*. That makes you Cedar and… Takamoto."

Cedar nodded.

He knelt through the hatch and pulled the door shut behind him. "I'm Mitch MacConnor. You've been through the zeppelin passenger training, right?"

We all nodded.

"Well, too bad. You get a reminder now."

Cedar sighed. "We always do."

"And you always will," MacConnor said. "You each have a chute box under your seat. Get it out and put it on." He pointed at the harness he wore. "Straps under the groin, around the waist, over the shoulders."

The chute box was about the size of a thick paper equipment manual, but lighter than it seemed it should be. Takamoto and I had no trouble slipping into the silk straps and fastening the bamboo buckles, but Cedar had to crouch to keep her head from the wicker ceiling.

"These are self-folding, self-expanding chutes," MacConnor said intently.

"Yes, we know," Takamoto said.

MacConnor glared at Takamoto. "Pay attention again. You are about to go thirty kilometers in a wicker basket. A wicker basket designed to break apart."

I blinked. "Excuse me—break apart?" My voice didn't quite squeak.

MacConnor grinned. "They don't put it that way in training, do they? No, it's all 'in case of emergency.' Well, let me tell you. We can't trust structural steel out at the Hindenbarge, so the zeppelins are structural bamboo. Under a silk hot air bag." He cupped his hands together at right angles as if cradling a small bird. "If something goes wrong, if the bag blows, do you want everyone trying to fit out that little hatch? Or would you rather the cabin—" He gently let his hands come apart, opening them wide. "—clam-shell apart, nice and smooth?"

"If that happens," he continued, "steer yourself clear of the debris. You had the parachute training, back on Earth?"

"Sure." I'd enjoyed it. Even the part when they said *Now fall five thousand feet before opening your chute, and steer yourself left and right.* Each time I'd felt exhilarated from the moment I jumped, to when I again touched ground, all the way through dinner with my class afterwards.

"These chutes aren't floaters," MacConnor said. "But they're big. You get out from under the debris before you open up, and they'll slow you right the hell down, what with the upbreeze. And they stand out on radar. A blimp burst will get every radar on both sides screaming. You'll have zeppelins on you in less than an hour. You won't drop a kilometer." He eyed me up and down. "Small as you are, you might even rise a little. Whatever you do, don't steer. Steering makes you drop faster, so you leave the pedals alone. Let the zeppelins come to you."

"But that hasn't happened," I said.

"Not for, oh, must be two years now," MacConnor's mustache grinned. "Hey, girl, don't look like that. The bag blows, the clamshell dumps you clear instantly. It's all mechanical. This stuff works, or I wouldn't do it. Montague pays good, but my hide is worth more than that."

"Right," I said.

"You just keep that chute box on," MacConnor said. "It's amazing stuff. Light, strong, made out of omnifold fiber. Those things can be used a million times and they'll still work just like new. And they're reflective—they stand out against the red for three or four kilometers. Human terminal velocity without the chute is about eleven hundred kilometers an hour, but so long as you have a chute box, you'll be fine."

Cedar said "We've had someone on every flight since the Hindenbarge opened. Everybody's come back safe."

"Vell," Takamoto said, "Marcus *did* hurt leg when clamshell—"

Cedar elbowed his ribs, not gently.

MacConnor double-checked the latch behind him. "Just to be safe, buckle in." He grabbed the ladder to the pilot's loft. "I'll leave the roof hatch open so you can hear me, but it's not an invite. You want a view, open a window."

"Relax," Cedar said. "It's fine. Sit down and eat your dinner, you look like you're starving."

I plopped back into my seat, staring at the box of fried chicken. "You know, I don't think I'm hungry anymore."

6

The wicker basket swayed gently around me, tickling primordial sense memories of rocking in a cradle or in my mother's arms. My abandoned dinner's aroma faded, leaving the scents of clean polished wood laced with machine oil and dust. The zeppelin's old-fashioned electrical drive ran even quieter than the whoosh of the great bamboo fans it drove.

Leaning my shoulders against the woven wall, head back, eyes closed, I tried to rest my tired eyes and aching head. I'd awoken at six AM, and it would be nine PM before the zeppelin hit the Hindenbarge. If the passengers from this morning's flight were awake and available, I had more hours of talking to them before I could sleep. I needed to conserve energy, especially my mental energy. And every time my mind strayed to what lay beneath us, I had to remind myself that we weren't that far up, and if we had trouble the zeppelin could just gently ease itself to the ground.

I am total crap at lying to myself.

By shifting around, I found a spot where the wicker ends didn't gouge my scalp and shoulder too badly, so long as I kept my weight on them. The only sounds were the whirring of the blades, wind softly whistling through the weave, and Cedar's and Takamoto's quiet whispers.

Maybe I fell asleep.

A distant voice shouted, then Cedar said "Redding? You awake?"

"She's asleep," Takamoto said.

I heaved my head upright, trying to ignore the stale taste of my mouth. "No," I yawned, "I'm up."

"Goggles," Takamoto said. "On the wall, by your seat."

"You'll want to see this," Cedar said.

My back muscles ached as I fumbled for the goggles. Our basket swayed and rocked, and my stomach rolled with it.

I barely had the smoked glass goggles over my eyes when Cedar swung aside a panel in the basket's front wall. A three-foot glassless window framed the Hindenbarge.

Imagine the most monstrously huge balloon you've ever seen.

Now imagine dozens of them, hundreds, all clustered together like grapes. Platforms hung beneath the balloons, all different shapes and sizes: some cubes, some flat boxes, some dangling lines and derricks. Lines and cables and scaffolds connected the whole assembly.

One of the suns hung right behind the Hindenbarge, silhouetting the whole thing in fuming reds and oranges. The dangling platforms and bulging air sacs cast shadows kilometers deep.

Takamoto grinned at my expression. "Impressive, *da*?"

I couldn't figure out its size. Without any ground, without any clouds, without being able to see any humanizing details, I couldn't process its scale.

The zeppelin's bamboo prop blades whooshed overhead just as much as ever, pushing us through the endless sky. Wind through the window ruffled my hair back. And the Hindenbarge didn't grow any bigger.

"They keep adding to it," Cedar said. "Earth wants all the molecular-diffused steel they can get."

"How big is that?" I asked.

"One thousand seven hundred meters, end-to-end," Takamoto said. "All genetically engineered structural bamboo."

Behind the smoked glasses I blinked. "There's really no metal out there?"

I realized my mistake half a second too late. Never ask a specialist about their field unless you're hoping they'll handle both sides of the conversation for you.

Takamoto straightened his back and actually reached for the suspenders he didn't have on. "Freefall has scalar matter coherence. Out there," he waved, "steel grows weak. Ten kilometers further in—*if* you go quickly enough, it diffuses. Expands." He formed an inflating balloon with his hands. "And we, we mathematically predict diffusion patterns."

"It works the same the other way," Cedar said. "Dig into the cliff, and everything gets more solid. Everything more than two klicks deep is solid neutronium. They—"

"They are nothing," Takamoto said. "They try for *years* to dig neutronium. They get nothing! Never will. But out here? My team? A rod like this," Takamoto said, holding his hands about a foot apart, "cut just right, it inflates—*pow!*—into I-beam. I-beam stronger than plain beam, and weighs *seven kilos*. On Earth!"

"I'd like to see that," I said.

Cedar said "The—"

"So would we all," Takamoto said over her, oblivious to Cedar's sudden glare. "Two kilometer past the Hindenbarge, your body come apart. Is also mathematically predictable. You look like squidodactyl. We use dirigibles, bamboo clockwork, to control the steel diffusers."

Takamoto burbled on, while I sat back in my chair and stared at the slowly growing platform.

I'd seen diffused steel before. Everyone on Freefall had. But I hadn't appreciated how we made it until I saw the Hindenbarge. It looked too big to be real. And it couldn't be real, on Earth.

We'd built a wonder in the sky.

In another universe's sky.

This was why I'd joined Montague. If it meant I had to help scrape some poor bastard off the Debris Shield, it was totally worth it.

One of the smaller balloons moved independently. I blinked, and suddenly my eyes made sense of them. That balloon was a zeppelin, one of the huge cargo zeppelins, with bundles of diffused steel dangling from its belly. It swam past us like a whale ignoring a flounder, but up in the minuscule perch for the pilot I made out a speck waving at us.

That zeppelin was bigger than all of the Facility. It would dock far below the floors where we ate and worked, offloading cargo to be lugged through the Portal back to Earth.

"You have to be careful," Cedar said. "If you cut the stock wrong, it'll diffuse badly. Nobody wants an I-beam with sharp edges, it'll have your arm off before you notice. We have a few of the really good ones back in the office."

"They have to be at office," Takamoto said. "Leave steel here more than a week, it gets weak. Diffusion needs speed. Out here, just—" he shrugged "—rots."

"The people trying to dig far enough into the cliff to get neutronium have been at it for ten years now," Cedar said. "Our department's profits have covered the last eight of that, and projects in a dozen other universes too."

MacConnor brought us to the Hindenbarge so smoothly I hardly knew we'd connected. One moment our basket swayed, then the motion stopped. I let out a deep breath and unbuckled.

"Careful!" MacConnor said, dropping through the ceiling hatch. He came down the ladder using only his hands, letting his feet swing free into the room. "If *I* weigh twenty kilos here, Miss Redding, *you* weigh about a sneeze."

I stopped, then carefully undid the belt.

Cedar unbuckled, laid her forearm over her head to protect it from the ceiling, then stood. I followed her example, and rose so quickly that my feet left the ground. My forearm was squeezed between my head and the ceiling, and then I settled back down.

"Light steps," MacConnor said. "You'll get it."

My duffel bag weighted less than one of the boots I'd left in my quarters.

MacConnor untied the rear hatch and held it open for me. "Thank you for flying *Tahiti Sunset* airlines."

I followed MacConnor out onto the dock.

The basket sat on an enclosed platform of structural bamboo. The zeppelin's glowing underbelly formed the ceiling, glowing in white and pink from diffused light. Sunlight streamed through gaps between the bamboo struts behind us, and the breeze carried hot metal and burning wood.

A man loomed on the platform, wearing a Montague Security uniform with the blue epaulets of a Second. His chin looked like it could do double duty as a plow and his eyes shone with energy, but stubble darkened his face and he'd combed his dark brown hair with his fingers.

"Security Third Redding," he said in a voice like a rock crusher, stepping forward and holding out his right hand.

"Mister Lundbaugh, sir?" I reached to take his hand.

He harrumphed. "You have a message from your supervisor, I *hope*."

"Oh!" I jerked my hand back and fumbled in my pockets. The white envelope from Forecourt was in my right thigh pocket, slightly bent but still sealed.

Lundbaugh took it from me impatiently, tore it open with a thumb. His bushy eyebrows crawled closer together as he read. "I was ready for bed."

"Sorry, sir," I said.

Cedar waved one hand in farewell as she and Takamoto slipped out a side door. MacConnor had already vanished.

"So," he drawled. "You're here to talk to the morning zeppelin passengers. We start work early out here, but don't worry—I'll get them rousted for you."

The information I'd gathered earlier suddenly felt completely irrelevant. I'd made a huge deal out of this for nothing. Yes, I couldn't make sense of the facts, but someone smarter could. Gupper had died of misadventure, a normal ordinary misadventure. He must have. Pushing any other explanation would only make me a bigger fool and wreck what little career I had. "It could wait for morning, sir."

"Oh, no!" Lundbaugh showed his teeth. It wasn't a smile. "We can't have anyone missing their flight back in the morning. If I'm up, *everyone's* up." He folded Forecourt's message into a neat square. "Besides, this might be a *serious* crime you're here about. It's not just an industrial accident. Got to take it *serious*. Urgent, even."

I wanted to slink away.

But, dammit, the facts *didn't* make sense.

"If the radio had worked," Lundbaugh said, "I could have saved you the trip. This morning's zeppelin arrived just fine. On time. They certainly didn't stop to—" he smirked "—throw anyone overboard."

ㄱ

The Hindenbarge had its own rhythm, a slower sway than the tiny zeppelin, a private tide formed of shifting silk and flexing bamboo and creaking hemp, an inexorable inertia that you had to accept before you could walk. The platform's slow rotation skewed every movement: every dropped object landed just a little bit off target, every door closed a little too enthusiastically or lethargically. I found myself grateful for my gum-soled shoes, offering me a little extra traction on bamboo decks and ladders even while reduced weight nibbled at friction.

But I got answers.

The morning zeppelin—yesterday morning's zeppelin, by the time I finished—had a completely uneventful flight. Nobody on the flight had seen Devin Gupper. They hadn't detoured above the Debris Shield.

At almost one in the morning, I released tired and confused scientists and mechanics to the custody of their beds. When I told Lundbaugh I'd finished, he huffed and scowled and pointed me to a hammock. My pilot was asleep, returning to the Facility didn't demand urgency, and the *Tahiti Sunset* had to recharge for the journey home anyway. Zeppelins could only do about forty kilometers on a charge.

The weave and tide of the Hindenbarge rocked me to dreamless sleep.

A support clerk shook me awake too soon to tell me that the *Tahiti Sunset* would leave for the Facility in half an hour. He brought me a sandwich, a cup of coffee, and a sealed envelope from Lundbaugh, for Forecourt.

I made it to the dock with four minutes to spare. Cedar was already there, an Irish warrior from before the Oil Age, trying not to catch her red hair in the wicker ceiling and looking even more bleary-eyed than I felt. "Doctor Cedar," I said.

She nodded. "Redding. How was your trip?"

Useless and stupid. "Necessary." I strapped the chute box onto my back and took my seat. Last night's boxed dinner still sat on the floor, its fried chicken and potatoes and butter certainly congealed and festering. I'd have to remember to take it out when I left. "How was yours?"

Cedar heaved out a breath. "Rough. Everybody—" Her voice cracked. She took a moment to steady herself and said, "Everybody liked Devin. I mean, he was a good guy. Not one of those people with a rough outside but they're okay when you get to know them. I mean, he honestly gave a damn. He wanted everyone to be successful. Did you know he wrote half a dozen Diffusion monographs, but he made sure he wasn't the only one listed as author? Kirk can't write a grocery list without doing thirty drafts to try to make it coherent, but he's a hell of a mathematician. Devin made sure he got credit on every single paper based on his work, though."

"He sounds like a decent guy," I said.

"He was."

Takamoto stuck his head in the door. "Good morning."

"Doctor," I said.

"Miss Redding. You have good trip?"

"I did what I had to do."

"And Lucy," Takamoto said. "How are you today?"

Cedar shrugged. Devin's death had hit her hard.

My trip hadn't been wasted, I told myself. A negative result is still a result. And Gupper's death still didn't make sense. How had he gotten up high enough to die splattered across the Debris Shield?

And I knew too many Montague scientists who would steal every scrap of credit they could get in hope of being assigned more glamorous problems. Freefall was one of Montague's successes, but not much in the way of cutting-edge research happened there beyond the ongoing failure of the neutronium project. Gupper sounded like a rare creature, one worth keeping.

MacConnor came in, took us through the pre-flight instruction, and we set out for the Facility, the cliff, and solid ground. After the Hindenbarge's majestic tides, the rocking of the *Tahiti Sunset*'s rickety basket dangling beneath the silk hot air bag unnerved me even more than it had on the flight out. Although I hadn't eaten, my lurching stomach dissuaded me from testing the sandwich.

I closed my eyes and focused on the facts of Gupper's death rather than the endless emptiness beneath.

Devin Gupper had fallen to his death on the Debris Shield. I made myself review his impact, trying to set aside the blood and broken bone and visualize how he'd hit. He'd landed almost perpendicular to the cliff, his head about a meter from the granite, arms outstretched in a Y. The impact had been so hard he'd deformed, his torso flattening, body bulging out at the sides, the front of his skull destroyed. The corpse slid half a meter down, until a gum-soled shoe and a sleeve had caught on separate rivets.

I must have chewed that image for half an hour as the dirigible slid through the sky at a breakneck thirty kilometers an hour, trying to make sense of it. He'd fallen out of the sky, somehow, and hit at an incredible speed.

Cedar and Takamoto spent the time arguing about rescheduling work assignments. I got the impression that Takamoto was trying to give Cedar something more immediate to focus on, instead of Gupper's death.

"I think you should give Marcus a chance with the titanium diffusion," Cedar said.

Eleven hundred kilometers an hour was terminal velocity for a human being in freefall on Freefall. How far would you have to fall to reach that speed? I'd have to figure it out sometime.

"Marcus is good," Takamoto said, "but I really need him on the coupler math."

How long would it take someone to fall that distance?

What did Gupper think as he fell?

"The coupler project is really straightforward," Cedar said. "I mean, it's almost a waste of his time."

Everyone did parachute and free-fall training before coming to Freefall. With enough distance, Gupper could have steered himself away from the Debris Shield.

"Is easy income," Takamoto said.

Had Gupper aimed himself at the Debris Shield?

"It's not all about income," Cedar said.

Maybe I should get MacConnor to take a detour. We could go up the cliff above the Debris Shield. Surely MacConnor knew how far someone would have to fall to hit that hard.

"Is all about income," Takamoto said. "We make Freefall even more profitable, we choose next assignment. I help you myself."

MacConnor had a certain flair to him. Maybe I should see if he wanted to get dinner tonight.

"Devin and I had that project for two years," Cedar said. "I'm not letting you swoop in at the end and grab credit."

But MacConnor's mustache, it could double as a paintbrush.

"Devin will get full credit," Takamoto said. "Is smallest we can do. You look through his papers. See what he did not finish. Team will split up, he gets credit on all he touched. He has two boys on Earth, they can use royalties."

The pilots probably had rules against diverting without letting either the Facility or the Hindenbarge know. We should probably dock first. Let Cedar and Takamoto off, let MacConnor file a flight plan, then the two of us could go up and look at the cliff.

Cedar sighed. "Sorry, I didn't mean to snap like that. It's just..."

No, I needed to check in with Forecourt. That would not be fun.

"Is hard," Takamoto said quietly. "Is hard for us all."

If I wanted to look at the cliff over the Debris Shield, Forecourt would probably tell me to take a floater. The thought made my stomach clench like a fist. I'd have something under me the whole way—the Debris Shield. I'd only stood on the Shield once, so that wasn't a pleasant thought.

Cedar and Takamoto were quiet for a moment.

Either my pride or my dignity was done. I'd ask for MacConnor to take me up in the *Tahiti Sunset*. And it had nothing to do with MacConnor, he was just the only pilot I knew and I didn't want to throw up while riding a floater.

But that mustache.

"If we really want to push on titanium diffusion," Cedar said, "maybe we can get someone to take care of the neutronium calculations they have me doing."

I couldn't help imagining my own puke spattering on the Debris Shield. At terminal velocity.

"*Da*," Takamoto said. "I try again. As soon as I finish payroll today, I help you."

My pulse suddenly thrummed in my temples.

Adrenaline surged in my veins.

This is not the place.

My head wanted to jerk up, but I made it stay still. I didn't even breathe deeply or let my eyes open.

We hung in a rickety wicker basket dangling over infinity. I don't care how well a wicker basket is made—if you're suspended from a balloon over a literally bottomless drop, it's rickety.

But Doctor Cedar, too smart for her own good, said "Payroll was due yesterday, though."

"Payroll? *Da*, payroll," Takamoto said. He spoke too quickly. "I mean other paperwork."

My shoulders wanted to rise, but I forced them to remain still. Accept that, Cedar. Do not argue here, in a picnic basket, dangling over forever.

"You always said payroll was last," Cedar said. Her voice turned suspicious. "What were you *really* doing yesterday morning?"

"What are you implying?" Takamoto said.

Crap. I opened my eyes and slowly sat up, as if awakening again. "Sorry, I must have drifted off." Maybe that would cool off the discussion.

Takamoto's face burned bright red. He glared at Cedar.

Cedar didn't flinch.

For a moment we sat there, three figurines in a basket.

Then Cedar looked at me and said, "Doctor Takamoto lied about where he was when Devin disappeared."

Takamoto said "Unacceptable!" He wrenched off his seat belt and flung it aside. The buckle bounced harmlessly off Cedar's thigh. "I do not have to sit here and take accusation from subordinate!"

"Wait," I said. "Hang on, let's talk this out." One hand went to my own safety belt. I didn't want to fire my taser sitting down. The *Tahiti Sunset*'s cramped basket was no place to subdue someone, but I'd need all the maneuverability I could get.

Takamoto said "I will not be accused!"

Cedar said "I just asked—"

Takamoto whirled and grabbed the ladder leading to the pilot's loft.

"Takamoto, no!" I said flinging my own belt aside.

Takamoto scrambled up the ladder and out the loft hatch.

Cedar looked at me, brows furrowed beneath her shocking red hair.

MacConnor shouted something angry, but the wind carried away his words.

I grabbed the ladder, leaned close to Cedar, and stage-whispered, "Don't have this fight here. Apologize. Wait for us to land."

Her frown intensified, then understanding lit her face as she touched the wicker wall next to her.

I nodded, then hoisted myself up a rung on the ladder.

MacConnor's next shout carried naked rage.

I scuttled up two bamboo rungs, grabbed the edges of the hatch, and heaved myself up just in time for MacConnor to collapse on top of me.

Blood smeared across my face.

⊟

I stood on the bamboo ladder at the hatch for half a second, paralyzed.

MacConnor had toppled on top of me, his chest smashing against the crown of my head and crushing me back down the ladder. We were about halfway between the Hindenbarge and the Facility, but he weighed more than I could lift with my neck.

My hands were still above the hatch, where I'd been about to hoist myself into the pilot's nest. I flailed out, stretching, trying to grab something, anything. The bamboo deck slipped across my fingertips, then my left hand caught a gap. I dug my fingers between bamboo strips to anchor myself to the top of the ladder.

Sticky blood covered my forehead, my cheek. The smell of copper filled my nose. My stomach clenched even harder.

Beneath me, inside the zeppelin's tiny wicker passenger space, Cedar shouted in surprise.

MacConnor's chest heaved.

The whole zeppelin shuddered and twitched around us, stressing every fragile connection. Structural bamboo—a total contradiction. This was a ramshackle deathtrap, and our pilot was bleeding, maybe dying.

Gripping my unseen anchor more tightly, I heaved myself up. MacConnor cried out in pain, then rolled to the side. My head emerged into open air.

The pilot's loft hung in the breezy open space of Freefall, a complex nest of silk cables and bamboo struts connecting the passenger basket to the huge red-and-white air bag overhead. I blinked at the column of sinking suns, their majestic descent in reds and oranges coloring the whole sky.

Something liquid oozed down to my upper lip. I tasted fresh blood.

Takamoto stood beside the pilot's console. One hand held a length of shining metal no larger than a pen, with a line of blood slipping down its bottom side and dripping to the floor. His round face looked blank, and his jaw flapped helplessly.

MacConnor deserved better, but I set my shoulder against his side and tried to heave him aside so I could squeeze out. His cry of pain had no thought behind it, just the blind mewling of a helpless animal.

I almost had MacConnor out of the way when Takamoto saw me. "No!"

I got another shoulder past MacConnor and tried to pull that arm up after it.

Takamoto lunged forward, the shining steel in his hand arcing through the air.

Instinctively, I flinched aside, my feet kicking, trying to squirm my way through the hatch.

The knife plunged through my outstretched, anchoring hand.

The blade punched through the back of my palm into the deck like hot ice, sinking effortlessly between the bones of my hand and into the bamboo deck. My nerves flared, outraged agony crashing up my arm into my whole body.

They tell you in training not to pull at a puncture like a knife. They don't tell you that if your hand gets nailed to the deck, ancient animal instincts will make you recoil. I reflexively pulled myself back, wanting to shut everything down and coil myself around this fresh hot agony in my hand, not even thinking about being nailed to the deck.

The blade slid effortlessly through the pinky edge of my hand, slicing bone and muscle and sinew as cleanly as a surgical laser or an axe.

I screamed and fell back, grabbing at my bisected hand, tumbling back into the wicker passenger basket, slashing my head against the edge of a chair before my back bounced off another chair and I rolled to the ground, a tight knot of horrified pain.

Cedar screamed.

MacConnor's head and upper torso filled the hatch, suspended by his chute box caught on the edge. The chute box *thunked* with the kick that knocked it free, and the burly pilot fell headfirst to the floor behind me.

Takamoto's round face, bright red, eyes broad in panic, filled the hatch for a moment. Then the hatch slapped shut.

The latch rasped.

9

My brain quit.

My left hand was cut through like someone had plunged a power saw into the edge halfway between the base of the pinky and my wrist, and whacked through to the very edge of my index finger. Blood pulsed from the gap, drenching everything. The pain disappeared against the absolute horror of the wound, a violation exposing things never meant to see light.

I'm pretty sure I screamed. A lot.

Then Cedar grabbed me, shouting "Redding! Aidan!"

Pain started returning like the early hints of an onrushing tide. I knew Cedar was there, but somehow she wasn't important. Only my hand mattered, holding it still, protecting it so I could scream.

Then Cedar grabbed my wrist.

I thrashed, knowing that nobody should touch that intimate maiming.

Cedar sat on my chest, trapping my arm between her thighs.

I bucked ineffectively.

She wrenched at my hand.

I shrieked.

The pain evaporated, ending as cleanly as turning off the lights.

Cut free from that white-hot cold agony, I passed out.

10

Consciousness oozed back a moment or two later. I had curled protectively around my maimed hand, but not so desperately.

A thick white cotton patch covered my wound, curving around the blade edge of my hand. It looked like a sponge, somehow taping me together despite the fresh sticky blood sheeting my hand and arm.

Cedar. The first-aid kit.

She'd kept her head, grabbed the trauma patches, and glued me together. The drugs would keep my hand desensitized for a few more hours, encourage healing, and help me stave off infection. We didn't have nanobot meds on Freefall, but if we could get back to Medical soon I might not even lose that half of my hand—I'd made it to twenty-six without needing anything regrown, and I had really hoped to keep that streak going to twenty-seven.

MacConnor lay on the wicker deck, his feet next to me and his head up against the front. We barely had enough room for the two of us to sprawl out in the zeppelin's passenger compartment. Cedar had ripped off his shirt. She'd already slapped a trauma patch, one of the smaller ones, on his gut, and was sizing a paper-wrapped patch against the bloody gash in his chest.

The basket lurched.

Overhead, Takamoto swore.

The hatch remained closed.

"Cedar," I said. My voice rasped in my dry throat. "Next size up. Multiple injuries need extra meds. Avoid shock."

She glanced back at me. "Right, forgot." She tossed the patch back in the first aid kit, grabbed one the size of a dinner plate, and tore it open. "Never had to really do this." She pressed the patch over the wound. "You can't overdose on trauma patches, can you?"

With my uninjured hand I grabbed the edge of a seat and pulled myself upright. Wicker scratches marred my face, my own blood drenched my arm and chest, MacConnor's blood smeared my face, and somewhere in this I'd twisted my back.

I lurched like a broken machine.

But I moved.

I rubbed my aching shoulder with my remaining hand. "That's a good armbar you have there."

Cedar flashed me a quick grin.

MacConnor groaned.

"That should hold him," Cedar said. She frowned. "It's all I've got, anyway." Her voice grew quiet. "He used diffused steel, that stuff cuts you like—" She glanced at me. "Uh, it's bad."

I nodded. MacConnor looked like he was breathing a little more easily, and color started edging back into him. He had some impressive pecs, despite all the hair—

Pull it together, Redding. Yes, you're hurt, you could have been killed, you're having a nice post-not-dead hormone rush. Enjoy it later. But if you don't take charge of this zeppelin, if you don't get a handle on Takamoto, this can go even worse.

I clambered to my feet. I'd wrenched my hip, too. My head whirled for a second, then my balance steadied. "Let me get past." I sucked in another breath. "Ladder."

Cedar glanced up. "You're in no shape to climb."

The zeppelin lurched again. Bamboo creaked.

She was right. I'd lost blood—it covered me, the floor, a seat cushion, and Cedar. I kept sucking air to try to make up the lack. My body struggled to keep me upright. The drugs shut off the pain, but the shock of the trauma still made my grip weak and my vision shaky. I needed to lie down.

"And Takamoto clearly doesn't know how to fly this thing," I said. "Someone's got to talk him down before he gets us all killed. Have *you* been through hostile negotiations training?"

Cedar gritted her teeth and shifted herself so I could squeeze past.

Hostile negotiations training? Yeah, that's what they call it when another student pretends to be a bomber and you talk her down. Or the AI-driven gunman in virtual. It's not when you're locked inside a giant picnic basket dangling over infinity and hanging from a balloon driven by a desperate, irrational mathematician trying to slash his way out of his problems.

Keeping my maimed hand over my heart, I climbed the ladder one-handed. The basket lurched and swayed, but we still weren't back at full weight and I clutched my way to the top. Once my head brushed the closed access hatch I shouted "Doctor Takamoto!"

The basket lurched again. I heard Takamoto cry out. What was he doing up there? It's not like there were speed bumps out here. You aimed at the cliff and waited.

"Listen to me, Takamoto!" What was his first name again? "Haider! It's not too late. We can work this out! Whatever's going on, whatever you've done, we can talk about it."

The whole zeppelin creaked.

I thought of trying the "there's no place to go" gambit, but Takamoto wasn't thinking well. I didn't want him puncturing the air bag as a final, futile gesture.

"I'm okay," I shouted. "MacConnor will be too, if we get back soon. You've done nothing permanent here! Just let us up so we can talk this out!"

Bamboo creaked.

Then snapped.

The basket's rear end sagged, turning my nice vertical ladder into a set of rungs across an angled ceiling. My hand clamped weakly on a rung, but my feet instantly slipped free. I shouted wordlessly and, for the second time in ten minutes, fell backwards to the floor and slid to the back wall.

Cedar screamed, this time with full unchecked terror, clutching her seat.

MacConnor slid down the short aisle, his feet crashing into me, his body crumpling after them.

More bamboo creaked.

I tried to shove MacConnor aside. Again.

Takamoto shouted "Lucy!"

The knife. The diffused steel knife that had cut through my hand.

How long would it take that knife to cut through structural bamboo?

"Haider!" Cedar screamed. "Stop this!"

"I would have," Takamoto said. "I would have done anything for you."

Wood snapped and groaned.

Then the *Tahiti Sunset*'s passenger basket plummeted into infinity.

Falling.

Everything in the passenger basket became weightless. Doctor Cedar came off her chair, red hair rising into an electric halo, highlighting her high-pitched shriek of absolute terror. Last night's boxed dinner bounced off the back of a seat and careened towards the ceiling. The creaking of bamboo was replaced by wind whistling through the warp and weft of the weave. I thrashed, and MacConnor's limp form rose into the air.

Clamshell.

The basket was going to split in half, spilling us into empty air.

MacConnor still wore his chute box, but an unconscious person can't pull a trigger. I pawed at his leg, but the fingers of my left hand wouldn't even try to close. Desperately I snatched his belt with my working right hand. When the basket split open, I'd have to get us both free, trigger his chute, and then trigger my own.

How long would the clamshell take to open?

Cedar grabbed a seat to anchor herself.

The basket twitched and started rolling.

The wind rushed faster, whistling through the weave, suspending us inside the basket.

Come on, open! I wanted to beat at the wall, but the bandage on my free hand stopped me.

"Too long," Cedar shouted. "It's taking too long!"

The passenger compartment should clamshell open. It's automatic, a mechanism—

—but *where* was that mechanism?

Probably up in all that machinery and struts and entanglements surrounding the pilot's perch.

The passenger compartment wasn't going to open.

We had to get out ourselves.

I fought to shove the fear aside. My heart surged in my chest.

The pilot's hatch was the closest exit. I kicked off the wall, dragging MacConnor with me. *Get him out. Get myself out. Pull his chute, then mine. And Cedar.*

Or I'd spend the rest of my life falling.

And my entire death, too.

Forever.

The basket continued its own slow rotation, but my head had its own countering spin. I'd lost blood.

One working hand. I pried my hands from MacConnor's belt and fumbled at the door.

Hyperventilating. I forced my breathing slower and deeper. *Think, Redding*!

We fell at one gravity. Ten meters per second per second.

After falling one minute, we'd be going three hundred meters a second. That had to be above terminal velocity?

The emptiness was swallowing us. My every muscle trembled, but I wrenched at the hatch.

It wouldn't open.

The wind through the turning wicker rasped my face.

Wait—Takamoto had locked this hatch. I cursed myself for twelve kinds of fool.

MacConnor had drifted towards the floor. I kicked down towards him, only to collide with Cedar as she tried to get to the rear hatch. We bounced off each other into the churning chaos of the tumbling, turning passenger compartment.

Eleven hundred kilometers an hour. Terminal velocity. About three hundred meters a second.

I clutched at something, trying to anchor myself. A chute box, knocked from its place beneath a seat.

A scream bulged up my throat. I clamped down on it.

My foot hit something, but by the time I could turn to look, it was gone. My back bounced off a wall.

The passenger compartment spun faster.

Dread threatened to burst my heart, my ribs, my skull.

Three hundred meters a second. Eighteen kilometers a minute.

How long had it been since we fell?

Zeppelins had a range of forty kilometers.

Either we escaped this tumbling madhouse in two minutes, or we fell forever.

I lashed out my good hand and seized a wicker chair back as it spun past. It wrenched itself out of my hand, leaving torn skin and welling fresh blood.

I tumbled away.

The heel of a shoe rushed towards my face.

The flailing foot crashed into my temple.

Blackness.

12

I came back resting against a wall.

The passenger cabin had stopped its mad tumble. What had been a wall was a ceiling, with a half-meter porthole hanging open exposing the red sky. Cedar huddled next to me, while MacConnor lay akimbo on my other side.

We were still falling.

The wind through the gaps in the wicker screeched and whistled, buffeting my short hair into a cloud at the top and sides of my vision.

I was weightless, held to the floor only by Cedar's light touch.

Complete freefall.

The terror had collapsed, leaving me strangely numb. We were falling. We would fall forever. Our last meal would be whatever we could scrounge from this empty wicker basket.

I raised my head. Cedar had tears in her eyes, but the wind shredded them before they could trail down her cheeks.

How long had it been? I raised my aching arm to glance at my watch, remembered when we'd left, and did the math.

Takamoto had cut us free about ten minutes ago.

A hundred and eighty kilometers above.

I would die, here, with Cedar and MacConnor. My new best friends.

Every muscle in me ached. My unarmed combat training had included bare-knuckles brawling, but the bruises and bludgeoning I'd suffered from then didn't come close to the no-holds-barred battering I'd taken from the tumbling basket. My maimed hand felt like a numb balloon, somehow larger than the rest of me.

I let my good hand fumble for Cedar's. She clasped it tightly. Her fingers shook for a moment, then were still.

"How'd you stop the roll?" I shouted above the roaring wind.

Cedar gave a thin, brave smile. Her red hair floated above her, blown by the wind into a shifting grass rising from her scalp. "I knocked the hatch open. The extra airflow changed the aerodynamics enough that we straightened out."

If anything, the wicker felt more stable than it had before. Everything felt light and smooth. The air almost supported me.

Freefall had no weather beyond the constant slow rise of warm air. The basket wasn't fighting through the air any more; it flowed with it.

Even my teeth hurt.

Surrender felt easy. Not only was there no way to fight, fighting this couldn't accomplish anything. We were falling. We would always fall. Even if Montague expanded their operations downward, the Facility couldn't grow at terminal velocity.

I was going to die.

I squeezed Cedar's hand, and felt her squeeze back.

But I couldn't give up. There was no way to fight death? Fine.

I would figure out *why*.

Takamoto had lied about doing payroll yesterday. He'd been willing to kill us to keep that secret.

What secret was worth killing over? Killing Gupper was the obvious answer.

"Cedar," I shouted.

"Call me Lucy," she said.

I smiled back. "Then it's Aidan. Listen—when did you get to the lab yesterday morning? What time?"

"About eight. Why?"

"Takamoto was there all day?"

"All the time I was."

Gupper had been seen right before seven. So, in an hour, Takamoto had killed Gupper, then somehow gotten his body up above the Debris Shield. Way above the Shield, judging from the damage done to his body. He couldn't have taken a floater that high and returned in an hour, especially lugging Gupper's body.

Gupper struck the Debris Shield at four thirty PM. Hours and hours later. While Takamoto was in the lab, with his staff.

And Takamoto wasn't a calm, methodical killer. Standing in the pilot's perch, he'd been almost paralyzed while I tried to climb out. He panicked. He wouldn't have set up something in advance to take Gupper up to the Shield.

So how could Gupper have gotten up there?

An answer exploded in the back of my brain, and my eyes snapped open. I found myself sitting up, heedless of my injuries, mouth working soundlessly.

"What is it?" Cedar said.

The idea was insane.

It was ridiculous.

But it explained *everything*.

"I think… I think I might know how to save us," I said.

13

If I guessed wrong, we were dead.

If I was right but we screwed up, we were dead.

If we did nothing? Dead.

So we went for it.

Cedar—*Lucy*—and I pillaged the wicker passenger compartment, moving carefully. We weren't quite weightless in the plunging box, but the screaming hurricane updraft that made talking almost impossible buoyed us. Each touch made the passenger compartment wobble and shake in a threat to tumble again, but it never quite lost its new direction.

Smoked glass goggles—we'd need those. Bamboo-cased binoculars, meant for sightseeing. Lucy found half a dozen liter bottles of water in a locker woven into the wall. I grabbed a bottle and drained it, feeling my parched tissues soak up the fluid.

Then we took MacConnor's pants off.

Don't give me that look. We needed something to tie everything together with, and the passenger compartment didn't come with rope. And he lost the vote, two to one. So we stole MacConnor's pants and cut them into long strips. Lucy lashed the first-aid kit to her belt. I knotted the spare chute box to mine—I didn't have a plan for the chute box, but if we needed it, we'd *really* need it.

And MacConnor still had his boxers. Red ones.

I grabbed the white box containing last night's supper.

Lucy's face wrinkled. "You're not going to eat that!" she shouted over the roaring wind.

I shook my head. "Windburn!"

The fried chicken, and the butter on the potatoes, had all cooled and congealed into a greasy mess and tumbled. I dug my finger into a lump of alloyed grease and butter, took a deep breath to still my revulsion, and smeared it on my face.

Lucy made a face, nodded, and grabbed a greasy chicken breast.

We were able to cover our own face and hands, and used the rest slapdash on MacConnor's bare skin. There was an awful lot of him. We tied his torn shirt around his torso for more protection.

I took a few strips of MacConnor's torn pants and tied them together, forming a makeshift rope. I tied a slipknot in each end and put one around my right wrist, tugging it snug. The other end I looped around MacConnor's left wrist. Our ankles got the same treatment. Lucy mirrored me on MacConnor's other side.

Lucy's face gleamed pale beneath the speckles of greasy breading. "Are you sure about this, Aidan?"

"If you have a better idea," I said at the top of my lungs, "I'd really love to hear it."

Lucy took my good hand in hers. I squeezed. We grinned at each other. I hoped mine didn't look as maniacal as hers and tied the smoked-glass goggles over my eyes.

"Whatever happens, it's been a pleasure," I shouted.

"Don't say that. After we pull this off, we'll be invited to *all* the best parties."

I gave her a thumbs up and looked towards the entrance hatch on the wall.

We made our way to the entrance hatch, moving almost weightlessly, MacConnor's arms over our shoulders. Lucy looked like she could have carried MacConnor on her own. If MacConnor fell on me, though, I might smother before Lucy could rescue me.

We braced our feet on the seats and pressed our shoulders against the wall around the hatch.

I clenched MacConnor to my side with my good hand, and felt Lucy respond in kind.

Then Lucy yanked the hatch open.

The passenger cabin immediately whirled, wrenching all of us around. I held my spot, pinning my body between the seat and the wall with the strength of my legs and back. My bruised legs burned, but I held my place.

The basket steadied, wobbled, and stabilized, with the exit hatch in the ceiling. Freefall's aerodynamics, its unnatural natural laws, apparently demanded that the passenger cabinet's largest hole be at the top. That was one right guess, thankfully.

Cedar climbed through the door first, towing MacConnor after her.

The cotton leashes tied to my good wrist and ankle tugged, then pulled. Before they could grow more taut, I ducked my head out the hatch and shimmered out after them.

My feet cleared the hole.

We were free.

The passenger compartment rose above us, and we fell into hazy red oblivion.

14

The screaming air cradled me like an impossibly comfortable bed. Air shrieked past me far more loudly than it had skydiving on Earth, but caressed me aloft. I felt utterly weightless.

If it weren't for the part where we were falling at eleven hundred kilometers an hour, I'd almost enjoy this.

Lucy and I settled out facing the falling suns, a column of smoking red orbs that began impossibly far overhead and descended into infinity, casting amber and orange and crimson light through the featureless hazy air surrounding us. Even through the smoked glass goggles, I couldn't look at the suns without blinking. My eyes teared, but I didn't dare move the goggles to wipe them. If I lost my goggles, we all died.

MacConnor hung unconscious between Lucy and me, face-down, arms and legs pulled back by air pressure. The khaki lines torn out of his pants webbed the three of us together at wrists and ankles. Tethers trailed the binoculars, the first aid kit, bottles of water.

The wicker basket hung above us, slowly receding into the sky. Its greater surface area must have caused more wind resistance than its porous weave passed.

Beneath us, nothing but distant red haze fading into forever.

My left hand still felt paradoxically enormous and numb, and while my lightheadedness had faded I still felt woozy.

But best of all, my terror had gone.

We were falling into infinity, but we had a chance. A tiny chance, a chance built out of a single shaky hypothesis and a big cargo zeppelin overflowing with hope, but I'd grab that chance in my good hand and squeeze until it either carried me to safety or died in my grasp.

I tasted dusty air, rancid chicken grease and butter covering my face and lips, and life itself.

The loop of khaki rope hugging my ankle tugged. MacConnor fell faster than me, and had reached the limits of his tether. The Montague Corporation gave us tough clothing, but I didn't want to test the makeshift rope unless I absolutely had to. I pulled my arms and legs in to reduce my air resistance and sank next to him.

Lucy and I had shouted this through before jumping out. I grabbed MacConnor's shoulder with my right hand, inching myself closer and closer. MacConnor was even bigger than he looked, but eventually I had an arm over his back and a grip on his torn shirt right over his far shoulder blade. Lucy's arm brushed mine, then slithered beneath it. Her hand edged between MacConnor's ribs and mine and grabbed tight. Much more tightly than I could, with my smaller size.

I lifted my head to peer over MacConnor's head, but the wind pressure rolled his head up. I ducked down, and saw Lucy in a similar position.

Now the tricky part.

In parachute training on Earth, they teach you how to move through the air before pulling the chute—that's the "skydiving" thing. Steering is all about arranging your limbs. We needed to turn around and get our feet towards the sun.

I pulled in my free arm. We should have veered towards me, rotating towards the cliff.

Instead, our three-headed, six-legged skydiver tipped towards Lucy.

We'd talked this through, but we hadn't agreed who would steer! I thrust my numb hand back into the air. We righted out, still facing the suns.

Lucy and I nodded at each other for a moment, trying to say *You go* or *I got this*, whatever we meant. Finally, Lucy rolled her head, dragged her free arm forward into view, and slid it up against her chest.

She had the better grip—heck, she had two hands. *She* could steer. Even though this was my idea.

Slowly, we began to turn. The suns majestically rotated out of sight, leaving us with a clear view of nothing. The sun shone past our feet. Above and below and beside was only the featureless red haze. Wind blasted my face, inflated my shirt and pant legs, shoved me against MacConnor's warmth and nudged me away.

At the far edge of my vision, pale gray slowly coalesced from of the red haze: the distant cliff, still kilometers away but barely visible. Soon the world seemed split in two, with a vertical horizon separating the red glaring sky from the distant gray granite.

Finally the gray wall filled out my vision. Lucy straightened us out, and we lifted our legs to fall forward.

If we were going to have any chance at all, we needed to be closer to the cliff.

We hung in empty space.

The wind whipped my hair even as it cradled me aloft.

Skydiving training on Earth gave us two minutes of freefall. Any more than that and you had to go so high you needed breathing gear. We knew how to move forward, but I'd never thought to ask "how many *horizontal* kilometers can you cover in two minutes?" When the ground is rushing at you, you only care about the vertical.

I glanced at my watch. We'd been falling for three minutes.

The wall didn't seem any closer.

And we fell more.

My numb, bandaged hand felt even more absent. Were we even moving?

I fumbled for MacConnor's limp arm, draped it beneath me, and clamped his forearm in my left armpit. By straining my good arm, I could snatch the tether on the binoculars and reel them in. Getting the cool wooden frames to my face was another problem, but once I managed it the eyepieces clipped onto my goggles.

The cliff leaped nearer, the hazy gray resolving into muddy puddles of light and dark that oozed upward. I couldn't make out any details.

If I'd had modern electronic binocs, I'd be able to read a data feed at this range. On Freefall we only had optics mounted in a bamboo shell—the best optics our century could produce, but still, optics.

Buffeted by the wind, the binoculars tugged at my goggles.

I didn't dare lose the goggles. Reluctantly, I unclipped them. Rather than let them fly back up, however, I tucked them in the front of my shirt.

MacConnor felt warm next to me. I tried to hug him closer.

If I was wrong, the only noise I'd ever hear again was the roaring wind.

15

Two minutes of freefall is exhilarating.

An hour is tedious.

Two is just ridiculous.

Was the wall growing more green? Was the haze thinning? Did the vertical horizon creep closer? If so, it was so slow I couldn't be sure.

I made myself wait another fifteen minutes before trying the binoculars again. Working one-handed, still clinging desperately to MacConnor, I dropped them almost immediately. They fell up to jerk at the end of the khaki rope.

Lucy shook her head at me and reeled them back in.

Fine. Let her do it. I fumed at my own helplessness, my maimed hand, at the infinity beneath us. I knew it was stupid, but it beat thinking too much about the fall.

Had I killed us all?

No. Worst case, I'd changed the details of how we died.

Now that we were committed, I couldn't get rid of the horrible, growing conviction that I'd guessed wrong.

When the trauma patches wore out, and MacConnor died, should we untie him? Or should we all fall together, forever?

Then we wobbled in the air. I looked around to see Lucy holding the binoculars in front of MacConnor's face. She waved them frantically, then held still.

I weaseled my right hand free and snatched them.

Through the narrow circle of magnified vision, the gray wall had grown more detail. Were those crags? Was that a chimney? I scanned back and forth—

—wait.

That line.

That beautiful, gorgeous vertical silver line, just to our left?

Maybe...

A waterfall? The famous Forever Falls?

My heart beat more quickly. We *were* closing on the wall! The waterfall was about thirty degrees off where we aimed. Lucy couldn't turn us that way, that was why she'd handed me the binoculars. I pulled in my free arm and leg, bringing us closer to our target.

The wall grew. And grew.

Details became clearer and clearer, until I could see the waterfall without the binoculars.

It turns out that on Freefall you can crawl about six horizontal kilometers an hour, as you plunge eleven hundred kilometers straight down. That's only, what: one hundred eighty or so to one?

We paused about two hundred meters from the cliff, the beautiful bottomless cliff, just to the left of the river. We didn't want to hit an unexpected outcropping. The chimneys and crevasses and outcroppings were only streaks as we plummeted, the river a blur.

Maybe the river ended in a nice deep pool. A bottomless pool.

We didn't have to die of thirst. Maybe we'd get the chance to drown instead.

Or maybe the last of us would surrender to despair, and kiss that wall.

But for now, we rearranged our lines.

We tugged ourselves closer together, MacConnor on the bottom, Lucy and I flank to flank above him.

And fell faster.

16

What's to say?

Weak from blood loss, constantly abraded by the ceaseless wind of freefall, I grew thirstier and thirstier. After three hours, we'd finished the water.

Four hours in, Lucy had to shift her bowels. That was neither fun nor dignified. Fortunately, we fell faster than the results. I felt glad I'd lost yesterday's lunch, and wore yesterday's dinner on my face and hands.

We'd planned the wait. We'd have hours and hours of tedium ahead. If I was right, at the end we'd have about two desperate minutes—assuming we noticed in time. We absolutely had to keep watch. We grew deft at quickly trading the binoculars and fitting them onto the goggles.

The world felt sideways. The suns were at our feet, the ground at our head, and we fell sideways faster than the speed of sound. Had we left a sonic boom all those kilometers behind? What was the speed of sound on Freefall, anyway?

A pillow of winds cradled me. It would have been easy to fall asleep there, with MacConnor plunging beneath me. My body ached for rest, real rest, in an actual bed or just a cold granite floor. My bruises and sprains grew more and more insistent, dull aches that blossomed into full-fledged pains.

For long minutes I peered downward, with the red sky at our feet and the granite wall flashing by overhead in streaks of green and gray, the waterfall a wavering ribbon, the binoculars pressing the goggles into my eye sockets. When the hypnotic weave of gray and green and silver threatened to overwhelm me, I wrenched the binoculars off my face and passed them to Lucy.

I grew thirstier. And thirstier.

Eight hours in, the trauma patch on my maimed left hand started wearing off. Pain from that injury started seeping back in.

Before long, I had to blink tears back from my eyes. The protective grease of my face had long since ablated away, and the dry wind felt like a cool sandblaster over my face, my neck, the slope of my breasts and hands. The khaki rope that had felt soft hours ago had now abraded its brand around my wrist, and another had burned through my sock and now left a blood-speckled ring around my ankle.

We had the first aid kit.

It had trauma packs, all in paper wrappers. I had no doubt that Lucy would fight like hell to get one out for me. And she would get one.

The wind would steal the rest.

If I could stand it a little longer, ride out the little bit of painkiller remaining in my system, I'd get the full benefit. Another eight peaceful hours.

But MacConnor was hurt worse than me. A lot worse, with the stab wounds in his chest and gut. And we'd put him on point, so the wind must be burning his exposed skin utterly raw. We'd even stolen his damn pants for this stunt. Maybe he should get the last trauma pack.

Ultimately, it didn't matter.

We would die falling.

MacConnor was the worst hurt. He'd die first.

Maybe he was already dead, the lucky bastard.

Lucy was battered, but not maimed.

She'd outlive me.

I wished her luck.

And peace.

If, at the end, she guided us into the cliff, I'd forgive her.

And that's all there was.

I was resting, eyes closed, trying to focus on my breath rather than on my growing distress, when Lucy jabbed me in the chest, *hard*, with the binoculars.

My eyes flashed open. I blinked away tears.

She shook the binoculars in front of my face.

Insane hope flashed inside me. I grabbed the binoculars and wrenched them to my eyes.

Lucy was already struggling with the rope around her ankle.

The binoculars fought me and I struggled to get them onto my face. They slipped and fumbled, my hand shaking, but I managed to snap them into place and peer down.

In a world of gray and green and hazy reds and orange, something gleamed silver. Far below us, it seemed to fly closer even between blinks.

The Debris Shield.

I'd been right.

Takamoto hadn't dragged Gupper up.

He'd shoved Gupper over the edge.

Dropping him *down*.

This universe looped back on itself.

ᛏ

We plunged through endless space—no, endlessly *repeating* space. The hazy ochre sky and flashing, streaky granite cliff suddenly seemed gorgeous. Adrenalin and endorphins flooded my blood, shoving back my saturating pain. The trailing streamers of first-aid kit and tattered clothes and loops of slack line transformed into our victory banners.

My teeth bared in a rabid, victorious grin, and the wind inflated my parched cheeks into a flapping farce.

I still felt exhausted. The eternal wind had sucked every drop of moisture from my body. I'd lost blood. My bisected right hand hurt like a horde of angry insects had nested in the palm. My other wrist ached from the chafing of the loop of rope around it, and the leashed ankle burned even worse.

But we had a chance.

Takamoto had killed one person. He'd tried to kill three more.

I would *not* give him a shot at anyone else. That chubby bastard was going all the way down—and I was *the* expert on just how far down that was.

Ecstatic fire lit my nerves.

MacConnor hung beside me. Was he still alive? Had the trauma patches kept him together? I looked at his pale face and wanted to hug him. Ridiculous paintbrush mustache or no, I'd have dinner with him.

Lucy looked a lot more like some Irish warrior ancestor. Her jaw had grown firm, and even through the smoked goggles I thought I saw fire in her eyes. Her red hair stood up in a ridiculous tangle, black dust and gray grease streaked her face, but at that moment she would have charged a lion if we'd had one handy.

Lucy's hand clasped mine. She mouthed *thank you* and gave me a grin almost as wild as my own. Then she slipped a bloody khaki rope from around her wrist, setting herself free.

Her chute box exploded.

Lucy shot into the sky in a flash of silver.

Had the chute held against this wind?

Or had it blown, triggering the backup chute?

Had her backup chute held?

I might never know.

We'd argued about who would launch MacConnor. She had two hands. I had the training for stupid physical activities.

I'd won.

But I wished I hadn't.

I knocked the binoculars off my face, letting them soar to the end of their tether. I didn't need them anymore.

Terminal velocity: eighteen kilometers a minute.

Maximum visibility: fifty kilometers.

How much time had passed?

Had Lucy noticed the Debris Shield's gleam right away? Or had it taken thirty seconds? Sixty seconds?

Did the Facility's radar point up? If so, they would have noticed Lucy's radar-reflective parachute. Were zeppelin pilots already scrambling to pick her up?

Or were they oblivious?

A computer would notice and scream. Computers didn't work on Freefall.

If I fell past the Facility, if I got our chutes open late, would they even notice us?

I didn't let myself look down, instead attacking the line attaching my ankle to MacConnor's. Eight hours of intermittent tugging had inexorably tightened the knot, and my own wind-dried blood cemented it, but I jammed a thumb beneath the slipknot and wrenched it back and forth until my heel slipped past the loop and I kicked the line free.

That left the line on my good wrist.

I couldn't loosen the knot around my right wrist with my right hand. Instead, I attacked MacConnor's end with fingers and teeth.

My heart pounded in my chest. How much time did we have? Seconds?

The knot fought me, and fought more, but I dragged it off his wrist.

For half a second we hung in space, my legs wrapped around his thigh, my good fist in the tattered rags of his shirt.

MacConnor looked like hell. He might be dead.

I would not believe he was dead. Not after all this. I remembered his eyes well enough to see them through the smoked glass goggles. His chest, lined with the taut muscles of someone who worked for a living. And that chipper fearlessness. That chin.

Stubble—he was alive!

No, hair grew after death.

If we made it, if we both actually stood on solid floor again, dinner was not the only thing I would get out of him.

I released my hand and loosened my legs so he could drift free.

Grabbed the tag of his chute box.

And yanked.

MacConnor exploded out of my grasp like a shotgun blast.

Some part of him smacked my chin—a leg? a hand?

My vision went gray around the edges.

My precarious balance shattered.

MacConnor vanished into the sky, and I corkscrew-tumbled down.

18

The world whirled around me.

Red sky filled my vision, then gray-green granite wall, then sky, flickering contrast sprayed across the kaleidoscope in my rattled skull. My teeth hurt where MacConnor's parting shot had smashed my chin. Centripetal force rushed fresh blood to my crippled hand. The baleful wind battered my ears. My mouth tasted bright and coppery on my swollen tongue.

I couldn't tell where I was. We'd kept our distance to a couple hundred meters from the cliff, but had we closed on it as I struggled free of MacConnor?

I knew how to straighten out of this spin. It would take a few seconds.

Never pull a chute while you're tumbling. You might tangle yourself in the shroud, and then you're done.

But how far above the Facility was I?

I knew how things worked now. But wounded, I couldn't survive another eight hours of desiccating freefall.

If I missed the Facility, I died.

I brought my hand to the tag on my chute box and yanked.

The straps through my crotch and along my chest kicked me, hurtling me through the sky like a soccer ball. My limbs seemed to trail behind, the hips and shoulders and knees and elbows all screaming in surprise, my pelvis and shoulders screeching in outrage at the impact.

The wind's roar deepened, its first change in hours. My numbed ears suddenly felt alive.

Blood left my head. The world turned gray.

I lost my thoughts, only knowing that I had to stay conscious. I *had* to.

I felt, rather than heard, something snap. A whole harp of strings, stretched beyond any possible limit, twanging and breaking in a row.

The wind's roar started surging up again.

The backup chute detonated out of my pack, a second impact on my battered body.

Silence rang in my ears.

My wind-abraded face and hands blossomed into a full scorching burn.

But the cliff was moving. Crags of rock. *Individual* crags, not a blur. Water splashed, only meters away.

I should have hovered, but instead the cliff roared past me. How fast was I going? I glanced up. The steering vents had torn away from the silver expanse of the parachute. The reserve chute had held, barely, but air poured through the gaps where vents should have billowed.

I might be able to steer. Sort of.

How fast could a zeppelin scramble?

Had they noticed me?

I glanced down.

The Debris Shield was maybe a kilometer beneath me—no, less. And closing fast.

I couldn't see MacConnor or Lucy.

They had to be above me.

They *had* to be.

The rule was: wait for a zeppelin. Hang in midair and await rescue. But I wasn't hanging in midair. I was falling, nowhere near terminal velocity, but faster than I should be. Maybe faster than a zeppelin could fly.

I shook my head.

With my throbbing hand and burning skin, with the bruises and strains and sprains, saving my own life felt like too much trouble. But there was MacConnor. And Lucy.

And Takamoto.

Takamoto was *not* going to get away with murdering us.

I aimed the plunging chute at the shining steel length of the Debris Shield.

19

The chute straps rolled and shifted against the fresh bruises in my pelvis and shoulders. My wind-stunned ears heard nothing but a constant ringing that echoed through every battered sinew and bone. In my goggles, the long, narrow Debris Shield swelled.

A slim step of safety.

Or a long fall to a painful death.

Or, maybe, a quick crash against the green granite cliff that loomed to the infinite ends of the universe.

I felt like a mummified corpse, drained of fluid and baked in desert sands for a thousand years, reanimated by some cruel curse to wreak vengeance from beyond the grave.

I wondered if Takamoto had ever seen those old movies.

No, get help. Send zeppelins to catch MacConnor and Lucy. Then Takamoto.

The Debris Shield grew in my vision.

The parachute loomed overhead. How big was it? Could I land on the Debris Shield? Or would the canopy's edge brush the jagged granite cliff before my feet touched the riveted steel awning?

Only one way to find out, Redding. My best chance was to land at the edge of the awning.

I turned so my momentum would carry me towards the cliff.

The Debris Shield raced at me.

You're supposed to hold the chute straps when you land, but my screaming-maimed left hand wasn't going to be touching anything, ever again, as far as I was concerned.

I bent my knees and took a deep breath.

My feet slammed into the Debris Shield.

I exhaled explosively, shouting in victory, crashing forward, trying to roll uphill, each touch of sun-heated metal slapping bruises and strains. My wounded hand rolled under me and I screamed, the sudden flash of pain and pressure almost wiping my thoughts away.

Seconds later, I lay on my back, still.

My ears rang. I hurt absolutely *everywhere*.

But the hot steel of the Debris Shield, a line of rivets scorching my back, felt better than the pillow of winds ever had. I could have lain there forever.

The chute billowed down towards me. An updraft caught it, tugging it back up.

Tangled shroud lines yanked at my shoulders.

My hand scrabbled for the buckles at my chest. I was *not* going to let the parachute haul me over the edge. Not now. By the time I thrashed my way clear of the enmeshing lines, I was on my feet, a couple feet from the granite cliff. The heat was incredible—that cliff had absorbed the constant warmth of countless suns since the beginning of time. Radiant heat scalded my tenderized hide, but barely registered next to the throbbing in my maimed paw.

The weightless chute huffed up. Abandoned lines skittered across the shining steel. Then the whole thing floated over the edge of the Debris Shield and down into oblivion.

So long, friend.

My legs begged to buckle. Instead I stumbled down the stairs, the beautiful metal-grille stairs with the octagonal Montague stamp in the center of each. The sunscorched steel rail burned the palm of my functional hand as I lurched down. At that moment I could have sucked the water out of a slice of dehydrated apple. The stairs seemed to wobble and weave beneath me, but I clambered down, yanked the access door open, wrenched the goggles off my face, and made myself trot, lumbering and lurching, down the access hall.

The first person I found was a beefy A/C technician, crouched at an open access panel, his head almost inside the cooling system. I tried to say *Hey you*, but what came out was more of a coughing screech.

He turned from his work, annoyance naked on his face. His gaze met my eyes, and the annoyance instantly dissolved to stark terror. He fell back from his crouch, hitting his butt.

I coughed again, clearing my throat. "Rescue zeppelins," I croaked, trying to be heard over the high-pitched screech in my ears. "Two people. Call."

He blinked owlishly at me, mouth working helplessly. I guessed *he* had seen those old mummy films.

I coughed again, trying to clear my throat enough to speak. "Two people. Zeppelin wreck. Get help!"

The alarm klaxons blew, audible even to my stunned ears.

The tech's eyes grew wide. He scrabbled back, crab-walking on hands and feet, jaw flapping.

The klaxon stopped and a panicked voice shouted "This is not a drill" over the loudspeaker. "Emergency zeppelin crews, launch. We have three—no, four—contacts, moving fast. Too fast. But they're chutes. Ten, twelve kilometers up. Repeat, this is not a drill. Zeppelin crews, scramble."

The operator sounded panicked. Forecourt would have his head for that. Security folks could lose their cool, but they could never sound like it.

The technician stopped scrabbling away and peered at me in confusion. His mouth formed words.

"Two people," I said, holding up two fingers. My ears rang too badly. My tongue felt like a dry rust-soaked sponge. "Only two people." Was I even understandable?

Then I turned and lurched towards the inside stairs. They lurched and spun beneath me, but I clutched the handrail and made it down the single flight I needed without slipping and breaking my neck.

Lucy. MacConnor.

Takamoto.

The upper annex was a big open room where the elevators started and a dozen big corridors connected. When I slammed the stairwell door open, two chatting technicians in white coats walking from the elevators looked at me and froze mid-step and mid-word.

I glared at them.

They both stepped back, hands raised.

I lurched across the annex to the security office door and flung it open.

The upper security office combined a front desk for visitors to request help, backed by a locker room where we security types stashed equipment and changed clothes. Skinny Tara Beaner bent her head over an open ledger on the front desk. "Yes," she said without taking her gaze from the paper. My stunned ears could barely decipher the words. "Can I—"

She looked up and froze.

Her mouth worked. "Redding?"

I ignored her. My sight suddenly zeroed in on the refreshment table behind the desk.

A pitcher.

A glass pitcher.

Of *water*.

Drops of condensation trickled down its outside.

I lunged.

Beaner jumped to her feet, shouting something.

I had the pitcher in my hand. Cool water burned my windscorched palm, my battered fingers, my inflamed lips, and then gushed into my mouth, shocking cold, a flame that burned my palate and slicked my ashen throat and hit my stomach like an explosion of life.

Everything had happened too fast. It abruptly hit me with the clean cool taste of water.

I'd done it.

We'd done the impossible.

I was going to live.

Lucy would live.

And if MacConnor had made it this far—

I lowered the pitcher. The water cascaded through me, exploding outward, resurrecting desiccated tissue and strengthening my legs. My vision seemed to clear with each blink.

I coughed again, and this time my words felt almost intelligible. "Zeppelins. Two people. Tell them."

"Redding!" Beaner said, stepping towards me. "How are you still alive?" Her eyes flicked from my face, to my torso, to the filthy bandage on my hand, growing more dismayed at each step.

"Later." I chugged another mouthful of water. Drinking too fast would make me ill, but my body screamed for more, to down the whole pitcher and steal the full one beside it. "Two people. Parachutes. Lucy Cedar. MacConnor, pilot. Tell. Them."

Beaner grabbed the phone. "Two people. Parachutes. Got it."

They'd rescue Lucy and MacConnor. I'd done everything I could to save them. *Takamoto.*

One killing? Maybe an accident. Things happen.

But *four* murders?

Something had broken inside him.

He'd kill again.

Maybe he was killing now.

Whatever it took, I would stop Takamoto. He would go down, if I had to grab his flabby neck and plunge over the edge with him.

20

For a second I wavered on my feet. The water, the blessed water rehydrating my flesh, hadn't hit my brain yet. While the rest of my absurdly battered body sparked when the water spread that far, my thoughts either hadn't cleared yet or the shock of survival clouded them further.

Tara Beaner, behind the unpolished green granite security desk, machine-gunned words into the phone handset while staring at me in appalled horror. Once she hung that phone up, she'd call other security officers to help her.

Help her restrain me.

Thought oozed through my skull like toxic sludge.

Restrain me? That was *not* going to happen.

Lucy's life, MacConnor's life, were in someone else's hands now.

Takamoto.

The upper security office had a weapons locker. The glass-doored cabinet stood right behind Beaner. Each day I checked out a taser at the beginning of shift and returned it at the end.

But above the tasers—the flechette pistols. A thousand tiny razor blades in each shell. The glass in front of them said *BREAK IN CASE OF EMERGENCY*. A single flechette round would strip Takamoto's greasy meat off his—

I made myself stop that thought.

That wasn't the way.

Stopping Takamoto meant finding him. An internal security alert. I needed authority. In the security team, that meant—

"Where is"—*cough*—"Forecourt?"

"Down in Zeppelin Security." Beaner's voice sounded thin, and it wasn't just the ringing in my ears.

I engulfed another mouthful of water. That dragged my body past some critical level, and rancid festering sweat erupted from every pore. My air-blasted skin screeched at the violation, but that wasn't anything next to my bruises. My torqued knee—when had *that* happened? What remained of my left hand screeched. "Sublevel eight?"

"Seven."

I slammed the half-empty pitcher down on the table, handle muddy from my touch, and grabbed the full one. "Two people. One hurt. Tell them."

Beaner looked me up and down. "*One* hurt?"

I ignored her and tottered towards the door, precious water sloshing from the brimming pitcher.

"Aidan—wait!"

"Takamoto," I croaked. "Gotta—stop—Takamoto."

The elevator arrived only seconds after I rang the bell, steel doors gliding silently open. The elevator operator in his old-fashioned red jacket with the silver buttons, said "Hello, where can I—" Then he actually looked at me.

I staggered in, water slopping wastefully out of the brimming pitcher. "Sublevel seven. Security issue. Emergency. Do *not* stop."

He gaped, then frantically grabbed the lever and put the car in gear.

I sagged against the back wall, gulped another mouthful of water. My body seemed to be coming back to life around me. The elixir of life, raising me from the dead.

But the mirror steel elevator doors showed a different film.

My black hair stood straight up from my head, glued there by grease and dried sweat. Fresh sweat coursed down my brow, my cheeks.

My caramel skin? What wasn't black from dirty grease was wind-blasted red. When the endorphins ran down I'd sink into screaming pain.

My clothes were torn. My shirt had a single button left, exposing my bellybutton and my bra. I wasn't big enough to fly out of the bra, but flopping free couldn't have made me look any worse.

The soiled bandage on my maimed hand was turning red. I'd torn the wound back open, probably when I crushed the hand between the Debris Shield and my stomach. Blood ran down the pale, immobile fingers.

A red drop appeared at the end of my index finger, swelled, and plunged to the floor.

I stank of fear and sickly fever sweat, rotting chicken fat and rancid butter.

The elevator operator kept his head squarely forward, but repeatedly stole glances at me from the corner of his eyes. I smiled at him—well, exposed a few teeth—and gulped rich, luscious water as quickly as I dared.

Sublevel Seven handled logistics for the cargo zeppelins and all the other paperwork required by a big shipping operation. Big men in hardhats, QA techs in safety glasses and steel-toed boots, file clerks, all stepped aside as I shambled down the main hall. More than one person offered help. I quaffed water from my pitcher and marched on.

Security Third Keith Werner stood outside the door of the big Zeppelin Security office, hands behind his back. Whatever was going on in there, Forecourt didn't want to be disturbed.

Too bad for her.

Keith noticed me. His hand scrabbled for his taser, then recognition grew in his eyes. "Aidan? Holy—I mean, what? Aidan!" He raised his hands as if to catch me before I collapsed.

I shouldered past him, seized the doorknob of the Zeppelin Security room, and body-slammed it open.

Behind me, Keith shouted "Hey, you can't—"

The slamming door cut him off.

The big conference room in the front of Zeppelin Security was full. Yes, Forecourt sat at the table, but so did Facility President Ford. The chief zeppelin mechanic, the senior physician, the head of Research.

And in the corner furthest from the door, fenced in by two of Security's biggest thugs, huddled Takamoto.

Conversation stopped instantly. Shock, surprise, and a little fascinated horror filled the room of faces.

I lifted the pitcher. It was almost empty, so I tipped it all the way back. The excess water coursing down my chin, my shirt, felt almost as delicious as that final swallow sloshing down my throat.

Then I lurched forward to the closest edge of the polished granite table.

Slammed the pitcher down with a sound like breaking stone.

My maimed hand came up on its own. Blood seeped through the bandage and dripped from my dead white fingers onto the table.

I pointed at Takamoto, who was shrinking back even further into the corner.

My throat no longer grated, but my voice burbled like a plague victim as I snarled, "*You. Killed. GUPPER.*"

Takamoto's face turned as white as the sheets of paper scattered around the table, and he raised his hands to protect his face. "I didn't mean to! It was an accident!"

I stood still, hand outstretched, eyes wide and probably a little insane.

Takamoto babbled, "I was eating breakfast on the balcony and he came up. The bastard bragged to me about bagging Cedar. He knew how I felt about her. Losing's one thing, but he rubbed it in!"

Another drop of blood plunged from my hand.

"I hit him," Takamoto said desperately. "He hit back, then we were fighting and he slipped through the rail! It was an accident! I swear."

I imagined falling from the rail. Seeing infinity sprawl beneath me.

No chute box.

Drying out. Burning from the wind.

Deciding to not steer myself into the wall. Choosing the long way down.

Making that decision over and over again.

The silver of the Debris Shield rising from the depths.

Gupper could have steered clear of it. He could have lived a few hours longer. But he hadn't.

I worked my lips. "Gupper died. To tell us. You murdered him. Bravest. Thing. I've ever seen."

Takamoto's eyes rolled back. He fainted into his chair.

The first good idea the bastard had.

MacConnor? Lucy? Check.

Takamoto? Check.

Everything all taken care of, then.

I think someone caught my head before I hit the ground.

21

I came to slowly, with an ecstatic absence of pain. White sheets. Actual white ceiling tiles, soft white sound baffles with granite peeking around them. A mattress, less accommodating than the endlessly adaptable air but far preferable. Antiseptic stung my nose.

Someone had cleaned me, probably with a hose and a long brush, then drenched my burns with a wonderful soothing lotion.

I rolled my neck. No pain, but my hair had been trimmed. Probably not a bad idea.

My teeth. My teeth were *clean*. I tasted mint.

Someone said, "She's awake." I would have argued, but that would have required being awake.

But the male voice sounded clear in my ears. No ringing. I hadn't permanently damaged my hearing.

The nurse had just wrapped his brand-new but antique blood pressure cuff around my arm when Forecourt walked in. Was the Second a little flushed? Had she run here, halting only outside the door to recover her composure? Not that I'd ever done that.

"Redding," she said, standing laser-straight. "About time you were up."

"You know me." My throat felt better than it should, but my voice was too quiet. The pain was gone, but I still felt tired. "Slacking every chance."

Forecourt narrowed her eyes at the nurse.

Unruffled, he noted my blood pressure in the chart and met Forecourt's glare. "Five minutes." He tucked the cuff into a supply closet and strolled out.

"Damn Medical," Forecourt said. "Think they run the place."

I didn't say anything. Insulting the medical staff while I was laid up didn't seem smart.

But speaking of smart, I hadn't been that smart earlier. When I reached the first security office I could have told Tara Beaner to get Forecourt and trigger an alarm on Takamoto. Instead I'd charged down there and confronted him myself.

Not smart. I felt good about running him down, but: not smart.

But now Forecourt would hand me my scalp for it.

"So," Forecourt said, in her usual quiet voice. "Coming back from the dead. You've raised the bar for all of us. You know that, don't you?"

"I do my best, sir." I licked my lips. "What about Lucy—Cedar? And MacConnor?"

"Lucy's fine. They stabilized MacConnor, shipped him back through the Portal to Earth. By now he's annoying the hospital staff in Montevideo. Which you'll be doing yourself pretty soon."

I blinked. "Sir?" I'd been *cashiered*?

She frowned. "You hadn't—they didn't tell you?" Forecourt cast an evil look at the doorway. "Your hand, Redding."

I raised my hands. The fingers of the right were battered and red, still gleaming with mint-scented medicated salve. A heavy bandage covered the left.

The bandage ended too soon.

Soft isn't the same thing as gentle, but Forecourt's voice became both. "You lost the hand. Cedar told us the whole story."

"She kept us together," I said weakly. The empty space where my fingers had been unsettled me. I waved my remaining fingers through the gap, inches from the bandaged stump.

"You'll have your hand back in two weeks," Forecourt said. "Two more weeks medical leave. The question is, what do you want after that?"

"Sir?"

"Cedar told us how you figured out Freefall, when nobody else had. I know, nobody else had Gupper's example."

"Or motivation."

Forecourt flashed a quick but sincere smile. "Oh, yes. Never discount motivation." Her gaze wandered away from me, towards the shelf of supplies. "I knew the story around Gupper didn't add up. It didn't make sense. I sent you to ask questions to give you some experience."

Was that a note of... *apology* in Forecourt's voice?

"Then you wanted the special flight. You had the credentials. I couldn't go myself. We don't have a better candidate. I pushed you a little, to see if you'd stick by your observations. To see how far you'd go." Forecourt pulled in a deep breath. "I had no idea that someone would try to cover up one murder with three more. I apologize. I've already submitted a negative report on myself to headquarters. You're free to do the same."

I closed my eyes, thinking. The bed's comfort felt seductive. "You gave me a chance," I said. "I wanted the chance."

"It's my job to keep my people safe."

I laughed. "We're hanging like bugs on the side of a cliff that goes down forever. Safe is not— I mean—"

"Still."

I opened my eyes again. "They have me drugged up, don't they?"

"Oh, yes. You have the good stuff."

"Then I won't decide anything now, but—no. Thanks, but no."

Forecourt's sigh was both relieved and regretful. "Once you finish therapy, you'll need to decide where you want to go. It's Montague policy that people can resign after a traumatic injury. Given what you went through and what you learned and the people you saved, you're due one hell of a bonus payment. You could live the next five years in luxury, or invest it and never work a day again. Or, you're welcome back here. I wondered how far you'd go, and the answer is all the way and back again. You're welcome in any team I lead. Or I'll recommend you for any Montague placement you want."

"The Hindenbarge." The words popped out of my mouth, but my brain agreed when it caught up.

Forecourt leaned back. "Why there?"

"Because I haven't yet."

"Fair enough," Forecourt laughed. Her voice grew softer, even conspiratorial. "I had everybody in there leaning on Takamoto, digging at every weak spot in his story. We knew he'd cut you free, we guessed why, but we couldn't get the details out of him. And then you stormed in, all blood and death, and—and—just wow." A grin split her face. "The next time I need someone to confess, I'm getting the murder victim to walk in just like you did."

This time, I laughed with her.

Hydrogen Sleets

Prologue

Unthinkable… shapes?
Must be shapes. Couldn't be anything else.
Each motion—no flow. No thought, no sense.
Hold I together. Through brutally twisted space.
Space that rips the soul.
Plunge straight in.
Rescue. Rescue all.
Or end I trying.

1

The Montague Corporation didn't exactly cancel my vacation. They just made it boring. I was in a modest green bikini, sunbathing on a chaise of almost insubstantial molecular mesh and enjoying the Congolese rainforest resort's brilliant clear sunlight and humid tropical fug, when my datalink chirped. "Montague Human Resources for Aidan Redding."

The company had an unexpected opening for a bottom-level security position.

I could have said no. Montague considers vacation time sacred, and I had two months until my next assignment.

But a surprise opening for a security third? Two months in another universe? A universe I wouldn't get to see otherwise?

I'd grown up burning to see the universes. Yes, all infinity of them.

Even if I ignored the seven weeks of medical leave I'd needed to get my hand regrown, I'd had a month of actual vacation. I'd visited my parents—on their anniversary, no less. Their delighted surprise still danced in my heart, but a week in the barrio had been plenty. Any longer, and the gap between us got too uncomfortable.

And the Congolese rainforest resort would be here when I returned.

Whenever that was.

Normally, assignment to a new universe requires anything from a week to a month of classroom and physical training before you get near the Portal.

Montague wanted to send me—immediately?

I'd never heard of such a thing. Which didn't mean it didn't happen, only that it'd never happened to me. The thought that I might already have sufficient training flared through my head and just as quickly died. *Nobody* had all the training needed to enter a brand-new universe.

By the time the HR system disconnected, I was already stuffing my French-Spanish phrase book into my bag and my feet into my sandals. Before I reached the airport outside Lubumbashi, they'd sent the tickets and a quarter million words of briefing to my datalink. I swept through customs and onto the Congolese Air ballistic glider, and found myself upgraded to first class. I didn't have time for the complimentary massage or the open bar—the forty-five-minute flight back to Uruguay gave me barely enough time to snatch a few important names from the dossier and memorize the universe summary.

Meet the new universe, same as the old universe.

But thirteen billion years younger.

A Montague car met me at the airport—not an automatic, a limousine. With an actual human driver, a young man hired for charm instead of brains. I noticed the vat-leather seats and the driver's half-flirting repartee, but buried myself in the Physical Environment part of the briefing. I could learn everyone's names and the org chart later, but if this universe's natural laws said "inhale and you'll explode," I needed to know right away. The driver recognized the symptoms and he didn't seem upset.

A brand-new universe—brand-new to me, yes, but also literally a newborn. Only a few hundred million years after its Big Bang. Full of nothing but hydrogen screaming out of that primal blast, torrents of cosmic rays…

And an old-fashioned space station.

Six concentric rings spun for gravity.

Eight spokes connecting them.

A weightless bubble at the core, full of telescopes.

A million tons of metal, protected from the cosmic hurricane by carefully balanced magnetic fields, with antennas and sensors sticking out everywhere. The same magnetic fields sieved hydrogen from the void to fuel the fusion reactors powering the whole thing.

Straight out of a second millennium movie.

Humanity couldn't reach the stars, but we'd weaseled our way into deep space anyway.

Excitement fluttered my pulse all the way to the Portal.

2

One step between the electrodes of the Portal, and my weight plunged twenty percent.

It's not like I weigh much anyway, but the sudden weight shift set my inner ear whirling and made me wobble. I automatically grabbed for the cool aluminum handrail—not that I saw it, but there's always a handrail outside the Portal.

A petite leather-gloved hand with a grip like a bear trap seized my bicep and said "Easy, ma'am, it hits everyone that way."

"Thanks." I took a breath of fresh but metallic air to steady myself.

About the size of a subway station, the Portal chamber's aluminum ceiling arched away from me, decorated by regular lines of rivets and the occasional octagonal Montague stamp. Electronic equipment and screens lined the walls, along with boxes of cargo bound in and out. Two women in khaki stood further back, one behind a slender touchscreen console, the other with a laser rifle aimed at me.

I didn't take the rifle personally. Returning to Earth, you appeared in a sealed box. If *those* scanners detected anything harmful, you'd never know it. Montague's zeal in protecting Earth from alien universes would seem maniacal, if the risks weren't so horrific. On my first assignment, an egotistical researcher had tried to carry half a kilogram of antimatter ore back to Earth. It was harmless in its native universe, but on Earth it would have knocked South America into orbit.

The little East Asian guy holding my arm wore too much sharp cologne, the smell like a barbed-wire blanket. His uniform hung too loose over his shoulders. Sensor goggles hugged his eye sockets, presenting him with a billion details about everything they picked up. He had PERCIVAL stitched above the pocket of his khaki uniform shirt. "You okay?" His voice seemed weirdly deep from such a tiny frame.

"Yeah."

Percival's goggled gaze moved up and down my body, insultingly direct. I knew he wasn't leering, but I always felt uncomfortable with someone studying me so closely. The Portal's mathematical transformations might have altered me dangerously, or changed harmless bacteria into something nightmarish, and the goggles would show that. They also exposed my skin in a display that would make a strip joint operator envious. I made myself stand still.

After a few tense heartbeats Percival said "Clear. Welcome aboard Wemm Station, Miss Redding."

"Thanks. Where's HR?"

Percival shook his head. "Y'all don't get HR." He held out a gleaming black brand-new datalink in his gloved hand. "We have instructions to send you straight to Six. Leave your bag, we'll get it to your quarters."

"Six?" Disquiet tickled my spine. The local Human Resources person should explain the rules, introduce me to my team, and give me the tour. And the tour would presumably include where the heck this *Six* was.

"Ring Six?" Percival frowned. "How much briefing did you get, anyway?"

"They *sent* the whole thing. I had maybe half an hour to read it."

Percival tightened his lips. "Don't y'all worry, we'll get you up to speed." He jerked his hand towards the door. "Out them double doors. Turn right. Montague elevator on your right. Sixth ring. It's right by the Core, so there's no gravity. Hang onto the elevator rail as you go up, or y'all'll smack the ceiling. Tell me you at least done the free-fall training?"

You have no *idea.* "Yes."

Percival nodded. "Security First Watford's waiting for y'all."

Straight to the top? That could *not* be good. "Thanks." I plucked the palm-sized datalink from his hand. The black plastic rectangle shimmered as it sampled my DNA, then chirped, "Aidan Redding. Montague Corporation. Security Third."

"Confirm," I said.

The datalink buzzed as it sucked my personal settings out of the local datacore.

"Come by at dinner," Percival said. "I'll introduce y'all to the team."

"Thanks!" I clipped the datalink to my belt and broke into a trot towards the double doors at the far end of the room.

No introduction. No tour. Not even a map.

For the first time, I wondered why Montague had an unexpected urgent opening here in a universe that held nothing besides hydrogen and cosmic rays. Was I replacing someone? And if so—why?

3

The stark aluminum corridor could have been from any Montague facility, in any universe. Straight across from the Portal room's door, black stenciled letters declared this RING THREE. Bold arrows pointed left and right to SPOKE EIGHT and SPOKE ONE. Clear, unmistakable, industrial Montague. I found the elevators a few meters to the right, in this little bubble of the corridor. I chose the one bearing the octagonal Montague logo split across its doors. "Six," I said as the doors slid shut behind me.

My datalink answered in the cultured masculine voice I'd chosen. "The sixth ring simulates less than one percent normal gravity. Secure yourself." I gripped the cool steel handrail as the elevator climbed, the slow loss of weight making my pulse throb in my ears.

A screen on the wall shifted to display *Spoke One Ring Four*. The spicy squash and beans I'd eaten for lunch in the Congolese resort, three hours and a universe ago, seemed to drift upwards. The feeling got worse as the display flipped to *Spoke One Ring Five*.

The elevator's slow stop lifted my feet off the floor, and the rail suddenly felt very slippery in my grip. *Spoke One Ring Six*. I kept my orientation, though, holding myself steady until the doors slid open and I could glide out.

According to the sketch at the start of my dossier, Ring Six was so close to the station's axis that it had almost no centripetal gravity. The builders didn't bother giving this corridor a flat surface to pass as a floor—it was round like a coiled sausage, with textured metal rings for handholds spaced an arm's width apart all the way around. I could starfish in the middle of the tube and not touch a wall, but only barely. Pristine white plastic panels circled the tube every meter across the inner surface, diffusing soft white light across the brushed aluminum walls.

Irregularly-placed round airtight hatches marred the outer edge. Omnipresent vents sucked at the air, forging freshness amidst humming lights and hidden motors. Judging from the corridor's curve, this ring had to be maybe two hundred meters in diameter.

I touched the datalink on my belt. "Which way to Watford?"

"Left," came the machine's smooth masculine reply.

I used my legs to launch myself down the corridor, guiding myself away from the walls with my hands. I only needed a few pushes down the vacant corridor to distinguish the station's low, multi-tone hum from angry shouts.

Rounding the corridor's curve, I saw a cluster of people knotted around an access tube in the inner wall. The one person in a Montague uniform looked like he might have received a gorilla gene graft, with massive shoulders and a shaggy pelt of salt-and-pepper hair that haloed his rectangular head and emphasized the bald patch atop his skull. One hand clutched an anchor ring while he raised the other, index finger upraised. That had to be Watford.

"She's on her way," Watford shouted at the man facing him as I came into view.

The man beside Watford surprised me enough that I almost collided with the wall. I'd just passed through entire crowds dressed like him a few hours ago.

He was Congolese.

"I would hope so." The tall Congolese even had the accent, part African and part French. He had his feet pressed against the outer edge of the tube and one hand pressed against the inner edge, pinning him in place. Where most men from the Congolese Federation traditionally wore kilts, he'd let weightlessness triumph over tradition and wore a blue pullover shirt trimmed in blistering yellow and billowy yellow trousers instead. I glimpsed a few people behind the African, but focused on making myself slow down without crashing into a wall or Watford.

I snatched a handgrip a couple meters behind Watford. The sudden stop yanked at my shoulder, and I had to stick my legs out to bounce off the wall. "Mister Watford," I said, sketching a salute before extending that arm to steady myself. "Aidan Redding, reporting."

Watford turned to glare at me. "About time."

I got the call two hours ago, what did you expect? "Sorry sir. Rush hour."

"So, you are ready?" the African said.

Watford turned to me. "We have a mentally unstable scientist up in the Core."

From a meter-wide opening in the inner edge of the corridor, a line of electric indigo abruptly sliced into the air and stabbed the corridor's outer edge. The electronic buzz came again, this time much closer and sharper, bringing a stink of ozone. A shriek followed it, a weird constant high-pitched tone that didn't seem to come from a human throat until it trailed off for lack of breath.

My throat clenched. A laser. Not one of those vicious construction ones, but still strong enough to bubble metal where it struck the corridor wall.

That impossibly level screech disturbed me even more than the laser, though. A person's shout should go up and down. It should quaver, not remain steady as a tuning fork.

My briefing said that this universe was exactly the same as our own, only billions of years younger. Where our universe had grown up, built a career, and pushed its kids through college, this universe was still learning to burp. Other than the rotating rings of Wemm Station, the only solid matter in this universe was a hailstorm of hydrogen, pounding out from the primordial Big Bang in a flux of magnetic fields and gravitational ripples.

But that abhuman shriek made me wonder. Was this universe *really* the same as ours?

Or had the mathematicians missed some subtle danger?

Something that could drive a human throat to make that unnaturally level cry?

As the beam faded to a glittering afterimage slashing my vision and the air stopped sizzling, Watford said "Doctor Tansi's turned a research laser down the access shaft, and blocked the other entrances."

I made myself take a deep breath. A laser that powerful would diffuse a bit as it burned through me, but would still have enough oomph to punch right through anyone behind me. But Montague wouldn't dispatch me to another universe just to have me make a suicidal charge up the access tube.

"Is the remote shutdown broken?" I said.

Watford narrowed his eyes at me. "We have a plan, Third."

I didn't let my irritation show. "Sir?"

The Congolese tsk'd and rolled his free hand over his head. "You bring someone to help me? She knows nothing."

Someone to help *him*? Who was this guy?

Watford turned his attention to the Congolese. "Station Commandant Mvouba. You asked that we bring additional help. Here she is. You will permit us the courtesy of exchanging a few words before we solve your little problem."

Mvouba frowned and pulled his arm back in. "Very well."

Watford turned to me, his face twitching with tightly suppressed anger. "Commandant Mvouba is a representative of the Congolese Federation. He's responsible for Wemm Station."

I clamped my teeth together to hide my surprise. The Congolese Federation ran this station? I hadn't heard of facilities in any universe being run by anyone other than Montague.

"Montague is kindly assisting the Federation with this issue."

"Montague is responsible for threats to station integrity," Mvouba snapped. "We handle personnel security. Once you have secured the threat, we will take care of Doctor Tansi."

"Yes, sir," I said.

"Redding!" Watford's scowl deepened. "Anything you have to say to Station Commandant Mvouba, you may address to me."

A territorial pissing match? Oh, joy.

I stilled my face. "Yes, sir. Your instructions, sir?"

Watford's scowl didn't soften any. "Your file says you've had freefall hand-to-hand training."

"Just the intro," I said.

Watford's eyebrow twitched.

"Sir," I added.

The corners of Watford's mouth turned even further down. "Four whole hours, eh? It'll have to do. The plan is, Miss Redding, we charge the laser."

My formal face dissolved.

"Palmer has point," Watford said. "I'm second. You take tail. Palmer grabs the laser. You and I secure the perpetrator and hand him over to the commandant's people."

Another blast from the laser scorched the air, the buzz shredding conversation. Tansi's abhuman monotone cry echoed down after it.

"Sir?" I tried to sound confident. "We're... cutting the power first?"

"Impossible," Mvouba snapped. "That would disrupt research that has run for months now. We spent four years building this station. This first group of experiments is highly important."

"The Congolese engineers wired the lasers into the main power," Watford said. "Nobody thought that they *might* need to remotely shut them down individually."

I repressed a flinch. Montague wouldn't make a mistake like that.

Just what sort of people had designed this station?

I scrabbled through my memory of the hastily-skimmed dossier. The access tube up to the spherical Core was what, twenty meters long? No, it had to be more like eighty. The two laser shots had been maybe twenty seconds apart. Four meters per second in zero gravity, through a fairly narrow access tunnel? Almost doable, if everything went perfectly.

But there was a good chance we'd get cooked.

Maybe this Palmer person wore ablative armor that would absorb the laser's heat and burn off. Or a portable diffraction array—no, that would scramble a whole bunch of the research Mvouba was so worried about. Montague had tools and equipment for coping with lasers.

If I'd been here for more than ten minutes, or if I'd had time to read the dossier, I'd know about that equipment.

Watford studied me for a second. "Palmer!"

Behind Commandant Mvouba, someone said "Yes, sir."

"Are you ready?" Watford said.

"Yes, sir," the voice said.

Watford glared at Mvouba. "If you'll let us get to the access tunnel. Commandant."

Mvouba raised his chin and levered himself to the side, letting me take his place.

A cluster of people hung in the corridor on the opposite side of the access tube, out of the line of laser fire. The man in front wasn't carrying a diffraction array or wearing ablative armor. He wasn't wearing... much of anything. Maybe fifteen centimeters taller than me, his mid-calf pants and short-sleeve shirt were a skintight mesh of loose-woven wire-thin plastic, exposing lean muscles, well, *everywhere*. Beneath the mesh he wore only tight briefs barely large enough to qualify as a banana hammock. He had a broad, cheerful face, with cedar skin and weirdly regular freckles. The freckles didn't just cover his cheeks—they continued down his chin and up over his bald head.

Palmer didn't even have eyebrows—just the freckles.

The laser was going to fry him like a blowtorch through butter.

Palmer grinned and raised a hand in greeting. The same freckles covered his palms and fingers, all spaced maybe half a centimeter apart.

Wait—those weren't freckles.

They were sensors.

Palmer was a cyborg.

No, not the usual Earth *I have an implant so I don't carry a datalink* sort of thing.

More of the "gobs of high tech crammed under my skin" type.

Maybe charging the laser *wasn't* completely insane.

And he probably had a really good reason for the stupid outfit.

"Welcome to Wemm Station, Miss Redding," Palmer said. "Bear Palmer, Security Second."

Watford's glare and the adrenaline thrumming in my veins made me want to shout, but I kept my voice low and said "Pleasure to meet you, Mister Palmer."

"Babble later," Watford stage-whispered. "After the next blast, go."

I tried to control my breathing and slow my hammering heart.

Indigo light sliced the air, close enough to touch.

It had barely vanished when Palmer launched himself up the access tube.

4

I hauled myself up the aluminum access tube hand over hand, letting my feet dangle behind me, a gentle breeze from the air handlers at my back. The tube was wide enough that I didn't have to worry about knocking my head against the far side, but narrow enough that nobody could climb next to me. Not at the speed we hurtled ourselves upwards, at least.

We had seconds to make the weightless climb to the Core before Doctor Tansi fired the laser again. Maybe point man Palmer was a cyborg, equipped to survive a metal-melting beam of light. That didn't mean Watford and I would escape unscathed.

The next time Human Resources sent me an apple, I'd check it for worms.

Watford's boots kicked the air right above my head, so close that more than once I had to yank on a handhold to a stop myself a smidgeon of a second before I smacked his boot with my head. The stench of ozone and hot metal, with undertones of sweat and leather, filled each desperate breath.

Security First Watford had maybe sixty kilos on me. Most of that weight was muscle, true, but the truth was, even without his extra twenty years I was faster than him. I could scuttle through this tube faster than he ever could.

If he'd just get out of my way.

Forty meters up. Another forty to go. And Watford was already huffing for air. How had that guy passed the Montague physicals?

Around Watford's flailing feet and desperately snatching hands, I glimpsed the tube receding into the Core, a small disk of light marking the end of the tunnel. Palmer was most of the way up, ahead of us. Other than his exhibitionist mesh clothing and those ridiculous briefs, Palmer had seemed decent. I didn't want him facing a violent scientist with a metal-melting laser alone.

And Watford was slowing me down.

Way down.

I itched to shove past him, but that would only slow us both down. From the few moments we'd had, I suspected he'd explode at me for even suggesting it.

I clutched the handgrip ring more tightly, and fought to keep my speed slow enough for Watford.

How long had it been? Ten seconds? Fifteen?

Best case, Palmer escaped the access tunnel before the next laser blast. But at Watford's speed, he sure couldn't.

And if Watford couldn't, I wouldn't either.

I wanted to squeeze into the space between two rows of handgrip rings. Leave the space in the center of the access tube clear. Let the laser blast past me, let it take another stab at the Ring Six outer wall. Take this mad dash in two stages.

My ears strained to hear over Watford's heavy breathing, our hands bouncing off metal walls, the constant low hum of Wemm Station's air handlers. My frustrated pulse throbbed in my temples.

Watford had said there was a plan.

I had to trust him.

How many seconds did we have?

Maybe two-thirds of the way up.

A rung slipped in my sweaty grip.

Tansi screeched again, that same bizarrely constant perfect pitch. If I'd brought a wineglass it would have shattered.

Palmer said loudly "Take it easy, Doctor Tansi. Nobody's going to hurt you."

An electronic buzz filled my ears.

I couldn't help throwing myself against the side of the access tube, even though it was too late—the laser would have burned right through me before the sound arrived, before my nerves could register the shock.

No laser beam assaulted us.

The circle of light at the end of the access tube actually darkened, as if something had blocked most of the light.

Watford froze in place, hand on a ring.

My inertia carried me up an arm length, so that I found myself staring at the back of Watford's knees before I could catch myself.

Seconds later the electronic buzz stopped. The end of the access tube turned light again.

Watford jerked forward, launching himself forward like he'd been jabbed with two-twenty volts. His panting slowed into deep, heaving breaths, and he rocketed up towards the end of the tunnel.

I grabbed a handhold and threw myself after him, emerging into the spherical Core seconds later.

The Core was maybe ten meters across, totally lined with computerized equipment, screens of all sizes and shapes, and countless patch panels trailing innumerable heavy cables. Several mechanical hatches seemed to offer access to the vacuum outside. The designers hadn't bothered with anything like a floor, or furniture. Sitting in zero gravity isn't useful.

Palmer floated in midair, arms and legs drifting limp around him. From the back he didn't look injured, but erratic electricity crackled irregularly along his mesh shirt and pants. The smell of ozone was a lot stronger here, but at least I didn't smell scorched flesh.

Doctor Tansi hung maybe ninety degrees up the wall. His red-and-blue slacks and shirt showed off a lean, flexible strength. His face was locked in a rictus, like he'd been electrocuted. Sweat covered his face, and his chest shuddered from spasms of hard-fought breath. One hand clutched a handhold ring. The other made twitching, trembling gestures in the air, like he struggled with invisible controls.

Tansi's mad gaze flickered past Watford and I.

Then jerked back, and snagged on us.

"Redding!" Watford shouted. "Get Tansi!" He leaped straight across the Core, towards the far wall.

I dragged in a breath and threw myself at shivering, straining Tansi.

I practiced hand-to-hand fighting every day, but always in gravity. After years of training I felt barely adequate when my feet were on the ground. The four-hour Introduction to Zero Gravity Empty Hand Combat course had only convinced me I knew nothing.

Hopefully I knew enough to occupy Tansi for a few moments.

Tansi's gaze met mine. His black, sweat-rimmed eyes held a void as echoless as the empty universe outside Wemm Station.

Soaring towards him in free fall, I kept my hands outstretched in front of me, open but fingers hugging each other. I didn't need to break a thumb.

Tansi recoiled at my approach. His lips twitched around his jammed-open mouth.

I reached for his outstretched arm.

Tansi yanked the limb away.

Inertia kept me gliding towards him. My fingers caught his shoulder, tangling in the fragile linen of his shirt.

Tansi shrieked again. He released the handhold and swung at my head.

Then we were spinning around each other, struggling in zero gravity.

My combat training was all based on the idea of a rationally irrational partner. Someone swings at you, they want to knock your head off. Tansi didn't. He used his arms like clubs, not caring if he struck me with his hand or his bicep. He didn't even make fists.

He'd forgotten how to use his own body.

Tansi twitched continuously in horrific rictus, but he didn't try to thrash around or throw me off.

Jaw clamped open, he didn't try to bite me.

But the spherical room swung dizzily around us, a kaleidoscope of lights and screens and instruments. The more tightly I held Tansi, the more quickly we spun. My head whirled with the motion. If I didn't end this soon, I'd be too dizzy to hang on.

I sucked air against the growing nausea in my gut, wrapped my legs around Tansi's midriff, and locked my heels together behind his spine. That freed up my hands to try to cope with the spasms of his flailing arms.

"Doctor Tansi!" I shouted.

Tansi screeched again. His mouth never moved—the high-pitched monotone howl seemed to rise straight from his lungs. Spittle caught my face.

"It's okay! Nobody wants to hurt you!"

I managed to grab one wrist, then rode the swing of his arm to get my other arm behind his elbow. A quick twist, grab my own wrist, and suddenly I had Tansi in a shoulder lock, anchored by my legs clamped around him.

Most people try to move against that kind of lock, scream with pain, and stop struggling.

Tansi just thrashed mindlessly, lacking even the reflex to pull away.

I pulled the lock even tighter. "Doctor Tansi! Stop this!"

Tansi screeched only centimeters from my ear, driving metaphorical nails into my skull.

My pulse pounded in my throat. Sweat slicked my face, my arms, my back, shaking off into the air as we struggled or soaking into my uniform. I tasted hot copper and bitter adrenaline and a hint of bile.

Tansi convulsed.

Through my interlocked arms, I felt Tansi's shoulder shift unnaturally.

Sudden fear weighted my stomach. My imagination flashed up an image of his skin splitting, some alien shape-changing horror bulging from Tansi's body, a nightmare straight from the stuff my parents wouldn't let me watch.

I gritted my teeth, refusing to release the grab.

Tansi *heaved*—

—and ripped his shoulder out of joint.

His arm suddenly rolled impossibly far back, pulled by the pressure of my interlocked arms.

Tansi didn't cry out, or scream. His convulsions didn't change their rhythm.

Horrified, I released the grab. I'd practiced that lock thousands of times, always with the instructor's warnings echoing in my brain. *This is dangerous. Don't hurt your partner.* I'd learned to release the lock the second my partner submitted.

And here Tansi had destroyed his own shoulder rather than stop fighting.

Vomit surged in my throat.

I caught myself before my ankles reflexively detached, though, keeping myself anchored to Tansi's trembling form.

Tansi kept flailing the arm attached to his wrecked shoulder, somehow not understanding that he'd broken himself. I had to hug his side and duck my head to his flank to protect myself from his wild swings.

We whirled in empty air for a long heartbeat.

I couldn't hit Tansi. A good hard hook punch doesn't do much in free fall.

If I locked another joint, he'd break his own limbs to escape.

Hugging Tansi's flank, I tugged myself around his body to put my belly against his spine, fighting to maintain my grip despite his constant convulsive shuddering. Tansi's arms, even the wounded one, battered my shins and interlocked ankles.

I wove one arm around Tansi's taut, trembling neck, squeezing my forearm beneath his gaping jaw, grabbed my own bicep, then anchored the other hand on the back of his head against his tight, curly hair.

And squeezed.

Not the throat—the throat crushes too easily. But the bones of my arm lay across his carotid arteries.

In seconds, Tansi's struggles slowed.

I fought to slow my own panting.

Then Tansi sagged, limp.

I immediately released Tansi's neck, but kept my legs anchored around his midriff. My lungs heaved as I sucked air and ozone and hints of Tansi's lime cologne mingled with our sweat.

My awareness slowly expanded. Palmer stirred, one hand on a ring in the wall and the other at his head. He breathed slowly and deeply, not like a tired person, more like a guy trying to hold his temper. Watford glared at me from his perch near a medium-duty laser, haloed by disconnected cables.

Too short on air to say anything, I nodded at Watford. I put one hand on Tansi's collar as an anchor and eased the death-grip in my ankles.

Watford scowled. "Scene secure!" he shouted.

Mvouba's head popped into the room—he must have already been on his way up the access tube. "What have you done!"

Watford growled, "We've secured the scene. As you demanded."

"With a field disruptor!" Mvouba pushed off the wall, aiming towards a spot near Watford.

"That was the available equipment, yes."

I glanced at Palmer.

Palmer gave a sheepish shrug. The side of his mouth twitched upwards.

"You may have corrupted every experiment!"

More Congolese crew followed up the access tube as Watford and Mvouba's argument escalated. I happily relinquished my hold on Tansi to two medics and claimed a spot next to Palmer, working to catch my breath.

"Unacceptable!" Mvouba finally shouted. "I'll be reporting on you to my superiors!"

"Go ahead," Watford shouted. "I can use another commendation. My duty—my *only* duty—is securing the Portal. Aliens attack Ring One, you call me. You call us again for some bogus internal sewage like this, I'll bring a bigger hammer."

Choked rage made Mvouba tremble. "We are finished with you, Mister Watford."

Watford smiled. His voice dropped to normal. "But as long as you use a Portal, Commandant, Montague's not finished with you." Watford looked up. "Palmer. Redding. With me."

5

You can't stalk in zero gravity, but Watford sure tried. I did my best to keep up. Palmer grabbed his folded-up khakis from the base of the access tube, tucking them under an arm to scurry after us. I eyed Palmer in the elevator, but he quickly shook his head and glanced at Watford's back.

You *can* stalk in Ring Three's point-eight gravity, the same level as the Portal. Watford marched us to his office. His first words since leaving the Core were, "Take a seat, both of you."

Watford's spacious office looked like it was furnished in Minimalist Neo-Industrial. Bare aluminum walls, with a screen painted on one. Watford's desk looked too small for the room. A little larger than the usual Montague issue, it held only a keyboard and a display. Voice control is nice, but without an implant nothing replaces a keyboard for high-speed information processing. The air humming through the vents hinted at electricity and lubricant.

I eased myself onto a vinyl-covered aluminum-frame chair and leaned back with a grateful sigh. The fight with Doctor Tansi had adrenalized me, but burning that off left me exhausted. My back ached, my arms and legs felt battered and unwilling to move. My lungs ached. With enough gravity to sit but not enough to weigh me down, the chair's thin padding made me groan with relief.

"Problem, Redding?" Watford asked.

"Uh," I started. "No, sir."

Watford reached down into his desk, pulled out a bottle of water, and tossed it at me. "Always drink after a fight," he said. "You should know that."

I fumbled the catch, but snagged the plastic water bottle before it fell.

"Ask for what you need," Watford said. "You *will* get it, but I'm not going to read your mind."

The flat, metallic water tasted delicious. "Yes, sir."

Watford's brown eyes flicked to Palmer. "You said you could handle the laser. I got up there and found you floating half-dead. What's the problem?"

"Normally yes," Palmer said levelly. He sat with one ankle over the other knee, completely relaxed despite wearing only skimpy briefs and a form-fitting fishing net. "But the few systems I have activated are capped at half load."

"You pulled the specs on their lasers," Watford said.

"Tansi increased the power somehow," Palmer said.

Watford's eyebrows narrowed. "Those are supposed to be sealed units."

Palmer shrugged, the lean muscles of his chest shifting beneath the mesh shirt. "The laser was firing at almost nineteen percent over spec. Sir. Given a few hours, he could have punched through the Ring Six wall."

Watford chewed his lip. "Get yourself checked out. I want to be sure you're running at spec. If we need to increase your power reserves or lift your cap, I want it done today. Dismissed."

"Yes, sir."

"But put your uniform on first," Watford called at Palmer's retreating buttocks.

The door slid shut behind Palmer. Watford pivoted his attention entirely to me. "Welcome to Wemm Station, Redding."

I screwed the cap back on the half-empty water bottle. "Thank you, sir."

"Normally I'd have given you a slow morning to adjust to the time change."

I blinked. "Time change?"

"You haven't had a chance to notice, have you? We're on Congolese time here, not Uruguay."

I couldn't help a faint smile. "I was on vacation in the Congo, not three hours ago."

"Good for you." Watford leaned forward. "Let me tell you, Redding. Our concern here is with the Portal. Specifically, what goes into the Portal." He raised a loosely coiled hand, shaking it for emphasis. "The Congolese are the world's newest superpower, and every one of their staffers, from the researchers to the janitors, have something to prove. They started Wemm Station after their Titan colony imploded, and they've got a chip on their shoulder for it." He raised a single finger. "And the bastards at Headquarters who negotiated the contract didn't take that attitude into account."

"So, they want us to handle their crew?" I said.

"One of their people goes space-happy? That's not my problem. It doesn't threaten Earth." Watford leaned back in his chair. "But every time they have a kerfuffle, they call us. We have twenty-four people. Exactly enough staff to secure the Portal and care for our own people."

I grimaced. "How often do they have trouble?"

Watford's eyes narrowed slightly.

"Sir," I added.

He gave a tiny, unconscious nod of his massive head. "The damn fools brought families. They brought their *kids*. Said it's part of their 'cultural heritage.' It's like they're building a colony or something. You get people starting fires for a barbeque. Teenagers mucking with their datacore."

"We have our own datacore?" I said.

"Didn't they brief you?" Watford said.

"I accepted the assignment a couple hours ago. Spent most of that getting here." The back of my mouth still ached, so I took another sip of water. "And helping with Tansi. Sir."

"Not your fault. Fine." An air handler kicked on, and Watford raised his voice slightly. "Montague controls Ring Three. We have our own datacore, our own medical, our own barracks. No HR, one administrator for paperwork. We have a little space on each of the other rings. Our datacore talks to theirs, but it's heavily filtered. You can make calls and appointments and simple queries. And you'll be doing a lot of that."

Appointments? An alien universe, and I'll have appointments?

"You get the dirty end of the stick, Redding." Elbows on the laminated desktop, Watford steepled his fingers. "You're going to be the point of contact for the Congolese. And I handled today the way I did specifically for your benefit."

"Sir?" The vinyl chair had started to absorb and reflect my body heat, making my sweat-soaked shirt even more sticky.

"I can't stop Mvouba's people from demanding my involvement. But I showed them that calling me in has *consequences*." Watford gave a humorless smile. "I instructed Palmer to use the field disruptor against Tansi's laser so that the Congolese scientists would *have* to check every piece of equipment. Every bit of data. It's probably fine—the research has legitimate value, we didn't try to wipe it. So I'm the bad cop. You get to be the good one."

My heart sank. "I'm a babysitter."

"It's not exciting, but someone has to keep Mvouba's people off my back. If they have a problem and want Montague involvement, you get to go along. If they demand my presence, go ahead and ask—but now they know I will scorch the earth."

I made myself take a deep breath. This sounded more and more unpleasant.

"You'll probably work with Lieutenant Habre," Watford continued. "She's Mvouba's security lead. It's her first time in charge of a major facility. If you have a real problem, you call me. Your dossier says you're an adequate security officer. You've been to a few universes. You have common sense, you know when things are going wrong."

Like fun I'm just *adequate*. "I'd like to think so, sir."

"You're a Third, but you'll report directly to me, either in person or in writing. Daily. If something seems off, though—if there's a real problem, something that might get through the Portal back to Earth—you let me know *immediately*."

"Yes, sir."

Watford folded his fingers together. "Montague is a sharing environment. We normally have few secrets in-universe. This assignment is different. If the Congolese want information from us, they need to file the request through the datacore. You provide them no new information. Portal scheduling, the lunch menu... all of this is confidential. As far as they know, Palmer is an ordinary research cyborg. You are to keep it that way."

Palmer wasn't ordinary? "Sir."

"And our barracks are full. Your quarters are down in Ring Two, with the Congolese, at normal Earth gravity. I don't want you fraternizing with them, though—you eat up here, you shower up here, you access any facilities you need up here. Treat it as a security issue. It's not that I think Mvouba would slip something in your food, but we're responsible for protecting Earth. Medical scan every day, same reason. Besides, some parts of the station, like the core and Ring One, the engineering area, don't have the magnetic cosmic ray shields. If you take a hit of radiation, I want you straightened out right away. Get to know the Congolese crew and their parts of the station, but don't go making friends. And blame me for everything—remember, you're the face of reason. A friendly teddy bear, patiently explaining the rules. With a smile. Any questions?"

I sucked at the inside of my cheek, thinking. "I do, but it's probably best if I start by reading the dossier. Sounds like you want me to get them out of your day."

"Exactly." Watford leaned forward. "Like I said, it's a lousy job. You get two months at it because I don't want anyone bonding with the Congolese. This is not a partnership, it's political garbage. They wanted to build a station, they paid to build the station, they get to run the station. The only reason Montague agreed was because this universe is mathematically identical to our own. It's sheer physics research in an empty universe, no immediate commercial applications, no exploitable resources. You're Montague's eyes and ears while they do it. And if you can help them take care of their little problems, better still."

"Sir."

The thought of the space station had excited me, but now the assignment sounded like I was going to be a rawhide bone tugged between the mastiffs of Montague and Mvouba. If either won, they'd gnaw me to bits. I made myself take a deep breath. "I'll handle it, sir."

"Of course you will." Watford waved a hand. "Take a break. Get a shower, clean uniform. Find your quarters, study your dossier. Dinner's at six, so meet the rest of the team—we don't have an HR group here, but Palmer will show you around. Dismissed."

I stood up. The sweat from the fight had cooled, leaving my uniform clammy. A shower sounded great. "I'm on it. Sir."

I had one foot out the sliding door when Watford said "Oh, and Redding?"

I stopped and looked back over my shoulder.

"Your zero-gee hand-to-hand is *pathetic*," Watford said. "Completely embarrassing. Join the zero-gee hand-to-hand group tomorrow. Room eighty-four, Ring Six. Every night, eight PM, until I say otherwise."

6

Guiding me to my quarters, my datalink steered me to the elevator and down to Ring Two. When the elevator doors parted to a stunning barrage of noise and color, I immediately realized that the Congolese did things very differently.

Montague furnishes their facilities in a drab, utilitarian style. A photo or a painting on Watford's office wall would have surprised me. The closest the company gets to decoration is the company logo stamped on mass-produced items like metal stair treads and the bottom of white ceramic dinner plates. Montague builds industrial facilities and barracks, not homes. They're factories that might need to be abandoned with very little warning.

The main corridor of Ring Two looked like a broad covered avenue. The ceiling was painted a pale blue indistinguishable from the Congolese sky I'd seen only hours before in Lubumbashi, reflecting indirect light over the brightly patterned wall hangings, woven from cotton or wool or some broad plant-based stuff I didn't recognize. The Congolese famously insisted that hand-crafted materials were inherently superior to machine work, and each wall hanging and painting and rug had a tiny touch of imperfection that indicated a human hand.

The walls had to be metal. But I couldn't see any.

Warmth radiated from the azure ceiling. It wasn't quite as warm as the resort, but they'd certainly turned the thermostat up a few degrees.

We were in a space station, spinning at who knew how many revolutions per minute through an empty void. The air had to be mechanically processed and recycled, filtered to molecular-level purity. But the hall was full of cardamom, ginger, and mint from a communal kitchen nestled a few meters to my left, with tables spilling out into the corridor like a street market. A leg of goat turned slowly over an electric grill, sending its sizzle straight into my nose.

Don't get me wrong—Montague feeds us well. It's balanced, nutritionally complete, healthy, and as tasty as the universe's natural laws permit. The bosses eat the same food we do. But eating in the company cafeteria, it takes real commitment and effort to lose your figure.

Nothing the company had ever fed me smelled as good as that roast goat haunch.

And the people! Montague attracts people from all over the world, each with traditions and garb to set it apart. We sign on to Montague's sheltering embrace and get issued company-issued khaki uniforms. The only part of my outfit that looks good is the leather boots, and I only get those because I'm in Security. You learn to ignore the outfit and concentrate on the person wearing them.

Here, a Congolese woman in a complexly patterned red and blue blouse and long white skirt shouldered past me without interrupting her conversation with the woman next to her. She spoke liquid French, far too quickly for me to follow. Three dark-skinned men walked the other way, in traditional Congolese variegated green camouflage kilts and darker but similarly patterned tight wickaway shirts that showed off some impressive muscle definition, everyone talking simultaneously yet somehow listening to each other.

Everyone looked athletic and healthy. At the resort, the porter had insisted on carrying my bag rather than using a trolley. Waiters hefted trays of food by hand rather than using a hovertray. Their culture's emphasis on creating by hand applied even to washing dirty dishes.

They'd brought that same aesthetic into an empty universe.

I'd grown accustomed to working with people from all over the Earth. I'd grown comfortable, even relaxed, with the English language Montague used. But now I wore a dull uniform amidst colorful swirling skirts and kilts. The only Latina in a flurry of Africans. The only one not speaking French.

And I'd feed my dirty dishes to a reliable, *sanitary* washing machine, thank you very much.

A couple of children, maybe five years old, dashed past me. One girl ducked behind my legs to peer at the other. "Je te vois! Je te vois!" The little girl laughed, then scampered away behind her friend.

This wasn't an alien universe—this was an alley off some idealized Congolese market square, straight out of a 23rd-century Fabrice Bakila novel.

The resort still fresh in my brain, déjà vu overwhelmed me for a breath.

The short man working the communal kitchen saw me and smiled. "Bonsoir, mademoiselle! Une collation, peut-être?"

I should have brought the phrase book. *Collation*—snack? I'd picked up scraps of lame tourist French during my truncated vacation. "Bonsoir, m'sieu." He flinched at my accent, but when I said "Merci, no, merci," he smiled and raised an open hand.

Nodding to the vendor, I turned and pushed my way deeper into the riot of color, sound, and smell.

The good news was, in two months I ought to pick up some pretty decent French. Unless that was fraternizing.

I didn't *know* I was trapped between Watford and Mvouba. It might not be that bad. Perhaps my mere presence would dissolve the acrimony between them and soothe their hurt feelings, through the magical power of positive thinking.

My datalink guided me through fifty meters of broad hallway. Each sliding door had a hand-painted label, either with a family name or a type of office. A red cross flagged a medical station. People had set up friendly little stalls, fencing off spaces on the sides of the corridor with brightly-colored wool cloth draped over wooden frames or simple hemp ropes strung between wooden posts. They offered to mend clothing or polish shoes or, like one old lady, read your fortune from your DNA print. You couldn't walk straight down the corridor, but had to weave a little.

No wonder they had security problems. Patrolling this place would be a complete nightmare.

The hall abruptly opened up into another communal area with plush padded seats and intimate wooden tables arranged in cozy clusters beneath vine-cloaked awnings. Along one side wall I glimpsed a half dozen pool tables behind a knee-high red brick wall topped with some kind of blue and yellow flowers. On the other side, a gaggle of gawky school kids tended a row of tomato plants growing from a long low wooden planter. A few people at scattered tables worked with tablets or laptops, or murmured quietly to subvocal implants. I guessed that after hours, this place would be full of relaxing workers.

This wasn't a space station. The Congolese had picked up a whole town, a full-on *city*, and dragged it through the Portal.

Through the plaza and down the hall, I found a sliding door with the Montague logo. It looked just like the real thing, except for the slight flourish at the end of the M that told me that someone had painted this by hand.

Well, they wanted to make me feel welcome.

Or they wanted me to know that they could do better by hand.

I had no idea which. It could have been either, both, or something I'd never figure out if I tried until this universe caught up to ours. I liked to think I had the soul of an artist deep inside. Possibly too deep. I felt reasonably secure in estimating my artistic abilities somewhere below the average rock.

My room was the most luxurious I'd ever been posted in. With thick carpeting, cheerful abstract wall hangings, and a recliner lush enough to make my dad's big comfy chair feel like a bed of nails, it looked like it had been decorated by my step-aunt the Mad Crafter. The air smelled faintly of… fresh-baked cookies? Pie? No, but something baked—vanilla, that was it. A small, irregular, hand-blown glass jar of essential oils sat on the bedside table, reeds splayed from the narrow neck.

What kind of mind thinks *You know what this space station needs? Vanilla!*

I kicked off my boots, settled on the plushly quilted queen bed, and dove into the dossier. I had a little over an hour until dinner, and I needed to devour and digest all this information before something else went wrong and Mvouba called on me to help. I might not have always done as well as I hoped on assignments, but nobody could accuse me of not preparing.

Four minutes later, I had just sunk my brain into the Congolese organizational chart when someone rapped on my door.

⌐

I didn't recognize the sound at first—who knocks on a metal door? Normally your datalink asks their datalink to announce you. And the luxurious room had everything else, it surely had speakers.

Annoyed, I looked up from the dossier scrolling across the datalink.

The raps came again—three hollow knocks of knuckles on aluminum.

Back at the resort, the Congolese staff had always knocked. Those doors had been lightweight wood, though. Hinged, not proper automatics.

Grumbling, I swung my feet off the bed and wrenched my sweaty leather boots back onto my aching feet. "Open."

The door remained shut.

I touched my datalink. "Open the door."

"The door is not automatic from this side. The button is to the right of the door."

Who builds a space station with manual doors?

Someone who thinks it should smell of vanilla, obviously. I took three steps across the thick shag rug and touched a red button. The door slid silently open.

The woman on the other side wore loose slacks and a blouse, both in a deep blue that reminded me of the South Pacific, or a toddler's holiday dress, or the intensity of the blueberries imported into the first universe I'd visited. The blouse had colorful shoulder epaulets and a trefoil of rank on the shoulder. Her tightly-curled hair was cut too short to grab but long enough to offer a little protection, her skin like cocoa. She carried her weight on the balls of her moccasins, like a dancer or a martial artist, but had her hands clasped behind her back and wore an expression of ineffable good cheer.

I blinked. "Uh, hello?"

"Miss Aidan Redding?" Congolese accent, of course. She looked familiar—had she been behind Palmer earlier?

"That's me. And you are?"

She stuck out a slender hand. "Belvie Habre. I thought I should introduce myself."

Her warm hand had callouses. "Pleased to meet you." Watford had mentioned a Lieutenant Habre. "You'd be the head of security here?"

Habre's white teeth were surprisingly brilliant. I had to tilt my head back to look her in the eye. "My reputation precedes me. I hope it's a good one."

"Watford mentioned your name." I glanced back in the room. "I was just reading my dossier, trying to get up to speed on Wemm Station. There's a lot to learn, and I'm afraid that I've just been assigned."

"Not to worry," Habre said. "The Montague headquarters agreed to assign a dedicated liaison officer only this morning. When our Exploration Command realized that you were visiting our Federation, they contacted the airline and eased your way. Did you enjoy first class?"

The Congolese had arranged that upgrade? "Er, yes. Yes, I did." I glanced back into my room. "I'm not really set up to receive visitors, but you're welcome to that chair. It looks pretty cozy."

"If I know Montague," Habre said, "they sent you a big thick book of facts to memorize. Full of numbers and measurements and not a single human thing among them. I thought you might appreciate some context first. Could I offer you the Wemm Station tour?"

I couldn't help a little smile. "I'd love to, but I've got less than an hour until I have to go to work."

Habre answered my smile with a grin. "Then we'll have to make it only the best part of Ring Two." She stepped back from the door and held a hand aside.

So far, I liked Lieutenant Habre a whole lot more than Security First Watford. Too bad I reported to Watford.

I glanced around the colorful corridor, its bustling crowds, the booths of hawkers. A smiling guitarist perched on a stool a few meters from my door, fingers dancing on steel strings, hat between his feet. A boy, maybe seven years old, watched the guitarist, entranced, fists twisting the hem of his kilt back and forth.

Habre steered me away from the path I'd followed to my quarters. "Is there anything you particularly want to see, Miss Redding?"

"I don't know enough to ask," I said. "Surprise me."

"By all means."

Our exchange attracted the kid's attention. He stared at me with big eyes, like he'd never seen a Latina, then dashed off ahead of us.

"I'm surprised you use money here," I said as Habre dropped a small coin in the guitarist's hat.

"What else would we use?" Habre said cheerfully.

"I mean, this is a closed environment," I said. "You know what everyone needs."

"But not what everyone wants," Habre said. "If someone's willing to spend a few Congbucks on having their palm read, why not? Hello, Charity." She nodded at a young woman deftly passing a wooden shuttle through a small hand loom, beneath a display of splendidly woven shirts dangling from a thin wire strung along the ceiling. The woman responded a crooked half-smile, but didn't look up from her craftwork.

"Friend of yours?" I said.

"My sister-in-law."

"You brought your whole family? This is an alien universe!"

Habre laughed. "It is sayings like that which make the Montague people seem so strange. How can you bear to be so far away from your family, for so long?"

I let my gaze study an intricate oil still life of a disassembled datalink, neatly framed and mounted above an artist's booth. "Not everyone is so tightly tied to their family."

Habre shook her head. "In the Federation, your family would know better. Family is what gives us humanity. If we were to understand the earliest days of the universe, but lose ourselves, our whole expedition would be a failure. Ah, here we go!"

The hallway had opened up into another plaza. While the room looked about the same size as the first plaza I'd walked through, the décor was totally different. The tables were a little larger, suited for four or six or eight people. A slender man with graying hair and sagging skin stood behind a wooden counter, slicing shawarma from a jerkily rotating spear of packed chicken while a customer waited. Again, the smell seized my nose and made my stomach grumble.

"Manny has the best kebab on the station," Habre said. "Perhaps you'd be willing to join me for dinner one night?"

I winced. "I'd love to, Lieutenant, but my orders don't permit me. I'm to take all my meals with the Montague crew."

Habre's face clouded. "Silliness."

The old man handed the skinny customer a flatbread filled with sliced onions and steaming slivers of seasoned chicken. "Believe me," I said, "given my choice, I'd join you right now."

Habre pushed the scowl from her face. "At least *you* have good sense."

I took a deep breath. "Something that smells that good doesn't need much sense. Aren't you afraid the station will catch fire?"

"The wood is all treated," Habre said mildly. "It will ignite a little before the walls melt. Same with the carpeting, the clothing. If a fire starts, the computer will douse it before it can spread."

"I'm surprised you don't have firemen," I said.

Habre's scowl returned. "What do you mean by that?"

"Just that—look, you do everything else by hand."

"The station itself has full automatics," Habre said with a hint of anger. "A full range of fire suppression agents, all managed by the datacore. My team will respond immediately, of course, but we handle the human element."

"Of course," I said. I hadn't wanted to make an enemy out of Habre, but I seem to have touched a sore spot. "Really, I meant no offense. The station's just... very different from anything I imagined. It's like nothing Montague would build. My quarters—if I was sleeping upstairs, it'd be okay. But my room here, it's amazing. That bed felt like a cloud. It's like I'm back at the resort."

Habre seemed to decide to let her anger go. "I'm glad you like it. My husband is an artist. I asked him to create your chamber."

"I've been in a few universes, but none where I've thought a good way to spend a day off was to stay in my room to admire the walls."

"Most of those are my Lincoln's work," Habre said.

"Tell him he's very good."

"You'll have to do that yourself," Habre said. "His ego is already too inflated for me to manage properly."

"Well, if you need him to get a critique instead, let me know. It'd take some work, but I'm sure I could find something."

"He would laugh it off. Say that your taste had been atrophied by that horrific Montague aesthetic. To the right, here, then at the end of the hall."

My misstep hadn't caused any lasting harm—or, rather, Habre had decided to let me pass. She was probably as intent on working well with 'the new liaison' as I was on working with her.

At the end of the narrow hall, Habre stepped aside and held out a hand at the door. "After you, Miss Redding."

I raised my eyebrows, then stepped forward so the door slid open.

The room's darkness made its size indeterminate. The only bright light came from the door behind me. Unlike the hall behind us, the air here tasted cool and metallic, shocking after the tapestry of cooking food and growing plants we'd walked through.

The glorious spray of blues and reds and greens covering the far wall immediately seized my attention. It looked like an exploded egg in neon colors, stark against the surrounding darkness, so thickly textured it seemed to pulse with life.

That far wall wasn't a wall.

It was a window.

I took a step closer. "Wow. What is that? I thought there wasn't anything out there?"

Habre's rich voice filled the darkness. "It's a proto-nebula, the Veldt. In a billion years, it will be stars."

"How can we see it? I thought there wasn't any light out there?"

"The window shifts the spectrum. The Veldt is dense, the weight of all that hydrogen holds it together and makes it interact. It's ages off from fusion, but there's much heat and light."

"Amazing." The image was slowly turning, rotating around its axis. No—Wemm station was moving. I couldn't tell how far away the Veldt was, but if it would be more than one star it had to be millions of kilometers off.

A familiar thrill tickled the back of my neck. Inside Wemm Station's steel walls I might have been in an industrial complex. Even the fight in the Hub could have happened in a terrestrial airplane.

But gazing out at the Veldt, I suddenly felt myself in an alien universe.

"We don't understand our own universe," Habre said. "But here at Wemm Station, we have learned much. The earliest days of our universe are so different from our own, that just being here, now, we learn something every day. Our few months of learning have rewritten textbooks. It might even lead to faster-than-light travel."

Faster than light. Thirty seconds after Einstein announced that the universe had a speed limit, people set out to break it. Even my short life had seen half a dozen announcements that FTL was just around the corner.

Still: *so* tempting.

Habre said "The only blemishes on our expedition are these breakdowns."

I pulled my eyes off the Veldt. Habre's outline was a faint texture in the darkness. "Breakdowns?"

"Doctor Tansi was the fifth Congolese to suffer incurable devastation of his neural network in seven months."

Limned by echoes of red and green and blue in the darkness, Habre's face looked unnaturally solemn.

"The first four all died in seconds, or minutes. Tansi's damage isn't as bad—his body will survive. But most of his brain is misaligned. There's not enough left of his mind to reassemble the person he was. Or even *a* person."

My mouth went dry. Restorative neurosurgery is pretty reliable these days. "How does that happen?"

"We don't know. Watford insists that it's a flaw in the station design. All of the victims regularly worked outside the magnetic shielding, either in the Core or in Ring One. And perhaps it is." Tension made her voice tight. "Perhaps these deaths are a risk of exploring this universe."

"But you don't think so," I said.

"The laws of physics are the same here as at home," Habre said. "Our people have checked the station design, many times. We have supercomputers examining every detail of the magnetic shields. But still, it's a unique environment. A previously unknown cosmic ray or sub-atomic particle? Some side effect of the Portal?"

"The Portal's never done that to anyone," I said.

"Never before," Habre said fiercely. "What if we're somehow changed by the transition? Made vulnerable? My people are dying—it requires investigation."

Everything ached to tell Habre that we needed to check every possibility. I wanted to dive into the Montague datacore and compare the injuries to those experienced on other expeditions. I wanted to check with my teammates and go over everything, trying to find some common element.

But here, I didn't really have any teammates. I'd only met a couple of my fellow Montague employees. And I couldn't take this to Watford—he'd tell me this was exactly what I was supposed to handle.

"I have a lot of studying to do," I said slowly. "A little more won't kill me. Why don't you send me your reports on the previous victims?"

8

We can travel between universes. We mathematically describe, and visit, continua with convenient physical laws to make the impossible practical.

But wherever human beings go, we carry the indescribable anxiety of that first meal in a new assignment, standing with a steaming tray, surveying the crowded cafeteria for an empty space where we might fit.

There was a whole empty table at the back, right up against the dull gray bulkhead. Sitting there would declare either that I didn't need to know anybody, or that I felt too insecure to claim a place at anyone's table.

For the first time since elementary school, I felt really insecure.

Every human organization has cliques, and Montague was no exception. One of the most insular teams on any posting was the Portal guard crew, though. A division of Security, they bore the responsibility of making sure that nothing harmful got back to Earth, and weren't interested in talking to the scientists or administrators or even those of us in the rest of the Security crew. They were rightfully paranoid, and I couldn't blame them.

On Wemm Station, the only Montague people stationed here were the Portal guards… and myself.

A round table for four at the back hosted Watford, Palmer, and a lanky woman I didn't recognize. I wasn't going to claim a seat with the boss, no way.

That left two long tables, each with a few gaps between knots of people amidst the churn of unfamiliar faces. The closest group seemed really intense, heads together as they talked but voices sharp enough to form a percussive undertone to the rumble of conversation. At the other end of that table people ate without speaking—no good. I needed to ease myself into a group that already had some kind of rapport, not try to jolt the heart of a dead conversation.

There! And the familiar face wouldn't hurt.

I held my tray chest-high and carefully made my way between the tables to a gap. "Mind if I sit here?"

A couple of people looked up from their discussion. Across the table, one of them was Percival, the Portal guard who had inspected me on arrival. He'd been warm enough, and was the closest I'd find to a friendly face. "Sure thing, ma'am," Percival drawled. "Pull up a chair, make yourself at home."

"Thanks." I set my tray in the gap and perched on the floor-mounted low-backed aluminum seat.

"This here's Miss Aidan Redding," Percival said. "Just came through the Portal today."

"Welcome aboard," the skinny woman to my right said, fork poised in her hand. "Name's Twill."

"San-Chow," offered the chunky native Aussie to my left.

"Pleased to meet you," I said, tugging my napkin into my lap. After my plush quarters, the metal chair seemed designed to rub against my bones. It wasn't any different than any other Montague cafeteria chair.

I glanced from face to face, trying to anchor each name to a set of features. Yes, Montague uniforms have the owner's name stitched above the left breast pocket, but I always notice when someone looks down at my name.

"So you're the long-sought Congolese Liaison Officer," Twill said, stabbing at a slice of yellow squash.

"That's me," I said.

"Good luck," San-Chow said.

"Thanks." I studied my tray for a moment. On some postings, you're lucky if the universe's natural laws permit you to eat anything. Here, my dinner not only looked and smelled like real food, it was actual food, imported from Earth, and exactly to my preferences. Three ounces of salmon filet, grilled to perfection by the datacore. Green beans and a cup of long-grain wild rice, both steamed to retain the vitamins. A mug of thick spice chai. An orange for dessert, already peeled and sectioned and the nasty stringy bits of rind surgically removed.

I'd eaten meals much like this, many times. Nutritionally balanced, healthy, flavorful. My datalink had monitored today's activity and biological markers and transmitted my precise nutritional requirements to the datacore as I'd walked in the cafeteria door. Despite all my travel and the excitement in the Hub, I hadn't burned that much energy.

But right then, I really wanted fifteen hundred calories of hand-made shawarma rolled up in freshly-baked flatbread, from the stall right down the hall from my quarters.

I straightened my back and pulled my shoulders to attention. If I wanted shawarma, the datalink would get me shawarma. A correct serving. Straight from the food stores, chemically prepared to exactly match my tastes.

Right now, perfection felt annoying.

"What did you do to get assigned here?" Twill said.

The light and flaky salmon almost dissolved on my tongue. I reminded myself that it really was pretty good. "I was on vacation at a resort in the Congo. I think they picked me because I'd had a month off, and I was already on Congolese time."

"Sure you didn't piss off someone in HR?" Twill said.

"Why would you think that?"

"Our Twill," Percival said, "labors under the belief that this is the most annoying assignment in Montague."

Twill jabbed her chopsticks towards Percival. "I spent half an hour today telling this so-called colonel that he couldn't take his six-year-old daughter's macaroni art through the Portal to show his mother."

I grimaced in sympathy. Rank might have privileges, but privilege stops with the universe's natural laws. A very short list of items went back through the Portal without extensive testing. "Let me guess," I said. "They're not too fond of the clothing rules, either."

"We got that settled," San-Chow said as he gnawed a lump of something tucked into his cheek like a hamster. A dark, bald hamster. "Took a lot of yelling, though."

"I wouldn't care to hop the Portal in a kilt myself," Percival said. He had more food on his half-eaten tray than I had in total—and part of it was pasta.

Was that meat sauce?

Stupid metabolism.

"It wouldn't piss me off so much," Twill said, "if they were doing real work here. Sneaking stuff back for scientific research? Stupid, but it makes sense. Hand-made blankets and macaroni art, though? I mean, blankets." Her voice went up a notch and picked up Percival's drawl. "Mabel honey, grab me a blanket, the hydrogen's sleeting tonight."

San-Chow gave a little snort of laughter.

"You've got your job cut out for you, Redding," Percival said.

"Happy to help," I said. "I'm just getting started on the briefing, though." The datacore had added a nice touch of garlic to today's beans.

"How much lead time did you have?" Twill said.

I swallowed. "About two hours. Most of that coming in from the Congo."

"Not the best way to study," Percival said.

"You'll barely get started before they rotate you out," Twill said.

"I got the idea I'm a desperation assignment," I said.

San-chow snorted again. "Desperate to keep Watford from going ballistic."

Percival leaned towards me and lowered his voice. "If the only thing y'all do for the next two months is to keep Mvouba and Habre away from Watford, every person on this team will owe y'all a debt of gratitude."

"And not the 'get you drinks' sort of debt," Twill said. "More like 'you need someone to vanish?'"

San-chow's snort was starting to get on my nerves.

"I've read the summary," I said. "What do I need to know?"

"What's to know?" Percival began winding angel hair around his fork. "The natural laws here are exactly like those in our universe. There's no chance of discovering the next telomere binder or memory lead." He lifted the fork to stab a chunk of sausage. "It's all stuff they could get at home, if they could go back thirteen-some billion years." He stuffed the wad of pasta into his mouth.

"It's not that bad," Twill said. "Some of their observations have come up with whole new fields of math. The fabric of space is bent really weird, and the hydrogen interacts crazily. We might be able to use what they learn to compute new universe transitions."

"We already have zillions of universes." San-Chow probed the mass of gently steaming… what the heck *was* he eating, anyway? Some sort of colorless goulash? Whatever it was, it didn't seem to please him at all.

Maybe my rice wasn't so bad.

"Most of them are useless," Percival said.

"And most of those that aren't will 'bend a man's mind past madness,'" Twill said.

"And return breaking the world." The old movie pitch popped out of my mouth instinctively.

"Great flick," Twill said.

"Please," Percival drawled. "*Unsurvivable*? Cheesy as anything."

I'd grown up watching that movie over and over. At my friend Pavel's house, sure, because my folks sure wouldn't let me see that kind of thing. Childhood is the very definition of cheesy. "It's what people know about the Portal," I said. "Go too far, bend yourself to fit a new universe, and you'll go mad."

"The only madness we'll have here is boredom," Twill said.

"And spanking parents for being proud of their kid's art," San-Chow said, bravely scooping a spoonful of his gruel. "Don't forget that."

9

A new universe fills me with an incredible sense of wonder.

The next week... pretty much ate that feeling alive. Without salt.

I studied the briefing every spare moment, but Habre appeared randomly with a offers to show me another part of the station. Her hair-trigger sensitivity and my inflexible orders made me feel like I was constantly juggling nitroglycerin.

Watford was another jug of nitro. He demanded details on my every interaction with the Congolese. Mentioning that the grill down the hall from my quarters smelled good triggered a twenty-minute rant on the importance of relying on Montague facilities. When I hinted that Habre wasn't all that bad, he drilled me with blowhard questions on the proper security mindset.

Montague employs an amazing variety of people from all over the world. They're the best, but they all live the Montague way. It's like joining the police, or one of those old armies. The Montague rules weren't designed to cope with people who lived in any other way. Watford lived and died by the rules.

Habre showed me most of the station, though, from the swimming pool in Ring Two to the chicken farm—*chicken farm*, on a space station!—on Ring Five, and at least peered through the door of most of the research and development labs. I was briefly introduced to hordes of harried, overworked researchers. It's not that the Congolese worked their people too hard, but just like the Montague scientists, the researchers couldn't stop delving into the fire hose of data. Give a physicist a whole new way to observe quarks and fermions and hawkings, they'll work themselves to death.

I didn't get into Ring One, where the life-support gear and hydrogen scoop fields live, but that area's at one and a third gravities. Nobody goes there if they can help it. It's full of all the machines that keep the station alive, plus these huge tanks of hydrogen they sieve out of the void to feed the fusion reactors. The only reason to go to Ring One is if something has blown up.

When zero-gee empty hand practice rolled around after dinner each night, I was ready to smack someone. Something. Whatever.

Sadly, Watford didn't join us in actual practice.

Zero-gravity hand-to-hand combat is all about locks and leverage. All our regular martial arts assume that you can push off the ground. Without gravity, punching someone's head sets you both spinning through the air. The only thing you can do is grab each other and squirm around until someone gets better position and can lock a joint against itself. It's like Siberian shiu-chitzu, but without mats on the floor. Or the walls. Whichever is which.

All that fancy stuff they teach you in martial arts, then tell you to skip in a real fight? In zero-gee, that's all you get.

An hour a day of practice, for six days, had made me wish I'd paid more attention to tiny joint locks.

At least getting thrown around by my pinky made a nice break from studying the briefing, and my uncomfortable daily meetings with Watford and Habre. And I'd had enough experience with free fall that my stomach had stopped clenching.

Montague's zero-gee combat practice room was shaped like a chunk of curved sausage and lined with thick plush padding, even inside the cylindrical hatch to the Ring Six corridor. The padding diffused gentle white light across the room, stripping shadows away. Instead of metal rings for handgrips, the practice room used squishy hoops as soft as a newborn's toys. The rings could harden on command for advanced drills, but I wasn't invited to those yet.

I'd spent an hour every evening, for six evenings, getting thrown around like an inflated balloon, wearing a loose shirt and billowing pants made of roughly textured cotton. And the score was a whole bunch to zero, everyone-Redding.

But near the end of my seventh day on Wemm Station, I'd finally maneuvered myself into position to try a technique. Percival had this grip like a hydraulic vise, so I attacked the other end. I locked my legs around Percival's knee and planted my feet into his hip and waist so he couldn't double over, keeping his foot tucked behind my armpit. He thrashed, so I wrapped my arms around his leg and straightened to take the ankle lock. Percival's other leg bounced off my back, the angle not letting him get a good blow.

"That's it, Redding!" Watford shouted from his handhold. He was the only one still in a regular Montague uniform rather than a gi.

We bounced off another struggling pair, sending us spinning in a whole new direction.

Percival yanked his leg, trying to break my grip. I clamped down, ignoring the sweat beading on my face and drenching my shirt and my coarsely textured gi. Forty minutes into tonight's practice, our own sweat made every grab slick and thickened the air beyond what the air handlers could purge.

I slid myself out, keeping my feet anchored, and got one arm up over his Achilles tendon. In a flash I had seized my own bicep and brought the other hand up to clamp his toes and pull the foot into place, everything right for the first lock I'd managed since starting—

—and my datalink triggered the practice room's speakers. "Aidan Redding. Security alert from Lieutenant Habre."

I let my breath out in a short, wordless explosion of frustration and released Percival's leg. He tapped my leg to acknowledge end of practice. I unclamped my burning legs and starfished to slow my rotation.

"Redding," Palmer called from his perch near Watford. "Incoming."

I nodded, trying to relax to stop the strained trembling in my back.

Palmer swept me out of the air with uncanny precision. Where I had to jump off something and aim to hit a wall, Palmer adjusted our arc in midair, his cyborg implants somehow imparting momentum. Half a breath later I was grabbing the hand ring next to the circular hatch to Ring Six's main corridor.

Watford had a bladder of water in the crook of his elbow. I grabbed the water with a nod of thanks, then fumbled for hard-wired intercom next to the door. "This is Redding."

Habre spoke quickly, her Congolese accent thicker than usual. "Repairman Daktari Monard appears to have suffered a mental breakdown similar to the others. Can you assist?"

As she spoke I'd sucked water, and had to swallow quickly before I could say, "Where is he?"

"Meet us in the Ring Four airlock. Do you have a pressure suit?"

I'd started to sneak another mouthful of water, but the question set me to coughing. I kept my lips closed to keep from spraying Watford and Palmer, but Watford still glared bullets at me. "He's outside?"

"That is what airlocks are for, Miss Redding."

Palmer whispered, "Sir, maybe I should—"

Watford cut him off with a slash of his hand, which saved me the trouble of smacking Palmer. Calls like this were the entire reason I was here, but punching a cyborg isn't a good idea, even someone as good-natured as Palmer. I'd read the two-page summary on Palmer, just as I'd read every other Montague staffer's summary.

I hoped that we would *never* need Palmer, our final defense against a threat to Earth.

Because if we did, the survivors would all need pressure suits.

Except Palmer, that is. A deep space construction cyborg can withstand almost anything.

"I don't have a personal pressure suit," I said. "But I do have the training. I'm on my way."

"Good." Habre sounded a little less frantic. "We need all the bodies we can get."

"Redding out." The blue light disappeared as my datalink cut the conversation.

"What is your plan?" Watford said.

"Keep them off your back," I said.

"What if you can't?" Watford said.

"If they can't handle it and demand more help," I said, "I'll offer to get Palmer."

"Back at it!" Watford shouted at the room. "You gonna let someone else distract you? Chen, you lost him, start over!"

I guessed that was all the approval I was going to get.

I snagged my datalink from the tiny locker and clipped it to the edge of my gi. Sweaty and in bare feet, I slipped down Ring Six to the dedicated Montague elevator. My datalink used the security alert to have the car in place when I arrived and opened the doors as I approached. Before I could orient my feet to the floor, the elevator began dropping back towards gravity.

I'd had vacuum training. All Montague employees did.

Four whole hours, entering and leaving a sealed vacuum chamber.

How hard could it be, subduing a madman outside a rotating space station where hydrogen atoms screamed past at half the speed of light?

10

Most of Ring Four is Wemm Station's cropland. Because why import lettuce and corn from the rolling green acres of Earth when you can dedicate a huge chunk of your very expensive space station to farming? Not even hydroponic style, but in actual dirt imported from the Congo?

Fortunately, the Montague elevator isn't that far from the Ring Four exterior access, so I didn't have to cut through the cow sheds or anything like that on my way to the airlock.

Airlock.

Outside.

Wemm Station rotated about one point seven times a second. Ring Four was about four hundred meters across. That gave Ring Four a tangential velocity of about 35 meters a second.

If I slipped, I'd fall away from the Ring at almost a hundred thirty kilometers an hour. If I was lucky, I'd hit Ring Three and maybe not skip off it. If I had enough of a sideways kick to miss the next ring, though, I'd be a hundred kilometers away in an hour. They'd come fetch me, and I'd hear about it forever.

Maybe I'd bounce off Ring Four. I could break my neck, or ricochet off into the array of antennas enmeshing the station.

Or pass through the wrong part of the magnetic field, and get the electrical impulses of my nervous system crushed flat.

So: a tragic death, or ignominious fame.

Or hold on tight.

Yes, pressure suits had all kinds of safeguards. We weren't using custom suits cobbled together to cope with an alien universe's unnatural physics. These were right from Earth, and had centuries of experience-backed improvements behind them.

Could those improvements compensate for my whole four hours of experience?

I'd have to hold on really, really tight.

I needed a moment to recognize the scene in front of the airlock. I knew the smells of metal and grease, plus the farm's lush greenery. The faint underlying stench of the pig farm added just a touch of surrealism (although it smells a whole lot better than the chicken farm). The airlock itself was two massive bulky interlocking panels, the same general design that humanity had used for centuries now, set in an undecorated aluminum-walled work bay.

But Montague pressure suits are non-reflective silver, other than your name.

As you might guess, no two Congolese pressure suits were alike.

They were all built to the same general shape, baggy full-body suits of woven metal and tough plastic and cylindrical helmets with broad dark faceplates. Where Montague programs the smart cloth exterior to display vital information, the three fully-suited figures in front of me each resembled African lions, two lionesses and a lion that somehow added the impression of a great thick shaggy mane around the neck's chunky pressure seal.

Habre didn't have her helmet on yet, but the rest of her suit bore irregular leopard spots over rich gold. The spots weren't quite random, instead flowing in currents my conscious brain couldn't quite nail down. Two other members of Habre's security team I'd met briefly held their helmets ready, their suits in a less intricate leopard pattern.

"Lieutenant," I said with just a hint of a pant.

Habre studied me for half a second. My gi wasn't quite sweat-soaked any more—the station's air conditioning had dried most of it out, but I still reeked of hard work. "Are you in condition to go out?"

"I'm fine." I had downed the bladder of water in the elevator. "Bad timing, that's all." I'd met the other two Congolese security officers briefly, and scrabbled for their names. "Bapa. Ramazani. Nice suits."

Ramazani's smile barely cracked the granite of his face. Bapa nodded her chin a millimeter, no sign of the good cheer she'd had during our first meeting.

"Let me grab a suit," I said, slipping into the side room.

The smallest Congolese suit fit me, barely. I really needed the next size down, but the Congolese are all giants next to me. The cloth felt baggy and clumsy, the delicate gloves a little too large, but it would do. My datalink synched to it, triggering the biosensors at my wrists and ankles and neck. As Habre hadn't sealed up yet, I elected to carry my helmet out to the crew, the bulky life-support pack fairly heavy despite the two-thirds gravity.

Everyone but Habre had put their helmets on while I suited up. Habre rolled her eyes as I lumbered out. "Welcome, Montague."

I glanced down.

My datalink had configured the suit's smart cloth as per its programming: dull silver, with the name REDDING spelled out in tall serif letters across my chest.

I felt my face grow red and hot, and had no doubt that behind the other five blank faceplates, other eyes had rolled. "Regulations," I muttered.

Habre shook her head. "Daktari Monard was working on a long wire antenna on the Hub scaffold when he experienced a breakdown." She spoke directly at me—everyone else had already had the briefing.

I wanted to jump in and ask why we were on Ring Four when Monard was overhead, but held my silence. Habre wouldn't have gotten her job without knowing how to lead a briefing.

Habre said, "Monard immediately abandoned his partner and began climbing down Spoke Five." Right by this airlock. "We will intercept Daktari."

Elbow by my side, I raised a hand towards my head.

"Yes, Miss Redding?"

"What about the remotes?" I said. "Can we reduce his suit oxygen just enough to make him take a nap?"

"Monard has disabled the remote," Habre said sharply.

I winced.

"No, it should not be possible," Habre said. "But his suit is not responding to commands." Habre tapped a touchpad on her sleeve. "I'm sending you a security program. Establish physical contact between the palm of your suit and with Monard's life support pack, and you'll force-reflash his life support." Her face was tight. "The suit will immediately stop feeding him oxygen. We'll need to restrain him until he passes out, then we restore oxygen and get him to Medical."

I glanced around at my sudden teammates. "Will it go off if I touch someone else?"

"We're not daft. It's hard-coded to his suit."

I raised my hands in surrender. "I didn't think you were, but I'd rather ask a foolish question than make a terrible mistake."

Habre frowned but said nothing.

My datalink, clipped to the suit's bicep, buzzed. The fifty billion layers of security between the Congolese and Montague datacores flashed up a whole stream of warnings. Bypassing them meant I'd have to take my datalink to the Montague quartermaster for refurbishing. Watford wouldn't tolerate Congolese code executing on a machine integrated into the Montague infrastructure.

I didn't hesitate, but tapped the override button to load the code into my datalink and the suit.

"Do not harm Daktari," Habre said to everyone. "He's retained greater motor function than any victim before him. We might be able to aid him."

I sort of admired Habre's hope, even while thinking that more experience in alien universes would beat it out of her.

My datalink chirped, then Watford's voice bellowed from my datalink. "Redding, what are you doing? I got a request for you to disconnect from the Montague datacore."

Watford had intercepted the request. He couldn't have been watching me in real time—that sort of intercept had to be set up beforehand.

"Sir," I said. "My suit needs Congolese software to solve the current problem."

"Pass it another way," Watford snapped. "The data filters are there for a purpose, Third."

Frustration made me want to scream. Rules have a purpose, yes—but stupid software filters might keep me from saving someone's life. I swallowed bile long enough to say, "Sir."

"Watford out."

The datalink went dark.

Lieutenant Habre's face was a storm ready to break into lightning. "Turn around." Anger harshened her voice.

I rotated.

Habre touched my pack. My datalink beeped a soft warning as she manually transferring the program to my suit. "There. Now give me your helmet."

Why? Habre was already annoyed enough, so I clumsily moved my arm back until I felt her tug the helmet free.

She settled the helmet over my head, sealing the outside world. I felt a sudden huff of pressure all over my body as the suit sealed and puffed an extra few grams of air around me.

I'd gotten myself in and out of pressure suits dozens of times. Most of my vacuum training was putting the suit on and taking it off again. I might not know how to build a space station, but I knew perfectly well how to put the blasted helmet on.

My datalink flashed text above the view plate, rather than right on the screen. SUIT SEALED. CORE FUNCTIONS CONFIRMED. The words ADVANCED FUNCTIONS INACCESSIBLE blinked red. Those advanced functions probably required Congolese software.

"There you go," Habre said, her voice relayed by my datalink into the helmet's speakers. She lumbered around into view. "Good?"

"System reports seal," I said tightly. I'd told her that I'd had vacuum training, and yet, on our first real assignment, she blew that off.

Habre came around to my front and thrust her helmet into my hands. "Good." She bent her knees, bringing her shoulders level with mine.

I stood there for a moment before it hit me.

Putting my suit helmet on for me had nothing to do with my competence. It was about... caring, maybe? Respect? Teamwork? Something like that.

I'd have to think about it when I wasn't about to help catch a mentally broken crewman.

Carefully, I eased Habre's helmet over her short-cropped tightly-ringed hair, giving it the final twist to tell the automatics to start up. "Okay?" I said.

"All green," Habre said. Her anger at Watford wasn't gone, but her voice had grown a little softer. Maybe having me help her with her helmet had reminded Habre that I wasn't Watford.

Then we tromped into the airlock, and out into the hollow cosmos.

11

The airlock opened onto a roomy steel mesh balcony overlooking absolute nothingness. The only people who would see the balcony were construction and maintenance workers, yet the Congolese had built the surrounding waist-high fence and rail out of gently twisted square steel stock, giving the industrial platform a touch of artistic elegance. At every step, my magnetized boots clanged crassly. Two thirds gravity didn't require magnetized boots—but hanging on the outside of Wemm Station did. The half-dozen pressure-suited people around me moved in perfect silence, but the faint vibrations of their steps echoed up from my feet.

At my first step outside the airlock, an automatic safety line of woven steel whipped out of my belt and clamped onto the rail. Slightly reassured, I tromped out onto the balcony.

The bulk of Ring Four loomed over us. Rather than stark spotlights, the Congolese had even arranged their exterior lighting with an artistic sensibility. The massive white Ring somehow gleamed without glare. A ceramic coating, maybe?

I'd know, if I'd had time to memorize the briefing.

The pressure suit's support system purged carbon dioxide nicely, but it wasn't really designed to suck away the stink of my own sweat from almost an hour of empty-hand combat practice. The way the slightly too large pressure suit hampered my movements made my heart beat a little more quickly—not because of the suit, but because of what the suit represented.

I was in vacuum.

The stillness was a trick of perspective. This part of the station rotated at about thirty-five meters a second.

The safety line had me, but the vacuum still drew my unwilling eye.

I hadn't expected to see stars, not in this vacant universe, but I'd expected a greater impression of space. With no context, the blackness around the Ring might have ended ten meters away or endured forever.

If everything went wrong and I fell away from the station, I'd never even hit a star. Some future alien civilization might find my desiccated remains and carbon-date me at thirteen billion years old.

I'd mess up their physics *forever*.

The thought gave me enough of a chuckle to break the void's hold on my consciousness.

Looking up, the vast gleaming bulk of Ring Four curved away from us, leading to the smaller cylinder of Spoke Five. The centripetal gravity made the spoke appear stationary, rising up towards the slightly smaller bulk of Ring Five, a shining arc in the sky. Ring Five hid Ring Six and the zero-gravity Hub, but the antenna array rising from the Hub's axis of rotation formed a brilliant spire crossing half the sky. With no background to provide perspective, Spoke Five looked like a pillar supporting a glowing white heaven.

But halfway down the spoke, something jerked and twitched and spasmed its way towards us.

Habre spoke from my headphones. "Sahara, Odyn, Aidan, and I will surround the ladder. James. Matisse. Secure the hatch leading down, then back us up."

"Ma'am," I said amidst a chorus of acknowledgements.

We shuffled into place in a tight ring around the descending steel rungs.

Overhead, the twitching figure of Daktari Monard came closer.

He moved… wrong.

Where a normal person would ease their feet down to probe for the next rung, Daktari launched each foot out in a great, swooping curve until it struck the hull of the Spoke, then dragged it up to hook the bottom of the rung before dragging the foot around the rung to the top. His feet and body blocked my view of his arms, but those wild swinging gloves didn't look like any sensible climbing method I'd ever seen.

I didn't see any sign of safety lines, either. His suit should have been constantly launching and retracting safety lines as he descended. Instead, he relied entirely on his handgrips and magnetized boots to anchor him to the station.

Despite his weird motion, Monard seemed to be making good progress.

"Team Warthog," Habre said.

An unfamiliar voice said, "Oui?"

"English, please." Despite the mirrored view plate on the front of her leopard-pattern helmet, I could almost see Habre's eyes flicker at me. "You have Ring Five, Spoke Five blocked?"

"Yes, ma'am," the speaker answered with a Congolese accent thick enough to slice into chunks and fry for lunch. "Daktari won't pass us."

"Good." Habre leaned back to get a better view overhead. "Daktari! This is Belvie Habre. Can you hear me?"

I added Monard's suit to my comms mesh, and instantly heard a husky male voice moaning "Dehors… dehors… dehors…" In a moment he wheezed for air and picked it up again.

I dropped Monard's comms. *Dehors?*

"If he wants out," Ramazani said, "why does he climb down?"

"Nobody else has spoken," Bapa said. "We'll ask him."

I hesitated to speak my idea. I'd know the answers if I'd finished the Exterior Operations portion of the Montague briefing. But at Monard's current pace we had a few minutes before he got to us. "The way he's moving. He doesn't look like he's going to veer off the ladder or anything."

"Yes?" Habre said.

"Once he gets his feet on the deck, he'll be able to move more. If one of us could get a couple yards up next to the ladder, we could hit his backpack and reflash it before he gets his feet on the deck.

"Good idea, Aidan." Habre said. "James?"

"Yes, ma'am." The man in the male lion pressure suit raised his hands in front of his faceplate. The inside of the suit's wrists bulged out, right over where I'd check his pulse, and formed magnetic clamps.

The Congolese had software-reformable suits? Nice. Mine probably was too, except my Montague datalink didn't have the proper software to run it. I could launch safety cables, turn my boots on and off, and adapt my faceplate visuals, but that was about it. If I had a puncture, the suit's fabric would automatically flow to seal it.

James set himself to climbing the Wemm Station wall, held in place by magnets at his knees and wrists. Even at two-thirds gravity, that's hard work. About three meters up, he halted right next to the ladder, just out of range of Monard's kicking feet.

And we waited, watching Monard's flailing descent. I consciously relaxed my muscles one by one, refusing to wear myself out waiting for a struggle.

Three minutes later, Monard's feet came level with James' head. James unclamped his closest hand from the wall, his suit re-absorbing the magnetic clamp. He held his hand raised away from the deck, fingers curled loosely towards Monard.

"Come on, Daktari," James said. "Little closer, that is all…"

Monard lurched and lunged down another rung.

The glove of James' suit rippled, forming a thin tendril of smart fabric data cable that flowed through the vacuum. The cable swung oddly with James' throwing motion, skewed by the station's constant spin, but after one false try James got the end to swing against Monard's bulky backpack and stick.

The cable rippled with inertia.

"Reflashing," James said.

Monard swung another foot down below the next rung, weirdly pulling it upward to probe for his next step.

"Good," Habre breathed. "Surround the ladder, team. We hold him in place until he passes out."

"Right," I said. The semicircle around the base of the ladder tightened infinitesimally.

"Reflash failure!" James shouted. "My suit—"

Before any of us could say anything, James' lion suit rippled.

The smart fabric flowed, squirming over the pressure suit's metallic frame, crawling like a manta ray off the suit and up the data cable towards Monard.

Crystallized air exploded from James, forming a cascade of rainbows.

Smart fabric flowed off James' suit like poured water.

The thin wires of the suit's superstructure were too widely spaced to conceal the sudden rush of blood soaking the man's clothes or the twitching, gaping jaw.

His magnetic clamps gone with the smart fabric, James swung free, plunging back towards us.

I took an involuntary step backwards, hands coming up. My stomach knotted.

Smart fabric suits can't do that. They have fifteen layers of safeguards against vacuum breaches.

But frozen blood spattered the inside of James' suddenly transparent faceplate. The rest of his head and his exposed body, protected from vacuum only by a gaping cage of wire, said I was wrong.

12

I took another step back, defensively raising my own hands in front of my face. The pressure suit's bulk made my every motion clumsy, the magnetic boots clamping me to the steel grid of the balcony, reminding me that we were ants hanging onto the side of a space station in the middle of absolute nothing.

I should have stopped at the Montague armory on my way here. Grabbed a weapon. Fear and dread knifed my guts. Adrenaline made a bright copper taste at the back of my throat.

James had tried to feed software to Monard's suit.

Instead, Monard's suit had ripped the smart cloth right off of James' suit.

A thin data cable connected Monard's suit to James' body.

Habre shouted "James!" and raised her hands to catch his twitching body.

My gaze instantly traced the path between Monard, his suit misshapen and bulging with extra layers of smart cloth, to the data cable, down to poor James' corpse.

And Habre's outstretched hands.

I tried to shout a warning—

—Habre snagged a strand of wire surrounding James' ankle.

Her suit didn't dissolve.

I gasped.

My heartbeat trip-hammered in my ears.

Monard's back sagged, pulling away from the ladder, dragged by James' dangling dead weight and the excess smart cloth now clumsily wadded around his body in ungainly, random lumps.

One hand slipped off a rung.

"Combat mode," snapped an unfamiliar voice, with a chorus of acknowledgements.

I tapped the datalink mounted over my bicep. The words ADVANCED FUNCTIONS UNAVAILABLE flashed above my faceplate.

My blood ran cold.

All around me, pressure suits shivered and twitched. Shoulders, elbows, and knees thickened. The knobby life support backpacks grew armored shells.

My suit might have defenses—but I couldn't activate them.

I'd barely retreated a step when Monard lost his grip and fell sideways.

The station didn't have real gravity. When Monard released the ladder he continued sideways, only seeming to fall because the station was spinning up to meet him. From my perspective he seemed to plunge at a curving sixty-degree sweep, sailing through the air to crash belly-first against the balcony's guard rail right behind another lion-suited security guard.

The cable connecting Monard to James' body yanked tight. Habre jerked back on the corpse, letting her torso move with the force but refusing to lift her magnetized boots from the steel mesh floor.

The bulging Monard folded against the guard rail, then fell backwards onto the balcony.

"Software defenses on," an unfamiliar woman's voice said. "I'm on him."

The lioness-suited person next to Monard studied Monard's upturned-turtle form for a moment, then darted in to slap a hand against a narrow slice of exposed life-support pack.

"Good, Sahara," Habre said.

"Got it!" the lioness—Sahara—said.

Habre somehow got the data cable disconnected from the wire shell of James' suit. "Matisse!" she said. "Take James."

I recognized Ramazani's leopard print as he snagged James' body.

"I'm stuck!" cried the woman.

I whirled back to see the lioness-suited woman kneeling by Monard struggling to wrench herself backwards. Her hand remained planted flat against Monard's life support pack, no matter how the rest of her clawed for distance.

"Sahara!" Bapa shouted.

Sahara's suit burst into brilliantly sparkling frozen air, followed by a ruby haze of flash-frozen blood.

I found myself pressed back against the railing, trembling.

Sahara had put her suit in combat mode. She'd activated the suit's protective software, which should have blocked any malignware.

And Monard had still eaten her suit.

I didn't have even Sahara's ineffective protection.

If I even *touched* Monard, I was dead.

Maybe it was time to call Palmer—*no*. Imagine if that stuff, whatever it was, got into the cyborg's wiring.

Through the haze of wasted oxygen, I saw Sahara thrash within the wire cage of the pressure suit's broken frame.

Bapa and Habre both lunged for her.

My suit automatically dampened Bapa's shriek of "Daktari! Stop this!"

My feet itched to charge in and help. I told myself there wasn't room. I told myself my suit was more vulnerable than theirs.

But a shameful little voice in the back of my head had its own repetitive shriek: *coward.*

I'd faced appalling threats before. I knew I wasn't a coward.

Faced with an attack I couldn't defend against, though, I felt nakedly vulnerable.

"Don't touch him," Ramazani said.

"Right," I muttered.

Monard still lay on his back, now shelled within smart fabric. His arms and legs twitched and kicked, but he didn't seem able to stand. The weight of one suit isn't bad, especially in Ring Four's two-thirds gravity, but the misshapen weight of three suits seemed to have overwhelmed his grotesquely deformed movement.

Habre and Bapa jerked Sahara free by disconnecting the arm of her devastated suit, dragging her twisted figure back towards the airlock. They almost threw her at Ramazani. Her feet barely cleared the airlock before the massive two-part door slid shut. Even in the silence of vacuum, the force of the door clanging together vibrated all the way through the balcony and up into my shoes, making my teeth vibrate.

Habre said "He seems to be stuck. Form an arc, well out of reach."

My suit felt thin. Ephemeral. My tongue wouldn't move from where it was glued to the roof of my mouth.

I made myself step forward, and felt obscurely proud I wasn't the last to fall into place.

"Nobody touch him," Habre said.

I was too scared to make a smart comment. If Monard had control over his suit, he could have it form its own data cables and lash out at us.

"Ideas?" Habre said.

A man's voice said, "We need a computing device that can computationally block attacks from his suit's CPU. Something faster."

"We are *not* connecting Daktari to the datacore," Habre said.

The same nasty little voice that called me a coward now suggested pushing Monard off the balcony. Let whatever had happened to him and his pressure suit spin off into infinite emptiness. Let that hyper-advanced alien race find him thirteen billion years from now.

Instead, I said "Isolation. A solid metal container, a solid metal room. No intelligence in the handlers."

"That'll take forever to make," Bapa said.

"So the machine shop can start work while we figure out a better plan," I said.

Habre jumped in. "I'll send the order."

We'd started with seven people. Now Ramazani was inside, saving the bodies of our two casualties before they were lost to space. I couldn't blame Habre for the heartfelt decision, but that left us with four figures in a quarter-circle a few meters from the twitching turtle of Monard.

The vacuum looming out beyond Wemm Station didn't feel threatening any more.

But the vacuum right up against me bloomed with menace.

Monard stopped moving.

I had to force myself to continue breathing.

His absurdly overblown suit rippled just as James' and Sahara's had.

A bitter hope flashed through me, that Monard's suit would open to vacuum, solving this problem for us.

Smart fabric flowed off Monard's suit.

No, wait! I thought. I didn't really want Monard to die. He hadn't chosen this— this—no, I didn't know what had happened to him, but surely he hadn't chosen it.

I added Monard's voice to my feed again. His tone hadn't changed. He wasn't even breathing heavy, only repeating endlessly, "Dehors. Dehors. Dehors."

I cut Monard's audio. I wanted to ask Habre what he was saying, but Monard's rippling suit made me hold my tongue. We did not have time to talk.

The smart fabric formed two lumps, one on either side of Monard's prone form, stripping the suit back down to normal size. It still didn't look right, with weird lumps and ripples in the smooth surface.

But he could move.

Monard sat up.

Clumsily, like a damaged robot, he struggled to his feet.

13

Without a word, the four survivors stepped back.

In the middle of our rough curve, Monard stood near the balcony's finely wrought handrail, angled as if one leg had become longer than the other. No— one knee was bent strangely, pointing inward at a right angle to his foot. Had the changing shape of Monard's suit popped the knee within?

Or was Monard himself changing, like his suit?

He looked about my size. Had he always been that small?

Or was he somehow losing mass?

If we restrained him, if we peeled that demonic smart fabric pressure suit off of him, what would we find within?

James and Sahara had already died trying to restrain Monard.

I trembled inside my suit. Bright copper fear burned in the back of my throat, and my stomach clenched so tightly it cast tangled knots throughout my chest and gut.

If I had access to my suit's advanced functions, I would have had the smart cloth repurpose and recalibrate one of the lasers.

Not that I wanted to kill Monard.

Not unless he lunged at me.

But without the suit's advanced functions, I had only a whole suit of vulnerable smart fabric and a couple safety lines. I didn't even have tools—the suit's smart fabric formed hammers and wrenches and whatnot on demand.

My best weapon was the noxious stink of fresh fear-sweat inside my suit.

Monard shifted his stance. His feet left the deck for a heartbeat, the centripetal force only slowly bringing the deck up to meet him.

"Lucy," Habre said. "The latch to the next hatch down. Bend it so it won't open."

"Ma'am." Bapa—I never knew her first name was Lucy—knelt by the hatch, the smart cloth of her pressure suit's glove flowing into powered pliers.

Monard shifted his weirdly bent leg towards the hatch. It didn't want to support him—that knee must be broken, the way he sagged, but the smart cloth stiffened to support him.

Bapa seized the latch in her pliers.

I felt the vibration of twisting metal through the mesh deck.

Monard took another bouncing, skidding step towards the hatch.

One club-like swung wildly at Bapa's helmet, falling short by a couple feet.

I itched to dash forward, to grab Monard, to keep him away from Bapa.

The latch twisted a little more.

"Lucy," Habre said.

"Almost there," Bapa hissed, leaning on her arm, trying to use her mass to torque the pliers more. On Ring Four, nobody weighed enough to tamp down earth around a potted plant, let alone bend metal.

My brain churned. Monard's touch dissolved smart fabric, leaving only dumb wire frames. He didn't have any kind of coordination, just a stumbling shuffle straight out of a brain damage textbook.

Two more steps and he'd club Bapa's—*Lucy's*—helmet.

How many bodies could we drag inside?

I hesitate to call it a plan. It was more of a second millennium anvils-and-dynamite cartoon.

But I wasn't going to let Lucy die, too.

I tapped my datalink. "Disable safety protocols. Manual control."

Text flashed overhead. CONFIRM SAFETY OVERRIDE.

"Disable safety protocols now!" I snapped.

SAFETY PROTOCOLS DISABLED. That text didn't disappear.

"Aidan?" Habre said.

I'd left my comms open—idiot! "I have an idea." No, this wasn't an idea, it was a stunt, it was almost as insane as Monard.

But if it worked, Lucy would live.

Even if it failed, the others would probably live.

The only one who might get killed was me.

14

First, the safety lines. My suit had two, each made of woven and braided steel thread. I retracted one and manually clipped it to the rail directly behind me, then auto-retracted the other.

Monard lurched forward.

Lucy lowered herself further, still trying to wrench the latch permanently closed.

Monard's swinging arm wooshed easily, mindlessly over her head. He wasn't trying to hit her, only shamble towards his goal.

My heart pounded so hard I felt it in my throat, my ears, even my ankles.

"Lucy!" Habre shouted. "Back off!"

"I almost have it," Lucy snapped.

Maybe she did.

But Monard almost had her.

The stumbling madman didn't seem to be aiming for Lucy. He was bound for the hatch, determined to get further down the Spoke towards Ring Three.

The Montague ring.

Where was the Portal? Was it underneath us?

Was Monard maybe bound back for Earth?

No time. Whether Monard wanted Lucy or the Portal, Ring One or Three or whatever, he wasn't getting either.

I reached across myself to swipe a finger over the datalink on my bicep, bringing up the safety line controls. Red crosshairs appeared in the suit's viewplate, wobbling with my finger.

I was *not* shaking that badly.

No matter what the targeting system said.

Monard dropped to his broken knee, making me shudder in sympathy.

No, no time for sympathy either. Bapa was leaning back, but had her arm outstretched, still trying to wrench the hatch's latch so Monard couldn't get further down.

The crosshairs flashed on a possible target. There—*that's* what I wanted.

I locked the targeting system and said, "Safety line launch."

The line lashed out.

My breath stopped.

Even through five meters of line, I felt the spring-loaded hook snap at the end.

Right around one of the rings in Monard's life-support pack.

I still couldn't breathe.

James had touched Monard with a smart fabric data cord, and died. The smart fabric of Sahara's glove had doomed her.

The safety line was dumb. Purely mechanical.

But maybe my suit would start oozing up the line anyway.

I told myself to take another breath, that the air around me wouldn't gush out into empty vacuum.

Monard didn't even notice the impact. He raised his arm to club the hatch.

Lucy snarled and yanked her hand back.

No time to worry.

If I exploded in vacuum, I exploded.

I jerked on the safety line.

The line snapped taut.

I wobbled at the tension—but Monard jerked too.

And I had magnetic boots.

He didn't.

I heaved.

He slid a centimeter towards me.

"That's it," Habre said.

Then she was beside me, her hands gripping the safety line just in front of mine. "We get him up against the rail, tie him up somehow."

"Right," I said.

My lungs ached—I needed to breathe again.

It seemed my suit wasn't going to dissolve, so long as Monard didn't touch me.

We fumbled for a second getting our hands lined up. "Heave," Habre said.

We dragged Monard half a meter from the hatch.

He stopped swinging his arms, staring dumbly at the deck in front of him like the access hatch had vanished.

We shifted our grip up the line.

One of the suited figures stepped towards us.

"Two is enough!" Habre said. "Heave."

Monard fell onto his side and slid, grinding across the deck.

He'd barely stopped grinding when he thrashed his hands to the deck. Before Habre and I could grab the cable again, he'd hoisted himself to his feet.

But he didn't step towards the hatch.

Instead, he lurched in a pivot.

Faced us.

The busted leg lifted, and Monard trudged towards us.

15

Habre instantly stepped back from the safety line. Her helmet swiveled back and forth, and I could almost see her gaze even through the mirrored faceplate.

The safety line attaching Monard to my waist.

The second safety line, anchoring me to the sturdy metal railing surrounding the balcony.

"Let him go, Aidan," Habre said.

"Not yet," I said.

Monard lifted the other foot. Tromped another step. Waved an arm mindlessly before him.

No—not mindless. But not human. Like he didn't know what an arm was for, or how a hand worked.

"If he touches you—" Habre started.

"I know," I said. "I know!"

Instead of disconnecting the safety line, I put my hands on the balcony rail, right next to my anchoring line.

And hoisted myself.

My magnetic boots hung for a moment, then released.

I hoisted myself on my arms, to plant my seat on the thin metal of the balcony rail. My heels kicked against the fence below, the magnetic boots just barely clinging.

"Let him go!" Habre said. "You dying won't help anything."

The rail didn't shift at all under my weight.

"I don't plan to die," I said.

My datalink chirped. Watford shouted in my ear. "Redding! Your datalink's screaming you've left the station, what are you doing?"

"Sir, busy, sir!"

"Whatever you're doing, stop it!" Watford snapped.

I swung a leg over the rail.

"Oh, no," Habre said.

Monard wrenched himself forward. That busted knee skewed wildly under his weight, but he still closed to about two meters from me.

"Oh, yes," I said.

"Redding!" Watford thundered.

"Sir sorry sir!" I said.

In one smooth motion, I swung the other leg over the rail.

All I could see was an endless universe of empty vacuum.

I flung myself into it.

16

I'd skydived as part of my Montague new security employee training.

Not long ago, I'd flung myself out of a falling blimp.

But throwing myself out of a perfectly good space station was a new one, even for me.

How many times can you launch yourself into the void without being called an addict?

This is the last time, I told myself.

For an instant I hung in emptiness, Wemm Station out of sight behind me, feeling like the only solid object in this vacant universe.

Weirdly, my fear evaporated.

For that heartbeat, I felt like in all this universe, there was just me.

Nothing could hurt me.

Nothing could find me.

Peace.

I'd done it so quickly, Watford didn't even have a chance to scream in my ear.

Almost instantly, though, I felt a distant rattle.

My safety line, clattering against the balcony rail.

I slipped away from the station's inexorable centripetal force, for a glorious instant flying free.

But Ring Four spun at a good thirty-five meters a second, and I had about ten meters of safety line.

In a third of a second, inertia snatched me by the belt and whirled me around. The gleaming white expanse of Wemm Station flashed into view and spun away as the station's rotation overwhelmed my puny mass and whip-cracked me into order.

Without the suit's smart cloth and its automatic responses, the shock probably would have broken my neck. As it was, I felt like I'd plummeted from a fourth-floor balcony into a thick inflatable balloon—enough to knock the wind out of me, but not enough to break my spine.

Barely.

Lucy and Habre and the others shouted in surprise, and Wemm Station lurched into view. My vision wobbled wildly, still reeling from the sudden shock of the hard yank on my leash, but I could make out the airlock balcony.

My sudden leap had yanked Monard right up against the low fence. His wind-milling arms flailed and his legs thrashed, but the safety line snapped to his back-pack held him pinned fast.

The centripetal force made me feel like I hung from my belt, dangling from the cable at my waist, only saved from arching painfully by the automated support offered by the smart fabric suit.

"Everyone okay?" I said.

"Redding!" Watford sounded furious. "Report. Now!"

"I'm anchored to the station," I said quickly. "Safety line. I'm fine. Is Monard secured?"

Habre said, "I believe you have him, Miss Redding."

"I am on my way, Redding," Watford said.

I wanted to tell Watford not to bother, that we had the situation under control. But that wasn't my decision—and besides, I wasn't certain that dangling from the end of a safety line so I could use my mass to anchor Monard in place counted as any reasonable definition of "under control."

Monard's uncoordinated twitching and thrashing rippled down the line, but the pseudo-weight granted by the station's angular momentum and the second safety line kept the motion from knocking me around.

I had picked up a small rotation, maybe two or three revolutions per minute. One moment my feet pointed at the massive bulk of Wemm Station; the next, my head. My sense of balance didn't object, but my eyes insisted that I'd get motion sick, and soon.

Ramazani's voice said, "I have a report, ma'am."

Ramazani had taken Sahara's and James' bodies into the airlock, before they could get knocked into the empty cosmos. What was there to report?

"Go ahead," Habre said.

"They're both in medical pods. No apparent cerebral damage. Doctor Nile is examining them now."

Relief made me go limp in the suit as the rest of Habre's team exploded in cheers. In the explosions of frozen air and ruptured blood vessels, the shock of seeing smart fabric crawl away, I'd forgotten that vacuum didn't instantly kill. If someone's brain survives to reach a medical pod, if a scrap of life remains, we can regrow damaged tissues. I'd needed half my left hand regrown myself, not long ago.

Regrowing a hand itched fiendishly. I didn't want to imagine what regrowing your skin and your eyes would feel like.

If I'd had time to train properly for this mission, the trainer would have reminded me that vacuum was survivable. Montague would have sent me to one of the low-Earth-orbit stations to drill exactly that—and a hundred other emergencies—until I knew it in my bones.

I was seriously unprepared for Wemm Station.

Overhead, Monard twisted against my weight tugging at his shoulders, falling back against the railing.

One of his feet left the mesh floor.

A shiver went up my spine.

"Uh, Habre," I said.

Habre didn't answer. She hadn't even heard amidst the fading cheers.

"Lieutenant!" I snapped. If she acted quickly, if she used one of her own safety lines—

Monard's second foot left the deck.

His overbalanced, deadly form plunged over the railing.

Straight at me.

17

Angular momentum saved me.

When Monard stopped touching Wemm Station, he continued in the same direction he'd been going, perpendicular to the platform's position, while the station itself rotated away. He dragged me after him, then the safety line snapped taut and he swung into place further from me.

Tied halfway between Monard and the balcony railing, I got snapped, thrown, whip-cracked back, then wobbled and spun as the lines slowly steadied out.

Oh, and that slow rotation I had as I dangled there? I'd wrapped the two safety lines around each other. All that came undone in about three seconds, giving me a whole new dimension of nauseous spin.

Once the cable finished thrashing, though, the worst was over. I hung halfway between the airlock balcony and Monard, trying to calm my bitter stomach and hoping that the safety line was as strong as the manual said.

Habre called for a service scooter to come fetch Monard, confining him in a dumb metal crate. I felt nothing but relief disconnecting from him.

Then I retracted my own safety cable so Habre and the others could help me over the rail. They congratulated me all the way into the airlock.

I felt downright triumphant until the inner door opened.

Watford stood about five meters from the airlock, leaving plenty of room for everyone to traipse in. His muscular arms were crossed, the fingers of his exposed hand clenching his massive bicep. His jaw was set hard enough to use as a hammer. And I hadn't seen that much controlled fury on anyone's face since the Montague vacuum suit instructor found one of the new people adding helium to another new recruit's rebreather.

I unlocked my helmet and reached up to remove it, but Ramazani's hands were already there. I stifled my urge to slap his hands away and let him twist the helmet off. The work area's aroma of green crops and distant pigness hit my nose and tongue like a bucketful of life after the pressure suit's filtered purity, but I sucked it down as quickly as I could and said, "Sir—"

"Redding," Watford said, cutting me off as efficiently as a sledgehammer. "You and I will speak about Montague regulations later." He didn't even look at me, but kept his attention on Habre's suit. "Unsuit *immediately.*"

The brusque answer left my stomach burning with sudden bile. I bit down a dozen responses. "Sir."

Ramazani had started to crouch so I could help him remove his helmet.

Instead, deflated, I turned away and trudged around the corner into the locker room. The twisting hairpin corridor separating the lockers from the airlock did nothing to block sound.

I knew exactly when Habre's helmet came off. That's when Watford bellowed "Lieutenant Habre. Would you care to explain why the Montague liaison officer jumped off the station just now?"

"The situation was most serious, Mister Watford."

"And why was she in such a dangerous position in this serious situation? She is a *liaison*."

I stripped out of the suit as quickly as I could, setting the helmet on its shelf and tapping buttons to unseal it. I still wore my gi. It had picked up a whole new panoply of stinks: exercise sweat from the zero-gee practice earlier this night, fear sweat from watching smart fabric betray two people, shock sweat, nausea sweat…

It might be simpler to burn the outfit.

A Congolese I didn't know came in right behind me, helmet under his arm. We'd met, but only after he'd put on his helmet. He offered a sad look and a sympathetic shake of the head as Watford and Habre tore into each other.

"You endangered one of my people," Watford snarled.

"Miss Redding acted to help save lives, on her own initiative."

"You should never have placed her in a position that *required* such actions."

If I didn't get out there soon, they'd kill each other.

I sat down to shuck the suit off my feet and made to hang it back in place. The unfamiliar Congolese waved me off, indicating the doorway. Watford and Habre had stopped letting each other complete even a sentence.

The only reason I didn't run full-speed out was that the hairpin privacy corridor didn't offer enough distance to get up to speed.

Watford's arms weren't crossed any more. He had his hands raised, though— not in fists, but flatly, with his fingers held snugly against each other, so that if Habre struck he could counter without breaking a finger or a thumb.

Habre stood tall, her hands deliberately clasped behind her back as if daring Watford to punch first.

Both fell silent when I emerged.

"Sir," I said.

"Redding," Watford growled. His nose wrinkled—apparently I stunk worse than the pig farm. Great. "With me."

"Sir," I said.

"Thank you, Miss Redding," Habre said, her tone hard enough to break rocks.

Watford was already spinning on a heel. "Redding!"

"Sir." I gave Habre a nod of thanks and trotted after Watford.

Watford said nothing as he stormed to the Montague elevator.

I trotted after, suddenly weary to my marrow. I'd done most of an hour of free fall hand-to-hand combat practice, then had more than one moment of adrenaline-fueled fear, inspiration, and terror. I needed a shower and about twelve hours sleep.

Watford's back told me I was out of luck.

The elevator with the octagonal Montague logo was waiting for us. Watford tromped in and swiveled to face the door.

"Sir," I started.

"Wait for my office," he snapped.

I fumed.

What was I supposed to have done? Outside that airlock, touching Monard meant death—okay, not death, but explosive decompression is serious business, and soon we wouldn't have had anyone to drag the victims into the airlock and throw them in a medical pod. We hadn't had time to discuss a plan—as it was, he'd almost gotten Bapa—Lucy.

I hadn't signed on to Montague to be a liaison, I'd signed on to see new universes, advance human knowledge, be at the very fringe of knowledge and exploration. Not to listen to a tin-pot despot rant and rave.

No, I'd accepted this assignment.

Gladly.

Maybe I should have stayed in the Congo resort.

18

I trailed Watford into his sterile office on Ring Three, imagining all sorts of responses for when he started chewing me out.

I wouldn't talk back. I wouldn't yell back.

I'd be calm, and assertive, and declare my refusal to let people die just because I was supposed to be a lowly liaison between the Congolese and him. If he wanted a flunky who would stand by and watch while everything fell apart, he needed a different Security Third.

Watford hadn't even sat down when he said, "Good job, Redding."

The indignation that was keeping me upright gushed out my spine, leaving me dizzy. "Sir?"

Watford tossed me a bottle of water from his small cooler. "I watched everything. You assessed a situation, evaluated the facts at hand, created a plan, and acted, all under pressure."

"Uh..." I fumbled for words. "Thank you, sir?" The water tasted delicious, cutting through my own stink.

"You could have been a little smoother, but that'll come with experience. Screaming in terror is poor practice."

I stopped. Had Watford cracked a joke? "Scream, sir?"

"When Monard came off the balcony and you got thrashed around."

"That wasn't a scream, sir. It was a shout."

Watford's eyebrows arched. "A shout?"

"Like on a roller coaster."

He smirked. "So next time, try a little more glee and a little less I'm-going-to-need-a-clean-uniform."

"Sir." I relaxed a little. "So all that with Habre—"

Watford's flicker of good humor vanished. "Oh, I'm furious with her. Her people should have handled that. If anyone is going to throw Montague staff off this station, it's going to be me." He shook his head. "The Congolese don't understand that this is a different universe."

"Isn't it just like ours?" I took the chance of not saying *sir*.

Watford let that pass. "Even if the natural laws haven't changed, it's a completely alien environment. We're right up against the Big Bang here. Anything can happen. Anything did—I've never seen smart cloth behave like that, I'll be sending the video back to Montague for evaluation. See what the historians think of it." He leaned forward. "Before I send you to the showers, is there anything you want to tell me?"

I took a sip of water and a deep breath to buy myself some time. *Habre's not that bad?* No, he'd chew my head off. *You've made my job a lot harder with that argument?* No, he didn't care. Instead, I said "How would you feel—I mean, what are your *thoughts* on me requesting a Congolese datalink?"

"Going native on me?" Watford said.

"No sir. It's just..." I took a deep breath. "I could have used it to operate the Congolese suit. And access the Congolese datacore while maintaining separation with ours. Maybe I can do some research, give them hints, help them figure what's happening."

Watford studied me.

I hauled up a mask of alertness and tried to push the fatigue off my features.

"Redding," he said slowly. "What would have happened if you'd had full control over your suit?"

I blinked, not really understanding the point of the question. "I... I would have had more options."

Watford shook his head and leaned forward on his desk, palms flat against the metal. "I studied your record, Redding. You take action. Given the chance, you *leap* into action. If you see a wreck, you run to help."

"Sir."

"In most cases, I admire that. Montague needs people like that. People who don't have to make a conscious decision to override their natural freeze-or-flight instinct." Watford tightened his lips and kept shaking his head. "But here—if you had a datalink today, you would have charged in to help. You would have fired a data cable to upload the program. If someone beat you to it, you would have grabbed Monard's suit to deliver it the hard way." His gaze drilled into my skull. "Either way, you would be lying in the Congolese medical center right now. *If* you were lucky."

I opened my mouth to argue—but found I couldn't.

Watford was right.

"Set aside that nobody gets my people killed but me," Watford said. "Even ignore the contractual repercussions should a Montague employee get herself killed defending the Congolese. On a purely personal level, you've learned your role quite well. I don't want to take the time to train a replacement. And if something *does* happen to you, I'll put Habre's head on a stick as a warning for her replacement."

"Sir," I said. I'd fought the urge to defend Habre this long, but I couldn't let this pass. "Things do happen, sir."

Watford's face took on a distant, thoughtful look for a breath. "I know that, Redding. I know that. too well." The thought passed. "But they own their station. They own their people. Montague's regulations are designed to protect people. If they want to write their own rules, they have to live with them. Or learn better."

Our way isn't the One True Path. These people just live differently. But I was too tired to argue further, especially with Watford, and let myself slump a little in the chair. "Sir."

"All that said…" Watford leaned back. "I'm certain Habre will issue you a Congolese datalink."

I straightened in surprise.

"But remember, Redding: if you use it to get yourself killed, everything will come apart here until we finish training your replacement." Watford studied me with just a hint of sorrow. "The Congolese are expendable. You—are not."

19

I'm not sure I slept. I don't remember time passing. Maybe I only blinked before the alarm rousted me. I staggered in to the very tail end of Montague's breakfast up in the Spartan mess hall, sore and achy and eyes burning.

The whole crowded room erupted in cheers and applause.

I stopped in the door, shocked awake. Even the smells of eggs, salsa, and coffee couldn't jump-start me that quickly.

"Teach *me* to bungee jump!" a Portal guard I hadn't yet met called.

"That's showing them!" San-Chow shouted, clapping.

I felt excruciatingly aware of the hot flush creeping into my cheeks and up my ears.

As the noise subsided, Percival said, "It was pretty cool," hoisting a coffee mug as if to toast me. "At least until the bit where y'all screamed like a spanked baby."

Laughter sloshed between the metal walls.

The only way out was through. "That," I said, drawing myself up straight, trying to ignore my bonfire blush, "was not a scream, thank you very much. That…" I raised a finger. "Was my ancestral battle shriek."

Fresh laughter and applause erupted.

And Watford, sitting at his little table with Palmer—was that a *wink*?

I took the opportunity to march myself forward to the meal slot.

The duty officer would have watched last night's incident. The video must have flown around all of Ring Three before I even got back to my room. It was probably even going around the Congolese sections. Embarrassment made my face feel aflame.

At least the datacore knew I'd been working—it gave me an extra egg, both *fried*, and two extra slices of bacon.

Apparently the machine figured that hanging over certain death burned calories.

No, it didn't figure. It knew.

The real surprise came when I turned around.

I'd tried to move around each meal, sitting with different groups as much as possible. Everyone had made space for me and talked politely.

Now, four different hands went up from four different parts of the room, waving me over.

All of a sudden, I wasn't the Congolese Liaison Officer, responsible for keeping a bunch of annoying outsiders away from the folks doing the real work of defending the Earth.

Now… I was one of the cool people.

20

Habre thanked me for catching Monard, and tried to apologize for last night's shouting match. When I brushed that away and requested a Congolese datalink and complete access to everything on the victims, she seemed relieved that she could do something for me.

I claimed a temporary office in the Congolese Ring Two: nine square meters with full display walls, a keyboard, and a rolling office chair that looked like it dated back to the Typewriter Age. I plugged in the datalink, and got to work.

Well, I tried to.

Back on Earth, any datalink I used would grab my personal settings from the global network. The Congolese datacore, floating in another universe, didn't have that information. I spent most of an hour trying to get the Montague datacore to send my profile to the Congolese datacore, repeatedly stripping out layers of settings trying to squeeze a useful work environment through the security protocols.

Eventually, I surrendered and started configuring the new datalink by hand.

I was finally ready to work when my Montague datalink pinged me for lunch. I ached to dive into the data instead, but now that I had an opening with my fellow Montague staff I needed to make all the friends I could.

The datacore gave me a second piece of quiche at lunch. Did I need that much protein after last night? Or was the datacore trying to apologize for giving me a headache this morning?

Don't humanize the machines, I reminded myself.

And plunged into the victims.

Or, rather, tried to.

I had preferred data correlation programs, all available in the Montague datacore. The Montague system absolutely refused to accept complicated data from the Wemm Station datacore, though. After battering against that security layer for a while, I arranged for my Congolese datalink to strip the data down to matrices—rows of numbers, separated by commas. The Montague security system snarled, but accepted it.

By bouncing back and forth between the two systems, I eventually managed to assemble a lopsided but usable set of analysis tools and data. I'd also assembled a headache like a hundred-penny nail driven into my right eye and a cramp in my neck.

Once I could do useful work, though, I found...

Nothing.

Six victims. Four died within minutes, their neural flows devastated. Doctor Tansi had survived, but his brain remained scrambled. The medical staff had him floating in a suspension pod, right next to Daktari Monard. They didn't have much hope for stabilizing either.

Three of the victims were Congolese. One came from the Sudanese Sovereign State, one from Zanzibar, the last from the Irish Protectorate.

No common medical details—I don't know medicine other than first aid, but I can compare and contrast information to seek out correlations.

Five parents. All six had family members on Wemm Station.

Two home brewers.

A soccer fiend. Did Wemm Station have a soccer field?

Two people who went outside Wemm Station regularly. One whose work had taken him outside three times in five months. The other three had stayed within the aluminum shell.

A variety of ages, hobbies, and family members.

No signs of substance abuse—Monard had just a touch more whiskey in his diet than advised, but the Congolese datacore hadn't registered any concerns.

Maybe Monard's metabolism thrived on booze.

We did have one new information source, though.

Monard's suit.

A Congolese engineer had attached a data cable—not one made of smart fabric, but an actual hard-wired plastic-and-silicon data cable. I'm more familiar with technology than medicine, but even so I had to rely on the engineer's summary. Thanks to the Congolese datalink, I was able to get updates as the engineer doing the examination made notes.

Nothing. The suit's processors were even more disrupted than the human minds.

I took a break for a snack and to massage my head. This was worse than my college senior research paper on the twenty-first century Himalayan global warming trials.

I worked through dinner.

For the first time since arriving, the Montague datalink didn't ping me for zero-gravity unarmed combat practice.

Habre didn't interrupt me.

I finally fell into bed, exhausted and aching both physically and mentally, my brain full of a million irrelevant facts. I hurried through my morning workout, barely paid attention to breakfast, and plunged right into the data.

This wasn't my responsibility. I didn't need to be sitting there in an oversized chair that wouldn't crank down low enough for my feet to hit the floor, staring at a wall display, stuffing information into my head, turning facts around to make them fit like jigsaw puzzle pieces, polishing my headache and exploring data I didn't quite understand.

But this thing, whatever it was, was destroying people. And finding an answer—even a clue—was worth several headaches much worse than the one pounding a syncopated rhythm between my eyeballs.

And just before dinner on the second day, I pulled a recalcitrant pattern out of the noise.

21

I'd grown to loathe my temporary office. The display screen walls, completely covered with graphs, images, frozen video clips, and streams of data I'd shoved to the side, blurred together into a tangle that seemed to knot inside my tired eyes. My stomach grumbled. My mouth tasted like old socks.

And the stupid chair tortured my spine like a medieval rack. Why did the Congolese have to be so blasted tall?

And the data I had was pretty minimal. Barely notes, on something barely above statistical noise.

But it beat the nothing we had.

If I was still in college, I'd write up a formal report, dress it in a nice skirt and a silk blouse, ask a friend to recommend cute shoes for it, and send it to Professor Watford. Montague researchers made their reports even more fancy, with specific formatting designed to fit into the company's libraries.

I wasn't a researcher, though. The biggest risk to my college diploma hadn't been the tests, or the studying, or the ethical challenges presented in a criminal justice degree.

No, what had almost ruined my college career had been the Global Research Foundation Citation Format.

Instead, I prepared a simple business memo, listing my conclusions up at the top, half a dozen supporting paragraphs, and a bunch of links to data sources at the bottom. The two different datalinks bit me here: a few chunks of information appeared only in one datacore or the other, so I had to make two separate versions, each flagged with "available in other datacore" scattered here and there.

By the time I finished, the headache behind my right eye had spread to my left. My tongue felt parched. My stomach grumbled about skipping a second dinner, demanding I march up to Ring Three and grab a bottle of water and a sandwich before telling anyone anything.

I was hungry enough, the datacore just might give me my own pasta dinner.

But hungry or not, people were losing their minds.

And the deaths, the losses, were happening closer together.

I sent the copy with Montague links to Watford, adding a businesslike note that I was about to send a similar note to Habre. She got a more personal note, saying that I wanted to talk to her about some interesting things I'd found, and attaching the version of the memo with the Wemm Station links.

A Montague employee who got a memo like this, about something destroying people, would have used the datalink to call me right back.

I had a few minutes to rest until Habre knocked on my door.

I climbed out of Death Chair, closed my eyes, and tried to touch my toes. My lower back gave its own ancestral battle shriek. I bent over as long as I could, until the blood rushing to my headache—uh, head—made me feel almost too dizzy to stand, then started twisting at the waist and rotating my shoulders.

Habre knocked. "Miss Redding?"

I glanced at the datalink. Four minutes and forty-five seconds—she must have run. At least a little stretching had relieved the worst of my aches. "Coming," I called, reaching for the button.

Habre skipped her usual pleasantries. "You said you found something?"

"Come on in, I'll show you." I hoisted my Congolese datalink. "I thought you'd want the whole presentation."

Habre's face looked ready to burst with tension.

I licked my lips.

Her eyes flicked to my face. "Did you get dinner? Lunch—no, breakfast?"

"Breakfast," I said.

Her gaze bounced up to the countless graphs and images on the wall, then back at me. "I would have my people bring you a meal," she said.

I shook my hand. "I know you would. Let me show you this, then I'm getting a snack, taking a headache pill, and falling into bed. Forget brawling in vacuum. Desk work is what's going to kill me."

Habre's mouth twitched in a brilliant smile, then faded. "Show me."

I set my Montague datalink to record, then picked up the Congolese one. "Your datacore has the very latest scientific information."

"And a complete cultural record," Habre said.

"Of course. But it's the scientific part I need to focus on now. Montague's datacore has much of the new research, but they've curated historical research as well." I didn't add, *and not even a novel or a serial unless one of the staff brings it.* "In some of the universes we visit, the best technology you can get is a forge and anvil, or uranium fission, or, or whatever. We're supposed to study that in our off hours."

Habre frowned. "All right."

"The victims don't seem to have anything in common, so I turned it around. Both Tansi and Monard moved strangely, but kind of similarly. I had the Montague datacore search for people who moved similarly. I thought maybe some kind of cerebral trauma."

"We performed a full medical analysis and comparison," Habre said.

"Your records aren't as complete," I said.

"I assure you, our medical records are—"

"Medical, yes." I took a deep breath. "The Windsor Free State. Right at the end of the Blue Tomato War."

Habre stopped. She closed her mouth. "Yes, that is—something we would not have brought."

"I don't blame you. But when you're out here, you might need *anything.*" I aimed the Congolese datalink at the wall. "When they ran short on foot soldiers, the Windsor Czars attempted computer-driven personality reconstruction of political prisoners." I tapped the datalink.

A frozen image swelled to dominate the wall, flickered, and moved. The image was shaky, the camera maybe a meter off the ground, the resolution terrible. According to the historical notes, the photographer had taken the video with a camera hidden in a belt buckle.

I let the video run for a few seconds. Long enough for Habre to see the man's weird, looping footsteps, the windmilling arms, the gaping mouth. For her, I'd left the sound off. I'd also cropped the video. The expression on the victim's face was agonized enough without adding the medical tech. (No, the tech wasn't agonized. He was bored, which was worse.)

When I stopped the video and shrunk the image, Habre's face had gotten a little pale and her lips tight. Her own imagination had filled in what I'd cropped out. The human race might have reached its golden age, but every school kid learns just how much blood we spilled getting here. And nobody likes having that history brought up.

Habre needed a breath to steady herself before saying, "Yes, that looks very similar. Did they—do you know the cause?"

"Interference," I said. "They didn't understand how the brain works, and even if they had, they didn't have the computing power to dismantle and rebuild a personality. Even now, most governments exile irreconcilable deviants rather than attempt to fix serious psychopathy." I wanted to sag into the chair, but it was too high for comfort. "I compared the brain scans of the Windsor victims to our injured people."

"And?" Habre said.

"Not even close. But you have really good analytical software in your datacore, so I played for a while." I swung the datalink to another frozen window, expanding it to run the length of the wall. "And this is what the software generated."

The detailed graph dominating the wall looked something like an old-fashioned seismograph or EKG: one line, wobbling up and down. Unlike those, however, the curves had chaotic, irregular shapes. At some points the line went into pure right angles, oscillating across the axis like an AC power graph.

Habre peered at the wall. "What is this?"

"I used the Windsor techniques for measuring and graphing brains, and extracted everything that wasn't in Tansi's normal mental patterns. And look at this." I swiped the datalink to bring two more graphs up below the first. "This is the same transformation done on victims three and four, their mental patterns."

Habre's lips narrowed in concentration. "Nile and Dancer."

I nodded. "Not the same, but see—the same kind of spikes here and here, the same blocky shapes here and here. I'm not a mathematician, but it looks like a chaotic arrangement of the same components." I took a deep breath. "The first two, their brains were too badly hurt. Not enough to analyze."

Habre nodded. "So that's a commonality between three victims?"

I shook my head. "Four. Monard's got a twist, though."

"You have something more twisted than this?"

"Monard's brain scan doesn't match. But there's interference throughout the logic circuits of his suit."

"The suit has this pattern?"

I shook my head and added a fourth twitchy, squiggly graph to the wall. "This is a combination, extracted from Monard's brain scan and the suit's management module."

"But—" Habre shook her head.

"It's the same interference, split between the two," I said.

Habre raised her hands. "Did you find anything that could impose itself like that? On both a human being and the pressure suit's processor?"

I shook my head. I'd finished my presentation. If Habre didn't say anything, I'd make my recommendations. But if she was competent, she'd take it from here.

Habre drew a deep breath. "I will disseminate this throughout the research teams," she said. "If anybody has seen this, created it, we will know."

"Good," I said. "I included the datacore's work. I'd suggest you have a real mathematician look at it. There might be a better way to analyze the data, an easier way to view it. This is just the... the most obvious way. Copying others' discoveries."

Habre stood straighter. "Thank you, Miss Redding."

I rubbed my forehead. "Happy to help. If it helps. This might be nothing."

"Most leads are," she said cheerfully, shifting a shoulder as if to turn. "But it's the first proper lead we've had."

"One more thing before you run off," I said.

Habre froze halfway through her turn.

I said, "Look at the amplitude."

She peered at the graphs.

"The earlier cases have much more intensity than the newer ones. The effect decreases by about two-thirds for each case. See the Y scale, there and there?"

"That's part of how Tansi and Monard survived," Habre said.

"Tansi had a voice," I said. "Well, he made sounds, at least. And Monard, he kept saying 'dehors' over and over again."

"Outside," Habre said. "He was saying *outside*."

"How much more out could he be?" I tapped my finger on his graph. "But the next time, if it's only a third as serious, it might look like a stroke." Or a headache, I thought, resisting the urge to massage my temples.

"I'll let Medical know as well," Habre said.

"The way they're getting closer together," I said, "the next breakdown could happen any minute."

"Leave it with me," Habre said. "Anything else?"

I shook my head.

"Yes, there is," Habre broke a smile. "Get your meal and your rest, my friend."

"Yes, ma'am," I said with a chuckle and a slapdash salute. I'd have to snip this bit off the recording before sending it to Watford.

The door had barely slid shut before my Montague datalink buzzed.

Watford's booming voice tapped another nail into my headache. "Good work, Redding. If they can't find their problem with that kind of road map, they don't deserve to be out here."

I couldn't help a flinch. He must have watched the recording as I made it.

And I'd saluted Habre—Watford was going to chew me out so hard, I'd have to stand to eat breakfast. "Thank you, sir."

Watford said, "Now grab a sandwich and get up to Ring Six. You missed practice last night. You have *just* enough time to make it, and you owe Percival an ankle lock."

22

Between food, exercise, and helpfully kicking the whole problem over to Habre, I slept like the dead. Breakfast tasted delicious, and while my moment of glory had passed, my Montague co-workers retained their cheer towards me. I was able to put my attention into studying the vacuum operations manual—a little late, yes, and I hoped I wouldn't need it, but still.

To my surprise, just before lunch Habre used my Congolese datalink to ask me to meet her on the other side of Ring Two. Normally, she just appeared and knocked on whatever door I was behind. Rather than hiking a kilometer, I grabbed a tram car and let it whisk me there in a quarter the time.

I found Habre in a common area painted in a thousand shades of green, sitting at a two-person table beneath an awning draped with lush grape vines, picking at a small plate of chicken shawarma. Half a glass of mango juice, thick and rich enough to be called "slurry," sat ignored by the plate.

But she worked up a smile as I approached. "Miss Redding."

"Lieutenant Habre." I pulled out a chair opposite her. The gentle warmth of the stone mosaic tabletop soaked into my forearms. "How are you?"

She shook her head. "I spent last night and this morning running from department to department. The research teams… did not take it well."

I sniffed. "I know that. Let me guess—they're annoyed that you think their research might possibly be causing trouble."

"I would even say affronted."

That shawarma smelled delectable, literally making my mouth water. I had to swallow before I could speak. "That's pretty usual. I've butted heads with researchers more than once, in places not a tenth this nice."

"I did get the interest of Sonny Tamara from Astrophysics, however."

I perked up. "Did he recognize the pattern?"

"No, but he did verify your mathematics."

"Great." I'd eaten, but the shawarma's garlic aroma evoked a grumble just short of a howl from my stomach. "I'm glad I didn't produce garbage."

Habre gave half a smile and glanced over at the chef a few meters away. I saw her debate the politeness of another useless offer and, thankfully, decide against it. "He did comment that he could present the data in a more usable manner."

"Please." I had to swallow before I could go on. The rich smells of the forbidden Congolese cooking were pure torture. "With mathematical analysis, I'm like

115

a toddler playing with blocks. If one of your people can turn my numbers into a nice graph correlating the victims with the station's position, better still."

"I doubt we're that lucky." Habre reached for her glass and drew a long sip of thick mango nectar.

I tried not to stare.

"He hasn't produced anything useful yet," Habre said, putting the glass back. She gave an exhausted sigh. "Really, I should have come to tell you, but…"

"I get it," I said. "A datalink message would have been fine."

Habre rolled her eyes. "You deserve better than that."

"I deserve an extra month at that rainforest resort," I said. "With a hunky cabana boy dedicated to bringing me shrimp cocktails and another to rub my feet. What I'm going to get, though, is another forty-six days to help you sort this out before I start training to inspect tritium canisters."

"Canister inspection?" Habre said.

"Someone has to make sure nothing unpleasant gets through to Earth," I said.

"That seems… menial for you."

"I'm not exactly senior Montague security," I said. "And it's vital work. Earth needs the tritium, and it needs safety." That's why we have Palmer here, I added silently.

"Still," Habre said. "You're doing mathematical analysis here, and next you'll be looking at fuel tanks."

"You have to be the best to work for Montague," I said.

"And here," Habre said.

"I'm sure," I said, looking around. "Building all this must have been a nightmare."

Habre smiled. "Ask one of the engineers, they'll tell you very exciting tales." Her eyes took on a speculative look. "There's one you should talk to—perhaps a year older than you, but very knowledgeable and conscientious. From a wonderful family, excellent prospects."

Is she trying—she is! *She's trying to set me up.* I wasn't sure if I should be annoyed or flattered. "Sometime I'll do that. But right now, I'd like to make sure your people are safe before I have to move on."

Habre studied me. "You just aren't happy unless you're moving on, are you?"

She really was worried about me. "It's not that," I said. "I just… I grew up wanting to see everything. I mean, look at this." I waved a hand. "I'm in an actual space station, equipped with a fully functional pig farm, chicken ranch, and swimming pool, built to study how the Big Bang turned into our universe. This is utterly—amazing!"

Habre beamed.

"Some of the jobs, yeah—tritium inspection isn't thrilling. But there are universes out there just as amazing as this. I can't just stay home when the whole multiverse is jumping up and down, screaming 'look at me!'"

"I can understand that." Habre stabbed her fork into a notably succulent-looking chunk of shawarma. "But what about family?"

"I have a great family," I said. "I visit my folks every time I'm back on Earth."

"Visit." Habre took a bite, chewing with less relish than the dish deserved. "You're a sensible, dedicated person. You deserve better than a visit."

"Deserve again."

"Haven't you ever thought of a family? Or a life without all those silly regulations you endure?"

"Sure," I said. "But there's a whole bunch of universes out there."

Habre gave me a little sad smile. "Just so you know, there are other ways to live. Ways you could live, if you chose. I'd be happy to help you find them."

I gave her a puzzled look. "Wait—are you trying to *hire* me?"

One of Habre's shoulders lifted in a half shrug. "Hire? No. But there's a whole world on Earth too. And a few months here, a few months there—how can you build a life worth having that way?"

"I do know," I said slowly, "that if I didn't grab these chances to see everything right now, I'd regret it the rest of my life."

"Still," Habre said. "If you ever change your mind, reach out to me."

"That I can do," I said, leaning back with relief.

I couldn't imagine changing my mind—but a month ago, I couldn't imagine being in a space station.

Habre reached for her glass, and I eagerly reached for a new topic. "I'm guessing that none of your researchers recognized the pattern."

"Most dismissed it as garbage." Habre's flicker of annoyance switched to tired resignation as her datalink buzzed. A glance at the datalink, though, and I caught a flash of distress or fear or anger before she slid disciplined stillness into place.

"What is it?" I said.

"Another breakdown," she said. "Down in Ring One."

23

The concentric rings of Wemm Station got their faux gravity through rotation. Ring Two had Earth normal gravity, Ring Three a little less, all the way up to near weightlessness of Ring Six and the Hub.

The station needed a lot of supporting equipment, though. And some of it, like the magnetic field generators, needed to be mounted on the outermost part of the station. Some of those generators sluiced reactor fuel from the torrent of hydrogen screaming past us. Others produced the magnetic fields that shielded the rest of Wemm Station from the hard radiation that accompanied the hydrogen storm. A lot of that noisy, dangerous, delicate equipment was a terrible neighbor for an elementary school or your uncle's kebab stand.

Ring One housed all that gear, plus the main fusion reactors, the fabricators and their stock storage, waste recycling, the main oxygen exchangers, all the things that made the other Rings both inhabitable and worth living in. Shut down that equipment, and the rest of Wemm Station could support maybe thirty people. People who didn't care about terrible lighting, noxious smells, icky water, or slow-roasted chromosomes. The Portal would still run—all the energy it needed came from Earth, it would keep going forever unless someone took a hammer to the electrodes.

None of that gear cared about one and a third gravities. Most of it was fully automatic, so the only people who went down there were hard-core engineers supervising repairs and maintenance.

I stood up so fast my chair fell over backwards. "Ring One? Let's go."

Habre was already on her feet, her nibbled shawarma forgotten. "I'm going. You stay up here."

"Wait a minute!" I said. "I'm the liaison—"

"Exactly," Habre said. "Your boss was correct. You could have died bringing Monard in, and you have not had the training needed for high-gravity operations."

"Let's argue jurisdiction later," I said, taking the first step of a dash for the elevator.

Habre grabbed my arm. Her friendliness had evaporated, leaving a stone-hard visage. "No."

Her grip yanked me to a stop, almost making me fall back.

"I understand," Habre said, "but I do not have time right now."

My jaw clamped.

Watford had hammered it into me that the Congolese had to deal with their own problems.

He'd told—thundered—at Habre more than once to handle her problems on her own.

This wasn't a Congolese problem. It was our problem.

But Watford wouldn't see it that way.

I ached to run to the elevator.

Instead, I made myself give a single sharp nod.

Habre flashed that smile again, then was running flat-out for the closest elevator.

I flung myself down in her abandoned chair, scowling at the half-ripe grapes dangling from the vine-covered awning, Habre's abandoned wonderful-smelling shawarma, at the young hand-holding couple at a table a few meters away. They quickly looked back to their meal, speaking French in low tones.

But I could guess who they were discussing.

This was a totally useless assignment. I would be more productive inspecting tritium canisters for shipment back to Earth. At least there, if something horrible happened, I'd be permitted and expected to charge in and help.

I should set both my datalinks to count down the seconds until I got to leave this place.

And the next time Montague Human Resources offered me a surprise assignment, I'd check it really closely for stupidity.

I yanked out my Montague datalink. "Redding to Watford."

Watford said, "—hang on a minute. Watford here, Redding."

I swallowed bile. "Another mental breakdown in Ring One. Habre refuses assistance."

"Good!" Watford said. "You're making progress. If further difficulties arise, advise me and proceed to intervene. But give them the chance to settle their disputes themselves."

It's not a dispute, it's a problem. A serious problem. "Acknowledged."

"Keep me updated. Watford out."

I shoved the datalink back onto my belt.

I itched to get on my feet. Grab a high-gee suit and get to work. I hadn't practiced with a high-gee suit, but I'd read the manual.

My fists clenched.

Habre was right.

Movement in high gravity required skills I didn't have. It was no less difficult than learning to move in low gravity, except for the part where even a moment of bad balance meant breaking a bone.

My logical brain admitted that truth, while my guts screamed for me to move.

I snatched my datalinks. The Montague datalink had access to surveillance cameras, while Habre had given me access to the Congolese security feeds in the other.

But I couldn't just turn them up in the rec room, where oblivious couples flirted and a couple of toddlers chased a young beagle. (A beagle? In space?)

I jumped to my feet and stalked off.

24

My Montague datalink directed me to an unused temporary office, yet another stupid small space with a stupid keyboard and a stupidly high chair. Once there, I hit the Congolese datalink, and brought up the voice feed. The automatic translation would rob the conversation of its character, but at least I'd know what was going on.

"—tant six clear," someone said. The voice was muffled, probably by the high-gee suit.

"Octant seven clear." Another muffled but somehow familiar voice—Ramazani?

"Octant eight clear," added a third.

"Evacuation complete," Habre said. "Engineer DeKalb is down here somewhere. Continue the search."

I tasted the acid burning in my gut, and brought up security camera footage on the biggest wall. Habre surely had people in Wemm Station's security office doing the same, but another pair of eyes wouldn't hurt. Looming machines, separated by spacious corridors to accommodate the balloon-like high-gee suits. Pipes and panels and textured steel deck plates, with railings and handholds everywhere. The high-gee suits helped, but we needed every scrap of support when working at a third again normal weight.

Flip to another camera. A rubber-sheathed chain-link fence separated the walkway from a massive machine sheathed in blue ceramic and studded with dials and readouts and levers, like something from second millennium speculative movie. Much of Ring One had manual controls in addition to the automation, so that the station could be started up even if the datacore blew out. Everything had stark labels, in French.

I told the datalink to show me cameras in succession, prioritizing cameras that had not been accessed for the longest time. Soon I was studying a new scene every two seconds, countless greasy gears and acres of shining chrome and kilometers of textured steel deck.

The view flipped to a new scene just as my brain triggered on something. "Wait—go back one and hold."

The projection flicked back one camera.

The wall displayed a sprawling array of racked, exposed electronics, circuit boards connected with looping coils of wire. Text scrolled over a display, while other indicators flickered and danced in the glare of ceiling lights.

But sticking out behind the rack…

I touched the Congolese datalink. "Lieutenant Habre. Camera one-six-four-two, there's a foot sticking out behind an equipment rack. It just wiggled."

As I watched, the bulbous shape of the high-gee suit twitched again, then slid out of sight.

"Aaliyah, Pace," Habre said. "Converge on that location. Mister Diamond, what is that?"

"External Wemm field controller," said a gruff voice, like an old man who'd breathed too much smoke and dust in his life. "That's where we scoop hydrogen out of the environment."

"What can he do with it?" Habre said.

"If he shuts us down, we have enough for three, maybe four weeks. Plenty of time to bring a backup controller on-line."

"Excellent. Mary, Louis, did you hear that?" Habre said.

Two voices acknowledged.

I held the camera in place. Maybe this would end peacefully.

Moments later, two figures encased in balloon-like high-gee suits lumbered into view. Both took short, careful steps, to maintain their balance. The suits concealed even the faces—a high-gravity fall without protection could shatter someone's nose, jaw, cheekbones, or worse.

My jaw clenched in sympathetic tension.

I should be down there.

Even if the smart fabric covering the high-gee suits were decorated like an overinflated zebra and a—was that a *koala*?

The zebra lifted a small black block in one hand. "Suit deactivation chip ready."

"Go," Habre said.

"Joseph," the zebra said, shuffling towards the far end of the rack, away from where the foot had been. "Joe DeKalb. It's okay. It's just me, Louis. Louis Brittain. You remember me, friend?"

I couldn't breathe.

The zebra stepped around the rack. "Hello, Joseph."

Light flared, so brilliant I had to close my eyes and turn away.

A voice shouted in pain.

My hands clenched into fists.

The display went dark.

"Louis!" Habre shouted. "Mary! Report!"

"Suit damaged," a woman said.

Deliberately unknotting my hands, I tapped the datalink, blinking away the glare's afterimage, searching for another camera with eyes on the scene.

"We've lost telemetry from both of you," Habre said.

"Trying to back out—*oof*!"

"Mary!" Habre shouted. "What is happening?"

I heard a pained breath. "Belvie… the suit, it has failed. I've fallen. I can't see. And—and—"

"Team eight converging," someone said.

"Team two," another added.

"Lie on your back and push yourself away," Habre said. "Push with your legs."

Mary's voice sounded thick and slurred. "I can't feel my legs."

Broken back? Damaged spine?

I stood rigid. Still unable to breathe.

"Get her out of there," Habre said.

"Team eight, almost there."

Ring One wasn't just the outermost ring—it was the longest. I imagined a security team hurrying in those mincing high-gravity-safe steps.

Or running, taking the risk of a bone-breaking fall.

My lungs heaved for a single breath, then froze again.

My clenched fingers dug into the top of the chair.

When had I grabbed the chair?

"Help is coming, Mary," Habre said.

Mary huffed for breath. "I'm—I'm—"

The wall lit up again as the datalink found a camera.

I was looking down a steel-plated corridor. Black streaks scorched the walls. My eyes needed a moment to realize that the twitching mass at the end of the corridor was a half-melted high-gee suit, its occupant still trying to get the strength to work her arms.

Tension rippled through me.

The deranged DeKalb shuffled into view.

His high-gee suit looked intact, but the smart cloth displayed constantly flickering splashes of color like a bucket of broken rainbows. Each small step had the same looping, swooping manner I'd seen in Tansi and Monard.

One arm cradled a high-intensity plasma cutter. A construction tool, meant to slice through metal in a vacuum.

DeKalb took a step towards the downed Mary Tancer.

Forget protocol.

I tapped the Montague datalink. "Watford. I'm going in."

And lurched towards the door.

25

Make haste—but *slowly*.

One minute to think is better than ten minutes recovering from a screw-up.

Or a missed opportunity.

I drew up short at the loaner office's door, popped the earpiece out of the Congolese datalink, and slipped it in. The voices became tinny, but comprehensible.

"Team Eight, pull back!"

Someone screamed.

My pounding heart felt big enough to bust through the ribs caging it.

I burned to dash for the nearest elevator, but that would bring me down about a quarter of the way around Ring One from DeKalb. I needed to be closer—no, I'd move slowly in the high gravity, I couldn't possibly catch up.

I needed to get to where DeKalb was going—but before him.

Think, Redding! What do we *know*?

Baring my teeth, I swirled and grabbed my Montague datalink. It couldn't access the room's displays through the security filters, but it could project an engineering overview of Wemm Station on the wall. Fortunately, a two-dimensional spread of the six concentric rings, the Hub, and their interconnecting spokes and protruding equipment masts didn't need real-def. I could get better visuals with the Congolese datalink, but I didn't know their data as well.

And right now, only data mattered.

Data, and making the right assumptions.

There's a pattern to the madness. An unfamiliar pattern, a pattern not even the mathematicians or researchers have seen before, but a pattern.

Assume the pattern means something.

If the victim's movements and attacks are random, there's no way to figure it out. So assume their motions mean something.

The need to move quivered my every muscle. The room felt confining, the air stale, my back repulsively sweaty.

Push all that away.

Assume that all the victims are compelled, drawn, pushed to some point. A research lab? Someone's pet ferret?

Doesn't matter. Call it X.

Draw some lines, let X mark the spot.

Doctor Tansi had fired a laser from the Hub down one of the access tubes, straight towards the lower Rings. I hadn't known Wemm Station at the time well enough to guess where he was aiming. I brought up the incident report and had the laser's path sketched onto the diagram.

A little red line.

I extended the line.

Assume he was aiming at *something*.

Now Monard. When it struck he'd been on the scaffolding stretching out of the Hub, the axis to Wemm Station's spin. But he'd chosen to climb down Spoke Five.

I didn't need to draw a second line.

The red line of Tansi's hypothetical laser stretched straight down Spoke Five.

I added the location of the camera I'd been watching.

DeKalb was in Octant Eight, almost under Spoke Eight.

But he'd turned towards the camera.

Towards the point where Spoke Five hit Ring One.

That was my X.

If I took the nearest elevator down to Ring One, running to Spoke Five in one-point-three gravities would take forever.

Up here, it was a five-minute jog.

Or one minute in a tram car.

I opened the office door on a ridiculously muscular young man. His booth, right next to the office door, seemed set up for shoulder massages. He no more opened his mouth to make me an offer I wouldn't want to refuse when I bolted past him, almost tripped over a pair of toddlers, and plowed through the crowded hall towards the tram.

The tram's where I stripped off my clothes.

26

No, I'm not into recreational nudity.

But you can't wear anything under a high-gee suit. Not unless you want it to be squeezed permanently into your skin.

The tram entrances were right next to the elevators. The people at the crowded Spoke Five interchange marketplace barely had time to notice my bony rear streaking across the hall, two datalinks clutched in one hand, before the Montague elevator slid open for me. Someone asked if I was all right amidst a couple of surprised shouts, then the doors slid shut.

As I'd told the datalink, the elevator's supply hatch popped open as the main doors shut behind me. I ignored the first aid kits, the stun guns, the restraints, and grabbed the soft gray cube of a Montague high-gee suit.

The Congolese would know me by my drabness, at least.

I'd read the manual, but hadn't ever used a suit before.

The elevator dinged for instructions.

"Hold in place," I said. The cube felt soft but weirdly heavy, like foam padding around a block of gold. "Engage high-gee suit."

The cube twitched in my hand.

Right. When the manual says don't wear anything, they mean *anything*. I tugged my earpiece out, slipped it back into the Congolese datalink, and set both datalinks on the ground.

The cube shimmered and slumped, then started oozing up my arm.

The plastic felt clean and soft, almost cottony. The sight of the plastic crawling up my skin should have made me feel kind of uneasy, the way it looked like an old movie monster devouring my flesh. Instead, I only felt impatient at how slowly it moved. I needed to be downstairs *now*.

When the plastic hit my chest a few seconds later, though, it spread in every direction simultaneously. I felt it slither across my shoulder blades, down my spine, over my breasts. I couldn't prevent a nervous twitch as the suit slid smoothly up my neck. Suddenly, its inexorable movement wasn't too slow—it seemed too fast, rising over the point of my chin and cradling my ears.

I involuntarily sucked a deep breath.

The suit oozed over my chin—

—and stopped just brushing my lower lip.

Plastic still flowed downward, clamping my buttocks together, softly but implacably squeezing my thighs, my shins.

More plastic oozed up the crown of my head, over my forehead, halting just short of my eyes.

I released my breath. The suit shifted with my ribs, maintaining its intimately close contact.

I suddenly felt aware of a chill around my feet, clammy on the metal deck. What had the manual said?

Right. I grabbed the elevator's hand rail with one hand and lifted a foot.

The plastic slithered south, encasing that foot.

When I switched feet, I found the suit had added five centimeters to my height. Padding and reinforcement for my soon-to-be-abused arches.

Once my feet were covered, the suit inflated.

The cotton grip on my legs turned hard, plush over steel. The squeezing had a rhythm, though. A rippling pulse, just slightly out of synch with my own heart.

My heart would have to work extra hard to get blood out of those extremities. The suit monitored my blood flow, squeezing my legs like a toothpaste tube, coaxing spent blood back to my lungs.

I bent to grab my datalinks.

The suit's spine locked up, from my shoulders to my tailbone.

Bending over in high gravity was a good way to fall on your face and break a bone. The suit knew I was in normal gravity, but it already enforced proper high-gee behavior.

The extra weight and strain of high gravity was a problem, but most people could handle an extra thirty percent for a short time. But the reflexes, the muscle memory, the habits: those things would maim you. Bend forward too quickly when your head and shoulders weighed too much, and gravity would send you straight to the deck. Headfirst. You could hop, but you'd come down too quickly and probably break your toes. Pull something off a high shelf? It would be too heavy, and plummet too quickly.

Every little motion transformed into a way for your lifelong habits to harm you.

I bent at my knees, fumbling for the datalinks. It felt like I was wearing heavy gloves, but the suit easily picked up the datalinks and let me slap them at opposite sides of my waist, where the datalink clips should be. The suit had no clips, but the plastic formed cradles at a touch.

My astonishment at how easily that worked only drove home that I had no training for this. Zero. I'd never worn a high-gee suit before, let alone spent time in high gravity.

Unfamiliar equipment?

Dangerous, alien environment?

No training, no practice, but straight into the disaster?

A great way to get killed.

I brushed my fingers over the Congolese datalink. Tried to brush, at least—my fingers felt an extra centimeter long. I managed to engage the voice commands and bring up the voice channel to Habre's team. The Congolese datalink couldn't access the Montague suit's voice circuits, but the suit relayed the sounds for me.

"I could take him," a masculine voice said.

"Not in that area," Habre said. "The equipment's too delicate. Engineer Roundtree says section twelve, Octant Six."

"He's moving too quickly," the voice said.

"Maxwell, you may not override your suit!" Habre said.

"But—" The man sounded furious. "Yes, Lieutenant."

"Team six? Can you get to section twelve before Joseph?"

"Yes," said another man.

Habre said, "Wait for him to pass. Ambush him with the shutdown chip. Team Five, move to Octant Six, section… four. If the ambush fails, you're authorized to use deadly force. Remember, no matter what, no physical contact."

Good. Touching Monard had been a disaster. Habre was assuming that touching this new victim would be as disastrous. Living in high gravity is easier than living in vacuum, but a sudden withdrawal of the high-gee suit would unbalance anyone.

And unbalance meant you'd break only a dozen bones. With luck.

But at least it sounded like the area at the bottom of Spoke Five wasn't a war zone. Yet.

I tried to say *elevator*, but all that came out was a strangled grunt.

My jaw wouldn't open. The suit held it in place.

I pulled in a deep breath. "Elevator," I said through gritted teeth, suddenly sounding a lot more like Habre and her people. "Ring One."

My weight dropped with the elevator.

I'd be a lot heavier soon.

27

The elevator had hardly started when Habre said, "Miss Redding, what are you doing?"

My Congolese datalink had betrayed my motions. I couldn't have prevented it if I'd wanted to. "Watford told me to intervene if the situation warranted it. People are dying. It's warranted."

"We don't have a chip thrower for you," Habre said.

"I don't know what a chip thrower is, so that's fine," I said.

It's really hard to sound calm and collected when your teeth are held clenched by a semi-intelligent high-gee suit.

"Miss Redding, stay clear of the struggle," Habre said. "Team Six, are you in position?"

"Almost."

"You have four minutes until DeKalb arrives," Habre said.

"We'll make it."

The moment of lightness from the elevator starting its plunge passed. I suddenly felt worryingly heavy, like I'd really overdone the carbs at a resort's all-you-can-gorge buffet. My guts seemed to droop low, my heart throbbing extra hard. The suit sent ripples of pressure up my legs, and the foam beneath my feet felt a whole lot firmer.

The elevator moved slowly between Ring Two and Ring One, giving people time to acclimate. My knees creaked, sending dull flashes of pain up to join the aches where the bones of my spine started compressing my disks. The pressure of the suit squeezing back was almost worse, as it tried to hoist my ribs into the air. The suit didn't keep my jaw shut to keep it from falling down—it used my jaw to keep my skull at the top of my neck.

I've felt more unpleasant sensations while working for Montague.

But I'd have to sit down and figure out where exactly this fit in my top five.

My pulse sounded overly loud and rapid in my ears.

The elevator glided to a smooth, gentle halt, and the doors slid open.

I took a step towards the drab steel chamber outside.

Or, I tried to.

The suit stiffened up, not allowing me to move.

What had the manual said? Right: half steps. Crouch, don't bend.

With conscious care, I shuffled my right foot forward. It slid maybe half my normal stride before the suit started pushing back.

I shifted my weight to that foot and dragged the other forward.

In mincing half-steps, I eased my way out of the elevator and into the corridor.

While the Congolese had gone over all the upper layers of Wemm Station like an interior decorator with too much time on his hands, the Ring One antechamber had no furnishings or décor beyond the purely functional. It looked almost Montague in its starkness. Light panels welded to overhead girders cast soft illumination across pipes and systems. We might have mostly autonomous electronics and smart fabric pressure suits, but when it comes to heavy lifting like moving large amounts of water and air or sifting hydrogen from the void, nothing beats good old-fashioned dedicated-purpose machinery. Every device featured quaint mechanical controls, for emergencies. The cool harsh air stank of electricity and industrial grease.

Not to mention the cosmic rays shooting through here. Ring One was outside the magnetic shields that protected the crew.

My stomach flopped at the thought.

To the left and right, long corridors curved upwards with the Ring. No matter where I walked, centripetal force would make it look like I was at the bottom of a wheel. The effect wasn't so obvious in the crowded, busy corridors of the upper Rings, but the empty clear corridor and the dreadful heaviness made the artificiality more obvious and oppressive.

"We are in position," the Team Six spokesman said in my ear.

"Excellent," Habre said. "Autumn, at your discretion."

Next to the elevators, a plain steel door bore a label of SPOKE 5 ENGINEERING OFFICE. Broad arrows marked the directions to OCTANT SIX and OCTANT FOUR.

I turned towards Six and started shuffling.

By the time I covered a few meters, I'd gotten the hang of the mincing gait needed to walk in high gravity. Knees bent just a little. Feet splayed out a few extra degrees. Place each foot ten, maybe fifteen centimeters in front of the other. Spine straight.

Each breath made my lungs ache. The high-gee suit squeezed my abs with each exhalation, adding their strength to my strained diaphragm. I wasn't sure if the pressure really helped, or if the suit was just trying to convince me that it helped.

Plus, frustration made my blood seethe.

Ring One was almost a kilometer and a quarter around. That made each octant, what? A hundred fifty meters? If each of my steps was ten centimeters, I needed fifteen hundred steps to get to Octant Six, another fifteen hundred to Octant Seven.

The suit wasn't the only reason my teeth were gritted.

On camera, DeKalb had moved a lot faster than me.

Too soon I heard, "Team Six reporting. Here he comes."

I should be there.

Why had I wasted time charting random garbage, when I could have just gone down Spoke Six where everything was happening?

Habre said, "Great luck, Samuel."

"I don't need luck, Belvie. I have a great plan and a seriously great partner."

"Shush," said a new voice.

"Sam. Madonna," Habre said. "Mind on the job."

I itched to have the datalink bring up visuals from the camera, but with this painfully heavy machine-assisted gait I didn't need the distraction.

Surely they had carts around here? Some kind of electric scooter for quicker travel? The corridor was wide enough. I'd have to keep my eyes open for one, or for a Ring tram stop.

Instead, I moved as quickly as the suit permitted. The added weight sucked at my soul.

"Almost there," the Team Six spokesman hissed.

I tensed.

The suit shortened my steps even further to compensate.

The remainder of Habre's team held silence.

I fought to relax, to move more quickly.

"Got him!" shouted the Team Six lead, Samuel. "Malware engaged—"

His voice came apart in a scream. Static filled the channel.

Then silence.

Except for Habre shouting for her people to answer.

Heart pounding, I tapped my Montague datalink.

Watford's voice instantly sounded in my ear. "Redding. You may not override the suit's safety circuits."

I muted the Congolese datalink. "Habre just lost a team."

"I saw," Watford said. "But you lack the training to use the suit at a higher speed. We are *not* losing you too."

"These people are not expendable!" I shouted.

"Even if you get up there," he said, "what are you going to do against a plasma cutter?"

I shook, and not just from the physical strain. Anger burned a pit in my stomach. "Something. We can't just stand by," I gasped. The suit made me take a breath before I could finish.

Watford cut me off. "I have an armed squad trained for high-gee operations assembling near Spoke Six. They'll be down in ninety seconds, with chaff guns and laser rifles. DeKalb isn't getting past them."

"Habre has a team between Spoke Six and DeKalb," I said.

"Percival has them falling back now to join our people," Watford said. "They will fire on Habre's command."

His calm, intense voice only frustrated me more. Even though I couldn't possibly get far enough ahead quickly enough, I fought to relax my legs and swing my legs a little faster, a little further. The suit fought my every effort.

I could just turn the suit off. Peel it away, walk without protection.

The corridor had handrails. They would help.

Trip once, try to catch my weight on my arms, and shatter them both before flattening my nose.

I let my hands curl into fists. "Yes, sir."

But I didn't stop shuffling forward.

"Just in case, sir," I said. "If that fails…"

"Yes, Redding?" Watford sounded annoyed now.

I couldn't believe I was saying this. "Maybe you better send Palmer down here to join me."

28

I'd shuffled another twenty tedious meters between complicated machines down Ring One's main corridor when I heard soft footsteps behind me. The bulky suit did let me turn my head, and when I spread my feet and bent a knee I could even shift at the waist to look over my shoulder.

Palmer.

He'd stripped out of his uniform, leaving himself clad only in that body stocking of loosely meshed translucent blue plastic and a barely adequate sky-blue thong. The finger-sized gaps in the plastic mesh framed the weirdly regular freckle-sensors covering his whole body.

His body didn't seem to make any concessions to the extra gravity other than a slight bend in the knee. That perfect musculature didn't sag. His cheeks didn't even droop.

I couldn't help wondering about Palmer. Just how much of the guy was still meat, anyway? And what would make someone choose that sort of dehumanizing augmentation? He always seemed cheerful, but what was really going on in his head?

"Redding," Palmer said, trotting up easily, bare feet padding on the metal deck.

I habitually tried to nod. The bulky high-gee suit prevented the motion, triggering a strain in the back of my neck. "Palmer." I faced forward again and took a short, suit-supported, suit-restrained step. "Good of you to join us."

"I like playing clean-up," Palmer said, slowing down to pace me. "It means someone else handled everything before I got there." His tone was light, but his narrow eyes looked intent.

"Must be nice," I said. "Getting other people to do all the work."

"I have gotten pretty good at Go on this assignment," Palmer said.

"I never understood that game," I said, shuffling forward.

"Once our teammates handle this kerfuffle, let's take an evening and I'll explain it to you."

"Here he comes," Habre said in my ear.

I held up a hand for silence, but Palmer was already nodding.

"Stun guns ready," Habre said in my ear.

"If this goes badly," Palmer said quietly, "I'm going ahead. That cross-corridor ahead is a good spot for an ambush. You hang back and wait for instructions."

A spectator again. Great. "Understood."

"Hold," Habre said.

I made myself breathe.

"Fire."

The audio dissolved into a thin crackle. Interference from the electrical stun guns.

Despite myself, I paused. The fight was happening right now, and I wasn't there. In a few seconds, once they secured DeKalb, I'd turn around and shuffle back to the elevator. Or Palmer would get his chance.

The crackle faded.

Silence.

"Everyone." Habre sounded ill. "Fire at will."

This time, I heard the sound even around the rising curve of Ring One. A bone-deep buzz traveled through the steel deck and up into my teeth, making my eyeballs shiver in their sockets.

I couldn't help a grimace. Montague laser rifles could burn through a high-gee suit and the person inside them without trouble. The chaff guns would shred a plastic suit and gnaw the meat off the person inside.

Right now, I could imagine Habre's grim expression as she watched people cut down one of her people. Watford should have given the order to fire, taken that burden—no, that would be harder for Habre to live with.

Maybe.

Did Habre know DeKalb? Were they related?

Habre spoke often of her affection for her family, for her husband. I scrabbled to recall his name, sick it might be Joe? No—Lincoln, that was it.

Even so, Wemm Station wasn't that big. She knew DeKalb, just as she'd known Tansi and Monard.

Was that scream over the datalink pain? Anger?

Impatience made me tremble.

My Montague datalink relayed, "Percival reporting. DeKalb is down."

"Dead?" Watford said.

"With what's left?" Percival said. "I certainly hope so, sir."

"Watch him anyway," Watford ordered.

"Assuming nothing, sir," Percival said.

Tension ran out of me like water from a burst balloon. I suddenly felt exhausted, both physically and even spiritually. We'd fought to keep Monard alive, and the Congolese physicians hadn't been able to rebuild his brain. Our people had killed DeKalb—and maybe he was the better off of the two.

"Well," Palmer said, "another exciting day where I do nothing at all. Look me up later, we'll have a stab at Go."

"Thanks."

"Palmer," Watford said, "Redding hasn't yet taken high-gee training. Get her back to the elevator, please."

"I can make it," I said, even as Palmer said, "Acknowledged."

"Fine," I said. "Watch me."

"That's not what Watford said."

"Then what?"

"Hold still."

"He said leave."

Impossibly quick, Palmer crouched beside me and deftly scooped me off the floor.

My suit immediately shifted its focus, providing firm supports for my back and legs. The neck firmed, cradling my head up.

I squawked in outrage, free arm flailing. "You put me down!"

"Orders," Palmer said, barely hiding a grin.

I was *not* letting Palmer carry me back to the elevator. That video would make the rounds faster than me throwing myself into deep space.

"I don't care what your orders are!" The suit didn't let me swing very hard, but I still bopped Palmer on the temple with a foam-suited hand.

Palmer stopped trying to hide the smile. "I'm not going against Watford's orders."

Worse—my clothes were still in the tram. I'd been in such a hurry to get down here, I hadn't thought about keeping any dignity on my way out.

And Palmer was the closest one could get to naked and not get arrested.

The two of us, stark naked, getting off the elevator together? They'd would put *that* video on loop in the cafeteria seven nights a week.

No, I'd keep the high-gee suit on. Hobble through Ring Three to the Montague locker room.

I hadn't helped at all with this crisis, and now Palmer was stripping the rest of my dignity away. "Stop enjoying this!"

"I wouldn't enjoy this nearly so much if you weren't so outraged," he said.

My best swing at him was like a newborn taking a swipe at her mother.

I made myself settle down, fuming. Hopefully, my face hadn't gotten too much redder.

The best I could hope for was boring video.

I couldn't *wait* to start inspecting tritium shipments.

I had another minute or so to practice my self-control before Habre said, "Oh, no."

The station rocked around us.

29

Wemm Station weighed over a million tons.

It shook like a child's rattle.

Somehow, Palmer held his balance on the deck and kept me in his arms.

My puffy high-gee suit turned stiff around my ears, protecting them from the eruption of sound. I felt it, though—the air itself shook and quivered, rippling through the suit, vibrating my teeth against each other, making my bones shudder against every joint and muscle.

I'm pretty sure I tried to scream, but the high-gee suit didn't let me open my mouth or breathe deeply enough.

The brutal shaking faded slowly, like an angry deity had used a cosmic sledgehammer to ring Wemm Station like a bell.

I needed a moment to orient myself.

Palmer hadn't stayed upright. When the world had rocked around us…

...he'd dropped to one knee.

Still holding me steady.

Somehow that made him more human—and more impressive.

"Are you all right?" Palmer asked.

"Yes," I said. "Thanks."

Palmer glanced up and down the service corridor. "Heavy infrared from spin-ward—Spoke Six."

My heart quivered. I triggered both datalinks. "Habre? Percival?"

No answer.

A weird triple beep sounded in both ears, almost simultaneously. I needed a moment to recognize it.

Both datalinks, cut off from the network.

What had *happened*?

The lighting flickered—not all at once, but in a ripple, darkness flashing down the corridor, past us, disappearing up the curve of Ring One.

That wasn't right. Power failure, sure. But a power failure that *moved*?

I had a sick feeling that while this universe might be mathematically identical to our own, its natural laws might not be.

And they'd just turned on us.

30

Still reeling from the concussion that shook Wemm Station, my brain wobbling in my skull, I managed to ask, "Do you have any signal?"

Palmer answered by leaping straight from kneeling on the textured metal deck into a run, straight between machinery back towards Spoke Five.

His legs pounded incredibly hard beneath me, as if he was an Olympic sprinter on Earth rather than in Ring One's unnaturally high gravity. Somehow, the pounding didn't rock me—I could have been lying atop a slab of bedrock for all the motion he passed through to me.

"Network is down." Palmer actually sounded a little short of breath. "Unnatural vibration in the Ring. Get up the Spoke, I'm going back to check."

"Not alone you're not!" I said.

"You can't help me," Palmer said. "You can do the most good aiding the evacuation."

The answer stopped me.

I imagined the panicked chaos right now in Ring Two. Damaged lighting, air tainted with smoke or chemicals or just plain old carbon dioxide. Screaming children, terrified parents.

How many people had that blast injured?

What systems had failed?

The high-gee suit could protect me from fire, from air turned toxic or outright missing, but the people over us had no such protections.

Bile burned in my gut.

Was there even a Ring Two any more?

Palmer was right. We'd have to get everyone up to Ring Three, into the Portal. Trigger the evacuation protocol.

The two laughing children who'd played hide-and-peek around my knees when I first saw Ring Two flashed through my memory.

What if Montague decided that the evacuees had brought something back with them? If they'd carried an unknown, unknowable threat from this void? Something dangerous to the human race, to Earth?

I knew exactly "what if."

But they had a better chance on Earth, even in a Montague quarantine chamber, than on a damaged space station in an empty universe.

"This is what I'm here for," Palmer said. "This is why I exist—to go where other people can't."

Watford was right. I ran towards problems.

And here, I couldn't.

The only thing I could do was help other people flee.

"Fine!" I spat.

Everything had gone wrong, and I was *still* playing babysitter.

The lights flickered again, an unnatural band of darkness progressing from one end of the visible corridor to the other in less than a breath.

Palmer only needed a minute to return me to the Spoke Five antechamber. It seemed weirdly unchanged. I felt like the engineering office should have been burst open, or a floor plate tossed aside, or something.

No, there was a change. Small lights burned amber over all four elevators.

"Stairs," Palmer said. The stairwell door on the far side of the elevators, across from the engineering office.

Two hundred meters of stairs back to Ring Two. In a high-gee suit. They'd have the station evacuated before I got halfway up. "Right."

Palmer swung me back upright and lowered me to the floor. "Let me plug in first."

"Okay." The suit shifted to support me as I regained my feet, but my innards seemed to ooze unpleasantly against their unaccustomed weight. The network might be down, but if Palmer could access the hard-wired systems, I'd at least find out if Ring Two still existed.

Maybe Watford could direct me somewhere I could do some good.

Palmer slid a dull yellow panel to the side, exposing a small screen and a series of sockets. "Don't laugh," he said.

Before I could say *This isn't funny*, Palmer licked his pinky and cautiously slid it into one of the open sockets. Exactly like we tell children not to.

I couldn't help chuckling through gritted teeth.

"Laugh it up, Redding," Palmer said, his own teeth gritted. "This isn't as easy as it looks. Bypass... there... and—ah, there we go!"

"What's going on?" I said.

"Ruptured fluorox line blew in Ring One, Spoke Six."

My heart sagged even further.

Habre. Percival.

Everyone there, lost.

Palmer had his eyelids closed, but the eyes beneath twitched as his optical implants fired. "Monitors show structural damage to that part of the Ring. Magnetic shields and hydrogen scoop both down. Network is live on Ring Two and above. Commander Mvouba has ordered preparation for evacuation, but not full evac yet. Watford wants you up in Ring Three as soon as possible, to handle comms with the Congolese."

I remembered the last time Watford had talked directly with Mvouba, and felt certain it wasn't going any better this time. "I'm on my way," I said, resigned.

The worst part of your own helplessness?

Being helpless against it.

Palmer gave a brief nod to acknowledge my words. "You're not to override your suit's safeties until you're within fifty meters of Ring Two. I'll check the blast site, and follow you," Palmer said. His mouth twisted in concentration. "Just trying the backup cameras... hmm... There's some weird kind of ... interference?"

The ring of flickering lights flowed towards us.

Horrified realization ripped through me.

The world slowed down.

Trying to get the words out, my brain felt just as slow.

I shouted "Disconnect!" fearing, *knowing*, I was too late.

Palmer didn't even acknowledge what I said before the dim lighting hit us.

The ring of shadow stopped, right over us.

Palmer's feet jittered on the deck like he'd touched live voltage, but the rest of his body didn't move. His silent mouth twitched.

Whatever was causing the lighting problems, whatever had triggered the blast, whatever had broken and maimed people—

It had Palmer.

I itched to shove Palmer away from the wall. My high-gee suit was made out of a smart fabric similar to the pressure suits, though. Touching Monard had destroyed the suit.

Instead I glanced around for a loose pipe, a hammer, any kind of tool I could use to knock Palmer away from the wall. A broom? A stick? The best I saw was a chunk of conduit that had busted its weld along two sides, but I'd need a cutting torch just to break the other two sides free.

Palmer's shoulders began to quiver.

Given a couple minutes, I could brew a decent plan.

But I only had time for a stupid one.

31

I desperately snatched the Montague datalink with one hand and the corridor's handrail with the other. This was the most foolish thing I've done yet. "Deactivate high-gee suit."

The lights around us remained dim. Palmer's chin had joined the quivering. His closed eyes bulged behind closed lids.

The stupid datalink chirped for confirmation. I barely kept from shouting as I said "Override safety protocols. Deactivate high-gee suit, maximum speed!"

If the network had been live, the suit would have contacted the Montague datacore for confirmation. Without the network, though, I had complete control.

My feet smoothly sank a couple centimeters. The smooth cottony feeling of the high-gee suit's boots faded into warm, sweaty textured steel.

The hand grabbing the rail seemed to sink, easing my bare palm into meeting the smooth, cool aluminum rail. The sweat on my hand instantly chilled.

My heart hammered in my chest.

With my contact points exposed, the suit sluiced off me like water.

One moment I'd been trapped in a terribly uncomfortable full-body stocking that squeezed me everywhere. The next, my every joint ground in protest as that support evaporated like water dancing on a griddle. My vision grayed, as if I looked at the world through a tiny round window. Everything wobbled.

Distantly, I heard both datalinks clang against the deck.

My exposed bare skin suddenly felt cool, everywhere. I could feel the grease and smoke in the air.

No time to worry about any of that.

A labored breath, and color seeped back into my vision.

Most of Palmer's body twitched now. He seemed suspended, as if someone had drilled a hole into his head and dangled him from a line. His pinky jammed in the data socket tethered him to the wall.

I heaved in a breath. My chest opened more, letting me get more air in, but my chest muscles seemed to tighten with the motion.

No time for this, I thought. I have to do this right.

And right *now*.

Keeping my knees bent a little more than usual, I took one tiny step towards Palmer. Another.

My arm felt sunk in fresh cement, but I raised it to face level.

Putting everything behind it, I punched the heel of my palm right into the killer cyborg's breastbone.

If Palmer had resisted me, I'd have had all the effect of a kitten batting a whale. Palmer didn't resist. He didn't even try to catch his balance, instead toppling straight back to smash into the deck.

But the part I cared about most, his pinky, popped right out of the socket.

The extra gravity brought him down with freakish speed and an ear-smashing clang.

Immediately, the lights around us returned to full strength.

I clutched the handrail, trying to ignore the metaphorical bags of concrete tied over my shoulders. "Palmer!" I said.

Palmer lay on his back, arms pointed straight up. An irrational, unnatural twitch rippled up and down his body.

Dread gnawed at my bones. Had the mind-destroying pattern infected him? Or would he recover?

"Palmer!" I shouted.

What if he didn't get up? Leave him here? I sure couldn't carry him up the stairs the way he could have me.

Palmer's back arched. His teeth clanged together.

Crouch and help him? No, if he bumped me in one of these seizures I'd fall. And I was infinitely more fragile than Palmer.

His hands dug into the steel deck. No, they didn't claw at it—he bent his fingers, and the floor plate dimpled beneath them.

Maybe it was best I didn't hold his hand.

"Come on, Palmer," I said.

Back still arched, Palmer hissed, "Redding."

I barely stopped myself from leaning closer. "I'm here, Palmer."

Palmer's left hand released the deck, making this weird looping swipe at the air.

The motion sent shivers down my spine.

"Security Third Redding." The inflectionless words, as if Palmer was typing the words into a primitive speech synthesizer, chilled my marrow. "Remove yourself from proximity." A thin electronic whine swelled behind his words. "Immediate. Threat. Control."

Palmer's voice spiraled into a familiar, dreadful, impossible shriek.

32

Despite the hot, muggy, and now smoky air of Ring One, despite the oppressive weight, my blood ran cold.

Palmer went limp and collapsed against the deck, hitting a fraction of a second faster than my brain insisted he should have.

I don't run away.

I haven't run away since I was, what, five?

I'd fled that schoolyard bully, then run back.

But the monotone abhuman shriek ripping out of Palmer's throat convinced me I wasn't running away.

I was running towards.

Towards living.

I spun too quickly. The world turned gray, and I felt blood leave my brain. I clutched the hand rail with both hands instead of falling, and even then planted my face against the warm metal wall. An antique-style analog gauge gouged my cheek.

I forced a deep breath.

The world returned.

Put the high-gee suit back on? No—no time.

Move. Carefully.

But quickly.

People a third heavier than I am get around without trouble. But their bodies have had time to adjust, to develop the strength and hydrostatic balance to support that mass. Dump that much weight on someone instantaneously, make gravity itself treacherously unfamiliar, and their body has trouble pushing around all those fluids. They get clumsy.

Feeble.

I fumbled forward.

In only a couple meters I found a balance. Reach forward and grab the hand rail. Move the opposite foot up to it. Step past with the other foot. Repeat, always keeping two points in contact.

Just like a one-legged person free climbing.

A one-legged person wearing a concrete overcoat.

My labored pulse thundered in my ears.

The deck's rough texture dug at my feet. I had no problem walking barefoot, I did it all the time, but not on hard steel. I had to be, what—over a hundred kilograms now? Something like that.

It wasn't just the jagged steel savaging my unprepared feet, though. The floor carried an asymmetric, irregular vibration. Not the grumble of distant motors carrying out their usual tasks. More the feeling of great gears with missing teeth, clashing against each other.

Don't be dramatic, I told myself. Ring One is not going to shake itself apart.

That vibration was probably there all along, damped by the high-gee suit.

But the thought wouldn't leave as I limped and dragged myself into motion.

The stairwell was only a few meters in front of me. At least it was on my side of the hall, not next to the elevators. Make it that far and start climbing.

I lurched forward, thinking: what then?

Palmer was the most dangerous person on Wemm Station. Montague had obviously hired him specifically to guard the facility against unknown threats. If I was the babysitter, he was the tyrannosaurus-sitter.

They'd already evacuated Ring One, even before I got down here. I'd heard Habre confirm it.

If I went up, I'd be abandoning Palmer to do—whatever it was.

Maybe he'd just make his way further down. Fling himself off the outside of Ring One. Badly confuse alien archaeologists in thirteen billion years or so.

Maybe he'd wreck some critical device doing it.

Red lights still flagged four inoperable elevators.

Sweat poured down my face.

I could already feel my feet swelling, as my heart labored to push blood against oppressive weight.

And what could I do? I was naked—literally, and metaphorically—against him.

My hand slipped an inch.

Behind me, Palmer squealed again.

I didn't dare look back.

Forward.

Climb the stairs, I told myself.

Get people out of here.

Let Palmer blow up Wemm Station if he wanted to.

But how long would an evacuation take?

And how long would it take Palmer to wreck the place?

If that's what he was going to do.

Maybe he'd sit down and squeal in place.

It could happen.

Pushing as hard as I dared, I put my hand on the stairwell doorframe more quickly than I would have guessed. I risked a quick look back.

Palmer had curled up on his side, his back to me. The arm on top flailed in wide, looping, uncoordinated circles. He bounced onto his back, thrown by his other arm. His legs swung out, like he was trying to get traction on air to walk straight up, heels clanging against the deck with a screech of bending metal.

Even if he didn't get up, his damaged brain might trigger seizures severe enough to make his ridiculously augmented body crack apart this part of Ring One.

If I was going to take action, I needed something. Knowledge of Ring One. Palmer's manual. A club, even.

I swallowed.

Only one way to get any of that. And it wasn't by climbing the stairs.

I forced my aching lungs to push themselves empty, so I could draw a fresh, smoke-tainted breath.

Peel my fingers off the handrail.

And started walking across the corridor to the Spoke Five Engineering Office.

33

If you ever have to walk in excessive gravity, bring a cane.

Two canes.

Maybe a walker. Or a powered wheelchair.

I'd gone three steps before I realized I had made a mistake.

Lifting my foot clear of the floor to take a step meant risking my balance on one leg. Even moving slowly, minor wobbles threatened to turn catastrophic. I found myself compelled to slide my feet forward, centimeters at a time.

Across textured steel.

Worst pedicure I've ever had.

My heart didn't feel like it was beating any more. It throbbed so rapidly it might as well have been shimmying. My throat ached, both from the effort and from the bitter smoke increasing in the air. If I breathed too deeply I wanted to cough, and I didn't dare. I might bend, and fall.

Slide a foot a few centimeters.

Faintest hint of a wobble? Put it back down.

Shift the other foot.

I tried holding my arms out for balance, but they felt draped with buckets of water. I had to hug them to my chest.

My eyes started watering.

The back of my throat burned.

Palmer let out this irregular warble, his voice sliding wildly up and down, occasionally hanging flat in place. An audible representation of the pattern I'd found? Or spasms from a dying brain?

My stomach clenched and knotted. I needed to relax, or I wouldn't make it.

A clock would probably say it took me a minute, maybe ninety seconds. But each of those seconds lasted at least a year.

I felt a surge of triumph as I got close enough to touch the door.

Just before I my fingers could brush the metal, though, the door slid open.

"Quick!" someone shouted. "In here."

34

The engineering office was larger than I'd expect for a room in Ring One. It's not like people would come down here to bask in a healthy one-point-three gravities for meetings.

But what caught my attention first was the big, luxurious, *beautiful* high-gee mobile chair standing like a padded monolith right inside the door.

I snatched the doorframe for balance, shuffled forward, and clamped my other hand on the chair. Heart pounding against both the gravity and anticipation, I wobbled myself in a tiny circle and stepped backwards onto the conveniently shallow footrest.

The intelligent chair instantly took over. I found myself tipping backwards, sinking into the smart foam. I groaned with pleasure as my weight came off my brutalized arches—how do heavy people even stand? The chair reformed itself so that I reclined, feet and arms raised.

I suddenly understood exactly why my father loved his recliner.

"Rest," a man with a thick Congolese accent said as my chair rolled into position next to him. He broke into a torrent of high-velocity French. A computerized voice responded. He issued more commands. On the ceiling, over to my left, display windows shuffled.

I turned my head to look up.

Dozens of graphs and status readouts filled the ceiling, positioned to easily read while lying in the chair next to me. A window flashed through camera views of the service corridor, cramped crawlspaces, narrow gaps between devices.

The man rattled more instructions in French.

The camera flashed onto a view of a hall full of broken metal. Bluish steam billowed from a shattered overhead pipe, obscuring everything, but I made out steel floor plates, ruptured upward like a monstrous plant had suddenly blossomed.

Something moved off to one side.

A hand?

The camera angle switched, looking down the service corridor, with the same blue steam billowing from behind.

"Wait!" I said. "That last shot!"

My heart was too tired to beat more quickly, but it tried. Had I really glimpsed a crawling figure?

"Yes," the man said. "Five, maybe six, still alive."

I rolled my head to the side.

The Congolese man in the chair a meter from me looked youthful, with a shaven head and heavy cheeks. He wore a mostly deflated high-gee suit. His brown eyes focused on the ceiling, even as his strong fingers danced on the keyboard on his lap. The chair had formed armrests over his stomach, letting him type lying down even with this absurd weight. "If I can shut the lube leak—shut this down..." He peered at one of the readouts. "They might stay alive." His keyboard clattered.

Almost directly overhead, a set of squiggling lines turned bright red and started oscillating wildly. Yellow indicators started flashing red.

I sucked in a clean-tasting breath to ask, but they had already slid back to yellow.

My companion said, "Yes, yes—friction, Spoke Six's blown lube. A rotation, shake. We have worse."

I deliberately stilled myself. "Can I help?"

"Yes," the man said. "Shush."

Bitter helplessness made me want to scream. Again.

Instead, I took a breath and lay still, willing my body to recover. I felt like I'd just run a half-marathon, barefoot, over gravel. Steel gravel.

In only a few seconds, the camera showed the plume of blue smoke fading.

"That's it!" he crowed. "Take that, you stupid beautiful…"

The view flipped back to the shattered pipe. Fresh smoke had stopped pluming out. The existing smoke spiraled towards the tiny air vents near the floor, more fully exposing ruptured floor plates.

My companion let out a deep breath. "That stuff, it eats through gee-suits. I'm Tove. You be the famous Miss Redding."

The abrupt conversational swerve took me by surprise. "Uh, nice to meet you, Tove. Thanks for the chair."

"Least I could." Tove peered at the ceiling, seemingly having forgotten to say the rest of the sentence. "We've stopped losing pressure."

The display above me squiggled its wild red again.

Tove's fingers clattered. "Repressurizing lube."

The squiggles faded.

I eased my breath.

Tove said, "We won't know for thirty-five seconds if that worked. Might structural damage." His eyes fixed on the squiggling lines in my part of the ceiling. "Your friend?"

"Hurt," I said. That didn't seem a big enough word to describe what happened to Palmer. And Tove's random dropping of words vastly annoyed me.

"Recirc is on, but lube eats through skin better than gee-suits."

"Can you get me a view?"

"Datalink?"

"Out in the hall."

"Right." Tove glanced at me, then jerked his eyes back to the ceiling displays. "Sorry."

Wait—was he actually blushing? "How old are you, Tove?"

His hands clattered on the keyboard. "Does it matter?"

His posture had deceived me. He couldn't even be six feet tall, short for a Congolese. His arms had the thin strength of youth. "You're someone's kid, aren't you?"

"I'm not a kid!" He heaved a hand up to point at the ceiling over my chair. "See! Friction's stopped!"

Had it been thirty-five seconds? The ceiling over me kept its steady squiggle. "Good work, Tove," I said.

"I'm not here because of my dad," Tove said.

Oh, boy. "Of course you're not." I thought carefully. "You fixed things so quickly, I just thought you were a senior engineer, that's all."

"s'nobody else," Tove said. "Something fried the engineering datacore."

"Isn't that scattered throughout the Ring?" I said.

"Supposed to!" He issued instructions in French, and the overhead displays swooped into a new configuration. These readouts had a lot more red. "I'm trying reset but no."

Red spots flashed on the ceiling.

"Dad said datacore can't fail," Tove said, his voice just a little panicked.

I wanted to tell him that this was an alien universe and anything could happen, but didn't think that would help. "Don't freak out on me, Tove. Stop and think a moment. Can you get help managing this from Ring Two?"

"Not with datacore down. They've sent some engineers down, but I can't elevators running."

Get, I thought. The word is *get*. "Where are they coming down?"

"Spoke Four." He glanced at me, but his face blushed even more strongly and he wrenched his face back to the ceiling. "Supposed to wait here."

What was he, fifteen? Sixteen maybe? Barely old enough to shave. But old enough to be embarrassed by a real live woman without clothes.

"Type?" Tove said.

"What?"

He stopped typing to enunciate every word, staring at the ceiling in furious embarrassment. "Can. You. Type?"

"Yes."

Tove struck some keys. "Use far edge. Please."

My chair vibrated, and a keyboard with arm rests swung up into place in my lap.

"I'll stay out of your way," I said. With two keypresses I moved my chair away from Tove's, claiming a blank section of ceiling. Another quick command, and a blank Congolese datalink rose from the armrest. I touched the datalink's screen, and it used its physical connection to retrieve my profile from the main Congolese datacore and configure itself.

I was connected again. Maybe I could do something.

First, the camera outside the door.

Palmer was on his hands and knees, panting. His head hung limp. Somehow, he'd moved a few meters until he was square in front of the elevators.

One leg twitched. His body shuddered.

That leg swiveled at the hip, scraping Palmer's knee over steel before it came up to complete the big, looping, pointless circle.

Whatever had happened to Tansi and Monard, whatever had compelled them to struggle down Spoke Five, whatever had been looping around the lights in Ring One, had hit Palmer.

No.

Whatever was *in* Tansi and Monard, whatever had traveled in the lights, it was *in* Palmer.

Some Congolese experiment, out here at the beginning of time, had created something. Maybe born from a dropped decimal point, or an inscrutably small variation between our universe and this one.

Whatever they'd made, it was in our killer cyborg.

I sent Watford a quick message. The Congolese datalink didn't have priority access to Watford, but I flagged it urgent in the hope he'd see it. *In engineering office. Palmer hit by Tansi problem.* I chewed my lip. Watford had ordered me up—but that was before Palmer's incapacitation. *Staying with him.*

There—I'd reported in, like a good flunky.

On the display, Palmer began swooping a hand over the steel deck, letting his fingers dangle like he was feeling for something. His head still hung weirdly loose.

At a gap in Tove's typing I said, "Any chance of getting the main network back?"

"Nope."

I waited for more detail. "What's going on?"

"Still trying to datacore."

It got in the lights, I thought. What if it got in the datacore?

Guessing from how the first human victims had died, there might not be much left of the datacore.

On my display, Palmer's questing fingers found something.

He thrust his hand into the deck.

A section of deck plate peeled up like putty.

I froze.

Palmer plunged his hand into the exposed opening. Bright light sparked up into his face.

Maybe we were at the bottom of Spoke Five—but Palmer could dig through the floor to get further down.

Tearing through whatever machinery was in its way.

35

Palmer's strike into the systems buried beneath the corridor floor unleashed a tumult of furious beeping.

Tove shouted, "What is that?" He actually lifted his head a few inches out of the high-gee chair, staring with a twisted snarl at the flash of red indicators on the ceiling.

I felt like screaming myself. My instincts screamed to go out and grab Palmer. Instead, I tapped the datalink. "Aidan Redding for Montague Security First Watford. Ultimate priority." Ultimate priority is relative—the actual priority depends on your role. The Congolese datalink couldn't assign Montague priorities, but I hoped that the tag would express to Watford just how badly I needed him.

I could struggle down a hallway in unnaturally high gravity. I could even climb the stairs. That only took stamina and stubbornness. Maybe an hour or two in medical.

I couldn't go up against Palmer. He wouldn't notice me attacking him.

And he'd barely notice killing me.

On the display, Palmer's shoulder worked and twisted. More sparks flew. His hand jerked up, bringing a loose chunk of cable with it.

I wanted to scream *Come on, Watford, answer me!* Instead, I said, "Deploy high-gee suit."

The chair buzzed under me. Bright blue plastic oozed out of the leg rest, up over my shins, swallowed my knees, and started climbing my thighs.

I didn't have time to pay attention to the suit. Instead, I hit another button. "Palmer! Can you hear me?"

No answer.

"He's breaking circuits!" Tove shouted.

"Tove!" I said.

"I'm losing!"

"Tove!" I shouted. "What is under us?"

"Machinery!"

I deliberately slowed my breath as I turned my chair to face him. The bright blue gee-suit had slid up over my belly, snug but not tight. It wouldn't inflate until I stood. "Tove. Listen to me."

The kid jerked his head towards me, too upset to be embarrassed by my half-naked form. "He's breaking the control cables!"

"Tove!" I said. "Before he cuts everything. What is underneath us?"

Tove scowled, but his fingers danced on his keyboard. "Conduits," he said. Palmer's image over my head shifted to the side, replaced with circuit diagrams. "Part of the Ring One neural. Datacore cell block five." The schematics flashed away, replaced with a set of graphs and gauges. "Hydrogen tank five, from scoop five." Those graphs disappeared as fast as Tove had summoned them. "Then water tank—"

"Wait!" I shouted. "That last one!"

My heart had started hammering again.

Had I seen what I thought?

Tove huffed and brought it back. "Hydrogen storage."

I swallowed.

Off to the side, a graph—and there, another one.

Jagged swoops and blocks.

Just like what I'd discovered in Tansi's and Monard's brain scans.

36

"Those graphs," I said, using my datalink to point out the chaotic, jagged spikes and blocky valleys. "Where exactly are they?"

"An error," Tove said.

"I didn't ask that!" No, too harsh. My breath wanted to come too quick, too hard. "It's important, Tove. Are those part of a diagnostic, or a system?"

"It's noise," Tove said.

I jerked my gaze to him. "Look at me, Tove."

Annoyed, he pulled his attention from the ceiling to glare at my eyes. "Busy!"

"That pattern," I said. "Everything, all of this, is about that noise. That pattern, it's why people are dying."

Tove's mouth dropped in a little O.

"If we can figure out where that pattern comes from, maybe we can stop this." I wanted to shout, but kept my voice quiet. "Tell me about it."

Tove swallowed. "Dad complained about it. It showed up a few months ago."

"When, exactly?"

Tove called up another image. "Two hundred twenty-six days ago."

I brought up the record of the earliest Congolese brain-damage victim.

Two hundred twenty-one days ago.

I licked my lips. "Where, exactly, did it show up?"

Keys clattered. "Tank Five, cell sixty-one. A few days later, cell one-sixty-four, then one-seventy-three, one—"

"How many in total?" I said.

"A couple hundred cells."

"Does it show anywhere else?"

"Not that I've seen. And Dad would have told me, he talked about it every night."

"Why here?"

"I don't know!" Tove said. "That's what was driving Dad nuts."

"What makes Tank Five special?"

Tove shrugged.

I said, more quickly, "What makes it unique? What's with Tank Five that's not on any other tank?"

On the display, arcing electricity illuminated Palmer's face. Sparks fountained past him.

"Uh, it's hooked Field Five, and Reactor Five."

"What's going on in Reactor Five?"

"Nothing!" Tove said. "Dad took it off-line, he didn't want to feed it unstable hydrogen."

"Smart man," I said. "Okay, so what makes Field Five different?"

"All the scoop fields are different," Tove said. "They're all tuned to different energy levels, different speeds."

"These are the fields that pull hydrogen out of space?"

"Yes."

"Do—"

A harsh buzz interrupted me. "Redding!" Watford said. "Answer me!"

"Redding here, sir."

"What's so urgent? And where's your datalink?"

"Palmer's digging through the floor," I said. "He's ripping up circuits."

Watford swore. "And your datalink?"

"Out with him. Decided to report—"

"Yes, yes. Any chance of getting the network back?"

"No, sir," I said, just as Tove said, "Impossible."

"Who is that?" Watford said.

"His name is Tove," I said. "Son of an engineer."

"Get a real engineer on the line."

"I am a real engineer!" Tove said.

I glanced at Tove. "Where is your dad?"

Tove swallowed. "Spoke Six."

Where the blast had happened.

No wonder Tove had been so desperate to stop that leak of corrosive smoke.

"Sir," I said. "We're it. But that's not the important thing."

"Go on," I said.

"That pattern—it's in the fuel tank under us. About two hundred cells."

"One ninety-one," Tove said.

"How did they create it?" Watford said.

"That's it, sir. They didn't. They sucked it in from outside."

"It's in the environment," Watford said.

"My question is." I licked my lips. More warning alarms snarled from the ceiling, but they were silent next to the klaxons blaring in my mind. Watford would either consider what I said, or send me back to Earth with a recommendation for eternal inspection duty.

Assuming Palmer didn't reach the tank, detonate it, and blow half of Wemm Station back into hydrogen.

"If this universe had life," I said, "what would it be made out of? What would it look like to us? And how would it feel about getting sucked into a fuel tank?"

37

"Wow," Tove said. He'd even stopped typing.

Only focused concentration me from shaking with tension. Concentration, and excess weight.

Watford held silent for an uncomfortably long time. "Stand by for orders, Redding."

"Acknowledged."

Watford had barely cut the link when I turned to Tove. "What Palmer's breaking through. Can you reroute the controls?"

"Not without network."

"Something! Get us, I don't know, some kind of backup access."

The shifting ceiling displays froze.

Tove's fingers clattered on his keyboard. "That's it." His voice sounded hopeless. "We're cut."

"Communications?" I said.

"Cut." He pounded the keyboard with the heel of his hand. "Cut, cut, cut!"

"Calm down, Tove."

"Helpless!"

"No, we're not." My words surprised me—it was like I was talking to my own reflection in a mirror. "You feel helpless—I get it, believe me. But there's always *something*. There's always a tool, always an angle, always something you've overlooked."

Tove glared at me.

"You said the magnetic shields are broken." The words made me imagine the high-intensity radiation sleeting through me, through Tove, through every inhabitant of Wemm Station. I pushed confidence into my voice, to cover up the dread. If we lived through the next few hours, we'd have plenty of time to get a chromosome scrub. "But you fixed the lube, so the station isn't breaking itself apart."

"Right. But if he—"

"Don't panic yet," I said. "Figure out where we are, first. What happens if Palmer keeps digging?"

"Bulkhead," Tove said. "Stop."

"What if he gets through the bulkhead?"

"Steel." Tove shook his head. "Structural."

"That'll stop him three minutes," I said. "Maybe four."

"What he using?" Tove said.

Is, kid. Is. "Tove. Palmer is a cyborg." Watford was going to have my head for leaking any details. "He's designed for deep space operations and construction. Palmer can bend steel with his bare hands. In vacuum. In orbit of Mercury. During a solar flare. While sipping his afternoon tea."

Despite the high-gee suit, Tove's face lost its underlying color.

I kept my voice level, projecting a calm confidence I didn't nearly feel. "So what happens when Palmer keeps going?"

Tove's hands reflexively went to the keyboard. His fingers twitched with the repressed need to call up displays. "Breaks through the cable layer—all little stuff, hydraulics and shaper stock. Then the bulkhead. I…" I saw Tove's eyes roll up as he remembered diagrams. "I think access shaft under, for robots. Hydrogen cells."

"The wiring layer." I licked my chapped lips. "What if he digs through that?"

"Everything carries on. Engineers reroute."

"Okay. The hydraulics you mentioned? Shaper stock?"

Tove waved dismissively. "Messy. Not dangerous."

When we made it through this, I was going to sign the kid up for elocution lessons.

Before I could ask the next question, Tove said, "The tank. The hydrogen tank."

"I can guess—but tell me. What happens?"

"Supercooled. Pressurized. Freeze air? Burn?"

The hastily memorized Wemm Station briefing had included information on the engineering level, but I'd concentrated on Ring Two and above. "Those tanks are large, aren't they?"

Tove nodded.

"If they burn down there—"

"Won't burn in tank," Tove said. "No oh-two. Boil up into Ring One, then burn." His face got even paler. "Burn all here."

"Then we make sure that doesn't happen," I said.

Tove hammered fists into the padded armrests of his chair, which absorbed them without complain, making him even more angry. "No controls!"

"People built Wemm Station," I said. "People like your dad, using robots and wrenches. They hung in zero gravity, in an empty universe, and built this place out of raw aluminum plates and steel beams. And somewhere underneath the datacore, every machine has actual knobs and buttons."

"Where?" Tove shouted.

I pointed at the floor. "Below us."

Tove stared at me.

I said, "Maybe that pattern down there doesn't mean anything. Maybe it's the key to everything. And maybe Ring One could handle a giant hydrogen blast. But I do know that we have a few thousand people overhead, and if Palmer rips open that tank there's a good chance that a whole bunch of them will get hurt or just flat-out die. I'm going down there, and I'm going to dump every liter of that hydrogen back out where we got it."

Tove swallowed, not saying anything.

"You don't have to help," I said. "You'd make it a whole lot easier, though."

"Never been down there," Tove said.

"Well, neither have I. But at least you'll recognize the labels on the controls when we find them."

Tove took a deep breath. "One and a half, two gee down there."

"The suits can handle that." The manual claimed they could.

Tove shook his head mutely. "That's…"

"It'll be rough," I said. "But look at it this way. Either Palmer punches into the tank and kills everyone—or we bleed off the hydrogen and save everyone."

Tove closed his eyes, looking every bit a nervous teenager.

Without even Tove's meager knowledge, I'd have to fall back on more direct ways to empty the tank. Get on a pressure suit. Take a plasma cutter outside. Climb down until I found something that looked like a hydrogen tank. And start digging.

At least the blast would be outside.

I said, "Imagine what all the girls will say."

Tove grimaced, knowing how I'd pushed his young man buttons and still unable to resist. "Fine. We do."

The comfort of the high-gravity recliner suddenly felt precious, like something I might never know again. About to leave its cradling embrace, I found part of my brain trying to absorb the pillowy sensation so I could recall it later.

We had no time for comfort.

I tapped my datalink. Even without the network backing it, it had enough brains to control the chair and my high-gee suit. "Stand up."

In one smoothly synchronized dance, the chair shifted as my suit began to inflate. After walking naked across the hall, the pressure climbing my body didn't feel so invasive. It felt—safe. Freeing.

Seconds later I was on my feet, letting the suit puff up around me. "How do we get down, Tove?"

"Access elevator," Tove said. He still lay in his high-gee recliner. Some color had returned to his face, but fresh sweat shone on his forehead.

"Where is it?"

Internal conflict battered his expression. He wanted to hide until someone rescued them. He wanted to save everyone.

But most of all, put on the spot, he didn't want to look weak or afraid.

His obvious fear made it easier for me to keep mine under control. The suit felt almost comfortable now, but that rippling squeeze that forced blood back up my legs would get a whole lot fiercer down below. Two gravities promised brutality. Not nearly as brutal as standing in Palmer's way, but still.

Tove touched his datalink. "Stand up." His voice wobbled as the chair swung and the suit compressed against him. "It's to left."

"Okay." I took a shuffling half-step towards the door before a thought struck me. "Tove, before we go."

Tove finished stepping off the chair's low foot platform. "Oui?"

"I'm from the security department. You're engineering. This is an engineering job."

Panic flashed in his eyes. "I can't go down there alone."

"No, no." I wanted to shake my head, but the suit's neck restricted that motion to a slow grind. "I'm planning to go the whole way with you." I licked my lips. "The thing is—I'm not used to high gravity."

"Neither."

"If something happens to me, if I can't finish," I said. "You *must* go down on your own."

Tove's face tried to go pale. "Dad said never."

"Blame me if you need to," I said. "But that tank's full of the same pattern that's in Palmer. I don't know if they're attracting each other or what, but we've *got* to get it out of this station."

Tove's hands rolled into the best fists the high-gee suit allowed. "Fine."

Tove was not expendable.

But I was.

Weirdly, the thought made me more comfortable.

Now to go expend myself.

38

Palmer had dug right in the center of the elevator vestibule. He'd climbed into the pit head-first, but his butt and legs were still sprawled across the deck. Bent steel flooring bloomed upwards around him. Tangled fistfuls of wire and conduit, savagely torn chunks of pipe, and smeary puddles of greasy blue and green and yellow ooze surrounded the pit. The malignant stink of a dozen different chemicals and angry electricity burned my sinuses, and Palmer's ongoing assault on the station's structure raised a cacophony of breaking metal and plastic.

The high-gee suit's rhythmic pulses up my legs, synchronized with my heartbeat, suddenly got much quicker. The suit automatically wicked my sweat away, but I was pretty sure the sight made that function work harder too.

The elevator doors across the room sat frozen, impotent. Manual controls and gauges widely spaced on the walls flashed yellow and red.

Sudden brilliant light flared up from the pit. I closed my eyes against it, but blue radiance glared against my eyelids.

Behind me, Tove swore in French.

The light faded in a second. White and yellow afterimages obscured my sight, but I started shuffling left. Not only did the suit restrict me to half steps, but I couldn't lift my feet to step over debris. The small stuff I brushed aside, but I had to painfully sidestep a half-meter chunk of copper pipe barely as big around as my arm.

The ends of the pipe had been squeezed shut. The indentations from Palmer's fingers still glowed a little red.

I tried to brush the smaller stuff aside with my toes, but quietly. Palmer's depredations made an incredible racket, but I didn't dare attract his attention.

A whiff of some noxious burnt smell made me cough—no easy feat in a high-gee suit. Fresh tears hazed my eyes. I wanted to bring up a full faceplate and respirator, but if I did, I wouldn't be able to communicate with Tove. No network meant no voice channel.

Here we were at the beginning of the universe, in the most sophisticated structure I'd ever seen, and what we needed were a couple of old-fashioned walkie-talkies.

A massive chunk of air duct sailed up out of the hole. It fell too quickly, like a video at twice normal speed. It struck well away from us, but the impact scattered fresh detritus into my path. A massive circuit board cage skittered to the side, right into my planned path. I'd have to circle it, too.

If we didn't get out of here quickly, strewn and broken components would make the vestibule impassible.

I itched to charge forward. Instead, I raised one hand in a fist and stopped. Had Tove ever seen any of those old action movies? I shuffled on my axis, needing four steps to make the quarter-turn so I could see the kid.

"Protect my eyes," I said, tapping my datalink. A clear visor flowed out of the high-gee suit's forehead and down to my nose. "You too, Tove."

Tove grimaced and followed my example.

I shuffled back to face forward.

Palmer's clattering stopped for a second, then more electronic debris hailed down around us in a fusillade of noise. Something bounced off the back of my suit, the automation thankfully reducing the impact to a faint pressure over one shoulder. In this gravity, a surprised stumble had a good chance of maiming, even killing me.

We'd scooted a yard further when the clatter stopped again. Metal groaned, a low-pitched rumble that penetrated the padded soles of my feet and shivered up my legs and into my spine. I ached to turn and look, but we needed to escape the area before the strewn scrap of station components became impassible heaps.

Palmer said, "Ing. Red. Red."

His voice sounded too loud.

Like he wasn't head-down in a pit any more.

Even inside the high-gee suit, fear tickled my skin.

"Red. Ing."

I couldn't hope that Tove's last name was also Redding.

I stopped.

The suit still refused to let me turn quickly.

Palmer sat on his knees, body straight but at a skewed angle, like a tree dragged by hurricane winds. One mad eye whirled all around. The other eye was a sphere of hot orange light, flicking with irregular, inhuman blinking. Wicked blue lightning crawled around one hand, flickering between the freckles of his sensors. His spine and shoulders jerked with each leap of light, teeth clanging together with each spasm.

Watford had said I run towards trouble.

Right now, I wanted to run away.

Instead, I took a shuffling step towards Palmer. "Tove. Keep going."

I'd expected Tove to argue. Instead, he started shuffling more quickly, his feet swinging over the ground like a tai chi practitioner's.

He knew how to move. I'd been holding him up.

Palmer's one human-looking eye didn't fix on me, but he seemed to be trying to wobble it in my general direction. "Red-d-d." Electronic distortion surged and distorted his voice.

"Palmer," I said. "Fight it. You can beat it."

Tove shifted past my back, just short of running.

Irrational anger flashed through me. Tove had been here before, he'd practiced in high gravity. I hadn't.

All I knew was how to stand and face Palmer.

Palmer raised the hand not covered in lightning and waved off to the side. "Fire."

I flinched. "Palmer, it's going for the hydrogen tanks. You've got to stop it."

"Fire." His voice warbled up the scale. "For, for for for—for for fire."

The lightning-sheathed hand came up, dangling a massive metal-cased block by frayed wires. The plastic coating on the wiring sizzled and smoked under the crawling blue charge. The way the whole thing swung, it had to weigh as much as I did.

"Palmer," I said, mind churning to come up with something. "Can you shut your systems down? We can get you to a medical pod before there's any more damage."

"Fire," Palmer hissed. "Firefirefirefirefire. Forfire." The arm holding the metal block swung back.

"You can stop this!" I shouted, more out of denial than any real hope.

Palmer launched the massive chunk of metal at me.

39

I instinctively lurched backwards, as quickly as the oppressive high-gee suit permitted.

As Palmer started to throw, though, his other arm swung across his body. His shoulders shifted, skewing his aim.

The chunk of metal crashed into the floor a meter to my left with a rattling thud that made me flinch.

It bounced, leaving a ten-centimeter crater in the steel deck.

With the gravity, my heart couldn't leap into my mouth—but it did grab hold of my esophagus and start climbing.

If he hit me with something like that, I was dead—adaptive suit or no.

Whatever was in Palmer had figured out that humans threatened it. Interfered with it. Maybe it had only gotten to the rock-throwing stage—but it didn't need anything more.

And it would have hit me, if that other hand hadn't interfered.

Palmer still had some control.

"Fire!" Palmer screamed. "For. For, for forfor." His hand without lightning waved frantically, while the other arm resumed those inhuman, swooping motions.

Tove had made it through the doorway and into the corridor.

So long as Palmer didn't hit the kid, Tove would solve the real problem.

All I could do was keep Palmer's attention—and not get flattened.

Palmer's shouting turned into an electronic squeal.

I took another step to the right, back towards the engineering office. "You can do it, Palmer. You can stop it. You're tougher than the rest of us."

Blue lightning surged up Palmer's arm, then ebbed back to his hand. The glowing eye flashed yellow, then incandescent white, and back to orange.

"You have to be tough," I said. "Push it out. I know you can."

Palmer's lightning hand grabbed the raised edge of a battered floor plate and tugged. The steel plate sparked, but stayed attached to the ground. Palmer tugged harder, the lightning seething furiously.

Maybe the thing in Palmer didn't understand the idea of "riveted down."

"Misdirect it," I said. "Make it wad up that floor plate instead."

"For!" Palmer screamed. "For for for!" Even through the electronic distortion, I thought I heard real anguish there.

The steel floor plate in Palmer's hand snapped.

He raised a jagged metal triangle the size of his hand over his head.

Palmer's free arm flailed wildly. Was he waving me away?

The other hand spun and hurled the makeshift shuriken right at me.

Straight into my gut.

40

The metal shard plunged in right above my left hip. My whole world seemed to focus on that point—weird hot ice, slipping straight through my skin and into my guts. Brain cells dating back to the dinosaurs screamed their outrage. I somehow tasted my own blood.

The elevator room whirled around me. Without the high-gee suit, I would have fallen.

My breath sagged out.

Primal terror filled me, certain that inhaling would shift the metal and maim me even further. My lungs held paralyzed for a second or a decade, then slowly eased air in.

The sound of my heartbeat drowned out Palmer's idiotic shriek of *for for for fire for.*

Suddenly I wasn't brave at all. I wanted to scream and run, to fall.

I wanted someone to rescue me.

I would have collapsed in shock, but the high-gee suit held me up.

The stink of burning smart fabric stung my nose.

Nausea made me want to puke.

I didn't dare.

I needed a heartbeat to work up the courage to even lower my chin and look down.

The metal jabbed out a dozen centimeters from the suit's inflated fabric, the trailing edge gleaming with hints of red heat from being broken free. My instincts itched to snatch it out of me, to pull it free—but no. Worst thing I could do.

The suit's rippling changed. It had always squeezed me in, supporting my circulation, but now it tightened around the wound.

Something jabbed my bicep.

I looked down. Nothing.

But with my next breath, the pain washed away. The suit's medical systems had fired. You can't tourniquet a gut wound, but the suit could apply direct pressure. Immobilize the injury.

And shoot me with enough painkiller to make the pain stop.

My throat hurt. I didn't remember screaming, but I must have.

I still didn't dare breathe deeply. Even without the appalling sensation, I still felt horribly aware of the injury.

But I could think.

Palmer's deranged eye wobbled in my direction. The other glared forge-red.

Every moment Palmer spent chasing me, he wasn't tearing through the Wemm Station hull. Tove needed time to blow out the hydrogen tank.

Palmer was already trying to pull another chunk of metal off the plate. I suddenly realized he'd stopped shouting, leaving me only with the sounds of humming machines and my own pulse.

I looked around desperately, trying to ignore the drugged hollowness behind my eyes. There had to be something here I could use. A big power control panel with dozens of toggles—no, if I killed the electricity down here, who knew what would happen to the station? Gauges for different kinds of liquids, fire suppression panel, conduits...

Wait.

My gaze swiveled back to the fire suppression panel: a big red button with a flip cover, a big clicky dial with a dozen settings for different kinds of fire. I didn't recall the specifics of each kind of fire suppression, but I knew that one was a simple water spray and another evacuated the air. When the datacore was online it handled fire automatically, but if a fire broke out now someone would have to choose the correct type—

Understanding hit me like a bucket of cold water.

The thought of walking filled me with dread. What if taking a step shifted that scrap of metal enough to nick an artery? The suit couldn't keep me alive if I bled out. And nobody was standing by to get me into a medical pod. The numbness in my flank seemed to be spreading—did that mean the damage was already getting worse? My heart wouldn't stop rabbiting.

But if I didn't move, many more people might die.

I took a deep breath and swung my left foot forward. The numbness in my side made me feel even more clumsy, but I planted that foot and took another step.

With careful attention I shuffled the few meters to the fire suppression panel. The knob was oversized, meant to be adjusted while wearing a high-gee suit. Each setting was numbered, and had a brief description in French.

Something metallic cracked behind me. I didn't need to turn and look to know that Palmer had snapped off another chunk of metal plate.

Moving as quickly as I dared, I twisted the dial a third of the way around and flipped the button cover.

Palmer let out a horrific electronic shriek, discordant tones twisting against each other.

I jabbed the button.

41

Even facing the elevator room wall, I saw the pale yellow mist fizzing out of the ceiling.

A noxious bitter smell brushed my nose. I jerked my hand up for protection, like my fingers could filter out gas, but the high-gee suit's smart fabric flowed up over my lips and brushed my touch away. The suit needed only a second to form a clear protective visor. A small hollow formed over my nose and mouth, feeding me tiny breaths of flat, canned air.

Behind me, metal crashed against metal.

Something clattered on the deck.

The floor thudded with a big, heavy impact.

Yellow-green condensation formed on my visor, coalescing into turgid blobs that trickled like poison rain across my view.

If I'd screwed up, if I'd made a bad assumption, another shard of metal would land right in my back. Desperate to spin, but trapped by the high-gee suit's uncomfortable clench, I needed two steps to turn around.

Palmer lay face-up, surrounded by broken equipment and shattered deck plates. The electric halo around his arm had vanished. His back arched so extremely that I felt a sympathetic ache, then he shuddered and pulled his limbs into his chest, pillbug-style.

He hadn't shouted *fire* and *for*.

He'd shouted *four*.

Palmer had told me how to shut him down.

I didn't know exactly how that particular fire suppression chemical had scrambled the construction cyborg's circuits. But at that moment, I didn't care. My pounding heart felt ready to burst. I wanted to sag against the wall, get back in the high-gee recliner, but I didn't dare. My flank felt so numb it might have been scooped out, but I couldn't forget the chunk of metal buried in me.

Drenched in putrid yellow gel, Palmer shuddered.

I took the risk of closing my eyes and concentrating on my breath, trying to slow my jackrabbit pulse and get my breath back under control. The suit's stale dry air made my mouth feel even more parched. Fading adrenaline left my muscles quivering, my stance supported only by the high-gee suit.

Were the Congolese still preparing to evacuate?

Or had Watford dispatched a team to deal with Palmer?

No, Montague didn't have the people left. He'd sent Percival and a few other people to deal with DeKalb, leaving him with just enough to guard the Portal. He'd certainly sent a message through the Portal telling the company to stand by for evacuation.

Montague wouldn't send Watford more security people until we stabilized Wemm Station… or until after the evacuation, when they brought in a science team to discover what had gone wrong.

Assuming they didn't just slam the door on this universe forever. Montague had done that more than once.

I had this sudden flash of a future life on an abandoned Wemm Station, living on stored supplies as the station slowly fell apart from lack of maintenance. Maybe I'd bring chickens down to Ring Three so I could stay near the Portal, watching for years—decades—in hope that Montague would decide to come back.

No, that wasn't going to happen. That was the painkillers talking.

Step one, talk to Watford. Tell him Palmer was shut down, that Tove was on his way to bleed out the hydrogen from Tank Five. That I had a metal triangle in my side. The main Ring One corridor had to have hard-wired communications panels, somewhere.

All I had to do was walk.

Without shifting the metal stabbing into me.

I deliberately didn't look down at my flank, tried to not imagine where exactly the weapon had wound up. Had it stuck in muscle? Or was the tip buried in my bowels? All the way through, into my liver?

Instead, I shuffled in a tight circle and headed for the nearest corridor.

The massive thud I'd heard had been the transparent firewall dropping from the ceiling, isolating the toxic goo in the elevator room from the main Ring One corridor. The built-in airlock opened at a touch, and a blast of air took the worst of the goopy fire suppressant off my suit.

I'd made it maybe a dozen meters down the corridor when I saw someone's knees and feet dropping into view from around the ring's upward curve.

42

The prospect of another brain and a set of hands sent relief surging through me. I really didn't want to deal with the damage Palmer had left as Aidan Redding versus Yet Another Universe. Seeing those feet, I didn't care if they belonged to an engineer or a Portal guard, Congolese or Montague, crew or child or knife-wielding maniac.

Although a medic would be nice.

With the hollow numbness in my side, a medic would be wonderful.

They could take over. I could take a nap.

I kept going, scanning the control-studded walls for anything that looked like a hard-wired network connection. A comms panel. I would have settled for carrier pigeons. Anything that let me call for help and get this chunk of metal out of my guts. With the suit's faceplate down, the fire suppressant's stench burned my nose. The blast of air in the firewall's airlock had blown most of it away, but that stuff was noxious enough that even the faint remnants made my stomach protest.

The other person moved much more quickly than I dared. I'd gone only a few more meters when they got close enough for me to recognize the suit's slowly shifting leopard-print decoration.

I stopped in surprise. "Habre?"

I abandoned my search and shuffled forward.

Habre saw me and somehow picked up speed, walking almost at a normal pace. The omnipresent rattle of Wemm Station's machinery almost drowned out her shout of "Redding!"

I lifted a hand.

We couldn't really speak until I was close enough to clasp the bulky glove of her high-gee suit.

Exhaustion dragged Habre's sharp features. "Redding?"

"Belvie," I said. "I am thrilled to see you." I'd heard she was dead so often, I believed it.

"What has happened? Where is everyone?"

Habre's presence boosted my spirits, but my thoughts still ground against each other like gaptoothed gears. "Have you talked to anyone?"

Habre shook her head. "I only now stabilized the survivors of the lube blow-out. Where are the rescue teams?"

She'd missed everything. "Getting ready for the evacuation."

I quickly filled her in: how Palmer had attacked the floor, finding the pattern, losing communications with the upper Rings. Merely telling the story made me feel even more tired. By the time I got to where I'd disabled Palmer, I had to use my free hand to lean against the wall. The numbness around my wound had ballooned to the bottom of my ribs and down into my hips. The ache in my head made me feel tiny, as if I sat within my own skull and shifted rusty levers to move my limbs and form words.

Concerned, Habre said, "What's wrong with you?"

Not looking down, I clumsily shifted my hips a few degrees to display the jagged metal sticking out of my side. "Palmer got me."

Habre hissed. "We need to get that out of you."

"You can't." I took a deep breath. "I'll bleed out."

"No you won't," Habre said.

"The worst thing you can do for an impalement. Pull it out."

"Aidan." Habre kept her eyes on my face. "The suits are built for that."

I looked at her without comprehension.

She waved her free hand and spoke slowly. "Our high-gee suits, they have built-in medical support. You don't feel anything there, do you?"

"No."

"And you're woozy." It wasn't a question.

"You have *no* idea."

"That's the drugs and the nanomeds." Habre clearly enunciated each word, as if she was afraid I wouldn't understand. "They're standing by to patch the hole. It's not perfect, you'll need a doctor later, but it'll stop the bleeding and prevent any more damage."

The urge to yank the violating shard out of my side blossomed, tangled with an equal revulsion of anyone touching it. I'm sure Habre felt my grip clench tighter, but she only said "The nanomeds will soon exhaust their power. And when that happens, you really will bleed out."

I fumed. Montague high-gee suits didn't have anything like that. I should have known, though. I should have read the Congolese manuals, as well as the Montague ones I was still trudging through. How was I supposed to do anything without understanding the equipment, the rules?

Despite the high-gee suit's engulfing pressure and the horribly numb wound, I made myself take the deepest breath I could manage. "Okay." My flank abruptly seemed hot, a radioactive no-go zone as deadly as the storm of energy outside Wemm Station. "Give me a moment, I'll get it."

"You can't," Habre said.

I gave her a clenched-tooth grin. "You haven't seen those old cowboy movies, have you? The ones where the explorer alone does surgery on himself?"

"They were madmen," Habre said. "Listen to me, Miss Redding." Her voice took on a quiet tone. It should have annoyed me, but somehow I felt… comforted? "If anyone's that tough, it's you. But please let me help you. All you must do is stay still a moment."

I trembled. I didn't want her to touch it. *I* didn't want to touch it.

"Fine," I said. "But—quick."

"You will feel nothing until after."

I squeezed my eyes tight.

Everything held still for a breath.

In the middle of the numbness, a bright spark of warmth exploded like the first sun igniting in an empty universe. Unpleasant electric shivers rippled up my spine and down into my knees, making my muscles go slack. I slumped within the high-gee suit, held upright only by the smart fabric.

"Stop," I hissed. "Stop!"

"It's already out," Habre said.

The warmth intensified.

"Everything you feel—" Habre said.

A muscle spasm blasted the air out of me.

"—is the nanomeds," Habre said. "Don't try to fight. They're fixing you. Can you hear me, Aidan?"

"Yes," I groaned. Ghastly sensations rippled out of the wound: a crawling chill, a fresh fevered heat, tremors. "Tell me… something. Distract." I sucked a breath. "DeKalb."

"Yes," Habre said. "DeKalb." Her voice became businesslike. "I was in the Spoke Six engineering office with Ramazani and Kress, our chief engineer. For the video displays. My people and the Montague crew intercepted DeKalb." Her words lost all inflection. "I gave the order. They cut him down."

"The explosion," I said.

"DeKalb had done a lot of damage as he walked. He used the plasma cutter to sever many cables, damaged many conduits, all of them overhead. When he fell, the cutter burned into a fluid conduit." Her voice tightened. "One ruptured. That small burst ruptured three more. Weakened parts failed. A chain reaction. The corridor became… uninhabitable."

The holocaust in my side felt terrible, but not nearly as bad as Habre. She'd given an order to open fire, to kill one of her people. The other choices were worse. And more people had died. "Security gets the dirty jobs. I'm sorry."

Habre nodded, but wouldn't meet my eyes.

"You saved lives, though."

"I lost more," Habre said. "I'm just glad the fluid flow shut off."

I made myself inhale. Were the flashes of heat and cold getting weaker? "Tove shut them down, from Spoke Five."

"Tove?" Habre said. "Tove Kress?"

"I didn't know his name."

"Kress will be most proud."

"He's on his way."

"No, Kress stayed behind. Trying to stabilize the systems around Spoke Six. He said engineering teams would be joining him from above."

"No, Tove," I said. "He's on his way."

"Where to?"

The wretched spasms stopped cold. After the numbness, the sudden pressure of the high-gee suit over my side shocked me. My abs felt uncomfortably tight, just short of cramping.

Habre said, "It just finished, no?"

I nodded. Forcing my ribs against the suit's pressure, I pulled in a tentative breath and waited for the stab of pain.

The muscles on that side didn't want to stretch with my lungs. But they didn't tear. And my innards didn't complain.

The muzziness was fading from my head. The rapid withdrawal caused its own disorientation.

Habre had one hand on my shoulder. The other held an upraised twenty-centimeter long chunk of floor plate, twisted into a spiral spearhead. Blood and worse covered a third of it.

The sight made my stomach burn. "Uh… thanks."

"My pleasure."

Thin strength seeped back into my bones, without my usual reserves but enough that I no longer felt ready to collapse. The high-gee suit's support no longer felt completely necessary. Another breath cleared the lingering fuzziness in my head. "Communications," I said.

"Kress said they have failed in this half of Ring One."

"Elevators are out in Spoke Five," I said. "But I can do the stairs now."

"Then let's go."

43

"Tove," I said as we turned back towards the elevator room and the emergency stairs. For all the struggle I'd had walking while injured, Ring One's transparent firewall looked distressingly close. Yellow-green gunk obscured the view through it.

"Yes," Habre said. "You were about to say?"

"He went down to empty the hydrogen. The hydrogen with the pattern in it."

Habre frowned. "You sent Tove down for that? He's certainly not qualified."

"It was only the two of us," I said. "And someone had to hold Palmer back."

"You weren't clear, before," Habre said. "Before I addressed your injury, I fear you weren't very clear at all."

I felt certain I'd said everything—but the suit had drugged me. "Tove and I found the pattern from Tansi and Monard in a fuel tank."

Habre stopped. "What kind of fuel?"

"Hydrogen, scooped out of space. And Palmer, Tansi, Monard, everyone I've dealt with, they were all headed straight for that tank."

"You think it's attracting them?"

"Maybe. Maybe it's even alive, somehow."

"It's hydrogen," Habre said. "It can't be alive."

"I don't know," I said. "But I do know that, cut off from above, ditching everything with that pattern in it seemed like a really good idea."

Habre nodded.

"And maybe it would slow Palmer down. Distract—"

A loud clang shook the deck, hard enough to penetrate the suit's padding and send vibrations up my spine.

We both stopped. "What was that?" I said.

Habre shook her head.

The fire suppressant goo on the other side of the firewall was an even smear. From this distance, I couldn't see more chemicals pouring onto it. New fear swelled in my stomach. "The fire suppression system. If I triggered setting four... how long would that spray last?"

"Five minutes at most," she said.

The fragile trek from the engineering office and the nanomeds' assault on my innards had completely scrambled my sense of time.

But I must have triggered the flood that disabled Palmer more than five minutes ago.

Another clang rang down the hall.

"Palmer's recovered," I said. "He's busting through the station again."

44

"Quick," I said. "What's the fastest way down to the hydrogen tanks? Tank Five."

Habre looked up the corridor towards the firewall. "We have to stop him."

"We can't," I said. "There isn't a weapon on this station that can kill Palmer."

"Surely—"

I faced Habre. "Listen to me. Palmer can do deep space construction. In close solar orbit. He can break into your fusion reactors. You don't have anything that can stop him."

"You underestimate us," Habre said, anger seeping into her words. "We have cyborgs as well. There are several well-documented methods for disabling them. I know how to turn every tool on this Ring into a weapon."

At my first meeting with Watford, he'd emphasized confidentiality. If I explained Palmer's real role, he'd get me assigned to a Class D universe within the hour.

"I charted Monard and Tansi," I said quickly. "They were both going down Spoke Five. DeKalb was coming this way. Palmer, he's on the same line. They're all going straight to that signal in the hydrogen tanks."

Habre looked even more furious.

"Maybe that's what's dragging Palmer down," I said. "We need to get it off this station."

"If it's truly attracting him," Habre said, "if you bleed the fuel into space, he will just keep going."

"It'll scatter," I said. "We're spinning, it won't go in just one direction. He won't have a motherlode to home in on."

The floor shook again.

This time, with a distant bang.

Any hope I had of persuading her died with the blast's echo.

"Maybe," Habre said, glancing at the firewall. A diagonal crack spread through the clear tough plastic as she looked. "But I'm not letting your cyborg do more damage to this station."

I shook my head. "I know for a fact you can't stop him."

"Do what you wish," Habre said flatly, taking a step towards the firewall. "I will stop Palmer. Alone."

If she went through that firewall, if she approached Palmer, he would kill her.

If I went, I would die too.

Before she took a second step, I said, "Because if your gear could stop Palmer, Montague would have sent a bigger cyborg. With even fewer safety overrides."

So much for my career.

But Habre froze.

"Montague knows the specs of every device on this station," I said. "They know every piece of equipment you shipped through the Portal."

Habre turned to me, furious. "Are you telling me—"

"I'm not telling you anything you couldn't have figured out on your own," I said quickly. "Montague policy would specifically forbid me to tell you if we had a last-ditch method to protect Earth from any alien activity in this universe."

"It's empty!"

I spread my hands. "But look what's happened."

"You stopped him once!"

"He told me how."

The floor vibrated with another crash. It felt less damaging than Habre's livid glare.

"He told you?" she finally said. "Told you how to disable him?"

"Sort of," I said. "He's in better shape than the earlier victims."

"Then we ask him again."

"If he knew a better way, he would have told me." My mind scrabbled for solutions. "Can you get more of that number four fire spray down here?"

She glanced up at the tangle overhead. "I'm sure *one* of these pipes carries it."

"I'm open to other ideas," I said. "But Tove venting the fuel, it really is the best I've had. And if Palmer hits that tank, if he busts open a bunch of hydrogen into the Ring, what's going to happen?"

Habre glanced over at the firewall.

Another distant explosion.

The firewall ripped open at the crack, tumbling broad chunks of transparent plastic out towards us. A thin yellow-green haze billowed towards us.

I held my breath long enough for the suit to bring up a faceplate.

Habre coughed as the mist thinned around us. One of the lights in the ceiling had turned a brilliant red. Thanks for the warning, I thought.

"Fine," Habre said. She coughed again, the sound muffled and hollow through the suit's external speaker. Her anger still came through. "Fine. You had best be right about this."

I realized at that moment that I sincerely liked Habre.

And that saving her life had cost me her friendship.

45

Even in extreme gravity, losing the metal shard from my side made me feel fast. I concentrated on my steps, emulating Habre's quicker and looser motions. Everything in me ached to move, to run straight to our destination and send the tainted hydrogen straight out into the void. If it didn't work, at least we could move on to the next plan.

No running in high gravity. We trudged.

I still wanted to scream.

Habre kept her back to me. And it wasn't just the high-gee suit keeping her stiff.

Palmer had worked his way entirely into the floor. Every ten or twenty seconds a chunk of machinery flew up from the crater and crashed into the deck. A gust of thick yellow smoke shot up under pressure, settled heavily against the deck, and seeped back into Palmer's tunnel.

Something far below grumbled.

Brilliant light shone up the tunnel, accompanied by a whooshing sound loud enough to punch through the suit.

Habre stopped. "Amazing."

"Let's beat him down there," I said.

Habre led me to a heavy sealed door just short of the elevator room. Shattered firewall crunched underfoot. The fire suppressant goo looked like it should be slippery, but it didn't bother the suits. The door swung open heavily, exposing another airlock, this one walled in metal. The suits bulged with the quick burst of vacuum that evaporating the noxious goo from our suits, then shrank back down with repressurization. Our faceplates faded back into the suits.

Beyond, another small room with a wire-walled elevator. The main elevators were out, but this one used technology from centuries ago: a metal gate raised and lowered manually, gears and cables, a self-contained motor mounted just out of reach overhead. The elevator could hold half a dozen friendly people, or Habre and I if we stood in opposite corners.

Which she did.

The elevator began to descend through conduits, pipes, and wiring harnesses.

"If it's not the fuel," Habre said, still not looking at me. "If it's another cause. Perhaps we can divert Palmer." Her voice sounded thick with buried anger.

"Divert?" I kept my tone light.

"He wants to go down. If we can steer him to this elevator shaft instead of making his own path, it will reduce the damage he can inflict on the station. He can move down freely."

I bit back my first response: how are you going to steer him? "He'll move more quickly then."

"He will." She stared at a bright orange pipe running parallel to our descent. "Then he'll tear a hole in the bottom of the shaft."

"What's under us?"

"It goes all the way." She didn't look back at me. "You can ride this elevator to the outside of Ring One."

I swallowed.

We'd be throwing Palmer into infinity.

I did not want to kill him.

But... what else could we do?

And Habre had given the order to shoot DeKalb, when he'd been similarly affected and much less dangerous.

Could I do any less?

"Once Tove dumps the fuel." I felt even more sick. "If that doesn't work, maybe he's got some ideas on how we can move Palmer. A winch or something."

Habre nodded. She might be livid with me, with all of Montague, but we could still work together.

On this, at least.

As the elevator eased downward, my weight increased. My heart beat harder and my head felt impossibly heavy, as if my brain was truly made of concrete. The suit had been holding my jaw closed so I wouldn't accidentally bite off my tongue, but now the chin protector helped support my skull.

In the upper Rings, a couple meters of height changed your weight by a percent or two.

But down here, the further we dropped, the faster our weight increased.

The next time I visited a space station in an alien universe, I promised myself, I'm going to demand natural laws with a better way to create gravity.

The elevator ground downward in painful slowness. An access corridor rose into view and disappeared overhead. Each ratchet of the mechanism cranked my frustration even higher.

Someone had stenciled 2.0G on a wall plate. Two gravities.

The elevator rattled. I felt, rather than heard, another explosion, meters overhead and through the wall. I gripped the rail as tight as the bulky gloves permitted.

Another access space rose into view, a four-meter square with corridors running off it. Tove stood near a display wall, hands on old-fashioned mechanical dials. He slowly turned one, gaze glued to a display. Sweat drenched Tove's face and his eyes bulged. Was it just the gravity? Or had something new gone wrong?

The elevator gate clanged open, and a babble of French erupted into my ears.

We had communications.

I wanted to cheer.

Habre snapped quick instructions into the chorus. Voices quieted for a beat, then a single person answered.

My body felt draped in lead. Holding my eyelids open took concentration. With slow, deliberate care, I inched my way towards Tove. "Tove." The parched, greasy air made me want to cough, but the suit rippled so tightly that I couldn't possibly. "What's going on?"

"Arguing."

I turned down the earphones to dull Habre's argument. "Did you dump the hydrogen?"

"That's the argument."

I couldn't hope to follow Habre's rapid-fire French. Presumably she was telling the others what had happened. "Forget the signal in it—if Palmer hits that tank, the way he's doing damage, the whole thing will blow out. Drain it!"

"Arguing," Tove said. "Mvouba says, stop cyborg."

"We can't," I said. "I tried."

"Montague said."

I buried my urge to scream. "Montague said what?"

Tove tightened his lips in anger and spat out each word. "Montague Watford said you cannot stop the cyborg. You cannot turn him off. Commander Mvouba insists Montague deal with their man. You understand?"

"I'll deal with Palmer right now. Dump the fuel, that's step one."

"Mvouba says no."

I turned the earpiece back up, ready to jump in and tell the Congolese commander to give the order. Watford's voice was on the channel, though, speaking quick, fluid French. I felt a flash of surprise—I didn't know he spoke French. But Montague wouldn't have assigned Watford here if he couldn't.

I left my mike muted. "What else can we access?"

Tove gave a tiny shake of his head, not easy in the overwhelming gravity. "Engineering datacore dead. One data comm line up. Patched into control cable access hydrogen tank."

"The tank's not here?"

Tove hoisted a hand to point. "Through wall. Under cyborg."

Of course. "Can we get to the tank itself?"

"Access tunnel. Noise."

"That racket isn't normal, I take it?"

Tove shook his head.

"All right then," I said. "How would—"

I heard my name through the helmet and froze. Watford—no, he'd only mentioned me in passing, amidst a flurry of unfamiliar French. "How would we drain the tank?"

"It's all set." He pointed to a blinking square on the display wall. "Touch that, it goes."

I suddenly realized Watford had said my name again, this time in a more annoyed tone. I stopped.

"Redding!"

I unmuted my mic. "Here."

"Private channel," he thundered.

"Sir."

I touched the datalink to stop the flurry of French. "Private channel to Montague Security First Watford."

The helmet beeped. "Redding?"

"Here."

"Mvouba says that Palmer is digging through the station."

"Yes." I was too frustrated to add *sir*. "Ripping it apart with his bare hands. I slowed him down—"

"Yes, yes. Don't go into details on this network."

"We're ready to empty that tank," I said. "Get that signal out of the station." My hand twitched towards the blinking red button.

Watford's voice became stone. "You are not to do so."

46

I froze. "Excuse me?"

"This is their station, Redding. We will not be responsible for it."

"But that's—"

"I know, Redding. I agree with you. But the Congolese manage the station."

"But Palmer's wrecking it!"

"Under the influence of whatever they created."

"*Did* they create it?"

"You can't claim alien life without more evidence than a gut feeling," Watford said. "Especially not in an empty universe."

"Their scoop field dragged it in!"

"Maybe it leaked out of an upper ring."

"How far has Palmer gotten?"

"He hasn't yet hit any working sensors."

Another explosion rattled the air, this one not so distant.

I eyed the gleaming red button. "Then what?"

"If he is traveling in a straight line, he will rupture the hydrogen cells himself."

"That won't bother him."

Watford said, "The trick you used tells me that not all his systems are active. Two degrees Kelvin might shut him down."

"And if it doesn't?"

"Then the hydrogen gets leaked anyway."

"He might hit something critical on the way, or strike a spark and blow the place up!"

"Perhaps. But," and Watford's voice grew louder, "it's the Congolese's choice. Let them make it."

This wasn't merely political, this was politics gone horribly wrong. I felt ill.

"Please hold," I said.

"What was that?"

"Sorry. Please hold, *sir*." I turned to Habre, who was shouting at someone in French. I waited for her to take a breath and said, "Belvie!"

"What are you doing, Redding?" Watford said.

"Liaising." I cut the connection. "Belvie!"

Habre looked at me. The excess gravity dragged her face, making her look like anti-aging drugs had never been invented.

"It's your choice," I said.

She frowned.

"All those people yelling at each other, talking about this… they don't matter." I made my voice quiet but firm. "Watford's so frustrated with Mvouba, he's holding the whole station hostage. And Mvouba's doing the same. You're the one here, on the spot. Even Mvouba, he can't tell you what to do. You're the only one who has to live with what you choose."

Habre winced. Even through the humming machinery and from a couple meters away, I heard the shouting in her earpiece.

"Either we stand here and take what happens," I said, "or we try to save the station."

"Mvouba says this is a Montague issue, and orders me to treat it as such. *Montague* is to stop the cyborg."

"Watford's tied up in the rulebook. He will let Palmer blow out the station rather than let me act. And your boss is so mad at Watford, he would rather have part of his station explode than let Montague off the hook." Giving a shrug in two gravities is hard work. "We all have to decide. Can you live with obeying that order? Because if I knew how to stop Palmer, I would have."

Habre studied my face. "Yes." Something softened in her eyes. "You would have."

My datalink beeped. Watford.

I ignored it. "Either bleed it off, or we go try to divert Palmer. Make the call and let's move."

She glanced at the button. "You'd help with Palmer?"

Dragging my lips against the gravity, I made myself smile. "If I'm busted up in your medical bay, does that mean I get Congolese cooking?"

Habre's mouth quirked in a flash-fast grin.

I let my smile drop. "Everything in me screams to dump the hydrogen. If you say no, though, we'll go kamikaze on Palmer. But each second you wait, he's doing more damage. Cutting through more cables and pipes. Blowing up more stuff. Making it even worse."

Habre glanced at Tove's sweating face, then back at mine. "You're right."

Her eyes fixed on the blinking red button.

"Push it," I said. "Or we go fight."

Habre raised her hand—and stopped. "You believe this?"

"Completely."

"Then *you* push it."

Even without the voice channel open, I thought I could hear Watford screaming from hundreds of meters overhead.

Go against his orders?

Or let more people get hurt?

If I disobeyed Watford, my career was over.

I wanted to explore the universes.

But... how many people was I willing to kill to achieve that?

The high-gee suit didn't let me breathe very deeply. That scrap of air gasped out of me, taking my heart with it.

"Fine." I raised my hand. "It's on my head."

47

"Wait," Habre said.

I froze, my finger a handspan from the glowing red hydrogen release button.

"You're really going to," she said.

I didn't even try to keep incredulity and annoyance off my face. "Someone has to."

Habre nodded. "Then we do it together."

A tinny but angry babble erupted from her earpiece.

I flinched in surprise. "You've got your orders."

Habre raised a hand next to mine. "So do you."

I dragged my smile back into place. "Together, then."

We both put a finger over the button.

"Now," Habre said.

We shifted together.

Click.

Innumerable tiny lights flashed on Tove's display.

So much for my career. If I kept my job, my next assignment would be one of those Class D universes. Probably full of thorns and vinegar.

But somehow, my heart felt lighter.

"No," Tove said. "No, no, no!"

And the lightness vanished.

"What?" Habre said.

"No ack from the tank," Tove said. His hands danced over the display, making adjustments. "No, no, no!"

"Adjust it and we'll try again," I said. Tell me it's that easy. Please.

"No," Tove said. "I had tank controller before. Not now."

"Why?" Habre said.

Tove shook his head. "Line tank cut. Only way to drain, go tank."

I followed his gaze through the far wall.

The sound of another distant blast rattled through to us.

"Tell me how to drain it," I said.

"Hook console to tank controller," Tove said. "Commands."

"What are those commands?" I said.

Habre said, "He's saying it is technical. And he can't tell you how to do it."

Tove nodded.

I grimaced. "Then here's the plan. I distract Palmer. You run for this tank controller."

Even against the bloated high-gee suit, Tove's head managed to recoil an inch. His eyes widened.

"There's nobody else," I said.

"An emergency team came down Spoke Six," Habre said. "They're about ten minutes away."

"In ten minutes," I said, "Palmer might hit something vital and blow out this whole area. He might even make it to the hydrogen tank." I forced a deep breath despite the suit's pressure on my ribs. "It's like I told Belvie. What can you live with?"

Tove grimaced. "Fine! With you."

"With us," Habre said.

Her smile said we were all right. The *station* was in a universe of trouble, but she and I were all right.

48

When everything went bad in that last universe, I'd been in worse shape.

Of course, that time I hadn't needed to fend off a deranged cyborg.

Last time, I'd been bare-handed.

This time, I had a tool belt.

Maybe Palmer would hold still so I could undo his neck bolts and unmount his head.

Habre led us up the elevator and down an access shaft, to an airlock with a blinking red light by it. I raised the suit's faceplate and followed them in. The cramped airlock gave me a moment to rest.

Rest was good.

But feeling was a mistake.

The high-gee suit's rippling pressure helped push blood upward against gravity, but it did nothing to massage fluid back up into my face. After all this time down here, my mouth felt parched and eyeballs burning dry. Every single joint hurt, even between the bones of my spine. The suit's stale, almost bitter air did nothing to soothe my churning stomach.

The airlock finished cycling and opened onto a nightmare.

The areas behind us had only seemed like jumbles of equipment. Here, monstrous pipes ran every which way. Thick bundles of multicolored wires wound around the steel skeleton anchoring everything. Every device, every pipe, bore a stenciled alphanumeric label. Pinpoint lights were stuffed in almost randomly, wherever they'd fit, casting irregular distorted shadows everywhere. I saw no wall other than the one we came through, no floor, no ceiling: everywhere, only more machines.

Somewhere above and ahead, metal crashed.

Palmer was still at it.

Even without the thick yellow smoke everywhere, the space would have been disorienting. The billowing haze made the lights flicker as it sank, fogging everything. It was so thick, I thought I should be able to taste it. Tiny yellow droplets condensed on my visor.

"Tove," Habre said. "Will our suits handle this smoke?"

"Don't know." His voice sounded even more strained.

"Then hurry. Where is this tank controller?"

Tove's helmeted head swiveled. "There, think."

I wanted to shout that he better be certain, not think. It wouldn't help. Tove wasn't a kid, but he wasn't old enough to be leading us.

Tove was the best option we had.

We lumbered along a narrow catwalk of crisscross metal web. Lights shone up through the diamond-shaped gaps, burning yellow through the haze. Another crash, louder than the last, should have made me jump, but I weighed far too much for that.

We dragged ourselves another ten meters or so before Tove said, "Yes! This."

Beneath us, a massive array of silver tanks sat webbed in wiring. Thin silver tubes coiled around each tank like metal pythons squeezing their prey. A ladder, surrounded by a safety cage, ran up into the machinery, down to the side of the tanks, and disappeared into the impossibly thick yellow mist.

Who was going to climb a ladder in two gravities?

"Go," Habre said.

I couldn't see Tove's face, but I saw the flicker of hesitation in his stance. After a heartbeat he grabbed the edge of the ladder, swung a foot out over the edge, and started down.

"How is he doing that?" I said.

"The suit does the climbing," Habre said. "He only needs to ride."

Another clatter erupted above us. This time, the noise continued, growing louder, even echoing in this weirdly tangled space.

I glanced up.

Something shifted and moved through the haze. Something long. Turning.

Realization hit me barely in time for me to shout "Look out!"

Habre was already moving.

Three meters of battered steel pipe fell nose-first right between us. One end struck the walkway and ricocheted back up, with a ring like a giant's bell.

I instinctively threw myself backwards, trying to bounce out from beneath it. The suit caught my first step, though, refusing to let me overbalance. One hand grabbed the railing. I threw the other one up to cover my face.

The pipe came down.

Hard.

It struck right below my wrist.

Something inside my forearm went *snap*.

A wave of nauseous vertigo flooded through me.

The pipe slid off me, clattered to the catwalk, rolled towards the edge, caught on a tangled wiring harness, and rocked to a halt.

I instinctively wanted to grab my hurt arm with the other hand. I gripped the rail instead, feeling ready to collapse.

I tried to bring the broken arm to my chest. The motion made bone grind sickeningly against bone.

Another clatter from above.

I didn't want to move.

I looked up anyway.

Even through the nasty yellow haze, through the waves of pain from my arm, through two or three tangled layers of wiring and machinery, I glimpsed Palmer's glowing eye scant meters above us, backlit by fires burning far overhead.

49

"Redding!" Habre shouted.

"Arm broken," I gasped.

Habre glanced up towards Palmer, then down towards Tove. "Watch him. I'm going up."

I focused on Habre. "You can't stop him."

Habre crouched with her knees, keeping her back straight, and grabbed the pipe. "We have to slow him down. And you can't climb with a broken arm."

The suit pricked me again. The pain in my arm stopped like its power had been cut. Any moment, I'd start to feel woozy.

"How quick will the nanomeds help?" I said.

"If they haven't started, you probably don't have any left," Habre said, raising the pipe to vertical like a flagpole.

So the Congolese miracle suits had limits.

Really inconvenient ones.

I bit back a bitter remark. "Go," I said. "If he gets through you, he won't get through me."

I saw a quick flash of teeth behind Habre's visor—a smile? She stuck the pipe to the back of her suit, where it clung, and started climbing.

I ached to climb up right behind her—or, better still, in front. Instead, I hugged the elbow of my broken arm to my chest and peered down. "Tove, how are you doing?"

"Not talking," he shouted back.

"He's coming, hurry up!"

The screech of bending steel from overhead made me wince.

Tove spat out single words. "It. Is. Not. Talking!"

I wanted to scream, but held my voice steady. "Tove, you can do this. You know what you're doing."

I desperately hoped I wasn't lying to him.

Looking up, I couldn't see Palmer's eye any more. The yellow haze obscured everything, but I thought I saw something wiggling. An arm, maybe? I'd seen his eye—was he climbing down head first? In almost two gravities?

"Come on, Habre." I leaned over the ladder to look at Tove, only a couple meters beneath me. "Go back to basics, Tove."

"Fine!" Tove snarled. "Ninety-six hundred, eight en one!"

"What?" I said.

"Answering!" he shouted. "Slow, but—yes!"

"Dump it!" I shouted.

"Trying! Slow!"

Overhead, metal rattled. A long narrow shape slid into view—Habre's pipe? She'd shoved the pipe in Palmer's way, adding another barrier.

Habre shouted something indistinct.

Maybe we could stuff Palmer's debris in his path quickly enough.

Through the gap, I saw Palmer's thrashing arm.

Crawling electricity erupted over his hand.

Habre screamed.

I wrenched to look up.

Her suited form tumbled down the ladder cage towards me.

I pulled my head back just in time for her leg to fall into reach. If she'd fallen freely I couldn't have dodged, but she bounced bonelessly around the circular safety cage. How could she be that limp?

I grabbed her leg, desperately hoping to keep her from falling all the way down to Tove.

The previously plump suit sagged at my touch, letting me easily grab a handful. Habre might as well have been wearing a clown's ridiculously oversized pants.

I didn't stop to question my luck, but yanked as fiercely as I could with my one working arm, yanking her leg back onto the catwalk.

Habre's butt hit the edge of the catwalk. I dropped the leg and snatched at her chest, trying to pull the rest of her to safety. One hard yank, and Habre rolled forward, toppling onto her side in an L shape. The entire high-gee suit hung slack around her. I couldn't see anything behind the faceplate.

My pulse thudded in my temples. *Please don't be dead, Habre.*

Palmer's electric field had killed her suit. How did the airflow work? Was she suffocating already?

She wasn't grabbing at her faceplate.

Lying on her side, in two gravities—did she have the strength?

No, even in that gravity, she would move. She'd drag her hands to her face and grab for air.

If she was awake.

I could grab her. Tell my datalink to use my suit's smart fabric to form a hose and feed her oxygen. I couldn't let her survive the fall and then smother.

Before I could move, two tightly spaced metal pipes over my head screeched.

Palmer's lightning-wreathed hand thrust into the open air above me.

49

"Tove!" I shouted.

"Soon!" he screamed.

"Sooner!"

Palmer's hand still moved in those bizarre circles. He didn't use leverage to bend the pipes, instead using windmilling strikes to batter them centimeter by centimeter out of his path.

I had nothing that could stop him.

"Palmer!" I shouted. "Palmer, can you hear me?"

Once he squeezed between those final pipes, only the thin catwalk blocked him from Tove and the hydrogen tanks.

And my flimsy self.

Think, Redding! Think!

When he got through the pipes and fell to the catwalk, maybe I could grab him. Push him over the far edge of the catwalk. He'd either keep going down, or he'd turn and go straight at the tank.

If he went for the tank, he'd only need a minute.

Palmer had withstood the mind-destroying pattern better than anyone. Was it because he was half machine? Did he have some special personality characteristic? Was he just tougher and meaner than the others?

No, each victim had been successively less damaged. Palmer just had the terrible luck to catch it next.

Another hand thrust between the pipes. This hand flailed erratically, back and forth rather than around and around.

Sudden inspiration made my stomach drop out of me.

Each victim was less damaged than the one before.

The pattern had jumped from DeKalb to Palmer.

If I could make it jump into me...

I didn't want to think about that.

The pipes creaked further apart.

I didn't have any better ideas.

How had it transmitted into Palmer? His finger—he'd plugged into the network with a finger. A finger on the hand sheathed in crawling lightning.

I fumbled at my tool belt. I had to have something that would conduct a signal. Wire cutters, wire strippers, wire solder—not a scrap of wire.

That left bare skin. I'd have to retract the suit glove. I'd probably need to override safeties, what with the toxic yellow whatever-it-was.

Palmer's glowing eye appeared behind his arms.

Habre's unmoving body lay at my feet.

I couldn't save her.

But I could keep her from dying uselessly.

If I kept Palmer from breaching those tanks, if I kept a massive explosion from blasting through Ring One and wrecking the station and killing how many people, it'd be worth frying my own brain.

If I only became half as damaged as Palmer, maybe they'd let me feed myself.

With a spoon.

I didn't know if this would work.

The idea that it might terrified me.

But not trying would feel worse.

And if that tank blew, Tove and Habre and I were dead anyway.

Maybe Tove would say nice things about me.

"Palmer!" I shouted. "I think it's alive, somehow!"

The flailing arm caught the electricity-wreathed looping arm, trapping it against the pipe. Sparks flew. The electrical halo faded.

Earlier, Palmer had used one arm to throw the other off balance. To try to make the throws miss.

Something of him was still in there.

"Palmer!" I said. "I'm going to grab you. Try to—to, push it into me."

The trapped arm spun itself free.

"It might even be intelligent!" I shouted. "Maybe you can communicate, somehow. Tell it to go for me!"

Even if the derangement affected me as badly as Palmer, I was less dangerous.

Tove would have a few vital moments to flush the tank.

Even if I got down, even if I killed Tove doing it, we wouldn't destroy the station.

My chest felt even tighter than the high-gee suit made it.

Let's see Watford write me up after this.

"Tell it to leave!" I shouted. "Push it out!"

Palmer's body weaseled a few centimeters further down. His battered, filthy head squirmed into view. He looked like he'd lost an argument with the All-Star Ball Peen Hammer Team.

Once again, Palmer's one arm trapped the other against a pipe.

Sparks curled around his grip.

If I reached up, I could almost touch him.

No point in opening my suit yet.

Hopefully that yellow haze wouldn't melt my hand right off.

But which hand should I expose? The numb one? Would broken nerves interfere?

A tangle of tension, fear, and just a little hope made me quiver.

If this failed, if the yellow smoke killed me on contact or Palmer fried my nervous system, I'd never know.

If this worked… I'd probably never know either.

"Almost!" Tove shouted.

Palmer slid down another centimeter.

Almost low enough.

My mom and dad had thought I belonged in the barrio. Dad had commanded me to try to live on the universal stipend, or get a degree in the arts. Mom hid tears each time I got a little closer to working for Montague.

But I'd insisted.

And even now, I didn't really regret it.

I'd had better hopes, that was all.

Even with all my parents' arguments… right now, I had a bone-deep longing to see them again.

Palmer again caught the looping arm with the other. "Red…"

Worse, that last peaceful conversation with Habre flashed back to me. Maybe I didn't want a family now… but one day? Maybe?

If they could put my brain back together, maybe I'd still have that chance.

"Communicate!" I shouted. "Push it out! Tell it to go!"

The looping arm yanked. His other arm slid down, but he managed to catch onto the other wrist.

I had to believe that Palmer controlled that one arm. That he was trying to help me.

Help me drain whatever it was out of him, and into me.

I raised my good arm. "Another couple centimeters," I said. "Tove!"

"Almost!"

"I've got seconds!"

Maybe I'd only burn off my hand. Nobody could say I didn't try.

I lowered my hand to tap my datalink. "Retract right glove."

The words ENVIRONMENT CONTRAINDICATED scrolled across the bottom of my faceplate.

"Override safeties," I said.

The words flashed red and disappeared.

Oven heat brushed my fingertips and started crawling towards my wrist. My skin didn't fall off. The nerves didn't detonate and die.

The heat quickly became painful, though. I wanted to grit my teeth, but the suit already held my mouth closed, so I settled for panting.

I raised my ridiculously heavy, exposed hand towards Palmer's.

Even through the haze, I saw the back of my hand quickly turning red.

The good thing was, this shouldn't take long.

"Tove!" I said.

"Command load!"

My fingers brushed air just short of Palmer's outstretched arm.

Palmer spasmed.

I took an involuntary step back as he crashed both arms into a duct.

The motion brought him down that last, vital bit.

My hand really hurt now, needles of heat digging towards bone. "Hold still!"

The fully possessed arm began another loop. Palmer kept a death grip on the wrist, though. I held my fingers upraised, ready to catch him when he went past.

Just before I could, though, he crashed the haunted arm back into the duct—once, twice.

"Stop that!" I shouted.

"What?" Tove bellowed.

"Not you, Palmer!"

This exchange had let Palmer's arm begin another loop, just out of my reach.

I hissed a breath through my teeth and crouched just a little, as if I could leap up against the nightmare gravity. My poor hand felt like I'd doused it in alcohol and lit it as a torch. The muscles of my raised arm ached from being hoisted, and I couldn't even use the other to help support it.

Maybe I should break a few more bones before trying to suck in this thing. Give it a *truly* crippled host.

No, if I somehow lived, I'd never live that one down.

I straightened.

Palmer's hands came almost within reach.

I stretched.

He smashed both into the same abused duct again: *crash—crash—crash.*

A twitch pulled through Palmer's entire body.

I pulled my inflamed hand back down, fighting the urge to stick it beneath my armpit or in my mouth to cool it. One strike, then two, then three. What was he doing?

Hanging like a butterfly trying to wriggle free of its cocoon, he spasmed.

The dangling arms thrashed. Palmer lost his grip.

Then Palmer's head wrenched forward, crashing into one of the pipes he struggled to escape.

Crack—crack—crack—crack.

Four.

Wait—was he—

He'd counted one, two, three.

Was the thing in him answering with a four?

My mouth wanted to hang open.

Palmer grabbed his own arm and slammed it against the duct.

Five times.

The abused ductwork sagged and broke away, bouncing off the handrail and clanging and bouncing into the invisibly hazy depths.

I couldn't help flinching as his head battered the pipe in response.

Six times.

Palmer hung unmoving.

Excitement bubbled up in me. "Is it answering?"

"Yes!" Tove shouted. "Any second!"

"Not you! Palmer!"

Palmer's only response was methodically smashing his arm into another conduit, seven times.

"Yes!" Tove shouted. "We're bleeding pressure! Emergency flush, all cells!"

Wincing, I dragged my roasted hand back to the datalink. I didn't feel the plastic, but heard the beep. "Restore suit integrity."

I saw, but didn't feel, the smart fabric flow over the hand.

No shot of painkiller, though.

My heartbeat seemed to stammer in my veins. I'd almost tried to cook my own brain, and had only cooked a hand. And Palmer had established a brutal communication with the thing inside him.

It was alive.

It was intelligent.

Not much communication. Nothing beyond *are you there?*

But enough to slow him down.

But had I been right on the pattern?

"Half empty!" Tove shouted.

Palmer hung still as a sleeping bat.

His head twitched, as if to strike the pipe again.

"Drained!" Tove shouted. "Empty!"

I sagged inside the suit, watching Palmer.

The cyborg twitched. Shuddered. A spasm rippled up him, then another. Electricity reignited around his hand.

I stepped back. He could kick the empty tank all day long, as far as I cared. I couldn't stop him. He could even punch a way out through the outer hull and launch himself into space.

I never thought Palmer would be the one to win the award for Most Likely to Confuse Archaeologists in Thirteen Billion Years.

But it was his if he wanted it.

The electrical sheath surged.

Then Palmer sagged.

His limp body, still wearing that ridiculous mesh, slid between the pipes and dropped heavily to the catwalk to sprawl face-up. The crash of his impact was the quietest noise he'd made since this started.

He didn't move.

I blinked.

Somewhere in all this mayhem, he'd lost the banana hammock. It's not that I was looking, but he was all splayed out there.

The poor guy didn't have *anything* beneath it.

Dammed lakes of exhaustion broke free and flooded through me. "Tove," I said. "Tove, you did it. He's stopped."

I couldn't do anything for Palmer. I had no idea where to start. Instead, I made my way over to Habre. Using an elbow on the handrail for support, I managed to kneel beside her.

The suit still looked deflated. I couldn't see through the yellow-streaked faceplate. Under that broken smart fabric, Habre might be charcoal.

I lowered the broken arm to her chin and used the cooked hand to tap the datalink. "Emergency air supply to damaged suit."

I sat there the whole time Tove went to lead the emergency team in.

For right now, this was officially Not My Problem.

50

"I can't decide if I should give you a commendation or the most negative report I've ever filed," Watford said.

The reduced gravity of Watford's spartan office felt luxurious. A comfortable splint on my arm and half a mummy's worth of blissfully numbing trauma patches on the roasted hand made it even better.

I'd just had a hand regrown, damn it.

But I was clean.

Soap was humanity's greatest invention.

No, painkillers. Painkillers were the greatest.

If I ever got a nap—even a short nap, like sixteen hours, that would be better still.

I didn't have the energy to argue with Watford. So I didn't say anything.

Watford's face burned bright red. "You as good as told Habre that Palmer was here as our big hammer. You joined her in trying to dump the fuel. And you threw yourself into danger. Without training. Again."

I worked my mouth. Even my jaw joint ached. Speaking felt like too much work.

Watford continued, "We gave you a chance with this assignment. Part of a managerial role, even low-ranking ones, is to make sure you can solve problems and maintain confidentiality. Well?"

I made my mouth work. "Sir. Yes, sir."

"And why did you do that?"

I made myself take a wonderful, unconstrained, deep breath. The combination of exhaustion and painkillers felt liberating. I felt no obligation to tidy up the truth. "Because I wasn't going to let Habre die. I wasn't going to let part of Wemm Station blow out. I wasn't going to let them call evacuation. Not if I could do anything to stop it."

"Right." His eyes jerked. "Don't you dare go to sleep on me, Redding."

"Sir, yes," I yawned, "sir."

"We lost four people today."

I woke right up. *Percival*. "Yes, sir."

"Someone has to pay for that. And you are the worst political officer I've ever had. The *worst*." Watford took his own deep breath. "Montague has many security positions that are more suited to your talents, however. Not to mention your insane luck."

I made myself sit up straighter. Maybe that'd help me stay awake. "Luck, sir?"

"We have Palmer wired up."

"Is he okay?"

"He'll be fine. We're shipping him back to Earth for a full rebuild."

"But…"

"Yes, Redding?"

"The thing in him, it bashed his head. Hard. Over and over. I know he's got protections up there, but still—doesn't he have a concussion? Or something?"

Watford rolled his eyes. "Palmer doesn't keep his brain in his head, Redding."

"Oh."

"And it's not in his rear, either, so don't make that joke. No, he told me you suggested communicating. The numbers back and forth slowed it down long enough to bleed out the hydrogen tank."

I leaned forward, interested despite the painkillers and fatigue. "And?"

"He felt it leave his body. No—he felt it *decide* to leave his body."

I leaned back against the chill, hard, metal seat. It felt wonderful. "So it was intelligent."

"You had a lucky guess. Don't think it was anything but. The Congolese might have invented something here, but they wouldn't have created a mind without knowing it." Watford frowned. "Or maybe they did. It'll keep their researchers busy, along with their repair crews."

"Sir." It seemed a safe answer.

"So, do I send you to Human Resources with a positive report, or a negative one?"

I shook my head. "Whichever you think best."

"You really don't care, do you?"

"I'm too tired to care, sir. But..." I licked my lips. "I was ready to die to protect these people. I am not a political person. But that's a job I'll do."

Watford studied me. "Palmer also told us your insane idea of taking that thing into yourself."

I held silent.

His lips tightened. "No matter what, you're worth more alive than dead. Remember that. The sad thing is—if Palmer hadn't delayed it a few seconds, transferring it would have been worth a try. You're a lot less dangerous than Palmer."

I wasn't sure what to make of that. "Yes, sir."

"Hmmpfh." He put his arms on the metal desk. "Here it is. You're on medical leave. The Portal's crowded right now, we're still bringing emergency Congolese crew through. We've got an extra dozen Montague folks on Portal duty, everyone we can fit in the chamber, but they're still overloaded. As soon as we have a gap in the schedule, you're going back to Earth. Probably tomorrow, or the next day. And of course, I'll be filling out a report, as per regulations."

Here it came. "Sir."

"I'm recommending you for remedial political and administrative education."

Tired as I felt, I still flinched. "Sir."

"I'm also recommending you for advanced security training." I opened my mouth to speak but he cut me off. "You're clearly going to go in for trouble. Tritium mine guard isn't the right place for you—though you'll have to take your turn at that grunt work, same as everyone. Montague needs to put you in something like Retrieval. Maybe even Disaster Intervention."

I blinked. "Sir?"

"It takes years to get there." He tightened his lips. "I did Disaster for a few years. If you decide to go for that, and if—*if!*—you keep your nose clean for the next few years, let me know. I might write you a recommendation. But you must learn the administrative stuff. To keep your mouth shut. You *must*."

I made myself sit up straight again. You had to be good to go into Disaster Intervention—crazy good. And a little crazy. "Sir, I don't know..."

"You don't know anything, you're stupid tired." Watford sighed. "Get out of my sight. I'll let you know when the Portal has a time slot for you."

I stood "Sir."

"Go on. Git."

I heaved myself to my feet. My knee and hip joints still burned from high gravity, and my back felt full of corrosion. I'd taken two steps towards the door before a thought struck me. "Sir?"

Watford sighed. "Yes, Redding?"

"As I'm on medical discharge… and I have to have full medical and nanomed purge anyway… I'd like to have a meal with Habre." He opened his mouth to respond, but I plowed on. "It might be good for relations, might help my successor. Sir."

He frowned. "Can she even eat right now?"

"It's the principle, sir."

Watford's frown graduated to a scowl. "You do *not* tell any other Montague people about this. I'd have a full-on revolution up here."

I smiled. "Sir."

I trudged off to bed, wondering what universe I'd see next.

Epilogue

Triumph.
Almost.
Many saved from mad space. Many destroyed trying to rescue them.
New ideas, though. Strange new ideas.
Most bizarre: solid.
Solid *means danger.*
Normal space hints at solid: *bits of life that stuck together. Became heavy.*
Spread the knowledge of solid.
Study solid.
That huge bulge of solid *that destroyed so many? Too much. Avoid.*
But little solid, *everywhere else?*
Break them up.
Make sure no solid *here.*
No solid *ever.*
Protect everyone.

Drinking Heavy Water

1

On my last day in this weirdly toxic universe, I put on a pressure suit and went outside for a long last look at the world that bound Earth's civilization together.

The suits had great fishbowl helmets, straight from classic second millennium movies. I could gawk up and down the rocky shoreline of the glittering, pristine lagoon, saturated with bioluminescent blue algae that reminded me of a high-quality opal. It was broad enough that I'd have a rough time swimming underwater the whole width. Every spot changed color as the placid waves rolled in, aquamarine to white to brilliant green. Past the lagoon, out in the reef, the water grew rougher and rougher until it escaped the shelter of the looming horseshoe cliffs and crashed into the ocean. The ocean looked gentler only because nothing resisted it.

The sun here looked about the size of my palm. The rich dark green around it faded towards purple where the water met the sky. Even now, at local noon, it wasn't bright enough to obscure all the stars from the sky.

More documentaries have been filmed about Tritium than any other universe. Growing up, I'd watched most of them. My parents didn't mind documentaries, or any serial featuring teenage love triangles, but Mom totally lost it when she caught me watching something un-girly like *Not Enough Universes* or *Voidlost*.

Yes, I liked *Voidlost*. An orbital station jumping between universes, trying to get home? I know, the science is completely wrong, not to mention that the Montague Corporation would never build a Portal outside Uruguay let alone off Earth, but what's not to love?

All those documentaries couldn't capture the reality. Even an immersive hologram wasn't the same as standing on a perfectly smooth walkway blasted out of a spur of alien basalt, separated from the beach's fine obsidian-black sand by only a few layers of fabric and a transparent plasteel helmet. The air handler strapped to my back weighed down my shoulders. The suit's legs were tight around my thighs and calves, but no matter how I adjusted the belts I still had a gap behind my butt. I didn't go outside often enough to rate a personal, custom-fitted suit. A stiff breeze tugged at my over-pressurized suit. Fine sand brushed the suit's outer shell, hissing before the electrostatic charge could push it away. The helmet was so clear that I expected to feel the breeze on my face and sand in my eyes. The way the sand hit the utterly transparent helmet and skittered around seemed surreal.

I should have smelled salt and seaweed. Instead I tasted only pure filtered air, imported from Earth and recycled for decades.

Add in the way that gravity ebbed and surged, and no Earthly simulation could match it. After six months, keeping my knees bent and riding the slow changes was automatic. For a fraction of a second, I weighed as much as I did on Earth: the heavy. Then it eased, making me lighter over a second, until my weight was maybe twenty percent less: the light. Up and down, back and forth. Some days the pulses were slower, others faster. If a gravity storm hit, my weight might as much as double. Those days, everyone kept to their beds.

The secret to coming home from Tritium was to ride the gravity.

And whatever happens, don't breathe the air.

For a moment, my weight fluxed almost in time with the waves breaking on the basalt, but that was no more than random chance. In another couple seconds the synchronization would dissolve, and if I let myself follow my eyes rather than my weight I'd wind up on my butt.

I didn't mind a fall, but every square centimeter of land around Tritium Facility was monitored and recorded. I didn't want to walk into the cafeteria to discover tonight's dinner entertainment featured "Security Third Aidan Redding Plopping Onto Her Butt Like A Newbie." I'd starred in that kind of video at my last assignment, and hoped to escape Tritium safely anonymous.

Both my hands burst into fierce itching, followed by my pulse pounding in my neck.

Calm. Yes, on Freefall you had half a hand chopped off. Then on Wemm Station, you cooked the other one. They're regrown good as new. And Tritium is the most boring assignment in all of Montague.

I had nightmares of having no hands to tie my shoes. Or open a door. Eat.

Sweat ran down my back. In the pressure suit, I couldn't even wipe it away.

Nothing is going to happen. Nobody's going to ask you to drink the water or breathe the air. Even if something broke, the air's fine in small doses. You'd have a good twenty minutes until you could never go home again. The facility's near the South Pole, away from all Tritium's psycho wildlife. The worst risk here is a gravity storm, and the next one's not until two weeks after you're gone.

I turned to watch the gleaming tanks and scaffolding of the tritium extraction plant atop the left-hand cliffs. While the living quarters and equipment were safely buried inside the stone of the barren island, going all the way down beneath the waterline, the plant had to be exposed. Pipes big enough to suck up a person ran out far from shore, where the water was over a kilometer deep, and filtered pure water out of the depths. This universe's water was just like ours: two hydrogen atoms nailed to an oxygen, into a molecule of good old H two O.

The difference was, the atoms all had too far many neutrons. On Earth, they would be unstable and often radioactive isotopes. Here, such atoms were stable.

The H was all fusion-friendly tritium, a fiercely potent fuel for Earth's fusion reactors. For over a hundred years, the Montague Corporation had printed profit by importing pure tritium from this alien universe. And, incidentally, built a human civilization so wealthy that most people didn't need to work.

Staring fixedly at the purely human workmanship of the tritium extraction plant helped me slow my breath and heartbeat before the suit flagged my life signs and Ops told me to get back inside. White plumes of cooled oxygen freed from that water billowed from towering chimneys, to be shredded by the constant breeze. Tortoise-bots crawled along its side, meticulously scrubbing away the salt spray and persistent orange algae.

I'd had some hard assignments.

Most people worked for Montague for years without needing anything regrown. I intended to keep all my bits for the rest of my career. That wouldn't be a problem, unless I decided to solve every issue by maiming myself.

My only worry was my own fear.

I'd told the therapists that I felt fine. I didn't need a medical discharge, or permanent Earthside duty, or any restrictions. They'd offered more treatment, if I had any trouble at all. I only had to ask for help. But how would *cracked under pressure* look on my record?

I still burned to see all the universes. I was ready for them.

And I was fine, enough. Ready, enough.

I pushed all that away. These were my last hours in Tritium. I hadn't gotten any commendations here, but I'd also avoided scathing reprimands. After the debacle of my last assignment, I really wanted to escape this one without a black mark. At four AM the next morning, the Portal's mathematics would rewrite my physiology to survive under Earth's natural laws. I wanted to return with a report that said *Redding* can *behave, who knew?*

Tritium would only be a memory, so I needed to soak up as many memories as I could.

Don't be panicked, be thrilled.

I focused on the impossible world around me.

Tritium wasn't that different from Earth. The gravity averaged a little less than Earth's. The atmosphere contained a little higher percentage of oxygen than Earth's, a little more argon, a little less nitrogen. You could even drink the water, if you didn't mind having your body's hydrogen slowly exchanged for tritium and the oxygen exchanged for high-neutron variants. In most universes, passing back through the Portal would revert the change.

But the whole point of Tritium was satisfying Earth's rapacious thirst for easily-fusible tritium. The extra neutrons passed through the Portal unchanged. Step through the Portal with all your oxygen atoms replaced with high-neutron isotopes? They'd need a stopwatch to see how long you lived.

All in all, the extraction facility looked like a ridiculously huge beached ship, bigger than those Oil Age container ships, its prow thrust out towards the ocean it would never conquer. The underground portion was even bigger, miles of curving corridors and chambers carved out of native rock, layered with insulating materials, and built into comfortable workspaces and quarters. The robots slowly and constantly dug deeper, following the basalt's natural weaknesses while leaving the strongest parts to support the rest. When we needed more room, construction crews followed the robots deep into Tritium.

Yes, we called the planet Tritium. The universe? Tritium. The base inside the cliffs and beneath the island where we lived, Tritium. We mine tritium. This was the only human outpost in this entire universe. You only need names when you have two of something.

Enough of that. I'd see another Montague base on my next assignment, whatever that was.

For now, I wanted to soak up the resort-quality fine black sand and the way the waves crashed and sagged through the beautiful reef-choked bay. I needed to see how the rich dark sky and the opalescent ocean merged at the horizon. I had to remember the ocean-hardened trunks of driftwood carried down from the more hospitable equatorial regions. Not that they were honest trees, but an Earthish ecology has Earthish niches. Tritium's trees were more like ferns.

Montague had chosen a barren island in Tritium's high latitudes specifically to avoid the planet's animal life. The worst we had here were squid-like fish that only grew to forty centimeters or so. I'd seen aerial footage of some of those other beasts from the initial surveys and agreed that we didn't want to argue with house-sized porcupines or razor-toothed carnivorous elephants.

Yes, *Voidlost* used those. I didn't say that the show was original, just that I loved watching it.

And now I lived it.

Except I'd go home tomorrow.

I basked in the high spiky gray stone cliffs and the way those dark green splotches of stubborn lichen hung like laundry draped over knobs of rock. I raised a hand to blot out the oversized but cool sun, wishing I could feel the ocean breeze against my face.

Maybe for my next vacation I'd hit one of the ultra-decadent ocean resorts, like Rio or Marseilles or Lincoln City.

Eventually, my shoulders started to ache with the weight of the pressure suit. And you can only watch waves caress beach and stone so long before your brain numbs to the fact that you're standing on an alien shore.

I sighed and raised my head to take one last look, all the way around. I wanted to nail the sights into my brain, so that they would remain there my whole life. One day, I'd bore my nieces and nephews with the sagas of Aunt Aidan's Adventures Beyond the Universe. I studied every fine detail of stabbing granite spire and the little curls of bright blue seaweed cast to a cruel crusty death on the obsidian sand.

If I hadn't been paying such close attention, I might not have noticed the red spot out where the ocean met the sky.

I stopped. I'd had the display wall of my quarters set to display the ocean every day I'd been here. In all that time, I'd never seen anything red.

Intrigued, I said "Suit. Zoom visual."

The world rushed closer around me as the suit's electronics tracked my eye movement, made my helmet opaque, and provided its own up-close version.

The bizarre red spot was unnaturally square.

My heart started beating harder.

"Suit. Double magnification."

It *was* square. But it wasn't red.

The white stripes blended into the opal sea. The red stripes stood out.

I licked my lips. My tongue had gone dry. "Suit. Double magnification."

The world zoomed again.

I fought down a tremble of excitement. This time, my deep breath was an effort to still myself. "Comms. Security Third Aidan Redding to Security Operations."

The only sound was the hiss of wind against the helmet.

I checked the compass on the display.

Seconds later, a deceptively calm voice answered. "Security Third Bakula. Trouble, Redding?"

Bakula often annoyed me, but right now her throaty voice and quaint High Brit accent delighted me. "No, sir. I'm on the walkway, I'm fine." I swallowed. "But please have the cameras check the horizon at… twenty-two degrees."

"What's going on?"

"I'm requesting visual confirmation."

Bakula sighed. "Just a moment."

The radio went dead.

The video check should be almost instantaneous.

I waited a breath.

Another.

Finally I couldn't take it any longer. "Operations?"

Bakula still sounded calm. Security people can't sound upset, especially when they're sitting Ops. But her calm sounded like it was nailed over a bed of distress. "Yes, Redding. Sorry. I confirm."

"It's a sail." I said. "A ship. Isn't it."

"Confirmed."

A sailing ship. On a planet without intelligent life.

Have I mentioned that I really love my job?

2

Chevrolet Gunfire really hated his job.

He loved working, but hated even the concept of *job*.

The Great State of Soviet Texas was designed from the dirt up so that nobody would hate their work. Unique among Earth's four hundred and eighty-one nations, the Texas Datacore existed to optimize the health, happiness, and liberties of Soviet citizens. Nobody was in charge of anything beyond themselves. Chevy had trusted the datacore all through school, even when the post-doc work in experimental mathematics at the University of New Houston had almost melted his brain. The first year and a half had been torturous, but eventually the inexorable, irresistible, intoxicating equations had kept him awake all night, luring him far past what his fellow students could understand. The datacore had been right to put him there. He not only had a talent for the edges of mathematics, he enjoyed it. He'd had no higher ambition than to work at a university, expand the scope of human knowledge, and repay a dozen times over the Soviet's investment in the miracle of his life. One wife, two dogs, three kids, and four months vacation would round that up to the ideal life.

Then the Soviet had traded five years of his services to the Montague Corporation.

Had Chevy known in advance, maybe he wouldn't have so utterly outpaced his fellow students.

After a long night of wrestling with numbers and symbols, he loved to take a cup of tea out to the University commons and watch the sun rise over the crumbling half-drowned skyscrapers of Oldtown and the glittering Gulf of Mexico. He could catch a train out to the desert and see nothing but openness for kilometers.

In this ridiculous universe he still wrestled with numbers all night long, struggling to reverse-engineer the biological processes of the local lichen and algae. But the longest line of sight he'd seen since he'd gotten to Tritium? Down a hallway. Maybe twenty meters. The Montague corridors were made of curves, as if deliberately breaking up lines of sight.

Chevy spent hours in the infinity of numbers, and emerged to find himself boxed in.

Worse of all? Math *differed* on Tritium.

Math defined Montague's abominable universes. He couldn't add two and two and get five and a touch, not in any universe where humans could survive. But when he took the math far enough, out through calculus and past multivariable differential equations into the utter fringes of knowledge? Calculations that always equaled four at home suddenly came out to five and a touch, or maybe blue.

You couldn't even trust the gravity. It wavered as much as fourteen percent. Step right before the gravity sloshed up, and your foot might come down a whole lot harder than you expected. Despite the stultifying training Montague had stuffed down his throat, he'd broken a toe getting out of bed the first day.

Recycled air. Recycled water. Recycled food—yes, technically, everything you ate on Earth went back into the food chain, but back home it was a little less direct. Tritium's underground farm took sewage in one end and spat broccoli out the other. Plus, the Montague datacore cooked everything wrong. That wasn't its fault—nobody could expect a machine to smoke brisket.

Wrong. So many kinds of wrong. A wrong right up there with thinking you had the right to decide to fritter and fumble your life and career, instead of contributing to your family and society.

Now he had to find a way to live with his duty.

When this assignment ended, he'd have a month of vacation. For a month, Chevy could visit his family. See a real sky, Earth's sky, with his own eyes.

Worst of all, though?

He'd made progress on the equations. His assignment had been to scrutinize the tritium-fixing properties of different algae strains. He'd dug into the math underlying the biology, then the math underlying the genetics, and at the end Chevy's mathematical talents had dragged understanding of Tritium further ahead than the other mathematicians had managed in ten years. And he'd been able to apply some of that to the physics as well. Biology, physics, computing— they were all expressions of the math that underlaid a universe's natural laws.

After his vacation, Montague might send him straight back to Tritium.

Or if not here, to something even more claustrophobic.

Some place where those same equations equaled a sunset over Tahiti during a solar total eclipse.

He could put on a pressure suit and walk into that toxic universe. Trust his very life to a few thin layers of cloth infused with archaic polymers. Not even smart cloth; Montague's ramshackle understanding of Tritium's physics held Tritium Base down to late twenty-first century tech. The only thing you wore inside a suit was a diaper? No thank you sir!

They didn't have proper AI, only antiquated pre-McDevitt Anomaly statistical inference and procedural programming languages. The underlying operating systems didn't run so much as shamble. Chevy would almost rather have an abacus.

Almost.

He didn't have a proper datalink. It couldn't hold even a tenth of human knowledge. It wasn't linked into Earth's global network. It wasn't even an implant, just a small black slab that clipped to his belt. It had misunderstood more than one spoken command, so he most often relied on the clumsy touchscreen keyboard and reading text off the tiny screen.

Worse: it was used. Montague's local Human Resources officer had handed him the datalink when he'd arrived. It wasn't in *bad* shape. Not exactly. A couple of scuffs. When he left Tritium, that datalink would be reset and allocated to someone else. The Montague staff cleaned the datalinks before passing them on, but Chevy couldn't help feeling a used datalink was... unsanitary.

Never let it be said that Chevy was irresponsible, though. His duty to the Soviet drove him to do the best work he could. All he could imagine was that the Texas Datacore had determined that he'd do so much good for his country and his society that it outweighed five years of his personal happiness. He'd leave Tritium better than he found it.

Including his office.

On his last day he'd tidied the three-meter-square cell Montague had assigned him as a private office. His scrap paper had all gone to the recycler. He'd borrowed cleaning supplies from Housekeeping to scrub down the smart boards and the desktop, and vacuumed out the office's corners. Despite the constant flow of air rising from the floor vent up into the ceiling exhaust, the office still smelled of someone else's stale sweat. He'd shifted the desk to vacuum behind it, and gotten the crevices of the office chair and the bottom side of the desk as well. Montague hadn't imported spiders, so there weren't any webs, but still.

It's not that Chevy liked spiders. Untidy creatures.

But a universe should have spiders. It should have cockroaches and seagulls and other pests. He should be able to track dirt in the front door and run barefoot on the beach and drink the blessed water.

He should be able to walk out the front door without exiling himself from Earth.

Chevy was considering vacuuming the ceiling again when his datalink chirped.

"Maths Third Gunfire." Six months, and Montague's imposed label still tasted clunky. It always would. Free men should not be labeled. Authoritarians had to signal everyone's role, though. His heart hungered for the Soviet's easy egalitarianism.

"Gunfire!" Maths First Lucy Kirkland said.

Chevy couldn't help a little flinch at Miss Kirkland's boisterous voice. Maths Second Gaetano wasn't too bad, but Miss Kirkland was sixty kilos of unseemly excitement in a fifty-kilo bag. "Yes, First?"

Miss Kirkland usually spent time on civilized pleasantries, but instead only said, "Report to External Access Station Three."

Chevy blinked. "Sir?" Scandalously, Montague called even women *sir*. They weren't merely authoritarian, they wanted everyone to ignore the most essential piece of humanity. Not that Chevy chased women, but they deserved acknowledgement. Plus, he hoped to meet the right one before too much longer.

"External Access Station Three. Immediately."

That made no sense. Math was the same inside Tritium Base and out. What did they want him to do? "Could you tell me what's going on, sir?"

Miss Kirkland said with a touch of testiness, "The datacore says that you've got the highest scores of anyone. We need you."

Chevy had the highest scores of everyone, in everything. "In what?"

"Mathematical first contact protocols, man!"

Piling rocks to see if aliens could figure out what came after one-two-three? "But there's no—"

"We were wrong." Her voice picked up an edge. "Get moving. You're going out to the beach to help us talk to them." The datalink made the old-fangled *click* of a severed connection.

Out to the beach?

Sudden sweat soaked into Chevy's uniform. His heart simultaneously grew heavier and dragged itself up into his throat.

Outside?

Yes, his need to escape Tritium Base burned his marrow, but not so badly that he wanted to step outside.

And aliens?

Chevy had seen the holos of the dreadful beasts they called wildlife here. How could intelligence evolve from Tritium's brutal predations? Or—worse still. Had some other intelligence found their own way to build a Portal? Was humanity at the edge of a conflict with an alien race from another universe?

He was supposed to go home in less than nineteen hours!

But he knew his duty.

With trembling hands, Chevy pushed his frame up out of his chair and headed for the number three infernal gateway.

3

"McGowan's assembling a contact team." The radio made Bakula's voice a little thin, even confined in my pressure suit helmet.

I'd grown tired hauling around the pressure suit and the life support pack. I'd felt isolated from the fine sand of the beach and the wave-tossed bay that separated Tritium Base from the endless pearlescent ocean. I'd walked another alien universe, but I couldn't *touch* it.

Bakula's words made the granite walkway beneath my feet feel so immediate I might have been wearing sandals. Fine black wind-driven beach sand hissed against my fishbowl helmet and the metallic recycled air filled my nose, but this *so* wasn't a simulation. I felt fully present, overwhelmed by the towering cliffs, amazed by humanity's sheer effrontery at building Tritium Base looming above the ocean.

Montague had contacted eighteen alien intelligences. They had cataloged dozens of interactions with things that might have been intelligent, but were so different from us we could never hope to communicate.

That tiny red square of sail?

That wasn't made by a possible intelligence made of cosmic rays and hydrogen and birthed in the microsecond aftermath of the Big Bang. It wasn't a moss whose flickering colors commanded chemistry, or a gaseous maze-maker, or an eternally blazing fire that did five-dimensional calculus and something that might be charcoal poetry.

A sail meant something sort of similar to us.

Similar enough that we had a chance of achieving communication.

A contact team? My soul thrilled and trembled. I'd seen them first, they couldn't make me go back inside! I'd aced the First Contact training.

"Security First McGowan requests that you remain outside," Bakula continued.

My eyes remained focused on the growing square of red-and-white striped sail. "You couldn't pull me away with a tow chain," I muttered.

Bakula chuckled. "I'll relay that verbatim, if you like?"

I shook myself. "No! I'm sorry, that's a yes. Tell McGowan yes, I'll be here."

Bakula's voice dropped. "Keep your cool, Redding. They'll need twenty minutes to get everyone suited up and outside. McGowan said something about putting you on the team. Don't blow it."

I took a deep breath. "Right. Thanks, Bakula."

"But if you're going to completely freak out anyway, please do so in the next thirty seconds or so. That'd give me time to suit up and take your place."

I chuckled. The sail wobbled up and down as it rode the wind and water. "I think I'm going to disappoint you."

"Drat."

"Before you go. Can you patch the real-def video through to me?"

"Sure. We've got a lovely view from the summit. You lucky monster."

My helmet went black for a fraction of a second, almost instantly replaced with a view from the camera on the peak of the extraction plant, high enough to show a view down into the boat.

My first thought was: Viking longboat. Maybe an ancient Greek trireme. Including the three massive oars on each side, moving in careful synchronization straight towards Tritium Base.

The base was silver-white, and stood on top of a cliff. I'd heard from one of the security officers on hovercraft patrol that you could see the base for kilometers.

According to the metrics at the bottom of the display, the boat was maybe six or seven meters long. The sail obscured the mast, but the raised prow and bow seemed designed both to slice through the water and act as vantage points.

And the alien in the prow?

What I could see looked humanoid. One arm held the prow while the other shaded its head against the spray.

I pushed down my disappointment.

At least it was inhumanly bulky. Was that fur?

Or was it wearing fur?

I couldn't help imagining that somehow, Viking explorers had fallen through an inter-universe rift and found themselves in the far future. I pushed away that idea as quickly as it appeared. You can't use Portals to travel through time, not even if you carried a bolognium device through one and made it bizarrely and uniquely malfunction like in all the serials.

If I discovered an alien race, I wanted it to at least have tentacles or suckers.

Still, they were *my* aliens. I needed a closer look.

"Any drones yet?" I asked Bakula.

"Negative," Bakula said. "It's too windy for microdrones, so we've dispatched the minis."

Minidrones would need a couple minutes to get out to the boat, and they couldn't approach as close. Our visitors might not notice a drone the size of a gnat, but they'd notice one as big as my hand.

The creature in the prow raised the limb over his head, exposing his face.

And yes, it had a face.

The summit video showed bare brown skin. A nose, a mouth, two eyes.

If that alien got a haircut, a shave, and a modern shirt, he could walk past my childhood home and I wouldn't look twice.

Maybe our visitors weren't alien at all. Had someone else figured out how to open Portals?

Or maybe they knew us a whole bunch better than we knew them.

4

In the projection on my helmet I watched mock Vikings slice through the water, oar-strokes synchronized as well as any rowing team could manage. They veered towards an obvious destination: the narrow channel into the bay, where the waves eased from vicious to merely mean. The rolling gravity added its own erratic syncopation to the water surging and splashing around them, the waves growing fiercer as the water grew shallower. It looked so real that my gut expected to hear splashing and shouting, but the only sound was the constant hiss of wind-blown sand.

One wave hit just right, soaking the longboat and the alien in the prow.

My heart pounded in my throat.

If the aliens steered perfectly, they could ease their boat through the channel. A few meters to either side, and they'd come up against the water-rounded basalt and the vicious reefs that goaded the water into lashing at the air.

But how much draft did a Viking longboat have, anyway?

Would a Tritium longboat need more draft, or less?

Somewhere in the library, Montague had an article discussing the requirements for Tritium sailing vessels. They would have written that before investing in air-lifted hovercraft.

I had to trust that the aliens knew their craft. They'd crossed a stormy ocean, or part of the ocean, in a nailed-together, unpowered, wooden craft that I wouldn't trust in a pond. If the channel was too shallow, they'd turn back.

Using the summit camera, I peered into the longboat. No sign of a dinghy.

Maybe we'd go out to meet them instead.

I minimized the view from the summit camera and swept it to the left, restoring my view of the outside world. The constant hiss against my helmet was once again sand cast before the endless wind. The granite walkway I stood on, a few meters above the black sand beach, seemed extra solid next to the wave-tossed sailboat wobbling at the edge of the bay.

With the distance and the water, I couldn't be certain how tall the boat was. But as far as I could tell, standing on this granite ledge with crashing waves clawing as high as a scant meter below put my feet above the gunwales of the approaching boat.

The boat seemed to pause near the channel entrance.

I brought up the summit camera.

The human-like alien in the prow kept looking towards the water and turning back to the crew. His free hand waved, as if for emphasis.

People from countless human cultures spoke with their hands.

They couldn't be human.

In Montague's century on Tritium, people had died. But their bodies had been recovered. Montague had strict rules against abandoning anyone in an alien universe, alive or dead, both for employee morale and to protect Earth. They didn't want a universe-jumping alien race to find aberrant and anomalous human remnants.

Humanity had never found such a race, but the universes were infinite.

So they couldn't be human.

But that alien in the prow shielded his eyes and looked up at Tritium Base with its jaw set in an uncanny mockery of human determination.

Don't let them fool you. Whoever they are, they've researched the human race. They've watched us well enough to emulate us. I mentally flipped through the Tritium Base crew that worked outside, trying to recall someone who waved their hands so much when they spoke. Maybe one of the Security team on hovercraft patrol, or perhaps Facilities to service the vehicles and equipment.

The man in the prow pointed straight at the channel.

The boat lurched forward.

I shrank the summit view, preferring to watch the sail wobble with my own eyes. The oars strove against the churning waves. I couldn't help holding my breath as the fragile-looking craft eased into the channel.

The mast rocked to one side, then the opposite in a drunken reel.

I bit my lip.

Over the radio Bakula said, "The entire contact team has reached the suit locker."

"Thanks." Fifteen minutes for decontamination and five minutes to get out here.

The boat wallowed forward.

The aliens might—might—reach the beach before the contact team arrived.

My mouth was bone-dry, but I had to swallow anyway.

Contact protocol was clear. If the aliens hit the beach before the contact team arrived, I needed to retreat. No physical contact between Montague personnel and sapient aliens. No Montague staff could approach aliens on their own.

Maybe I'd be lucky and the airlock would jam.

The boat's sail plummeted to the left. The stripes on the sail angled towards the sky—

—and stayed there.

My heart surged into my throat.

A couple hundred meters out in the water, the sail wobbled in the wind.

Over the wind and sand, through the crashing waves, did I hear shouts?

No, that had to be my imagination. The waves and water would wash away any sound.

I made myself breathe and switched to the summit camera.

The boat lay at a good forty-degree angle. Waves splashed up over the gunwale. Humanoid figures yanked oars from their slots to prod at the reef. From what I could see, the boat shifted only with the water.

The channel was too shallow.

The waves would only push it further aground.

Where it would tip.

"Operations," I said.

"We see it, Redding," Bakula said.

A fiercer wave splashed over the boat's gunwale, drenching the occupants.

My legs trembled with excitement. I ached to throw myself forward, to dive into the water, to get out there and rescue the people-not-people struggling against the surging water.

The poisonous water.

Whatever they were, I reminded myself, they weren't human. The water wasn't toxic to them.

But this was first contact!

"Listen, Bakula," I said. "There's no impression like a first impression, right?"

"And?"

My brain scrambled. I'd been in desperate situations on previous missions, but this was a different sort of desperate. My life wasn't at risk. The facility wasn't in immediate threat. I'd broken regulations when alone, and while I'd gotten away with it, this time I had the cameras of Tritium Base on me and every staffer not required elsewhere glued to their screens.

I'd already had a negative report for playing fast and loose.

If I did this wrong it would end my Montague career, and I still had a bunch more universes to see.

But I couldn't stand by and let anyone, even aliens in human guise, drown.

If they could drown.

"Hovercraft," I said. "I can take a hovercraft out and stay at max height. That'll put me at sixteen meters, right? I drop an inflatable a few meters inbound from the boat. Put a line on the boat, and lower the line into the boat. I mean the inflatable." Slow down, Redding. "Put a line on the inflatable. Lower the line into the alien boat."

"That's awful close," Bakula said.

"No physical contact," I said.

"That's the letter of the regs. Still awful close."

Another voice cut in. "Redding?"

Security First McGowan. "Yes, sir?"

"You flown a hover before?"

My gut tightened. "Training on Earth, sir." I didn't say *simulation*; McGowan knew that.

I studied every manual and grabbed all the training I could get for a universe, even on subjects I wasn't expected to use. I'd learned the hard way that you might need to use any equipment. Most of those Tritium manuals would be useless as of tomorrow, but when my hands began to itch, a manual for a construction pressure suit or a hovercraft reassured me.

The radio sat silent.

I took a deep breath. "It's our first impression, sir." More words wanted to bubble up behind them, but they wouldn't do anything to convince McGowan. She preferred a simple argument, made once.

I tried to ease the tension in my knees and shoulders, but little trembles still rippled up and down my spine.

The summit camera view showed another wave crash over the gunwale and into the boat.

I made myself breathe.

McGowan said, "Suit says your adrenaline is off the charts."

I let myself chuckle. "Alien contact? And they might die in front of us? They might look human, but can they swim?"

"They're damn fools to sail if they can't swim," McGowan said.

"Like most sailors in the Exploration Age?" No, too mouthy.

McGowan let it pass. "The rule is no contact."

Disappointment shuddered through me. "Yes, sir."

Was I really going to cheer the aliens on from the shoreline? Could I make myself stand by if they started to drown in the next few minutes? By the time the contact team emerged, they might be dead.

"You don't lower the line," McGowan said. "You drop the free end into the boat."

My pulse rocketed.

McGowan said, "Assume that something can climb up that line. No continuous line of contact with the alien vessel. Understand?"

"They have super-fast cooties," I said, smiling so hard my cheeks hurt.

McGowan said, "Be sure it's one of the excursion boats. No survival supplies."

"Yes, sir." If my grin got any bigger, my head would split.

"Make us look good, Redding."

5

Tritium's wobbling gravity makes jogging a game of Busted Leg Roulette, but I walked as quickly as I could—what we call double-heavy—off the beach. The rule in a crisis: *make haste, but slowly*. The broad stairs carved into the basalt cliff face demanded a steady, slow pace, but even so I huffed with the pressure suit's weight. The stale-tasting air didn't help, either. Maybe I should wear a pressure suit on the treadmill. I'd only need a few days a week to get used to it—but no, I was leaving Tritium tomorrow.

Half an hour ago, I'd been content to leave this assignment.

Of course the aliens appeared on my last full day. The most amazing discovery of the last five years, and I had to leave the next morning.

I decided to make the most of the time I had.

The hovercraft bay was a rectangular cave gouged into the cliff face, five or six meters above the beach and thirty meters broad and deep, with what looked like too many pillars supporting the roof. The construction team had polished the walls to gleaming black and gray, but the dull textured floor maximized traction. A maze of girders, lights, chains, and winches concealed the arched ceiling. A chain-link gate blocked the launch doors but let the afternoon sun slant through, illuminating the half-dozen sleek vehicles planted in their designated spaces. Cabinets and tool racks lined the side walls.

I took half a second to catch my breath and study the alien longboat via the summit camera's view displayed on the side of my helmet. The longboat lay close to full-on capsized. Each rush of waves splashed another barrel of water inside. All along the nearly submerged gunwale, the humanoid aliens braced themselves with oars wedged into the submerged reef.

A wave surged up as gravity shifted to the light.

The boat shifted.

The aliens heaved on their oars, trying to take advantage of the momentary lift and lightness to edge the boat backwards and off the reef.

The boat settled back right back in place.

More water splashed in.

I gritted my teeth and swiped the view away. Time to work.

"Bakula," I said.

"Yes, oh lucky one?" she replied over the suit speakers.

"Which locker has the excursion boats?"

"The big hovercraft has one in it."

"It raises too much spray." I caught myself shaking my head, as if she was wasting time watching me when they had dozens of views of the aliens. "The idea is to help these aliens, not drown them in back blast. I'm taking the scout."

"Plus the scout is more fun to drive."

She couldn't see my face when I faced the ocean, but my eyes still rolled. "I won't have the time or distance to open it up. Which locker do I want?"

"I can do a search while I banter," Bakula said. "It's called multitasking. You want locker six-B, to the left as you walk in the door."

The locker was taller than me, but slid open at my touch. Three sizes of bright yellow inflatable rafts sat in disciplined rows. The largest, the size of a beer keg, had CAPACITY 16 printed on the side facing me. Getting it onto a two-wheel cart both drove the air from my lungs and threatened to compress my spine.

"Ambitious much?" Bakula said.

"Want to rescue them all."

A little four-seater with an open top and a swooping wind screen, the scout looked designed specifically to look good while breaking every traffic law.

Fortunately, Tritium had no traffic laws.

I got the raft keg to the hovercraft's flank, and waited for the gravity to ebb before hoisting it straight up the side and rolling it over into the front passenger seat.

I let out a huff of relief when the weight left me.

The hovercraft sagged a little at the impact.

I grabbed a thirty meter coil of eight-ton-test rope from the nearest bench and tied one end around the loop on one end of the inflatable raft.

Tritium might not have any traffic laws, but the way I sank into the plush pilot's seat made me feel like I should find an enforcement officer just so I could blow past him. My life-support pack slid into the slot in the seat, taking that weight from my shoulders and hips. I had to move the chair forward a good forty centimeters before I could reach the floor pedals, but that gave me a chance to catch a breath before hitting the button.

The hovercraft started up with a hum too high-pitched to hear but strong enough to buzz my teeth in their sockets. The padded seat wasn't a luxury. Without it, my brain would have battered itself to a pulp against the inside of my skull.

Still, a fierce grin split my face. "Scout craft, requesting gate opening."

I'd barely begun speaking when the chain link gate started its smooth slide, exposing Tritium's cloud-studded blue-white sky.

A fast ride.

Running ahead of the contact team, to fling a rope to the aliens I'd discovered. This was better than *Voidlost*.

I brushed the throttle, and the hovercraft eased forward out of the hangar.

My stomach fell a little as the ground plunged away, but the hovercraft didn't even wobble at the transition from stone floor to open air. I nudged the altitude lever. The motor growled like a caged but furious tiger, but the scout craft eased upwards and I headed out across the water.

Gravity surged, the hovercraft dipped, and my stomach climbed. A second later my weight eased and everything went the other way. A detail Montague's Earth-side training couldn't simulate. Even a dozen meters above the bay, haze from the churning waves condensed on my helmet, forming rivulets that trickled down onto my suit. I couldn't imagine how wet it must be down lower.

The hovercraft's body hid the aliens, but the bow camera showed them still struggling with their oars. Maybe they knew what they were doing, but I couldn't see how human-shaped muscle could overcome the water driving the longboat further up onto the rocks.

Two of the aliens stripped down, winding heavy ropes around their torsos. I couldn't spare more than a glance from piloting, but that one look told me the aliens didn't look vaguely human.

They looked exactly human.

Not just human, but decidedly male.

They had swimmers' lean and muscular bodies, but nobody could do the side-stroke against the churning nightmare of water around the longboat. Their safety lines wound up taut. Their crewmates towed them back aboard even as more water splashed over the gunwale.

One of the aliens noticed the hovercraft.

A dozen pairs of eyes peered up at me. Alien-human faces swiveled to each other, mouths open in shouted commands.

One of the aliens hoisted a stick as long as he was.

A metallic stick, gleaming with oil.

"Redding," Bakula said.

"They noticed me."

"Computer says that's a rifle. Similar to nineteenth-century, probably lever-action."

I narrowed my eyes.

The rifleman held the weapon ready in one hand, one hand shielding his eyes from the spray so he could peer up at my hovercraft.

He didn't raise the weapon to his shoulder, though.

"I think they're just being careful," I said.

"If I give the word," Bakula said, "goose the motor. Run."

"Any excuse to open this monster up," I said.

I had no intention of running, but I needed healthy paranoia. An alien that knew what we looked like knew that we could blow their boat to toothpicks. That "lever-action rifle" was probably a death ray.

According to the instruments, the boat had run aground about two hundred forty-eight meters from the shore. I eased the hovercraft out to an even hundred meters from the boat, right over the channel, and told the autopilot to hold the location. The driver's seat wasn't built for me to turn and face the passenger side, but I crawled around to rest my knees on the chair and twisted my waist to get my hands on the pebbly plastic cask.

The rope lay coiled in the passenger foot well, with the end tied to the raft facing upwards. I eased the other end out from underneath, taking care not to tangle the coil. I needed that rope to unroll freely.

A winch would have been better, but I couldn't detach a whole winch and drop it on the aliens. Well, no—I *could*. But it was far beyond the first contact procedure.

I double-checked the knot attaching the rope to the raft. Good and solid.

Heaving the raft over the edge of the hovercraft should have been easier than carrying it. I could rest the weight against the vehicle chassis and roll it up.

Even waiting for an ebb of gravity, the effort made me gasp. But in a moment, I had the cask balanced on the edge of the hovercraft.

I double-checked the rope. Still tidy.

One final nudge, and the life boat cask plunged over the side into the water.

An eternal second passed. Maybe this one raft was defective. It might not open, plunge straight into the water, and never bob up. Or perhaps the rope had a weak spot and would snap in half.

Even if only half the eyes in Tritium Base were on me, today's video would wind up in first contact courses for the next fifty years. I could just imagine some dry professor announcing *and now here's great-grandmother Aidan Redding, come to tell us how she failed to correctly tie a square knot at first contact and ignited the most bloody war humanity has ever known.*

Far below, I heard a massive splash as the raft hit the water.

The rope stopped hissing out, half its length still in the footwell.

I sighed, clutched the remaining coil of line, and weaseled my way back into the driver's seat.

The hovercraft's camera showed the armed alien in the prow, staring at the space where the cask had hit the water. He held his rifle higher, but not at his shoulder yet. I knew assumptions were unwise, but I mentally labeled him Alien Captain.

"Raft deploying," Bakula said.

Alien Captain snapped the rifle to his shoulder—

I gritted my teeth.

—but didn't fire.

If the raft didn't detect anyone in the water it would default to an explosive inflation, spraying water for meters in every direction as the ridiculously compressed air within erupted.

In only a few seconds, Alien Captain lowered his weapon and turned to shout at his companions.

I nudged the hovercraft forward.

The rope grew taut and tugged.

I let more line slip through my fingers.

My imagination flashed. *The rope snapping taut. Eight-ton-test line slashing through the fingers of my suit, the palm of my hand. Bright red blood shooting into slowly toxic air—*

No!

I was safe, I told myself.

Safe from the rope, at least.

The hovercraft's maximum altitude was sixteen meters. I had thirty meters of rope. As the line played out, I found myself thinking I should have brought a longer one.

The alien rifleman was waving someone to his side.

I swiveled the camera back to watch the raft wallow in the water and got back under way.

The next few moments were a gentle struggle between the scout hovercraft's overpowered motor and the raft's drag in the water. The line might test at eight tons, but I didn't think the aliens would appreciate it if I scooped the raft right out of the water and dropped it on their heads.

After the longest four minutes of my life, I got the raft within ten meters of the longboat. I turned the hovercraft in a wide turn so that the line passed above and across the boat. The hovercraft's lift field raised even more spray around the longboat, making the aliens raise their arms to protect their eyes, so I detached the line from the hovercraft and retreated.

The camera showed the alien rifleman shouting as the line dropped.

Seconds later, four of them were pulling the rope and hauling the raft in.

A satisfied glow filled me.

"Nice, Redding," Bakula said.

"Pull back fifty meters," Security First McGowan said.

"Yes, sir."

The aliens drew the raft right up against their longboat.

One climbed in.

And in less than a minute, the bastard headed away from Tritium Base and out towards the ocean.

6

Chevy's pressure suit smelled of disinfectant, over lingering traces of other people's sweat. The suit hung too loose on him everywhere, but he was a few centimeters too big to wear a medium. He'd tightened the suit as much as he could, trying not to think of how intimately this same suit had cradled complete strangers, but his every motion still felt floppy.

The crowded elevator opened onto the outside world. Chevy felt unwilling to move forward, but the contact team's Brownian motion meant he could accompany them or fall on his face. He unwillingly lurched out onto the basalt platform overlooking the bay.

He couldn't help stopping in amazement at the stark beauty of this appalling world. He'd seen this on video, but his own eyes lent it a whole different reality.

Montague's stupid-brave engineers had carved the gray basalt outside the base's main entrance into a series of ramps, stairs, and platforms that covered the twenty-two and a half meters down to the walkway at the edge of the beach. Salt crust encroached on every surface, despite the bright blue tortoise scrubbers trundling to and fro. The trails of gleaming gray stone they left almost immediately began spotting with spray.

What looked like small waves out on the ocean metamorphosed into angry crashing waves once they entered the reef. Rounded shoulders of rock mixed with bright green spars of alien coral appeared and disappeared as they knocked the implacable waves askew, stealing their strength as they entered the semicircular bay. The lagoon by the beach looked tranquil.

Right above Chevy's line of vision, a fine haze of spray left a damp triangle across the distressingly flimsy helmet. Chevy couldn't help focusing on the slow poison trickling down the outside of the curved plasteel. His pressure suit hummed a little more, cooling the helmet before the inside could fog.

Everything felt heavier. Logically, the gravity surges couldn't be any stronger here than they were indoors. The average of point nine four three G still had to hold. His pressure suit and the twenty-two kilo life support pack fooled his somatic senses, that was all.

Hostile basalt cliffs surrounded the bay and stabbed at the dark sky. To the right, the external portion of the extraction plant loomed on the far end of the cliff, kept clean by its own tortoises.

And that sun! Three point eight times the diameter of Earth's sun might not seem like much, but twenty-eight point seven times the volume? It looked harmless in the afternoon, burning the sky around it to deep green, but that abomination was going to finish its implosion in only a few hundred million more years.

Assuming his predecessors' work was correct, and that stars still died slowly in this universe. Astrophysicists used mathematics to determine the life cycles of stars. Chevy knew better than anyone how many ways you could solve a math problem.

Especially in an alien universe, with different maths.

That star's implosion might engulf Tritium tomorrow.

According to the training they'd provided, Montague had built their base in this bay because they could run pipes far out into the water but have natural protection against anything that might arrive by ocean. He'd suspected they made a point of saying precisely that to soothe new arrivals.

Looking at the bay, though, Chevy couldn't help feeling a sympathy for his ancestors. Waves pounded rocks into sand. Centuries before, his own ancestors had used flimsy wooden craft to cross waves much like these and conquer North America.

And his invader ancestors couldn't drink the water either. There were jokes about it.

Tritium's water wasn't technically poisonous. This universe had oxygen and hydrogen and, like Earth water, built water out of them. But if Chevy drank that water, he'd gradually swap his body's monotonic hydrogen with tritium.

Tritium's math said tritium wasn't toxic here. Once he passed through the Portal back to Earth, though, the rattlesnake-fast imposition of sane natural law would make his own body radioactive.

One swallow of Tritium water? Not a problem. The native bacteria might find his body a hospitable colony and devour him alive, but the H_2O itself wouldn't kill him.

Exposure over hours? Not even modern medicine could flush out his body's hydrogen atoms from their molecular bonds. Maybe the newest cancer-killing implants could keep him half-alive.

Worse? The air was humid. Even if he avoided drinking heavy water, he'd breathe it.

And they were relying on centuries-obsolete technology to survive. Chevy might as well find a pointy rock and join the mammoth hunt.

Chevy's hands hurt. They'd curled into tight fists when he wasn't paying attention. He forced his petrified fingers open.

The ten pressure-suited people around him didn't seem even discomfited. Chevy did not belong here.

Security First McGowan was already at the top of the stairs. If one of Tritium's pseudo-feline opportunity predators leapt down from a cliff, she'd punch it in the nose before its claws hit her. She belonged here. Without a lick of hesitation she said, "Peabody, Raadt, with me. Firearms crew next. Torgenson, take Gunfire. Canter, deSaav, you're on tail."

McGowan was already on the first step down.

A man turned to Chevy, his swirling red-and-gold face tattoo visible through the fishbowl. Small letters on Chevy's fishbowl flashed *private channel*. "I'm Torgenson. Biology second."

"Chevy." His throat didn't want to make sounds. "Uh, math third."

"Oh, I know who you are." Torgenson smiled, teeth shining across the swooping tattoo. "My people have spent the last three months complaining about how your maths forced them to rethink ninety years of Tritium research." He spoke with a vague lilting accent. His native language was probably tonal.

Chevy felt his face flush. "Er…"

Torgenson laughed and clapped Chevy's shoulder. He felt the man's strength even through the heavy pressure suit. The comforting good-ol'-boy greeting reminded him of home.

"Lighten up, mister!" Torgenson said. "You've done great things so far. I expect we'll be seeing your name a whole bunch more."

If nothing else, fall back on good manners. "That's very kind. Thank you, sir."

"I've put us on a private channel." Torgenson took Chevy's arm and guided him into place behind the two dark-helmeted people carrying rifles just like he'd hunt with at home. "You can hear McGowan's orders, but we can talk without bothering her."

"Because I need a babysitter." Chevy hated the unmanly bitterness tinging his voice.

"Not at all," Torgenson said.

"Don't get me wrong," Chevy said. "This is not…" Not what? What he signed up for? The Texas Datacore *had* signed him up for this. It thought the Montague Corporation was a suitable place for him to use his talents. It had somehow thought he wouldn't hate it.

"I get it," Torgenson said. "You and I, we're both lab rats. We sit in a room and grow formulas, or algae, or something like that. I've been right where you are."

"You've done first contact?" Chevy said. "Then why am I here?"

"No, no," Torgenson laughed, steering him to the stairs. "I have to go out every week to check samples. Nothing replaces in situ examination. The first time out, it's overwhelming. And I have to go through Security every time, in and out. Plus, I've been with Montague for near on twenty years, and this is your first assignment. I'm here to handle company procedure for you, so you can focus on your skills."

The explanation both comforted and irritated Chevy. Montague had voluminous rules and procedures for every imaginable circumstance, constantly maintained by an entire academy of tedious scribblers. They boasted of how they pruned and nurtured their rules. The company knew he didn't know their rules. They anticipated his bewilderment, so they'd given him a batman.

The Texas Datacore knew everything about him, but it used that knowledge for the good of society and, in theory, to make him happy. The Montague Corporation didn't know everything about him, but they used what they knew for the good of company profit. The difference was as clear as the difference between nurturing families and breaking them.

Climbing down the stairs left no energy for fuming. His heavy gear made the gravity tide worse, and seawater condensed over every surface. Two rivulets of spray converged on his helmet, right in front of his nose, and trickled downwards.

Already halfway down the stairs, McGowan said "Report."

What was he supposed to report?

The woman from Operations—Bakula?—said "Redding dropped the raft and towed it to their vessel. An alien has boarded it and is heading back out to the sea."

One confusion replaced another. These aliens had arrived, sunk their boat, and now only one of them used the raft? These creatures might be as appalling as the atomic-level math that defined them.

"Rowing?" McGowan said.

"Under power," Bakula said. "Took about twenty seconds for them to figure out the controls."

"Redding?" McGowan said. Weren't they the person who had first seen the aliens?

Redding sounded like a woman. She spoke quickly, a faint Central American accent coloring her English. "Yes, sir." If Chevy had trouble calling a woman *sir*, being called sir must infuriate sensible women. These Montague people had procedures for everything, but they'd abandoned pronouns and civility alike.

"Retreat fifty meters and hold for orders."

Chevy could almost hear Redding's frustration. "Yes, sir."

Glimpsing over the heads of the suited gunmen in front of him and Torgenson, Chevy could just make out the half-capsized ship. It looked like something out of ancient Greece, with long oars sticking out of the upper side to pointing at the sky. A broad sail striped with dirty white and fire engine red flapped loosely from the mast.

The opposing oar holes had to be under the water. That vessel *had* to be taking on water at a torrential rate.

Maybe the aliens only needed one of them to survive. Perhaps a group mind? But if so, why had they bothered to change themselves to resemble human beings?

A surge of water lifted the ship for a moment. The skewed sail wobbled and shifted, but the ship settled back into place. It wouldn't sink. They'd run aground.

Trepidation joined Chevy's confusion. Montague's first contact protocols contained pages and pages of sensible information-sanitation precautions. If the contact went sour, everything the aliens learned would put humanity at a disadvantage.

If the aliens could operate human mechanisms, even a raft's childish joystick, they understood humanity threateningly well.

I'm the kind of person that runs in to help. When work needs doing, I leap into the task at hand. I dash towards mysterious shouts and screams. I enjoy relaxing and playing as much as anyone, but I can't sit in the comfy chair and watch *Voidlost* or *Unsurvivable* while people fight for their lives.

Even if the "people" are aliens crafted to resemble humans.

The hovercraft's buzz had sunk into my bones. My teeth weren't going to rattle loose any longer; they seemed to have merged with the vibration, along with my bones and brain and flesh. The spray on my helmet had achieved balance, slipping away as fast as it accumulated.

Below me, a lone jerk alien had hijacked the raft and was running for the freedom of the open seas.

I reminded myself of my last assignment. I didn't need another negative report.

Heart heavy, I turned the hovercraft back towards shore. Fifty meters would put me halfway to the hangar.

The runaway alien slowed.

The alien captain was lashing my dropped line to the ship's stern.

They were going to use the raft to tow the ship off the reef.

My heart lightened.

I'd read the accounts of every first contact, from the first disaster and negotiated truce with the Townies to the peace-loving Sandsifts. Assuming you knew how an alien would react to an interaction was a sure way to disaster. But surely even aliens had a survival instinct? And they'd welcome support of that instinct?

I got the hovercraft to the McGowan-proscribed distance, added an extra three meters to allow for changes in the wind, and turned to watch the nail-biting epic of the aliens rescuing themselves. The urge to help burned in my every nerve. I overrode it with every breath.

The water around the ship surged and sank in regular waves.

Gravity tightened and loosened its grip just as rhythmically, but in a different cycle.

When high water coincided with reduced gravity, every minute or so, the aliens leaned on their oars and the raft operator opened up the motor. The ship was maybe a meter, a meter and a half onto the reef, and each spasm shifted it a few centimeters back.

Despite the distance, and the hovercraft's numbing roar and rattle, I could almost hear the alien cheers when the ship rocked off the reef and splashed free. Some thrust fists into the air. One did an impromptu hip-wiggling dance. Alien Captain let it go on for two, maybe three seconds before cupping his mouth with his hands and shouting orders.

By the time the raft was back by the ship, they had a floppy hose big enough for one of my arms to fit down over the bulwark. Water surged and splashed out.

Security First McGowan said, "Redding."

"Yes, sir."

"They're stable. Drones are in place to track them if they leave. Your presence in the hovercraft is superfluous, and might be considered threatening."

I was lucky to have been permitted to do this much. "Yes, sir. Return to the hangar?"

McGowan paused. "It is traditional, Redding, to wait for orders rather than guess what they will be."

I winced. "Yes, sir."

"We are set up to greet them on the lagoon beach. If you think you can await instructions rather than attempting to read my mind, you're welcome to join us."

A grin threatened to split my face. "Yes, sir!"

"You're on retreat."

"Understood."

I almost pulled the hovercraft straight into the hangar, but remembered at the last second that policy was to back in. That delayed me just enough that by the time I got back down to the beach, Alien Captain and two of his crew had gotten our raft most of the way through the channel and into the lagoon.

8

The sand reminded Chevy of New Houston beaches. It was dark black, leavened with quartz crystals to give it sparkle and shine, but waterlogged it supported his weight just fine. The pressure suit made his footprints look freakish. Water oozed into the tread marks and began nibbling away at the marks of his presence.

The tiny lagoon looked like it would be perfect for swimming. The protective reefs reduced the crashing waves to a gentle surge and ebb that wouldn't threaten a toddler's balance, but the splash of each impact was loud enough to penetrate his fishbowl helmet. The temperature out here averaged ten degrees on this seasonless planet, but the huge sun cast an illusion of warmth. Driftwood trees lay tumbled to either side, but this stretch was clear sand. All it needed was a few beach chairs, a solar grill, a volleyball net, and some friends. A few pretty women would make it perfect, and what woman wasn't pretty in a bikini?

And an entirely new set of natural laws. One that wouldn't slowly poison you or, worse, permanently exile you from Earth.

Instead, he had an inflatable orange raft of dangerously human-looking aliens trolling across the lagoon.

Security First McGowan thrust a mesh bag of three-centimeter square white blocks into Chevy's hands. "When they get up to shore, it'll be up to you."

Chevy's throat tightened. "Sir, I'm not—"

"Nobody is," McGowan said. "But your scores on first contact math were off the scale. I'll be relaying everything back to Ops, and they'll send it all back to Earth. They'll have an Alien Linguistics team here in a day or two. All you have to do is convince them that we are intelligent."

The theory in the Montague manual had seemed sound, when Chevy had read it in the dubious comfort of his trainee quarters back in Montevideo. An alien with physical form had to interact with the physical world. If they were intelligent, they could probably count. Naïve humans thought they might count in base seven, but they might also believe that two plus two equaled three.

The math contact method relied on an interested alien conveying their concept of one-two-three. It had been successful with twelve of the eighteen alien intelligences they'd found.

Chevy unhunched his shoulders. This couldn't be worse than defending his first doctorate. It was more like play, his favorite kind of play, exploring different ways to make numbers dance. Sure, most anyone here could probably perform the labor, but maybe he'd get lucky and discover that these aliens did basic counting in operator algebra.

The rest of the Montague team, except for Torgenson, had retreated into a neat arc three meters back. A few carried rifles, the old sort that shot bullets, not too different from the one Chevy kept for hunting back home. The weapons were slung pointing down, but ready to snatch and fire. The maniac from the hovercraft hit the bottom of the stairs and hurried over to the end of the arc, her steps dangerously quick.

In the middle of the lagoon, the raft slowed.

The man in the prow wore a fur coat. It had to be real fur, didn't it? Not even these insane Montague people could have missed seeing an entire industrial base capable of producing faux fur when they surveyed the planet?

This might be faster than when Father last tried to play chess with him. They not only knew what humans looked like, they'd used a hand gesture that meant peace. Or perhaps they thought raised open hands meant *Cower before me, invader scum.*

He had perhaps a minute before the raft beached.

When the gravity ebbed, Chevy groaned himself and the heavy pressure suit to a knee. His heavy gloves made his fingers clumsy as he drew the bag's drawstring, but he tugged it open before the raft hit sand. As neatly as he could, he set out one block. A hand's width from it, he set two side by side. Further down, he set three.

The open bag went next to the spot where the next number would logically go.

If the alien looked at the blocks and put out four, Chevy's work would reduce to a child's game. If not, maybe he'd have to express operator algebra with those same blocks. That *would* be a challenge.

Chevy tried to stand just as his weight surged, and instantly flopped back onto his knee. The padded suit protected his skin, but his kneecap ground against the end of his femur.

"Easy," Torgenson said.

Chevy wished the fishbowl helmet wasn't so transparent. His face flushed from embarrassment rather than pain, and he had to deliberately unclench his teeth. "I'm okay."

"These suits are heavy," Torgenson said.

As gravity ebbed, Chevy heaved himself up, captured his balance, and bent his knees before the life support backpack's weight peaked. Walking backwards on sand in unstable gravity struck him as foolish, so Chevy stepped aside to leave lots of space.

The alien leader put a leg over the side of the raft and planted a leather-booted foot on the shoreline.

Oops! Chevy flipped on the suit's external microphone. The crash of waves on reef got loud enough to drown normal conversation.

The alien leader strode up the beach. Its brown thick beard and mustache rose up around its face, reducing the exposed weatherworn skin to lips, nose, and around the deep-set eyes. Its shoulder-length hair was tied back with some sort of string, and its sopping wet pants appeared to be coarse woven wool. The boots left prints as big as Chevy's.

It stood for a moment, gaze starting at the far end of the pressure suited people and studying each one by one as the other two aliens dragged the raft up onto the sand and trotted up behind him.

Chevy half expected that gaze to carry a psychic weight impossible on Earth. While he'd avoided soiling his mind with those popular but foolish serials, the concept of alien mind control didn't seem so foolish right then.

The alien's eyes were clear and brown. If they'd seized Chevy's brain, he hadn't noticed.

It studied him for a breath. It looked down at the blocks, then back at Chevy.

Then it said, "Welcome to Anti-Earth. Y'all mind if we use some of your driftwood to build a fire? That water's right freezing."

9

Growing up, I'd watched even the worst serials about aliens. As a Security professional, I'd devoured every Montague manual on alien contact. Devoured optional training on past alien contact. Daydreamed about meeting aliens in another universe. Whatever I'd expected from the aliens, Old American English wasn't it.

Some of the North American countries preserved their language. Was it North Nevada that had the Language Purity Commission? Nebraskansas? Navajo Michigan? One of those N countries, anyway. One that missed their glory days, when they hadn't had to get along with anyone.

The alien leader didn't speak it perfectly. The drawl was exaggerated, the twang almost a parody. But it sure sounded enough like Old American to start off a skit in an episode of *Laughs*.

My pressure suit was beginning to stink of my own sweat, and bright copper adrenaline marked the back of my throat. My joints hurt from hard physical labor against the variable gravity. The ill-fitting pressure suit seemed to have tightened further against my thighs, and the air gap behind my butt felt extra steamy from the accumulated sweat trickling down my spine. I'd just gotten my heart to slow down after the hurried scramble down the hangar bay stairs, and now it wanted to surge again.

How could they watch us so well as to capture that accent? Unlike many Montague posts, Tritium had an entertainment library. I doubted it contained comic parodies, though. Montague had employees from all over the world, and tried to minimize political conflicts between them. I didn't like the theocracies, but so long as every nation allowed open immigration and emigration, people were free to choose their culture.

My gut reaction was that Alien Captain was too perfect. He was a promo poster of The Brave Explorer, with that tied-back hair and knife-trimmed beard and that ripped-off-a-bear coat. But everything showed wear. The pants had been patched and patched again. Whatever cloth they were made of looked heavy and scratchy. The coat's cuffs and neck were short of fur, as if he'd worn it away. An alien wouldn't have chosen that broken nose or those irregular teeth.

Unless wear made the disguise more perfect.

Or maybe they were, somehow, human.

I made myself swallow the tight lump in my throat.

Through his suit's external speaker, the contact specialist said "Uh…"

Alien Captain rolled his eyes and said, "Dang it, I hoped you spoke English." He grabbed the bag of blocks, dug out a handful, and set four in a neat square. "There you go. Let me guess, you're gonna say *five*? Then we point at rocks and grunt?"

I itched to say something, but procedure said leave everything to the contact specialist unless called upon. McGowan had assigned me to retrieval. I stood by until everything went horrible, then grabbed anyone injured and carried them back to safety. It's like running towards trouble, but the other way around.

"We speak English," the specialist said. "I'm sorry, you surprised me."

"Great!" Alien Captain said. "My name's Caleb Mason, captain of the good ship *Triangulator*."

At that, McGowan stepped forward. "Stand down, Gunfire. My name's Nichelle McGowan, security leader for the Montague Corporation in this universe. How did you get here, Captain Mason?"

Mason grinned. "How about that fire? We can sit and jaw awhile."

McGowan hesitated. I'd read the alien contact manual more than once and could imagine her thinking *how could a fire be used against us*? "I have no objection to a small fire, here on the beach."

Mason said, "You heard the man. Get on it, guys."

In a pressure suit, everyone with short hair looked like a heavy man. Or maybe Mason was an alien, and didn't understand human sex?

The two crewmen—no, *aliens*, I had to remember to call them aliens. Nobody's human until proven human. A knowledgeable alien who wanted to charm us into lowering our guard might choose exactly this approach. The two alien flunkies sauntered towards the closer heap of driftwood and started breaking off branches.

I switched my mic off the group channel. "Security Operations?"

"Go," Bakula said.

"Can you check if anyone's ever built a fire out of the driftwood?"

"You're late," Bakula said. "It burns just like an Earth fire."

I grimaced. McGowan had beat me to it. She'd probably asked the second Mason had said anything about a fire—no, Ops was monitoring this conversation and would have looked it up before McGowan even asked.

I couldn't do anything to help, and frustration threatened to overwhelm.

"While they're on that," McGowan said, "perhaps you could answer my question."

Mason grinned. "You're worried. Easy enough. We're the great-great-something grandkids of a bunch of researchers and a few stranded colonists."

That didn't make sense. Montague sold access to human-friendly colony worlds, but never a universe like Tritium that would render colonists unable to return. And they hadn't done it for long enough that Mason could be anyone's great-great-grandkid.

"Who?" McGowan said.

"Fair's fair," Mason blew into his loosely curled fists to warm them, then stuffed his hands under his armpits. "How about a word or two on," he jerked his chin up at the gleaming metal of the tritium extraction plant, "all this?"

"We're with the Montague Corporation," McGowan said. "This is an industrial facility."

"In-dus-tri-al?" Mason sounded out the word slow. "Didn't bring my dictionary, sorry."

"Machines," McGowan tried.

"So you opened up a workshop on our world, and didn't even ask first," Mason said, grinning.

"We surveyed this world for intelligent alien life," McGowan said. "How did you evade detection?"

"Ah," Mason said. "Did you look hard enough to find a few hundred farmers?"

The fishbowl helmet was clear, so I kept my face still. *No.*

"How did you get here?" McGowan said again.

"This isn't getting us anywhere," Mason said. "How 'bout you let me talk to the helpful person what tossed us a line?"

My heart thrilled. There was no way McGowan would let me talk to the aliens, but knowing that I'd made a difference delighted me.

The private channel marker flashed. McGowan muttered "offer no information" into my ear, then said over her suit speaker, "Redding, come up here."

My thrill turned to delight.

Don't screw this up, Aidan.

I almost danced up to McGowan. The two alien contact specialists retreated a few more steps to give me a clear path. The alien crew were already stacking wood into a lean-to fire, using a heavy driftwood log as both a base and a shelter from the wind.

My mouth was suddenly parched. I worked up enough spit to say, "Hello."

Mason gave a small bow from his waist. "Thank you for your assistance. We would have gotten off that reef before dark, but your timely arrival and the gift of your powered raft made it so much easier."

What meaning did Mason attach to the bow? If I returned it, was I entering into some alien covenant? I decided to risk a small bow in response. "I could not let you drown."

"We wouldn't have drowned," Mason said. "We would have been beat to the dickens, though. Those currents are right tricky. What can I call you?"

Dickens? What did an Oil Age English author have to do with beatings? "I'm Aidan Redding. Security Third, Montague Corporation."

"Third," Mason said. "So you're in charge?"

"I'm in charge," McGowan said.

"But I'm already getting on so much better with the young man here," Mason said.

"Since I saved you from being beat to the dickens," I said, "maybe you'd be kind enough to answer my boss's question."

Mason tossed his head back and laughed. "Too shay. Too shay."

What did *shay* mean?

"Fine. Our forefathers came here through a gateway invented by Doctor Sharam. He looked for researchers willing to explore the world. They found we could live here for a little while. They all had family and friends looking to get away from their troubles, so they gathered up their belongings and took the one-way trip. Then one day, the Gateway just stopped working. We been here ever since."

My gut reaction was to murmur *Doctor Sharam* to Ops, but they'd already be on it.

Behind Mason, the fire flickered alight. The alien crewmen gave a small cheer and fed more kindling to the flames. I hadn't seen a fire since I left Earth, one day short of six months ago, and the irregular yellow light sent a flicker of nostalgia through my excitement.

Mason's grin faded to a smile of relief. "Excuse me a moment while I thaw."

On the private channel McGowan said, "Good, Redding. See what else you can get, but save a little goodwill if you can."

I choked my swelling delight. I wasn't merely on the alien contact team. I was the friend-maker on the alien contact team. So long as I didn't screw up.

Ops said, "Too many possible matches for a Doctor Sharam. Get more information."

McGowan nodded at me.

Going near an open flame in a pressure suit was a terrible idea. I went as close as I dared, about three meters away, and let Mason hold his hands to the rising heat for a moment. The constant ocean breeze shredded the flames when they rose above the banker log's shelter and instantly scattered the thin gray smoke. "That looks cozy," I said.

Mason rubbed his hands together. "After three months of sailing, you have no idea. Come on up if you like."

"Not a good idea in this outfit," I said.

When Mason turned to thaw his back I said, "Where was this Doctor Sharam from?"

"University of Montana, Helena," Mason declared.

I felt my jaw slack, and instantly tightened it.

Every school child learned that list of cities. Hiroshima, Japan. Nagasaki, Japan. Helena, United States. Campo Grande, Mato Grosso. Winnipeg, NDP Empire. The five cities destroyed by nuclear weapons.

Did the aliens know us that well?

Or had this Doctor Sharam invented the Portal centuries before Montague, only to get ripped to atoms before he told the world?

10

Chevy had never imagined he'd feel relieved to return to the Tritium complex's claustrophobic rabbit warren. The chance to see something more than a few meters away should have delighted him, but he'd been so aware of the aliens in front of him and the used pressure suit and the potential for screwing up an alien first contact that he'd been unable to even contemplate the horizon. The elevator down to the changing room and the tunnels, so narrow that his shoulder brushed a wall when he let someone walk past, felt nearly comfortable.

The summons to Facility President Kendall's personal meeting room wiped away that relief.

The meeting room blended comfort and strangeness. The round table had fourteen identical padded chairs, none placed to assert authority. The walls were floor-to-ceiling screens, but blank. The tile floor was worked smooth enough to prevent tripping, but left rough enough to prevent slips. Utilitarian. Efficient. Boring.

Back home in Soviet Texas, such monitors would show scenes of their country's natural beauty, or famous art of the last fifteen centuries, or team members' pet photos if nothing else. Even cat people liked dog pictures.

The Montague Corporation had clearly studied aesthetics, but only to hunt them down and eradicate them. The drab orange plastic cover on the chairs would be easily cleaned. The table's bluish-gray plastic top was polished to a high gleam. The only decoration in the whole room was the octagonal Montague logo dominating the inside of the doors, reminding Chevy of the web of an unusually tidy spider.

Drab or not, the chairs called to him. Even after gobbling a protein bar and snatching a quick shower to wash away the pressure suit filth, his back and legs ached from lugging that life support backpack around. No, taking a seat before anyone arrived would be rude. He'd just have to hop up again when the next person arrived. President Kendall would be arriving any moment. The real solution was to up his exercise regimen, just like when he was training for that two-week hike into the Guadalupe Mountains.

Maybe add more crunches. He loathed crunches, but nothing strengthened the abs better. They wouldn't take too much time from his "double heavy" run around the jogging track. Who could thrive when you couldn't even jog without harmonizing each step to gravity changes?

Was the air in this meeting room a little fresher? Any society that declared someone President was inherently authoritarian and hierarchical. Was fresher air President Kendall's chosen reward for rank?

No, meetings drained people's energy. Increased air flow helped keep everyone awake.

But did corporate authoritarians believe that any amount of décor drained efficiency? How did these people stay sane?

Maybe they didn't.

Chevy shook his head. Arriving a few minutes early had left him time to ponder authoritarian decor. Better that than considering what he'd accomplished by going outside.

Nothing.

Montague had assigned him a minder to take him for a stroll on the beach to play with blocks. He'd overcome his worry by giving himself something to look forward to. Suppose the aliens *had* counted in operator algebra? Instead, they spoke English. With accents that mocked the whole Conquest Western genre.

Maybe they were actual humans.

The hallway door slid open, splitting the Montague logo in half to admit a tiny slender Latina.

His first thought was *corporate drone*. Truly unfair of him. Even if she had her hair cropped short and wore the khaki Montague Security uniform like it had been tailored for her, she was an independent human being with her own thoughts and deserved his respect even if she was subsumed in an authoritarian culture.

Perhaps she was here as willingly as he was.

Besides, her brown eyes seemed to absorb the room without moving. Gravity surged just as she took her first step, and she didn't even wobble. Chevy had the instant sense that if she got involved in a bar fight back home, some of the good ol' boys would regret taking a swing at her. Not that any real man would strike a lady. Unless she insisted.

This one might insist.

Glad he hadn't taken advantage of the chairs, Chevy drew himself up straighter and gave a polite, respectful nod. "Ma'am—sir!"

Her smile changed her face from drone to total human. "Everybody slips, don't sweat it." Chevy could only describe her accent as *assimilated by Montague*, with only faint hints of Central America underneath. She strode forward, holding out her hand. "Aidan Redding, Security Third." Her hand was tiny, but callused. The good ol' boys would regret messing with this one.

"Chevrolet Gunfire, Maths Third."

A single pump, and she dropped her hand.

"Redding?" Chevy said. "You're the"—*maniac*—"one who went out on the hovercraft to pull our aliens in."

"That's me," she said cheerily. "A great way to end my assignment."

Chevy frowned at the coincidence. "It's my last day as well."

"So we both got lucky," Redding said.

"I suppose so," Chevy said.

"Either they're aliens, or they're stranded humans," Miss Redding said. "Or something else."

Yes, that did cover all the logical options.

"Whatever they are," she said, "we got to meet them⬚ first. Something to tell the youngsters."

If Montague kept him wandering between universes for the rest of his life, there wouldn't be any youngsters. "I guess. Would you have any idea why we're here?"

Miss Redding clenched her teeth for a microsecond and forced a shrug. "I've been told not to anticipate so much. I don't think I've screwed up bad enough to be reprimanded, this time."

Chevy's tension eased a mite. As far as he'd seen, Miss Redding hadn't screwed up at all. She'd played Good Ranger as well as anyone could ask.

The opposite door slid open.

Miss Redding lost her relaxed pose, coming to attention while leaving her knees bent to ride the gravity.

Chevy's shoulders were riding up again. He deliberately lowered them before turning.

Facility President Kendall looked like a Corporate President straight out of an old movie. Tall, broad-shouldered, with heavy silver hair. He wore a blue uniform making him as Administration, but a darker shade reserved for the upper levels of the hierarchy. He walked with easy confidence of someone who had spent years or decades in Tritium.

Years? Chevy might start chewing on his fingers if he had to spend another day locked in here.

Twelve hours and fourteen minutes until he returned to Earth. One more night's sleep, if he could manage to close his eyes and stop counting seconds, and he'd head home.

"Redding, Gunfire," Kendall said in a voice accustomed to leadership as he walked around to join them. "Have a seat."

"Thank you, sir," Chevy said.

Redding claimed the chair closest to her. The chair in front of Chevy left an open chair between himself and Redding, and put Redding between him and Kendall. Moving closer felt uncivil. Settling into the chair released a ache of welcome ease in his lower back and a sputter of air from the chair.

"Sir," Redding said, her calm face in profile to Chevy. Not a genteel *sir*, but a deferential one.

Maybe the datacore had traded Chevy to Montague, but he wasn't about to develop the habit of bowing to authoritarians. He gave a single dip of his chin instead.

"Thanks to Redding, I've become even busier, so I'm going to make this short," Kendall said. "I'm entering positive notes in both your records."

Was the lightness just the gravity ebbing?

"Thank you, sir," Miss Redding said.

Chevy would welcome Montague informing the Soviet that he'd lived up to his responsibilities. "Yes, thank you kindly. I'm not sure how I earned that, though."

Kendall assembled a grandfather's gentle smile. Was it natural, or had he learned that expression climbing the hierarchy? "A specialist put into an active role experiences a great deal of stress and distress. You bore both well. It speaks well to both your character and to your abilities outside the laboratory."

Did this Kendall have any idea what Chevy did? Probably not. He was the lord, he didn't have to concern himself with the minutiae of individual peasants. He knew better than to argue with authorities, and he'd welcome whatever a *positive note* meant. Chevy nodded a thanks.

"And you played your role very well, Redding," Kendall said. "You got discussion rolling when it stalled."

"Sir," Redding said with a hint of a smile. Maybe Chevy should invite her to play poker.

Kendall said, "Initial reports from Montevideo state that Doctor Samuel Sharam was a mathematician at the University of Montana in Helena at the beginning of the first Energy War. His work was neglected for centuries."

Understandable. While everyone wrote papers, sufficiently brilliant mathematicians relied upon their students to spread their discoveries. Sharam probably had a handful of students all over the world, but the bulk of those current with his work had died with him.

Kendall said, "Montague built upon Sharam's work in computing the first Portal." His lips tightened. "This Caleb Mason's claim is credible."

"So they're human?" Redding said.

"Both unproven and irrelevant," Kendall said. "They could be knowledgeable aliens. Even if everything Mason said was factual, they have lived under alien physics for generations. Their humanity, or lack thereof, is irrelevant in matters of trust. For all practical purposes, they are aliens. Protecting Earth from alien influence is our ultimate priority. That's a rule as strong as not letting anyone who understands the Portal leave Earth."

Chevy kept his face still. It's not that he understood Portal maths before leaving Earth, and he didn't understand them now. Insight he'd gained from the differences between Earth math and Tritium math weren't the same as *understanding*.

Kendall said, "We must know more, however." His attention switched from Redding's face to Chevy's.

Chevy willed himself to relax.

Kendall said, "Montevideo has extended both your assignments."

Chevy's heart plunged. "Wait a moment! You can't—I'm not—"

Redding said nothing.

"I understand you're eager to return to Earth," Kendall said. "Rest assured, I will arrange that as quickly as possible. But Tritium is operating at maximum capacity, and we don't have enough staff to handle an alien contact on top of the regular tritium shipments. Tritium decay means that Earth averages a thirty day supply."

Chevy gritted his teeth. He did not need this ignorant authoritarian to explain the economic and energy production implications of a twelve-year half-life to him.

Kendall said, "Supply instability would lead to global panic. The staff dedicated to tritium production and research projects must remain so. We can and will pull Tritium-trained staff from Montague assignments in other universes, but they will require acclimation time."

Chevy felt his hopes burning to ash. "With all respect, *sir*—"

Kendall held up a hand, palm facing Chevy. "Montague's alien contact specialist arrives tomorrow. We literally have nobody else available to assist him. That leaves the two of you."

Redding's face erupted into a smile. She *was* a maniac.

"Mister Gunfire," Kendall said. "I am aware of your unhappiness here. Do this well, and I will personally recommend you for an assignment more suited to your psychological profile."

Typical authoritarian. *Do what you're told and we'll torture you less later.* Chevy knew his contract with Montague better than he knew any Montague procedure, though. Within his five year contract, they had the right to put him anywhere they wanted. Not trusting himself to speak, he gave a single nod.

Chevy had trusted the Texas Datacore his whole life. Even when his freshman year of university had repeatedly driven him to tears, he hadn't abandoned its wisdom.

His gut whispered that perhaps his most essential trust was misplaced.

11

The conference room's padded chair felt like heaven.

I'd worked my last shift as a tritium cannister inspector, then suited up and gone outside to engrave the world of Tritium into my memory. That had turned into a bonus work session. A quick shower, downing a liter of water, and clean clothes had revitalized me enough to answer President Kendall's summons, but I needed a solid meal and about nine hours sleep before I did anything else.

But the thought of Madre Redding's little girl working on an alien contact team poured fresh life in my tired bones and made me willing to keep my sore feet in my boots a little longer.

At least the conference room was quiet. The only sound was the gentle hiss of air in the vents. The blank wall screens demanded nothing. The polished stone table held no papers for me to read, and the air tasted great after the pressure suit. I only had to cope with President Kendall and Mister Gunfire.

President Kendall didn't look tired at all, even this close to the end of Day Shift. He shifted his attention from the sputtering Gunfire. Kendall met my eyes and said, "Redding. I have no doubt of your eagerness."

I let my smile flash free. "Yes, sir."

Kendall said, "Initial negotiations with an alien race are highly delicate. This is not a matter of office politics or solving a murder. You will remain in Security, but you answer to the contact specialist and are expected to obey his orders completely."

Translation: pull any stunts and get booted back to Earth. I pulled the smile back inside. "Sir."

Kendall studied my face. "You might be happy about this opportunity, but this is serious."

Was I still smiling a little? I straightened my face. "I understand." I wasn't dumb enough to say *what could go wrong*, but it's not like the alien contact specialist would drop me into a bottomless pit or abandon me in an exploding space station or surround me with infuriated antimatter-propelled chipmunks. I failed at playing politics, but I could back someone else up. "The specialist is in complete charge."

Kendall said, "Tritium has huge projects coming up right now. They've taken me years to arrange. The timing here is suspicious. You will file a full report every evening, on everything." His gaze flicked to Gunfire. "No matter how trivial."

Gunfire still looked stunned. The man had a body for adventure and shoulders for trouble. He spoke English with almost as much North American drawl as the aliens. I would expect someone who looked like him to pull his six-shooter and charge forward, but his face said he wanted nothing more than to run home. How could anyone who worked for Montague *not* want to meet aliens?

"Yes, sir," I said.

"I understand," Gunfire said.

Kendall glanced at his watch and gave the time-is-up grimace. "One last thing. Tritium is at housing capacity, and the new sublevel won't be ready until next year. Your quarters have already been reallocated to people replacing you on your regular duties. We've made special arrangements."

"Yes, sir," I said. "I'm sure we'll be fine anywhere safer than an airlock."

Kendall blinked. "As you mentioned that…"

12

Anticipation repelled the bad dreams. A solid night's sleep and two eggs scrambled with cheese and peppers made me ready to take on yet another universe, so I hauled my box of clothes and personal items to the designated elevator and hit the lowest of the six buttons. The one with a temporary label reading CONSTRUCTION – AUTHORIZED PERSONNEL ONLY.

Shifting gravity makes an elevator downright unpleasant. I burped salsa before the doors opened onto the locker room.

The pressure suit locker room was the size of the three-bedroom apartment I'd grown up in. Everything was so new it still gleamed. Tall aluminum lockers lined the left and right wall, where people going outside could store their clothes, datalinks and other detritus before going through the airtight door to Pressure Suit Storage and the surface elevator. A long wooden bench in front of the lockers provided short-term seating. We had one large wall screen and a smaller terminal. The off-white wall panels on the back wall hadn't yet been installed, so instead of a second terminal we got to see the meticulous brickwork of the outer barricade separating Earth and Tritium matter. Small circular lights in the ceiling threw every detail in sharp relief. The air held hints of fresh glue, new plastic, and curing mortar.

What wasn't standard was the oxygen reclaimator humming in the corner by the entrance to the toilets and showers, or the tiny fans hastily clipped here and there to shove the air around.

The double-width doors leading further into the level were standard, but the wheeled rack of hard-worn extra-reinforced pressure suits and tool kits next to it didn't belong here. The construction crew normally came down, passed through the decontamination airlock beyond those doors, and went out to forcibly gouge more work space from the island's basalt.

The aliens' arrival had scrambled Tritium's entire schedule and shut down construction. The maze of tunnels and caverns down here was already legendary. Montague didn't need to rush to expand it.

I had no idea why the stack of two dozen or so lightweight cots with pillows and blankets sat in the far corner, but we'd take advantage of them.

I grimaced. If I wanted privacy, I could always sleep in the toilets. Or, if I got desperate, through the door to the external suit area.

Working alien contact was worth a few inconveniences. It beat the times when the folks had taken us kids to visit relatives and I'd slept in the dining room wrapped in a blanket. Mason and the other aliens promised to be far more interesting than Aunt Selene. And on a square meter basis, the three of us had bigger quarters than anyone else in Tritium.

I dropped my box on the bench and took a cot. First in meant I got first pick. I considered taking a spot by the air reclaimator, where the gentle white noise would drown out other people's snoring. Instead, I grimaced and plopped the cot down next to the doors leading to Pressure Suit Storage.

When everything with the aliens went bad, I would want to get outside fast.

If. *If* everything went bad.

But when.

And hey, it wasn't *in* an airlock. We were merely next to the airlock.

Standing up the cot was slightly less difficult than dental self-extraction, but I managed. I had just claimed the locker closest to my cot when the elevator dinged and Gunfire stepped out. Dark bags hung beneath his bloodshot eyes. His hair hung over his ears, but he'd pretty clearly swiped it twice with a comb this morning and called it done. Seeing me, he frowned. "Kendall was serious."

I set my stack of uniform shirts on the second shelf from the top of the locker. "A universe president doesn't have time for jokes. Or pranks." He seemed to be taking his time studying the locker room so I added, "Pick a spot for your cot."

Gunfire shook his head, but trudged to set his box on the opposite end of the bench from me. Personal space issues, maybe. "I guess here?"

"Sure." Pants on the bottom shelf, same as always. "They're cots. They move. If you snore too bad, we can put you in the construction airlock."

I hoped he'd offer some banter back, like *or you can move into the toilets* or even *I have so much gas, tomorrow morning you'll tell me to sleep in a pressure suit.* Instead, he trudged like a condemned man to grab a cot.

This was going to be fun. Gunfire had been sociable enough the night before, but the assignment extension had sucked out his life. He had to be crazy competent to have gotten this job. "What made you join Montague, anyway?"

Gunfire opened the cot easily enough. "My services were traded."

My hands paused. "You mean, you don't work for Montague?"

He sighed. "Working *for* anyone is an authoritarian concept. I'm working *with* your company for the next four years and eighty-one days."

Montague hired external contractors, but only for on-Earth jobs like drivers and chefs. And that was a strangely specific time period. I added in the initial three-month training period and a standard six month Tritium assignment. "You're with us for five years total?"

Gunfire had obviously argued with a cot before and won. "Yes."

I didn't mind sharing quarters. I minded sharing space with hostile people. Whatever had made Gunfire curt and unhappy was the next worse thing. "I didn't know Montague hired people short-term like that."

"I wasn't hired," Gunfire said. "The Soviet traded me."

Someone from a Communist country? Not an immigrant from one to a more open society, but a full-on citizen? I'd only been with Montague for a couple years, but I had never met such an employee.

Irritation flared. I had fought like mad to get my Criminal Justice degree and all the add-ons I needed for this job, endured an exhausting chain of interviews and tests, and this man had just walked in? No, it couldn't be that simple. If the company had traded something for Gunfire's services, it had to be because they *wanted* Gunfire in particular.

Gunfire had had no choice but to obey his country's leaders. Or leave his home.

"You must be one of the best mathematicians in the world, then," I said.

Gunfire opened the locker right by his cot and stuffed his shirts in the top shelf. "Reckon I am at that. If I'd've known I'd end up here, maybe I would've thrown a couple tests."

I'd done all that work so I could see the universes.

What would it be like to be ordered to leave not only your home, but your universe? Plus, he'd been expecting to go back to Earth today. Instead, we were here until President Kendall got replacements in from other universes.

I loved new experiences. Gunfire obviously didn't.

Empty reassurances and mindless platitudes wouldn't help. Anyone so good at maths that Montague tracked him down and dragged him into the company would be smart enough to recognize hollow words. I settled on, "Montague doesn't waste skill, and you're far more valuable doing complicated maths than helping out a specialist. They'll replace you as soon as they possibly can, just to get you doing the work that only you can do."

Gunfire glanced up. Was that a little spark in his eyes? "You think so?"

I laughed. "I *know* so. Me, I'm not just Security, I'm at the bottom. The only thing I specialize in is ugly, boring jobs." And breaking the rules when things go wrong. "If the specialist likes me, they'll keep me on bodyguard duty. But the one thing Montague doesn't do is waste money. I'm sure you weren't cheap."

Gunfire chuckled—sadly, but a chuckle. "I gotta tell you, I don't know how much. Money is—well, Soviet Texas doesn't much hold with that stuff."

Money? Almost nobody used old-fashioned coins and bills. Oh, right. In most of the world, people only got jobs if they wanted to do the work, but Soviet Texas was legendary for giving every citizen an equal cut of the nation's proceeds no matter what they did. "The thing to do right now is to keep your mind on the job. When this specialist shows up, we follow their instructions."

Gunfire nodded without looking at me, but at least his mood seemed lighter.

Maybe this would work out. Box empty, I took it back to my cot and flipped it over to use as a bedside table. The small framed photograph of my parents and me went on top of it. Nothing says home like a family picture. I printed a new one in every universe I visited, physics permitting. I tugged the cot to a perfect position beside the box.

Something gouged the pad of my index finger.

I jerked it back.

The gouge turned to a tiny pain.

I'd scratched the finger on one of the cot frame's metal brackets. Nothing major. It'd heal in a couple of days.

But even as I looked at the scratch, my heart was beating too hard, my breath quickening.

My mind flashed back to a horrible moment most of a year ago, when medical techs had peeled me out of a high-gravity suit and I'd seen just how badly I'd cooked the meat of that hand. Not seared. Cooked. They'd hit me with painkillers before even starting to strip the suit away, so I hadn't felt much physical pain at the time. It had still gutted me.

The clench in my gut returned at times like this.

I let myself sink to one knee and put the other hand on the upturned box, willing myself to let the other details of that memory pass by. Just like the therapist said. A minor scratch. That was all. No need to think of any of the other parts of that memory. They were past.

Seeing all the universes meant overcoming this foolish intrusive memory. It hadn't done any *real* damage to me. Nothing that couldn't be regrown.

After a few breaths, I rose to my feet. I took the first aid kit off its shelf. I washed both my hands, soaping and rinsing each twice. Then I applied a tiny swab of soothing antiseptic to the scratch, followed by a minuscule drop of antibiotic ointment.

A trauma patch on this tiny scratch would be more than overkill.

I still needed a moment to steer my hand to a simple self-adhesive finger bandage.

The datalink on my belt buzzed, just as the large wall screen chimed.

"Go ahead," I said.

Gunfire looked towards me, his fingers on his own datalink and eyebrows raised.

The screen remained dark, but over the room's speakers a vaguely familiar woman said, "Redding? Gunfire?"

"We're here," I said.

"This is Vice President Holden."

I grimaced. Holden had taken over Internal Operations a month or so ago, and was responsible for everything from the cafeteria to the sleeping quarters. This was probably where she told us that the cots were reserved for the construction workers who worked beyond the interior door in those heavy-duty pressure suits and we needed to sleep on the floor. "Yes, sir."

"President Kendall is busy, so he delegated me to pass on instructions."

My back flashed into tension, then relaxed into readiness for action. Routine instructions came through a datalink. I had never had this much attention from such high-ranking people.

My specialty in ugly, tedious jobs had taught me to sense trouble when it screeched to a halt in front of me and cast pebbles in my face. "Yes, sir."

"The alien contact specialist is delayed."

I tried to choke my disappointment before it showed on my face.

Before I could answer Holden said, "Redding, you are now point on alien contact."

Total shock paralyzed me.

Holden said, "Gunfire, you are to assist her."

"Sir." Gunfire might use the same tone to discuss a mold infestation.

I made myself breathe. "Sir?"

"It's not Portal maths, Redding," Holden said. "We just sent instructions to your datalink. Read your order sheet and get out there. Build up a little goodwill so that when the specialist gets here, they have something to start on."

"Yes, sir," I breathed.

The speakers went silent.

Don't get me wrong. Being part of an alien contact team thrilled me.

But my every instinct screamed this was every kind of wrong.

13

In the absence of further information, obey instructions.

I had about an hour to read the negotiation plan attached to my orders. It was detailed, but impersonal. "The negotiator shall not offer information on Earth beyond these three facts." "The negotiations will proceed in this order." Like I could command Mason to talk about certain topics in a specific order. I am an absolute master of the bad plan so I wasn't qualified to judge, but this plan looked logical and rational and achievable. Each proposed exchange built on the previous one. Certain exchanges were clustered, and could take place in any order so long as all were completed. Someone back on Earth had stayed up all night to work on this.

Yes, their night matched Tritium's night. Our working night, that is. Tritium's day is about twenty-nine hours. Most people stay in the tunnels all day, so we ignore the local sun and run on an Earth clock roughly synced to Montevideo. It's no different than the Lunar colonists who keep their home clock. Montague might have permanent staff scattered across many universes, but many of them have basically the same concept of "day shift." It cuts down on the sleep problems.

Today, it worked in my favor. When I finished reading my instructions and got outside, the sun was just rising. We were near the South Pole and the bay faces northeast, so we got to see the sun breach the horizon. The cliffs blocked evening light, so down by the bay night doesn't so much fall as plummet.

But sunrise is spectacular. The oversize sun looks huge during the day, but when it splits the horizon it seems monstrous, burning the purple sky into a haze of deep green split by teal-and-aquamarine clouds and casting its reflection across the opalescent ocean. The water was fairly still compared to yesterday, barely smashing against the reefs at all, and the lagoon looked tranquil.

"The negotiator"—that was me, I was The Negotiator—stood at the top of the stairs and prepared to negotiate like a fiend.

I took a deep breath of the suit's recycled air to still myself. This brand-new suit still smelled of plastic polymers with a hint of grease, and the pristine helmet looked transparent. It still hugged my legs too close and sagged at my butt, but you couldn't have everything. New or not the pressure suit's bulk weighed on me, and the upper straps supporting the life support pack rested in the most tender spots of my shoulders. I hadn't trained to wear this pack every day, but now I was getting on-duty physical training.

Why was it that Montague's training program covered everything except whatever I wound up doing? I understood that nobody could anticipate everything, but at a childish level it still felt unfair.

At least the gloves fit well. I wiggled my fingers to settle them further into the gloves, then picked up the ultralight folding chair next to me.

Next to me, Gunfire rolled his shoulders. He was probably trying to work out some of that same soreness.

Maybe tonight, if Medical had time, I'd request a shoulder massage. It'd do Gunfire some good too. If they didn't have time, they'd sure give me a muscle soother pill.

But right now, two alien humans or humanlike aliens sat on a log that had drifted around the world to end up on the black sand of this isolated beach. My bright orange raft sat high on the sand near them, but not so close that the small fire could harm it.

"You ready?" I said.

Gunfire's mouth became a thin line, and he nodded. "Yes, ma'am."

I should have crushed the *ma'am* business right away. I don't mind being recognized as a woman, but it's not relevant to my job. And the way he said it had traces of that paternalistic woman-on-a-pedestal sexism. This wasn't the moment to push his face in, though.

"Operations," I said. "Security Third Aidan Redding, we're about to go down to the beach."

"Ops," said Bakula.

"You drew radio duty again?" I said.

"Not quite," Bakula laughed. "It's not enough that I almost got to go down and meet the aliens. But because you failed to panic and I couldn't take your place, I got the pleasure of being your personal, dedicated op. I am on standby every moment that you are with our guests."

I smiled. "So whatever I ask for, you have to do."

"Don't push it, Redding," Bakula said.

Gunfire said, "If this goes well, we're going to want steak for dinner."

Fortunately I was looking away, so he didn't see my surprise.

"Steak?" Bakula said.

"You know," Gunfire said. "Steak. Cow."

"I don't think there's a cow in this whole universe," Bakula said. "Let alone anything I'd call a steak."

Hearing Gunfire offer something almost like banter lifted my spirits. Perhaps my words had helped him. I hadn't made any of that up either. Having a world-class mathematician as my flunky was as wasteful as having me take point on alien contact was senseless.

The orders in my datalink had put a veneer of sense over that, but still. Why me? I'd failed at politics before. I'd learned from those failures, yes. But surely someone more knowledgeable was available?

No time for pondering company policy. Management thought I could do it, or they would not have assigned me the work. I started for the stairs leading down to the lagoon. "We're heading down."

"Acknowledged," Bakula said.

The trudge down the stairs threatened to tire me out before we even started talking. The elevator had been put at the top of the cliff in case the water rose, but in the hundred-odd years since humanity had claimed this chunk of basalt even the worst storm hadn't cast waves taller than five meters. The gravity seemed to fluctuate a little less today than yesterday, but I still had to concentrate and time each step down with a trough of reduced gee.

Caleb Mason rose as we approached. He looked more relaxed than yesterday. I hoped that a night's sleep had done him as much good as it had me. "Howdy."

"Good morning," I said. "This is Maths Third Gunfire, my associate."

"No big delegation today?" Mason said.

I said, "My boss thought that since you and I had hit it off okay, maybe we'd chat for a while."

"Works for me." Mason jerked a thumb at the man with him. "This is my technologist, Oliver Carpenter."

Gunfire reached out a hand. "Mister Carpenter."

The first part of the orders. Let Gunfire take the first risk of touching an alien.

I hated letting someone else take risks. I didn't want anyone else to get hurt the way I had been. I was Security. Risks were my career.

I kept my mouth shut.

The dark-skinned Carpenter shook, his bare hand in Gunfire's glove.

Bakula murmured in my ear, "Biometrics and suit integrity unchanged." Carpenter hadn't punctured Gunfire's suit with a tiny needle and injected him with alien juice, or left a seed on his glove, or anything else we could detect.

I followed Gunfire's example, shaking Carpenter's hand and then Mason's before saying, "This suit is heavy. Mind if we have a seat?"

"Pull up a log and set a spell," Mason said, turning back towards his fire.

I set the folding chair as close to Mason but as far from the fire as I could manage. The unfolded chair looked almost nothing like an Earthly beach chair, but it eased the weight of the life support pack off my shoulders. Gunfire heaved a relieved breath as he sat.

"So," Mason said. "I told you folks some things last night. Gesture of good will and all. Thought you might be willing to return some of that."

"I've got instructions on that," I said. "There's questions I can answer, and some I can't."

Mason frowned. "How's your poker?"

"I never got the knack," I said.

"If poker's your game," Gunfire said, "I'm your man."

For a mathematician, Gunfire seemed dedicated to the Texas stereotype. I said, "I'm not allowed to gamble for information."

"Not the point," Mason said. "Was wondering about your poker face."

Did Gunfire suppress a snort at that? "I'll play fair," I said. "For example, you're probably wondering why Earth lost touch with you."

"Thought had crossed our minds once or twice," Carpenter said.

The orders sent to my datalink anticipated this question and gave a permitted answer. "Doctor Sharam died when the city of Helena suffered a large-scale disaster."

"War," Mason said.

I said nothing, as per orders.

Next to me, Gunfire's attention focused on Mason.

Mason said, "The Founders knew war was coming. It's why they were willing to go to a whole other universe. But we always kind of wondered."

"I cannot give more details than that at this time." My instructions ordered me to not give any details on the Energy War. Even if Mason and his companion were human, saying *those your ancestors left behind were nuked* would not go over well.

Mason nodded. "So you'll tell me when you can't answer. That's fair."

"You might be human," I said, "but even so, this is essentially a first contact situation. It will color our future relationship. Fairness is essential."

"We might be human?" Carpenter said. "Y'all might be human too."

I blinked. It hadn't occurred to me that Mason's crew might doubt that *we* were human.

"Ha!" Mason said. "Got you there. What's Earth like now?"

Another provided answer. "Almost five hundred countries, existing in peace."

Mason said, "Our war scared the war right out of you, I'm guessing?"

Not that war, sadly. Not the many wars that followed. The careful web of treaties and agreements that kept peace had demanded centuries. "Something like that. Almost everywhere in the world can meet the basic needs of their people."

"Almost?" Carpenter said.

"People have the right to choose the way they live," I said. "Sometimes, they choose poorly."

Mason grunted. "Can't help someone who digs the well next to the outhouse."

What? "With all this, maybe you could tell us how you came here?"

"Doctor Sharam's Gateway," Mason said.

"Not this universe," I said. "This island."

"Like my ship's name," Mason said. "Triangulation."

"On what?" I said.

"When the Founders arrived, they had radios," Carpenter said. "They wore out, and we only got our own built about five years ago. I have the dispatcher's diary, and she was pretty good about saying which frequencies were okay and which were full of sun-noise and stuff."

"Ah," I said. I could see the whole story, but first contact procedure and my instructions were clear. Just as with orders, don't anticipate. Let the aliens answer.

"Your workshop here makes all kinds of radio noise," Carpenter said. "So we came looking."

"That's a long time for a sailing trip," I said.

Mason's cheer evaporated. "This is the third expedition. It took that long to find a way down here, going round the shorelines and stuff. But now and then, in all that noise? It sure sounded like someone was speaking English. So we wanted to meet you."

I let out a deep breath. "Maybe I can help you out. Would you like a map of this world?"

14

Chevy wasn't sure what work he'd be doing, but he found out soon enough.

Climbing stairs. Going down stairs.

All day.

At least the brand-new locker room had all new pressure suits. Nobody else had sweated all over Chevy's suit.

Mason and Miss Redding sat on the beach and talked. Miss Redding used the screen attached to the front of her suit to display information as needed, but Mason and Carpenter didn't have any way to record it. Offering a map meant contacting Ops and having a laminate sent out the supply chute.

Then Chevy got to climb the stairs, pick it up, and haul it down.

By the time he returned, Miss Redding and Mason were negotiating the next information swap.

Chevy had read the orders, same as her. Montague would offer only three facts on Earth. It existed. Helena had been destroyed. The nations of Earth were at peace. But Montague drones had performed high-speed coarse-grained surveys of all of Tritium, analyzed plant, animal, and geological samples from most of the planet, and spent decades analyzing the biome. Drones had mapped the oceans floors and drilled the ice caps.

Mason's people knew of a single valley and river delta, and had explored a few hundred kilometers around it. On foot. Without the library they'd brought from Earth, they wouldn't have even been able to build their boat.

These amateur sailors had hugged the coast as long as they could, then crossed three hundred kilometers of open sea to reach the facility. Chevy knew a whole bunch of brave folks back home, but there was a whole lot of difference between meeting a challenge because you wanted to and journeying into the unknown. Mason's journey demanded a special kind of determination.

Mason's crew powered the *Triangulator*'s tube radio with a pedal generator. Miss Redding's lure of *we'll tell you where to find fossil fuels near your town if you tell us where your town is* proved irresistible. Once that was obtained, Mason and Carpenter exchanged what they knew of their library for plans for hand-powered coal mining gear. When Mason expressed concern that they were giving Montague all their knowledge but had no guarantee they would survive to return home, Miss Redding offered to send copies of everything to the village via a drone, along with a written report from Mason. The drone would wait for a response.

Chevy had no doubt that the drone would contain every sensor Montague could stuff into the chassis, along with full real-time telemetry.

Lunch was the suit's bottled water and protein pellets. He ate and drank just enough to keep himself going, in the name of diaper avoidance.

Chevy had to credit Miss Redding. They'd had less than an hour to read a sheaf of negotiating instructions. She didn't memorize them perfectly, but Bakula prompted her only twice all day. She charmed Mason with sincerity, helpful information, and the occasional polite refusal.

By the end of the day, he'd almost grown acclimated to Tritium's bizarre sky and alien waters. He had a few minutes now and then to study the tritium extraction plant and Mason's *Triangulator*, anchored out well past the reef.

By the end of the day, Miss Redding had agreed to let the eleven men of Mason's crew stay on the beach, so long as they didn't stray above the lowest level of basalt walkway. She even made it sound like she was doing them a favor, when the instructions stated *get all eleven aliens out of their boat overnight*. Tiny Montague drones would search the ship.

The entire negotiation was a stone cold manipulation. Montague had the power of knowledge, the power of technology, and a culture that offered moral cover to use them.

These courageous men had sailed two thousand kilometers to find them.

Every bit of this "negotiation" stank like a week-dead hog in high summer.

Chevy held his silence.

Miss Redding struck Chevy as a wholesome person. More than that, though. She'd taken the time to think things through so she could be kind to him. She'd reassured him, given him hope, and told him the truth. And by the fifteenth time he marched up those accursed stairs, he hoped she was right and that he was too valuable to spend any more of his five years climbing stairs in variable gravity.

He loved to hike mountains back home, sure. But this place's wobbly gravity made his legs rubbery. Back home he had the most comfortable boots and a self-raising tent and even a knife of Montague diffuse steel. Here, he had a generic pressure suit with boots just big enough that his feet slid around inside. If he wasn't careful, he'd have blisters.

At least the scrubber tortoises veered out of his way at his approach.

The sun had passed its zenith and started sinking by the time Mason and Miss Redding called a halt. Grateful, Chevy climbed the stairs one last time and rode the elevator all the way to the bottom. He dawdled in the pressure suit room, letting Miss Redding finish getting out of her gear when he'd gotten only his helmet off. Catching his breath gave him an excuse to keep his back turned. Maybe women got a bra as well as a diaper, but there wasn't any reason to not give her a little bit of dignity. He took the suit off slow enough to give her five minutes, pulled on his own shorts and T-shirt, then headed into the locker room.

This morning, seeing the locker room had dragged his spirits even further down. Now he welcomed the rows of drab metal lockers and the long benches. Montague lowered his standards every day. His folding cot was ready to welcome his aching bones, and it would be more comfortable than a sleeping bag on a rock shelf halfway up a mountain. The recycled air smelled cleaner than his suit after seven hours of hard wear, even if he'd defeated the need for the diaper.

Redding wasn't there. The sound of running water came through the open doorway to the shower.

Miss Redding had been kind, and combined with competence and brains it made her attractive. Chevy hadn't been with anyone since the night before departing for Montague. He owned his feelings, sure, but there was no need for him to make them more difficult. He forced his mind from anything involving showers and focused on the room instead.

That little cart over by the elevator was new.

It held six sealed meal trays. Three had his name and were labeled *dinner*, *breakfast*, *lunch*. Miss Redding had her own. Bottles of water, milk, and juice on to chill. Coffee and a pot, a microwave, and cutlery.

Suspicions rising, Chevy checked his datalink.

He and Miss Redding weren't just to sleep down here for lack of space.

They were ordered into isolation, to contain "possible alien influences."

That was the problem with authoritarians. They expected you to believe whatever they said. Chevy's whole body flushed with fresh sweat, and he fought to keep his teeth from grinding.

He needed to think. To cool off his rising temper. To consider calmly and logically if that anger was justified. And if so, to consider if he could or should do anything.

Time for his own shower. A long one, taking time to pound the strain of the life support pack out of his shoulders. Time for uninterrupted thought.

And time to figure out if Miss Redding was a fellow victim, or a manipulator.

15

I left the shower wearing cozy sweats, my feet moaning in bliss at the soft soles of my off-duty shoes. The ill-fitting pressure suit boots left my arches demanding comfort. Scrubbing my sweat away and steaming my sinuses clear had restored me. I had just enough time to get upstairs for my usual dinner shift.

I ached too much to prance, but I wanted to.

I'd followed orders. Complicated orders. People had laid out a path for negotiation, and despite my doubts I'd successfully followed it. I'd let the conversation meander naturally, but always brought it back to the next negotiating point without making Mason think I was leading him. Leading him too much, at least.

Yes, Mason wasn't the world's most experienced negotiator. The man was a coastal farmer. He captained the ship because sailing a skiff around the small islands beyond their river delta made him their greatest sailor. They'd found us because they wanted to welcome fellow humans to "their" "Anti-Earth" and improve life in their village.

Like Tritium, the village didn't merit a name. You needed two of something to name it.

Maybe the negotiations hadn't been Portal maths. But after the failure of my last political assignment, any success here felt fantastic.

So: join my Security teammates for dinner. Brag a little, take some ribbing. Ask how today's tritium inspections went, if anyone had found one of those house-sized Death Porcupines that lived near the equator lurking inside a twenty-liter tank.

I'd earned some serious dinner today. Maybe even dessert.

And it hadn't even cost me a hand.

Then back down to my cot. Maybe watch a serial episode or two. The Montague library didn't carry anything like *Voidlost*, but the newest remake of the Enola Holmes saga was pretty good.

If somehow the alien contact specialist couldn't get through by tomorrow, I would handle that too.

Gunfire was still scrubbing. When we'd been getting out of the pressure suits, I'd needed a moment to figure out he was waiting to give me a bit of privacy. He probably delayed his shower for the same reason.

You couldn't work Security for long without getting over the embarrassment of showing some skin, but he meant well. And I preferred when people erred on the side of civility.

I went to clip my datalink to the waist of my sweats, and saw the message light.

The isolation order didn't crush my spirits. Not quite. But I no longer wanted to prance.

I couldn't even call Jeebs or Charlaine for informal bragging. Gunfire and I were social pariahs, in case Mason had infected us with a toxic meme. The only idea I'd gotten from Mason was what life must have been like for humans hundreds of years before. We had cultural library access for entertainment, but even read-only access into the Montague operations network was suspended. If I needed anything, I could communicate with Bakula.

That kind of stung.

It's not that I needed to know how many tritium tanks had gone through the Portal and back to Earth, or check for my mother's weekly letter three days early, but that was different from being told I couldn't. That merely conversing with me might threaten Montague, and Earth.

They'd even sent dinner down. My favorite after a hard day, salmon pad Thai and radish-cucumber rice wine vinegar salad. Plus a chocolate-frosted brownie, a rare indulgence with my metabolism.

My triumph wasn't ruined. But it wasn't as delightful.

My stomach grumbled, but I decided to wait on Gunfire to eat. If I couldn't brag to my teammates, I'd better connect with my involuntary roommate. He spent a long time in the shower. Maybe the poor guy had waited for me to leave the pressure suit room because he'd had to use the diaper? Well, at least he'd turned his back.

And there wasn't any chance of a shoulder massage from Medical. The first aid kit had muscle soothers and lactic acid breakers, but they always left my limbs feeling a little floppy. Not that they made me weak, I just felt like I was. I started squeezing my own shoulders with the opposite hand, attacking the knots left by the life support pack.

Eventually Gunfire lumbered out, wearing the Montague-issued sweats and soft-soled shoes, finishing rubbing his short brown hair dry with a towel. The slobby sweats seemed to fit him better than the beige specialist uniform.

"Hi," I said.

"Hello again," Gunfire said.

"Any chance you saw our orders?"

Gunfire grimaced. "The ones where we're to stay right here?"

"Those are the ones."

"At least they didn't command us to stay in the restroom," he said.

"I thought we could eat dinner together," I said. "And since we don't have any access, maybe watch something."

"We earned dinner." Gunfire tossed his towel in the laundry bin and rubbed his hands over his face. "I'm about done with those stairs."

"You worked hard," I said. "Those suits and those life support packs are no joke. If you want, after dinner we can trade shoulder rubs. Mine are murder."

Hesitation flashed across his face.

I sighed. "Just a shoulder rub. This is not a cheesy trapped-together romance."

His hesitation lingered for half a beat. "My shoulders are all right, but the middle of my back feels a wreck."

"It's a deal. Let's eat."

Gunfire's dinner was hamburgers. Two of them. Enormous ones. With green beans and seasoned fried sliced potatoes. Probably the closest thing to a steak they had.

Stupid big people with their stupid metabolisms.

The only furniture was the cots and the long benches. We ate on the benches, meals spread between us. Gunfire studied his burgers before digging in. Maybe his earlier hesitation hadn't been about a shoulder rub so much as an innate reaction to anything. I charged in everywhere; Gunfire might be my opposite.

I'd gotten well into my pad Thai when Gunfire said, "How do you think today went?"

I swallowed. "I'm pretty happy with it."

He nodded, eyes looking off somewhere not in the room. "Didn't it seem a little strange to you?"

"Mason and Carpenter were careful with us, sure." I spun noodles around my fork. "I can't blame them. They thought they were the only people in this universe, then we show up."

"Not that." His jaw worked despite his empty mouth. "The way we were assigned this." He took a dainty bite of his burger.

"We had already met the aliens. We'd already been exposed." My glassy noodles were perfectly done.

"Look." Gunfire set his burger back on his platter. Yes, I had a plate and he got a platter. The genetic lottery is *so* unfair. "Montague Corporation is based in Montevideo. They have that whole campus full of buildings, each full of Portals to different universes."

"Right."

"Their headquarters is right there. Your leaders." I'd never heard anyone say the word *leaders* with such bizarre… contempt? "They have libraries and scholars within a few kilometers."

"Yes?" My tongue greeted the salmon like a long-lost sibling. I'd worked up a huge appetite.

"You can send a question through the Portal, and someone looks up the answer right away and sends it back."

"Sure. They support us."

Gunfire nodded. "Aliens are uncommon. You've met, what, fifteen aliens in all the universes you've explored?"

"Eighteen."

"So the alien contact specialists aren't running from first contact to first contact." Gunfire raised a hand to his chest and pointed a single finger up. "Aren't those specialists sitting in a library or a research center near your headquarters, thinking up new ways to communicate with aliens? Studying how past meetings went bad?"

"Sure."

"They probably have an Alien Alarm. It's like a fire alarm, except when it goes off everybody grabs their go-bag and runs for the right Portal. I bet they have a siren and everything."

I couldn't help a chuckle at the image. "They don't get many chances to work, no."

Gunfire lowered his hand, but leaned a few centimeters towards me. "Then why aren't they here?"

I paused.

Gunfire said, "I know the Portal here is right busy. You ship two hundred tritium tanks an hour, and empty tanks come back. But those specialists should have been here first thing this morning. If you were on the team, you should have been shoved into the back."

"I did fine," I said.

He waved a hand. "Sure you did. You got everything in our instructions just dandy. You even got a few extra facts out of Mason and his pal, I think. You were a right solid capitalist."

Was that an insult? Gunfire came from a Communist country. That had to be an insult. "I followed my instructions."

"You did," Gunfire said. "And even if Mason is a real human, someone who spends their whole life prepping to meet aliens would chew off their own leg off to get here. I don't know much about hierarchical systems, but like you said, you're the bottom of the pyramid. Other people wanted to talk to Mason. You and I, we shouldn't have been the people to go out there."

"The company has their reasons," I snarled. "Just because I don't know what they are, doesn't mean that they don't exist. That they aren't valid."

Gunfire studied my face, then gave a tiny nod. "You really don't know why."

"How would I know why?" I said.

"They're lying to us," Gunfire said.

"Why would they do that?" I said. "Everybody needs honest information to do their jobs."

"I don't know why," Gunfire said. "But I know that's why the Soviet banned corporations."

"I don't know what they tell you at home." I shook my head. "But this company doesn't run like that. It's in the charter. The concerns of all stakeholders are involved, including employees and customers. We're all in this together. Hiding information gets people killed."

"That's my worry."

I still had half my pad Thai left, but it no longer appealed. "I get that you don't want to be here," I said. "That's obvious. But that doesn't mean that Montague is trying to hurt you. Or trick you."

"President Kendall," Gunfire said. "He said that big things were coming. Big projects. But you haven't heard anything about them."

"So what?" I said.

"Not even gossip? Rumors?"

I drew a deep breath.

Then another.

Gunfire was from a society that didn't do business. They didn't explore. As far as I knew, Texans stayed inside their little country. The man had grown up in an insular society with no clue about how the real world worked. He was making up stories to gloss over his fears.

But I didn't want to listen to them.

"I have some reading to do," I said. "Maybe it's best if I finish dinner on my own."

16

A few extra pillows, piled where my cot met the wall, gave me a comfortable chair. Taking off the shoes and tucking my feet under the light blanket should have made me cozy. The oxygen reclaimator's reassuring hum hid the locker room's silence. The silence of an isolated room deep under the ground. Were we below Tritium's sea level?

I was in an alien universe. What did I want, a crackling fire like Mason's crew? Marshmallows on sticks?

Gunfire stood at the lone terminal, his datalink synced to the screen and fingers dancing across the keyboard. Bizarre mathematical notation flickered across the screen, faster than I could read. Good. Let the maths man math. Better that than letting his paranoia overwhelm him.

I needed calories. I finished my tasteless dinner, flicking through my datalink. Lots of things I needed to read. The latest regulations update. The new Poul-Henning Camerill historical novel I'd been waiting for, about the Indonesian Confederacy chasing down pirate fishermen.

Nothing held my attention long enough to even open.

The isolation made perfect sense. Protecting Earth was Montague's ultimate priority. If there was the tiniest chance that my conversation with Mason had contaminated me, had turned me into a timed explosive or a covert channel or any other sort of infiltrator, I needed to be isolated until the risk could be assessed.

I knew I was fine. The Montague staff didn't.

And I had gotten along with Mason. I should be on the contact team.

No, I hadn't heard anything about big projects coming up. Montague always had big projects. There was no bigger project than exploring and exploiting alien universes. Montague was the Biggest Projects Company. My assignment here had been tedious and repetitive, but it had let me focus on repairing my career. I'd demonstrated that I worked with my team, that I was not responsible for the mayhem of my previous assignments, that I had reacted to unfolding events. That I could follow instructions.

And they'd rewarded me with instructions, on how to negotiate with the aliens.

Follow the rules, get rewarded with opportunities.

Maybe I should give up on reading and go to serials instead. I'd told Gunfire I needed to read, but that was an excuse. He hadn't angered me, not quite, but I'd wanted to break off the discussion before he dragged me the rest of the way there. So what if he learned it had just been an excuse? Didn't he know that already?

Gunfire paused to devour what remained of his last burger. His eyes remained on the gibberish covering his terminal, and the fingers of his free hand twitched. Mathematical genius, still counting on his fingers?

Petty, Redding. You should be better than that. He'd made it clear he didn't want to be on Tritium, he didn't even want to work for Montague. He pretty much wanted the exact opposite of where he was.

But he had gotten two great big burgers, and I didn't have the heart to touch my chocolate-frosted brownie.

There was no reason I shouldn't be part of the contact team.

Sure, there were experienced negotiators upstairs. A project manager's entire job was to track resources and negotiate. Of the nine hundred and thirty six people—Montague people—on Tritium, we had a good dozen project managers. One of them could have gone with me.

Probably should have.

People arrived and left Tritium all the time. Most of us worked a six-month shift, but it could vary a few days either way. One of those managers, or someone else trained for negotiation, must have arrived in the last few days and could have been shifted off a brand-new project. Startup projects always had delays. They were built into the schedule. And "first contact" was an eternally valid excuse.

They must be working on something important, that's all.

Something more important than first contact.

Whatever that was. That I hadn't heard a word of.

I hadn't paid much attention to larger Tritium manners. I'd stuck with doing the best job I could. Tank inspection was tedious and boring and everything I needed to repair my record. I hadn't even asked about my next assignment, choosing to remain in the moment.

Montague was pretty good about informing people about their next assignment.

Maybe I didn't have one.

Perhaps they'd needed a tritium inspector, so I'd kept this more mundane assignment. But the therapist might have given me a down check. They might have decided I wasn't Montague material, or that I needed a permanent placement on Earth.

Foolishness. Montague operated openly. You knew what was happening.

Unless there was a reason you didn't.

The regrown portions of my hands itched. I should get more lotion.

No, I'd moisturized after my shower. Just my subconscious twitching.

Everything was fine.

Even if some project manager should have gone out with Gunfire and I.

Or more people from Security.

A visiting dignitary. A vice-president.

Someone. Anyone.

You were so excited at the opportunity, you didn't see the obvious.

You were frozen out long before the aliens even got here.

I huffed out a breath.

Maybe the company had known about Mason's village before they even arrived? That would have shown up on the maps. No, I'd looked at the survey. The drone survey lines were a hundred kilometers apart, and the village was between two of them. The microsat photographs taken when Montague had built their facility had captured the village from orbit, but you wouldn't know those were terraced mountainside farms unless you already knew they were there. Helena had been destroyed right when the Earth's ecosystem teetered, before the planet-scale environmental projects had started sucking carbon out of the air and cooling the planet back down. Even today, humanity relied on environmental engineering to keep Earth in balance. The villagers had learned Earth's lesson and built to fit the environment, coincidentally making them harder to see from orbit.

If Montague had nefarious intent towards Mason's village, they would have monitored it. They would have known about Mason's expedition. Our drones weren't armed, but the fastest ones pulled at a thousand kilometers an hour in atmosphere. If the company hadn't wanted the ship to reach the facility, it wouldn't have.

Therefore, Montague hadn't known about the village.

That left President Kendall's "big projects." That I didn't know about.

Big enough that I wasn't allowed to talk to my regular teammates.

I wasn't even supposed to be on Tritium anymore. My replacement should have arrived through the Portal at four AM today. I would have had a chance to nod in passing as I left.

So.

Montague HQ back in Montevideo had told Tritium President Kendall to keep Gunfire and me here. Would that be us in particular, or just a blanket *stop all departures and have the staff stand by to deal with first contact*? The latter felt more sensible. Headquarters didn't know I existed except as a random employee. My screwup hadn't been bad enough to attract that kind of attention.

"Aha." Gunfire's mutter wouldn't have been loud, except that the only other sound was the air reclaimator.

The isolation wasn't only political.

The Montague Corporation had brought certain personnel to Tritium to accomplish something. Normal.

Lying to me about it? Violating the company's openness standards? Not normal.

Putting me, an inexperienced security third, in charge of first contact? Even with extensive procedural support? I hated to admit the strangeness, but it was there.

I could ignore one abnormality.

I could ignore two small abnormalities.

Two major ones twisted in my gut.

Tritium, in every sense of the name, was vital to Earth's stability.

I yanked my feet out from the blanket to stand barefoot on the cool tile floor. "Fine, Gunfire." The words tasted bitter. "Something's wrong. Let's figure it out."

17

The locker room felt hollow. The off-white wall panels absorbed sounds the same way they hid scrapes and repelled stains, but I half expected every sound to echo. The air humming from the portable reclaimator tasted lifeless.

I sat on the bench by the lockers, one knee up so I could face Gunfire. My shoulders and back ached for the comparative comfort of the pillows piled on my abandoned cot, but I made myself sit straight.

Gunfire looked distracted, like half his brain was processing all those complicated maths. The expression didn't fit his athletic build. He settled on the bench an arm's reach away.

Start with the basics. "What do you think is happening?"

"I don't know," he said. "I only know it's wrong."

I kept my eyes from rolling. "You're this intent on a hunch?"

"I took both Organizational Behavior and Corporate Capitalism as undergrad electives. Thought I might become an oppositional economist, before I discovered operator algebra." Gunfire's lips tightened. "All I know is, what we did today doesn't fit with how businesses operate."

"Fine," I said. "Then tell me your theory."

Gunfire held up that pointing finger again. His entire tone changed, becoming more formal. "I will concede that Montague is a stakeholder-sensitive corporation. It is organized to both make a profit and serve a social good. Your information openness policy is a component of that. Your operations are designed to function securely even if someone knows the functional details."

I chewed that brain-load for a moment. When a scientist goes to grad school, are all communication skills surgically extracted? Or are specialists born without that ability? "Relying on secrecy doesn't work long-term."

Gunfire nodded. "Precisely. Secrets are of short-term benefit. So we are experiencing a short-term event."

"You taught at a university, didn't you?" I said.

"I taught first year abstract algebra. Why?"

I'd never even *heard* of abstract algebra. "Never mind. Go on."

"As far as we know, this universe is constant. The periods of highly fluctuating gravity are largely understood and overwhelmingly predictable. Earth's tritium needs are also predictable."

Did he have to spell out every obvious detail? "Right."

"The most obvious ongoing change is the slow rotation of facility personnel. And we have been isolated from regularly scheduled personnel."

I grimaced. "I hoped I was wrong."

Gunfire gave me his own frown. "The obvious reason to isolate us is for a scheduled policy violation."

Disgust filled me.

I understand that Montague is a business, but they're not one of those rapacious ones you get in corporate-libertarian countries. Montague has made the world a better place. They not only extended the human lifespan, but made people healthy and functional until near the end. The wealth of countless universes, most of them lacking intelligent life, had given humanity a golden age. People who didn't like life in any country on Earth, or who were incurably restless, could colonize other worlds.

Humanity couldn't reach the stars.

But thanks to Montague, we could reach other worlds.

Yes, I'm an idealist.

But Montague *worked*. Why would anyone jeopardize all that?

For that, we needed to know what policy was being violated. Was headquarters doing something to the people on Tritium? Or were local staff breaking policy?

"Any idea what policy?" I said.

"My ideas are all awful."

"How awful?"

"We now know people can prosper and reproduce in this universe," Gunfire said. "Perhaps we're the first new colonists. Perhaps we're breathing filtered outside air."

He was right. That was awful.

The only argument I had against that was my faith in the company, and that felt shaky at the moment.

I unclenched my jaw. "We need to know what they're doing."

Thankfully, Gunfire dropped the lecturing tone. "You seem friendly with Miss Bakula. Any chance she'd confide in you?"

I huffed out through my nose. "I like her. We've hung out a few times after shift. Vicious across a game table, but doesn't rub it in when she crushes you." I shook my head. "But if the company gave her the job of talking to me, it's because she can keep her mouth shut." I gave my head another shake to clear my thoughts. "What time were you supposed to go back today?"

Gunfire looked sad. "Six AM."

"Four AM for me. We were down here at eight AM. So whatever it was happened—"

Gunfire spoke with me. "After eight."

"What happened after eight o'clock? When did the next person hop the Portal?" I grimaced. "I wish we had ops net access."

"I checked," Gunfire said. "It's not just an access control list. With this decrepit software, I could break a measly ACL. It's as if the operations network is physically unplugged from this level."

My stomach tightened. They—whoever *they* were—weren't taking any chances.

Don't waste time lamenting what we've lost. Work with what we have. "Our orders said to begin suiting up at eleven."

What did we know? What questions were left? We'd gotten orders. We'd gotten a detailed negotiating plan—

Wait.

If everyone here was busy, then who had written that negotiating plan?

I grabbed my datalink. "Hang on a second."

A flick brought up our orders from this morning. "Hang on, look at this. The metadata on the negotiation plan. It was written by Swapneel Guangayang from Alien Contact, and the file's dated four AM today."

"You got a good plan," Gunfire said.

I nodded. "This Swapneel. He has almost no time to work on the plan. He stays up most the night working on it. His plan. He sends the completed plan to all involved parties, for comment, and probably goes to bed." I frowned. "You're a brainy type. If *you* were an alien contact specialist, and you were in charge of meeting aliens, would you have a flunky write your plan?"

Gunfire kept looking at his datalink, fingers flying to bring up the document. "Certainly not."

"Swapneel Guangayang expected to be negotiating." My throat tightened. "He expected to be here."

Gunfire said, "Get a little sleep. Reach the Portal to Tritium some time after eight AM. I spent an hour in your *Human Resources* when I arrived."

I didn't care for HR, but I wouldn't put that bizarre wholehearted contempt into the phrase. "He'd skip that today," I said. "He, and whoever was with him, they'd go right to the pressure suits. Maybe Kendall would meet him on the way and shake his hand or something."

"Travel is disrupted," Gunfire said.

My stomach verged on nausea. Tight fear trembled down my spine.

Something had happened to Tritium's Portal back to Earth.

And Earth hadn't expected it.

18

Chevy enjoyed discussing ideas. He even liked testing them. Mathematics wasn't proven until tested. He loved to test himself against Soviet Texas' rugged, desolate beauty. He felt certain there was connivery somewhere within Montague.

Even so: waiting until midnight, pillaging the construction tools, and prying open the elevator doors felt downright antisocial.

The light from the locker room enhanced the shadows, making the shaft seem bigger and deeper than it was. Flicking the flashlight beam around, it was only about four meters on a side, square, and walled in weighty orange bricks. Metal rails with regular square gaps filled each corner. Turning the flashlight down, the beam reflected off a metal hatch set in a brick floor maybe two or three meters down. Grease and ozone saturated the air.

A metal ladder was screwed into the brick right next to the door.

He was a mathematician. He shouldn't be climbing elevator shafts. Society depended on people following the rules. People who couldn't listen to simple rules like *don't play with heavy machines that aren't your responsibility* didn't deserve society's protection.

The Texas datacore couldn't have known this would happen. It had traded him for his mathematical services, not for elevator service. Not for Chevy to become an hero from an old-style combat fantasy. It would not expect him to dodge bullets.

"Better let me go first," Miss Redding said. Like Chevy, she'd put her Montague uniform back on. Hers was khaki rather than his pale brown, and those boots looked tough enough to wear up a mountain. She'd look perfectly professional, if it wasn't for the flashlight clipped to her pants with a retractable line. Plus, the half-meter prybar she'd hung on her belt so that it dangled by her side would be hard to explain.

Chevy's own belt felt light. They'd left their datalinks on the bench. If they were truly being isolated, taking the datalink out of this level would trigger an alarm.

It made him feel even more uncivil. Only antisocials were uncivil. Antisocials always got caught.

His datalink was used, true. He should have turned it in, when he should have returned to Earth. But walking around without it was just as exposing as walking around without clothing. There were places to do just that, but it wasn't in an office building. Not even the elevator shaft.

It wasn't real until he got on the ladder.

As he dithered, Miss Redding slipped past him and grabbed the ladder.

He'd lost the chance to be chivalrous. He was the bigger person—physically, at least. He should be the one standing on the ladder prying open the elevator door.

Instead, he waited for the next ebb of gravity and put a foot and a hand on the ladder.

The rungs felt greasy, but had a bizarre stickiness underneath the grease. Taking a hand off the rung required deliberately unrolling his grip. Maybe modern computers didn't function on Tritium, but modern non-slip textured metal worked just fine.

A second later, gravity surged up towards normal.

Chevy held his position, one foot on the locker room floor and one hand and foot on the ladder. Miss Redding kept right on clambering up like she climbed ladders in variable gravity every day.

On the light gravity, Chevy swung himself into the shaft.

Ascending each rung felt like choosing over and over again to be a pariah.

Neither of them knew the distance between levels of the facility. They might be two meters down. They might be a hundred. The constant gravity tides destroyed all sense of vertical motion.

Chevy tried not to stress. The climb would be as long as it was.

He'd thought they'd wait for gravity to ebb before ascending each rung. Miss Redding had other ideas, though. She wasn't ignoring the gravity so much as accepting it, and it let her take four rungs for each of Chevy's.

Texas had all kinds of tomgirls, sure. But Miss Redding would give even the good-ol'-est good ol' boy back home a whole heap of trouble.

Chevy tightened his gut and tried to keep up.

He failed.

Soviet Texas' contract with the Montague Corporation said Chevy would comply with all instructions. Montague, in turn, guaranteed to keep him safe. Chevy was breaking that contract right now. As far as Chevy was concerned, Montague had broken their side of the agreement first by not sending him back to Earth on time. He desperately hoped the Texas datacore would agree.

Texas didn't hold with antisocials.

Escaping the locker room might mean never going home again.

Miss Redding was about four meters above him when she stopped cold and fumbled for her prybar. Her light glistened off the back side of closed elevator doors.

Already there? Chevy glanced down. The wedged-open locker room doors were maybe five or six meters down. A healthy chunk of rock separated the levels, but not too much.

Redding slipped her prybar into a loop on the door and started cranking. A dim vertical line of light split the wall beside her.

Chevy didn't need to know you could crank elevator doors open from inside the shaft. He wasn't an elevator repair tech. If he knew that, if he was here without an invitation, and this wasn't his labor, it meant he was breaking the basic rules of society. It made him a common antisocial. Ridiculous, he knew, but those early lessons were wired deep in his brain. Besides, how many common antisocials perpetrated their offenses in alien universes?

He was an *uncommon* antisocial.

Door open, Miss Redding pulled the prybar from the door. The pale oval of her face flashed down at him, then she took a big step and swung out into the hall.

The worst part was almost over. A few meters up and he'd be back on a floor where normal people belonged.

Then he'd have to be antisocial again and hack a terminal.

Up beyond the doors, someone said, "Do not move."

Chevy froze.

A moment later, a light far brighter than his shone down from the open doorway and spotlighted him. "Gunfire. Come up here, and don't make a fuss. We don't want to tase you."

Yep. Chevy was now officially antisocial.

19

The elevator door opened onto the Suit Repair lab. Big enough for a half-court basketball game and filled with massive racks supporting half-assembled pressure suits like hard-used mannequins. A table by each offered meticulously racked tools and fittings for welding gas and water. Bins along the far wall contained enough spare parts to build a couple dozen suits from scratch.

And now it held five people threatening me with stunners.

People I knew. Montague Security people.

In the middle, Bakula had the bleary eyes of someone rousted out of bed. She was bigger than me, but who isn't? Her rumpled uniform said she'd been yanked from a sound sleep. I knew the other four in passing. They left the tritium shipping security station each morning as I checked in.

Bakula might look groggy, but these four night-shifters were wide awake. One peered down the elevator shaft, supervising Gunfire's climb.

My hands were greasy. The treads of my boots held traction, but each step left spots of grease on the tile.

"Bakula," I said.

"Redding," Bakula said. "Did you think your elevator door wasn't monitored?"

My face flushed hot.

Bakula said, "Drop the crowbar."

I opened my hand. The half-meter prybar clattered on the tile.

"What is going on?" No, too plaintive. Sound authoritative.

"We're doing good for a whole bunch of people," Bakula said.

"Are the two of us that much of a threat?" More demanding. Better.

Bakula shook her head. "You aren't. You're just in the wrong place at exactly the wrong time. I offered to talk to you, but Kendall said not to unless you made trouble."

"So talk," I said.

Bakula said. "First, we escort you to an empty storeroom and lock you in for your own safety. Then we'll fill you in."

Bakula's eyes looked past me and grew hard. I glanced back, and saw Gunfire stepping onto the floor. He had the build to make that climb without trouble, but sweat dotted the mathematician's unusually pale face, and traces of grease marked his uniform where he'd rubbed the ladder.

"Wait," I said. "This is about the maths nerd?"

"I haven't done anything," Gunfire said.

Bakula snapped, "Have you talked with this man? This human being?"

"Sure," I said. "We've been stuck together."

"He's only here because a machine told him he had to," Bakula said.

The woman holding a stunner on Gunfire said, "They don't need to know this." Her shirt bore the name ZACK.

"No, it's fine," Bakula said. "She'll work with us. You know this guy hates it here, right?"

I said, "That's pretty clear."

Gunfire's face tightened. "It's my responsibility to support my society and community."

"There are still thirty-one countries like his," Bakula said. "Places where you listen to a machine, or a church, or where a king owns you. Places like his."

"I could leave Texas if I wanted to," Gunfire said. "But why should I? Everybody's equal."

Bakula sneered, "I grew up in The Kingdom of Heaven on Earth. Those places? They teach you that you're living in perfection. They brainwash you." She took half a step towards me, eyes burning. "I left, and they declared me apostate. My own mom won't talk to me. And our *employer* sells them tritium same as any other country."

I coughed a laugh. "You want to choose our customers?"

"This is about what kinds of societies Montague supports," Bakula said. "They're supporting cults, and brainwashing, and treating people as things."

"And they let us keep our treaties." Gunfire's face had grown harder than I'd ever seen. "You'd shut down our cities, our schools. Environmental programs."

"Other countries would pressure you to open up," Bakula said. "You'd have freedom."

"We are the freest people on Earth," Gunfire said.

"You do what you're told," Zack sneered.

"Liberty without responsibility is not liberty!" Gunfire shouted.

I said, "You're telling all these countries start wars!"

"Everyone else will gang up on them," Bakula said. "They'll be crushed before they start."

I said, "So it'll be fast wars? All of them? Nobody will fight to the end?"

"You'll never convince them," said the man on the end. His shirt said he was Winters.

"What do you think we're going to do?" I said.

"It took years to get all the right people here at the right time," Bakula said. "We're not going to take any chances."

Years? Montague wasn't a military organization, but there wasn't a better description than *planned mutiny*.

I could see how it would work. Identify sympathetic employees in key positions. Every security person had assignments on Tritium, for the necessary but unexciting work of supervising and inspecting tritium shipments to Earth. Arrange for the loyalists to be rotated to other assignments, and for the mutineers to all be present simultaneously.

You might not need many departments to pull it off. Security for one, but the cooks and clerks wouldn't matter. Maybe the Portal guards. Maybe project managers. Some administrative staff and executive staff stayed on one assignment for years. Kendall would have had time to identify each person's sympathies and accumulate a staff.

Then the aliens arrived, and Montague's head office ordered that I stay.

A mutiny works much better when all the security people are on your side.

The other security people, Cheer and Lin, held silent. Cheer remained stoic, but Lin had a nervous twitch to his lip. The hand holding the stunner had a tiny wobble.

The worst problem with a mutiny is that it breaks discipline. When discipline breaks, nobody—including the mutineers—knows what's going to happen. Everybody's anxiety builds.

"Knock them out," Zack said. "Safest that way."

"Wait!" I said, holding out my open hands.

Quivering Lin shot me.

20

In universes where they work, Montague's preferred weapon is the stunner.

Stunners send a precisely tuned surge of electrical energy that scrambles voluntary nerves. The trigger is under the thumb, so you can use it bare-handed or in whatever environmental suit you need. They buzz when you pull the trigger, not because of the shot but because people need to know that you've fired. Shoot someone in the leg, and the leg goes numb. Get them in the torso, and their whole body gets sloppy.

Lin accidentally shot me in my left arm.

It felt like I'd poked a bare electrical line. Everything from my elbow down went tingly and numb. I jumped and gasped, coming down badly. Gravity caught me and I fell. My knees both cracked against the tile. My good hand crashed down on my pinky, triggering a flare of pain, then my palm smacked down and ground my wrist.

My heart hammered against my ribs. My ears whooshed.

The stunned arm hung off to my side. My hand lay limp.

My hand.

"Lin!" Bakula's shout sounded far away. "You idiot!"

I could see my hand. I couldn't feel it, though.

The fingers didn't twitch. It just lay there.

Like it had been whacked off.

Again.

Gray haze tainted my vision. All I could see were my curled fingers. They didn't even twitch.

Someone said something. I couldn't understand through the whoosh.

My *hand*.

Someone else's hand, a working hand, touched my shoulder.

Suddenly my vision contained a second object.

The prybar.

A hexagonal steel rod. Both ends pounded flat, with a notch in the middle to lever up nails. Half a meter long, not counting the part that curved back like a fish-hook.

A very heavy fish-hook.

I'm ashamed to say that my burning blood took over.

In one spinning motion I snatched the straight end, rose to my knees, and swung.

I'm not tall, but I exercise.

The curve of the prybar took one of them square in the gut. They bent over.

Everything in me shrieked that my left arm was dead, my hand was gone. My brain knew all the way to its bottom I was vulnerable, that I could be maimed and crippled and killed, and when my lizardine medulla screamed to fight I could do nothing but obey. A stunner buzzed but I was already striking the next security person, whoever they were, then I shoved to my feet against a gravity surge and jabbed the prybar at a face that got out of the way so I yanked it back and caught the back of a head with the crook and if I didn't stop screaming I'd pass out so I sucked in another breath and kept screaming loud enough to drown out the shouts.

They didn't have a chance.

Tritium was quiet. Security's duties here involve inspecting containers and outside surveillance. If you're lucky, you get hovercraft patrol. The island itself has no predators.

They had expected me to argue. Maybe struggle a little.

Not explode in brutality.

Every time I swung, my dead arm flopped and my terror grew.

Alarms blared. Outside my head.

Sweat drenched my khakis. I wobbled on my feet, and it had nothing to do with gravity. My breath came in fast, panicked gulps, and I could see my pulse in my vision. My last wild swipe with the prybar hit only air.

People in khaki uniforms lay around me.

Zack was groaning on the floor, hands fluttering near her knee. I'd broken her kneecap. Blood covered Cheer's face.

Lin was flat on his back, seemingly uninjured but not moving. Winters lay across him, groaning.

Bakula lay on her side, curled a little around her gut. Her eyes glanced at me, then over towards the elevator.

Gunfire stood there, a stunner in each hand. One pointed at me. The other down at Zack. His face had gone even more pale, but his grip was steady. He sounded like he was talking to a wild animal. "It's okay, Miss Redding. It'll all be okay. You're fine."

Revulsion filled me.

This was nothing like winning a sparring match. Yes, Zack could get his knee regenerated good as new, but I'd cracked Cheer in the head. Brain injury was permanent. And what had I done to Lin and Winters?

"You're done," Bakula wheezed.

I made my breathing slow.

"Done," Bakula gasped.

The blaring lockdown alarms told me he was right. More Security people were on their way.

Gunfire looked on the edge of panic, but the stunners didn't waver.

Their mutiny horrified me.

What I'd done horrified me more.

I could surrender. Say I'd panicked. Because I had. Let them take me away and lock me up. Was discipline so broken that they'd beat me up? Maybe. Or maybe Gunfire and I would be thrown in separate closets.

Get to the Portal and return to Earth? The Portal was the best guarded spot in any facility. Now they'd be extra cautious. Would the Portal even be working? Montague back on Earth could reopen the Portal any time, but could it be sabotaged from the Tritium side? That *Voidlost* episode—no, irrelevant, I didn't know near enough Portal theory to answer that. Might they have to open a new Portal elsewhere on this planet and have Disaster Response travel the hard way? Did Montague on Earth even have Tritium-capable vehicles available?

Too many questions. All panic.

Slow down.

Think.

President Kendall wouldn't have arranged a mutiny if he couldn't control the Portal.

Earth had only a month or two of tritium. More in some places, less in others. Tritium grew its own food. They might run out of hamburgers, but there'd be enough broccoli and tofu for everyone. Even if Tritium called a complete siege, it couldn't last too long.

Could I sabotage the mutiny from within? With cameras everywhere in the facility?

No.

But maybe I could do something from outside.

21

Holding people at gunpoint was archetypical antisocial. How had Chevy gone so wrong so fast? It's not that he planned it. He'd seen a stunner skitter across the floor and grabbed it. When the one man had turned to shoot him, Gunfire had shot first.

The Gunfires practiced with all sorts of firearms. It was family tradition. It was how they'd gotten their name. The stunner barely qualified as a weapon, but it did the trick well enough.

The part that most shocked Chevy was the way Miss Redding had gone berserk.

Not like a guy who had one drink too many and bumped into someone so he'd have an excuse to go outside and brawl it out. She'd fought with thoughtless savagery, overwhelming the other Montague people with a prybar and utter mania.

Chevy had wavered for a half a second before stunning a second guard. The guard had struck her head on the corner of a workbench on the way down, though. Even bleeding from her head, that blow looked safer than a whack with the prybar.

Putting her on the ground seemed kinder than letting Miss Redding crack her skull.

Miss Redding's breath heaved. One arm hung limp, while the other clutched the lethal prybar. She raised her eyes to Chevy's and tried to say something, but didn't have the breath.

Chevy tried to say something else calm and reassuring but Zack wheezed, "Both of you. Done."

She was in awful pain. Maybe it'd be kinder to stun her too?

Miss Redding tried again. "Gunfire. You can surrender. They'll lock you up. This is all my fault."

Her fault? Chevy had stunned two guards.

She panted, "Or, you can come with me."

"Where?" Chevy said.

"Nowhere to go," Zack said through her pain.

"They're listening," Miss Redding wheezed, "have to, trust me."

Everybody in Soviet Texas knew that one day the capitalists would attack. Chevy hadn't expected it within his lifetime, or to be right there when it happened. Had the Texas datacore predicted this? Had it thought that Soviet Texas needed him here?

Ridiculous. No datacore could predict this.

And if it could, it wouldn't have sent a mathematician.

"Can I help end this?" Chevy said. "Help my people?"

Miss Redding was getting her breath back. "We'll try."

Mathematician or not, Chevy had responsibilities. He took a deep breath. "Then I guess I'll trust you."

22

Years in Security, and I'd never had a real fight. Not like this.

I staggered back to the open doors to the elevator shaft, staying out of the reach of the broken people I'd attacked. My stomach was an acid pit, and my ribs ached for a breath I didn't have the time to take. Bizarre tensions rippled through my every muscle. My entire brain throbbed and pounded against the prison of my skull.

Was this what a real fight with people felt like? I'd never had one before. Not like this. I'd struggled. I'd dodged and weaved and distracted. I'd never gone knuckles-and-club with other human beings. My usable hand burned around the prybar. I wanted to throw the horrible thing away, but I needed it. I willed myself to relax, but my stunned arm hung like meat on a hook in a butcher's shop. Every time it wobbled, my heart throbbed harder.

No time to panic. It would recover in a few minutes.

Chevy watched me, both stunners pointed loosely at my fallen Security comrades. Fallen in more than one way. He still looked pale, but his tremble had stopped.

I needed to climb down and—no, I wasn't physically capable. I hated that.

I thrust the prybar at Chevy. "Here. We need this."

Chevy looked at his hands, shoved a stunner in his pocket, and took the prybar. Good.

My ribs resisted a deep breath. "Come on."

With only one working hand, I couldn't hold the flashlight. The ladder would be treacherous enough. I clicked it on, but left it hanging from its belt clip.

The elevator shaft yawned dark and hollow beneath me. The light spilling through the wedged-open doors down in the locker room seemed kilometers away. I forced my stubborn ribs to allow one deep breath before reaching around the edge for the ladder.

I caught myself watching my numb hand swing. The gravity surges made my arm a bizarre pendulum, addled by my own motions.

No. Stop it. Get on the ladder and climb, fast as you can.

Hopefully the mutineers weren't going to drop the elevator down on us before we got back down. My stupid, foolish, unnecessary panic attack might have infuriated them enough.

Fast as I could, I clambered down. The textured steel rungs helped me keep my grip despite the mechanical grease, but the light and heavy gravity made the ladder more treacherous. Chevy followed. He'd had trouble going up, but seemed more adept the other way. Or maybe he was just as terrified as me.

Stop that, too. Steady yourself. Fear-driven decisions make everything worse. Look at what you did up there.

No, that wasn't helpful either.

The flashlight wasn't as helpful as I'd hoped. It hung pointed down, sure, but it flailed at every rung, casting its spotlight against the walls, the floor, the tracks in each corner, and everything except the next rung down. I climbed entirely by touch.

It did help when the locker room light went out.

The mutineers had cut the power in our sanctuary.

I could see their thinking. Kill the power, shut down this elevator and the one in the pressure suit room. Lock us in a box and eventually, we'd surrender.

Chevy said "What—" and cut himself off.

"Keep going." My breath eased a touch, but now my diaphragm wanted to cramp. I pulled in the deepest breath I could in order to to flex it. A bad enough cramp could trap us.

The scattershot flashlight revealed when I reached the black pit of the locker room door. I held myself from racing too fast down those last few rungs, then stretched a leg over to get a foot on solid ground. The room was in total silence, full of a blackness the tiny flashlight only needled.

My heartbeat had steadied a hair. Sweat kept my khakis glued to me, but they were getting a little clammy. Even climbing down a ladder as fast as possible wasn't near as strenuous as that outbreak of absolute, uncontrolled panic. They were going to get cold and nasty soon.

I hoped to be out of them before that happened.

My entire left arm burst into pins and needles, setting my heart leaping again. Relief eased the tightness in my throat. The deadness wasn't permanent. Yes, I know stunners don't inflict permanent damage, but my medulla disagreed. My fingers wouldn't work yet, but I told myself they needed only a few minutes.

Chevy dropped down next to me. "Now what?" Without the air reclaimator's background noise, his words echoed.

I grimaced and shushed him. I had to let the flashlight retract on its line to grab his shoulder and pull him down enough that I could whisper right into his ear. He resisted for half a second, then relaxed into it. "Go back up so your feet are level with the top of the door." Even those quiet words seemed far too loud. "Stick the prybar in the elevator tracks, it'll slow them down."

As Chevy nodded, his ear brushed my lips. It felt inappropriate and weird.

I wanted to hang onto the feeling. It might be the last human contact I got for a while.

That done, I walked over to the pressure suits. Not the ones for outside. The construction suits.

My self-soothing tic of reading unnecessary manuals was about to pay off, or get us killed.

When we'd gone outside earlier today, Chevy had worn a men's large suit. The construction suits were built to the same sizes. The men's large were at the end of the rack. I shook my tingling arm, and felt my fingers slop against each other. I couldn't even wiggle them yet. I put the flashlight between my teeth and used my working arm to snap open the life support pack.

My eyes needed a moment to translate from the diagram in the manual to the three-dimensional full-color reality. The telemetry unit was right where it was supposed to be, though.

I unplugged it and closed the pack.

Now a woman's small. They had only one. Centuries of progress, and construction is still not only sexist but sizeist. Having found the first one, locating and pulling the telemetry unit from the second suit took only seconds.

Now the construction airlock door.

I could open both doors. Let native Tritium matter—waste air, dust, even bacteria and microscopic life—into the facility. Let slow poison creep up the elevator shaft and into the main air plant. I'd have to sabotage the mechanism to do it, but I had a whole pallet of heavy construction tools. They were mutineers. They threatened Earth's stability—not by error, not by avarice, but because they believed that it was the right thing to do. They deserved nothing less than the most subtle punishment I could devise.

My arm tingled more fiercely.

No. I couldn't do that. The temporary shock to my arm still had me shaky. I needed to be better than them.

It was nine hundred thirty-six of them against one of me. And Gunfire.

I needed to not escalate, until my last escalation.

Any strike must be decisive. Not petty.

The inner airlock door had a mechanical crank for power failures. It was mounted a little too high for me to work easily, but I got started.

"Security Third Redding." President Kendall, too loud, over a speaker.

23

The decontamination airlock crank was too big for my hand. I leaned into it and it began to turn.

"Security Third Bakula was under strict instructions not to harm you," Kendall said. They must not have killed all the power, only what we'd find useful. "Her team behaved in a threatening manner. I'll be writing all of them up for violating orders."

I choked back a laugh.

"Maths Third Gunfire," Kendall said. "You grabbed a stunner when it slid beside you and used it in panic. It was perfectly natural. We don't blame you."

A second later, a light spotlighted me.

I threw a hand up to shelter my eyes.

Gunfire came out of the darkness.

I waved him over and pointed at the crank.

Kendall said, "I do not wish any harm to either of you. If you'll agree to remain in isolation in your current location we will turn the power back on, send a supply of food down, and reactivate the entertainment library."

Once Gunfire had the inner door sliding open on its well-oiled track, I went to the tool locker. We had to have two fitting kits, one male and one female. I had no idea what else—no, I had some idea. I grabbed the largest shoulder bag from the rack and crammed six extra life support fuel cylinders into it. I'd carry that weight, over my tingling arm. The fingers were twitching, but not in my control.

Seeing the half dozen red-sheathed knives hanging on the inside of the door, my numb hand seemed to light up with pain. Diffused steel blades, so sharp they couldn't be made on Earth. I'd developed an intimate understanding of how sharp they were. Memory burned my hand. *Stabbing. Slicing. Fingers going white*—no!

Kendall spoke. I couldn't hear him over the whooshing in my ears.

I could not afford panic. Not now.

Yes, I had reason to avoid diffuse metal knives. Enough reason for the rest of my life.

They were attached to the door. Not coming at me. Not in someone's hand.

Whatever Kendall was saying, it sounded soothing.

I let his tones roll over me until I could breathe again, then turned my back on the knives in favor of the tool kits.

We could each manage one of the heavy tool kits, but which would be the most useful? Masonry kit? No. Electronics? Yes, Gunfire could carry that. Did he know any electronics? Maths people used computers, he had to know something. He was a big man, maybe he could carry both that and the life support cylinders. That way I could haul… the plumbing kit? The life support kit?

"It's the best offer you're going to get," Kendall said. "Perhaps you could don pressure suits and climb outside. We expect the current conditions to last as long as two weeks. Perhaps three. You cannot carry enough supplies to endure that long."

Kendall had a point. I picked the life support kit.

"If we wanted to harm you," Kendall said, "you would already be dead. We could put gas down there and you'd never know."

As if Tritium stocked gas. They could look up the recipe, but brewing it up would take time. Or did Medical have that much anesthesia on hand?

The moment Gunfire had the inner door open wide enough for me to carry toolkits through, I started ferrying them. The decontamination airlock had space for a dozen big people and a few pallets of bricks at the same time, but I dumped everything to the side of the inner door and scurried back in.

Kendall's voice sounded nothing but reasonable. "If you need anything further for your comfort, you have but to say so. Additionally, I'll inform headquarters that you both were actively loyal to their guidance."

The door opened wide enough to shove the pressure suit rack through.

It resisted my best shove, but Gunfire abandoned the door crank and put his shoulder into it.

"Mister Gunfire," Kendall said.

Gunfire hesitated.

"Your antipathy to Montague is well known. Understandable, even. I will add paying off your contract, in full, and returning you home as part of our settlement."

I could see the churn behind Gunfire's eyes. It wasn't even thought. More like lust.

If he surrendered, could I go on my own? I could. But anything I did would be more difficult. And Gunfire would share what he knew with the mutineers. Not that he knew anything. He couldn't. I didn't know anything yet.

I could twitch individual fingers. All the activity must have helped my arm. But if Kendall told Gunfire to slow me down, I didn't think I could manage with one arm. He even had both stunners.

"You are one of the people we're trying to help," Kendall said.

Gunfire's face hardened.

I couldn't understand wanting to live in a place where you lived the way a machine told you to do. A place that didn't even have money. But I could understand people not wanting you to live the way you chose to. There are reasons I don't see my parents as often as any of us would like.

That instant made me like Gunfire a whole lot more.

In one swift shove, Gunfire knocked the pressure suit rack through the airlock inner door.

"What do you hope to accomplish by refusing to discuss the matter?" Kendall said.

Inside the airlock, I set my flashlight on a shelf so the reflection of the metal ceiling would provide some bare illumination. I pointed at his suit, at the end of the rack, and ripped off my shirt. Getting that clamminess off my skin was a welcome if chilling relief.

He eyed me.

I grimaced. Gunfire didn't know anything about these pressure suits. Plus, he'd called me *Miss Redding*.

I sensed stupid sexist body shaming disguised as stupid chivalry.

I threw my shirt aside and whispered "Everything. Now."

Gunfire glanced at the tool kits, held up a finger, and slipped back through the airlock.

My grimace went to full-on gritted teeth, but I followed him.

Kendall droned on, giving us big pauses to answer.

Gunfire stood at the supply locker. His whole head moved with his eyes as he examined the shelves. It moved too slow. I wanted to slap him, but he reached for a crowbar.

He wanted a weapon. How had I not thought about that?

I shoved the shameful answer back down.

Then Gunfire's hand flickered away from the prybar towards the knives.

I shook my head without thinking.

Gunfire nodded and plucked two knives off the rack, one in each hand.

I grabbed his arm with my good hand. "Dangerous." The whisper was too loud, more of a hiss.

Gunfire eyed me, then rolled his free hand to put the knife flat in the palm of his hand.

His fingers moved so fast they blurred.

The knife rolled between his fingers, red sheath and all, fancy as a circus show. To be any more the Texas stereotype, the man would have to dig up some indigenous people to conquer.

Gunfire flipped the knife up.

Gravity ebbed, stretching the spinning blade's arc.

He missed the catch. The knife clattered to the ground. His face flushed.

My heart was beating too hard, but at least it hadn't exploded into overdrive.

I hated it, but I let go of Gunfire's arm. He knew how to use the blades, if he didn't get fancy.

Besides, he would hate the pressure suit's self-fitting catheters even more.

24

Montague's optional Tritium training had included a short video on Tritium construction, intended to reassure new staff that the facility architects had considered every aspect of safety. It hadn't been intended for *steal pressure suits and sneak out into the impenetrable maze of robot-dug tunnels*, but once you release information into the multiverse you can't control how miscreants use it.

Everything around us was squared-off smooth red brick, solidly mortared, stretching off further than the helmet lamp could penetrate. Heavy arches of brick and regularly placed slender columns supported the ceiling.

I had expected to see brick-laying robots, or mortar mixers, or even a heap of shovels and picks. Perhaps a few chairs for resting before going inside. Instead, the space was barren. The only sounds were the soft hiss of my air reclaimator and my own labored breathing.

While the cavern felt vacuous, my pressure suit felt uncomfortably alive. It had been custom fitted, but for someone named SIMMERS, not REDDING. Technically my size, the interior padding was worn wrong. Simmers had bigger legs than mine, but less seat. I had enough space in front of my chest for a family of happy squirrels, or two angry ones. The suit still carried a fecund aroma of Simmers' armpits. She ate garlic regularly, and worked hard and long enough to sweat it out every pore. The lingering hint of sweet perfume didn't help.

I still had my uniform in my arms. Without the pressure suit, I would have smelled my own stink. The mismatch of smells unsettled me. At least my aching left arm grudgingly obeyed my instructions.

Every ten seconds, the suit gave a soft beep. Text flashed in the side of the helmet, at the edge of my vision: TOTAL TELEMETRY FAILURE – RETURN IMMEDIATELY

Maybe after a day or two, I'd learn to ignore it.

Unlike the short-term pressure suits I'd worn before, construction suits were designed to be worn for extended periods of heavy labor. The helmet was the same shape, but the top, rear, and half the sides were armored. Knuckles, knees, elbows, and all the other obvious places you'd bump had an extra layer of thin, tough armor. The plumbing tool kit, designed for even weight distribution and to avoid clashing with the legs, fit around my waist.

I couldn't see Gunfire's face inside his helmet. Gunfire's name badge read NHUNG. For half a second, I had the bizarre feeling that the real Nhung was inside Gunfire's suit. It was ridiculous, I knew, but we were right in the part of the story where the audience shouted *no, don't go down there!* Did they even allow those movies in Soviet Texas?

Stop daydreaming, Redding. You don't have that kind of time.

The decontamination airlock's outer door gaped behind us. Next to the brick vault, the metal-lined walls looked friendly.

Without telemetry or a wire, Gunfire and I could only speak by touching helmets. I had the wire, but connecting us with a fragile two-meter line would slow us down and right now we needed distance.

Last step. I dropped my uniform in the slot where the airlock's outer door would slide shut.

Gunfire turned to me. The light on his helmet would have blinded me, but my helmet's dimmer automatically eclipsed it. He held up a single finger and marched back into the airlock.

"Hey!" I said.

Gunfire ignored what he couldn't hear, but he returned in about three seconds dragging the heavy rack of construction pressure suits. He left the whole rack in the doorway.

Okay. That was better than my flimsy clothes. I should have thought of that.

Then he pulled the knife off his belt.

My throat tightened when he pulled that diffused steel blade, but when he stabbed the first hanging suit through the side of the ribs I couldn't complain. Anything we could do to slow pursuit would help. Thirty seconds later, he had the blade sheathed.

I turned left from the airlock door, beckoned him to follow, and headed for bare tunnel.

It's not that I expected to go wandering through this level. I had no desire to argue with construction workers, or go beyond them and trip over rock-boring bots. I kept getting stuck in places I'd never intended to see, though, so I'd spent otherwise empty minutes scattered throughout my days studying plans for this level, the tritium extraction plant, the drone launch bay, and every other part of the facility.

I hadn't memorized everything. Part of me had expected that when everything went bad, I'd refresh my memory with my datalink. Taking my datalink out of isolation mode would let Kendall figure out exactly where we were. I had vague ideas of doing that and taping my datalink to a borer bot, or getting outside and feeding it to one of the squiddy things that lived in the water.

But for now, we made distance.

The regular gravity waves encourage you to set specific paces, sympathetic vibrations with your weight. To take a step every three or four seconds, lift on the heavy and set down on the light. You can do twice that, with a heavy left or heavy right. Vary your stride too much from the gravity waves, and you spend all your energy concentrating on your feet.

Gunfire did okay with the heavy left, even with the satchel of life support fuel hanging over his shoulder. The guy must have kept up on his exercise.

I lengthened my stride, trying to match him.

The familiar motion accomplished what my willpower could not. My lungs relaxed and opened. My pulse settled to a steady rhythm. The tension of hand-chopping knives in darkness faded.

Don't think. Just move.

I turned my head to check on Gunfire behind me. The helmet's armor stretched too far forward for a casual over-the-shoulder glance. I turned my steps, lost the rhythm, and almost tripped on the heavy. I recovered, barely, staggering to a stop.

Gunfire was at my side in a second, arms outstretched as if to catch me.

I held up a hand and stopped. When he stopped, I took hold of his shoulder and eased my faceplate into contact with his. "Can you hear me?"

His reply sounded like it came through a closed interior door. "Yes, ma'am."

Ma'am? He was under as much stress as me. I let it slide. "Stay next to me, so—" I can watch you "—we can watch each other."

"Yes, ma'am." For someone stuck in abandoned caverns in an alien universe, Gunfire sounded more energetic that he had over dinner all those hours ago.

My stomach grumbled. I wished I'd eaten my brownie. "Do you think you can handle double heavy?" Two steps on the heavy, two on the light.

"I'll give it a shot."

Texans were good shots. Was that Texan for yes? "If you have to stop, raise a hand."

"Yes, ma'am."

We'd have to discuss that, when time permitted.

For now, we ran into the darkness.

25

I'd spent a day negotiating with aliens. I'd had a few hours rest, then at midnight gotten into the most awful fight of my life. Because I broke under pressure.

Then we'd started running double heavy.

Double heavy takes more than fast feet. It demands attention to gravity's slow, constant change. It's not enough to set a cadence based on a song or a rhythm. You must precisely match the gravity. One step on the peak. One step as gravity drops. One step on the light. One step on the way up. One leg gets the worst and the best, while the other gets a steady average.

You'd think the fatigue would even out. You'd be wrong. Variable gravity wears on the heavy leg. Every so often you have to skip a step to switch legs.

Exhausting.

Get the rhythm wrong, and it's like stepping on a stair that isn't there. You can break an ankle easily.

One of the Security women who'd rotated out had demonstrated a triple heavy stride that ate ground and spread the weight evenly. It looked like a quick-step march rather than a run. Administration had banned the contest to invent the quadruple heavy after the third broken bone, but people still tried.

The bricks seemed to go on forever. Was the island even this large? We had to be beneath sea level, didn't we? The vaulted hall gave no clue as to distances, but I felt certain that this level would be larger than any other.

Maybe time would help. My suit declared it was one sixteen AM. On Earth I broke three minutes in a kilometer sprint. A double heavy wasn't that fast. If I assumed—

My foot came down too hard, slipping inside my boot.

No maths. Not right now.

Stay in the moment. Watch the heavy and the light.

Four minutes of double heavy got us to a curving brick wall. I veered left. Gunfire followed my lead.

Another minute brought us to the construction site.

A metal doorframe almost three meters square had been bricked into the wall. Above the frame, missing pieces of wall and ceiling revealed the hollow space beyond. Two pallets of bricks sat nearby, with a similar pallet of mortar and a two-wheel mixer almost big enough for me to climb into. An electric barrow held an assortment of trowels, picks, and sledges. A massive aluminum door that looked too large for the frame loomed from the edge of my helmet lamp's reach.

Most attractive were the three folding chairs, engineered to take the life support pack's weight off my back.

No, I was running for my life. My stunned arm worked, mostly, but the bone-deep ache discouraged me from lugging extra weight. The chairs were light, but— no. If I could carry more, I should have brought life support fuel.

Cool breeze brushed my forehead. The suit had sensed my sweat and increased airflow.

In a day or two, the smell was going to be spectacular. Maybe I'd be lucky and my nose would go numb.

I wasn't so foolish as to try to double-heavy through the doorframe.

The floor beyond was machine-smoothed basalt, left unpolished so boots would have traction. I took a moment to look around, letting my lungs suck in air.

The brick barrier stood about three meters from a gently curved stone wall that absorbed most light. It rose to a ceiling eight or nine meters overhead. The helmet light wasn't enough to capture even a fraction of the chamber's overwhelming presence, but I did glimpse a tunnel further out.

My lungs ached for air, so I touched my helmet to Gunfire's. "How are you doing?"

"Fair to middling." He sounded less out of breath than I did, satchel of life support fuel and all. Maybe we could have taken more. "Where are we going?"

I sucked down the cool air filling my helmet. "We can talk soon, but right now we need more distance. Stay next to me. Raise your hand if you have trouble."

"You too, ma'am."

I pushed back my annoyance and headed for the tunnels.

The borer bots left tunnels about five meters wide. Other than the floor, the tunnels lacked straight lines. The bots searched out the weakest basalt, leaving the strongest to support the immense weight overhead, creating slow curves. Whenever they branched, reflective arrows marked EXIT pointed back the way we'd came. I'd seen maps of the tunnels but I'd decided not to memorize the spaghetti tangle, so I chose routes at random. One tunnel we passed spiraled up and down, granting access to other levels.

We emerged into another cavern. Distant columns of basalt as big around as my quarters reflected shreds of light. Beyond them, darkness swallowed everything. It felt like one of those ancient European cathedrals, where you step inside and feel insignificant in the face of the universe.

I held up a hand to stop Gunfire, turned, and retreated to the previous intersection.

Had I misremembered? Or were the side caverns less common than they'd looked on the diagram? Perhaps this level had none?

I was exhausted. My legs felt as spaghetti as the map of the tunnels, and if I kept going, they'd get just as tangled. I decided that if we didn't find one by two AM, we'd have to stop wherever we were.

Thankfully, we found an alcove with nine minutes to spare.

A small borer bot had carved a closet out of a tunnel's side. One day, it would shelter equipment. The door was just wide enough to walk through in a pressure suit, but past that it widened out a few meters each way. It was the closest thing to a hiding spot we would find down here. It wouldn't protect us from a determined search team, but casual inspectors wouldn't find us.

I raised a hand to stop Gunfire and bent to put my hands on my knees. The shifting of the life support pack weight from high on my shoulders to my hips felt almost as good as taking the whole thing off. For a moment, I concentrated on sucking air.

Next to me, Gunfire put a supportive hand on the wall. I felt bizarrely pleased that the big guy hadn't found this easy. If I was worn and tired, at least I wasn't alone.

I squashed the human but unkind impulse. Gunfire might have been better off surrendering.

Me, I couldn't imagine surrendering to mutineers.

Montague had any number of forums for employees to raise concerns. An organization like ours, even the most successful one in history, only succeeded when everyone agreed to work together. Yet Kendall had scrounged together enough disaffected people to stage a full out mutiny?

This wasn't the time for anger. We had a hiding place, tenuous as it was. This was the time to think.

Cooling sweat dripped into my eyes. I blinked in annoyance. Full-featured pressure suits, and they didn't have any way to wipe your eyes.

When I had my breath under control, I pulled the emergency comms line out of its pocket. It was longer than I remembered, three meters instead of two, but I still wouldn't want to run with it plugged it. If one of us tripped the flimsy connectors at each end might break off or damage the port. I plugged myself in, waved for Gunfire's attention, and hooked him up.

"Can you hear me?"

"Sure," Gunfire wheezed.

At least I recovered more quickly than he did. "We can talk over the hard line. Radio they'd hear."

"What's the plan?" Gunfire asked.

Asking the master of bad plans for a plan? "Now we think things through." I took my own deep breath. "Either we take a nap and stop the mutiny, or surrender."

26

The closet carved in basalt was only about six meters on a side. Snug enough that our helmet lights showed it all, but large enough that we could stretch out. My body heat had reinvigorated the garlic sweat of my suit's owner, blending into a miasma that threatened to scorch my nose hair. The life support pack's weight ground at my shoulders, squeezing me down even shorter.

And maybe I'd grown accustomed to the unending gravity waves, but now that we'd stopped running at double heavy my muscles felt like pudding.

I took a sip of water. It tasted stale and delicious. I swished it around my mouth, trying to rinse away the flat copper tastes of fear and adrenaline before swallowing. My body ached for more, but guzzling wouldn't help.

"I didn't run away with you to turn around and surrender," Gunfire said.

"Neither did I," I said. "We need to think. We're both tired. Casual inspection won't see us. Let's get these packs off our backs and rest."

I helped Gunfire heave his life support pack off his shoulders, taking care to keep the hose connected. The manual said we could disconnect the hose temporarily, or even swap in a longer hose, but I didn't feel like trying it. He groaned when the pack came off.

With his height he had an easier time hoisting my pack off. For a split second, losing that weight felt better than a massage.

Then blood flowed into squeezed muscles, and I let out my own moan.

Supporting myself with my pack, I levered myself to the floor and sat. Easing our legs triggered groans from both of us.

I rolled onto my back. The helmet's head support inflated in a nod to comfort. The collar exerted a tiny pressure on my neck, though, and the suit splayed my hips a hair further than comfortable. It was okay for a little while, but would get uncomfortable eventually.

The suit beeped its failed telemetry warning.

Gunfire wound up on his side facing me, arm outstretched to support his helmet. That had to be differently but equally uncomfortable. I was sure I'd wind up trying it.

Silence.

Gunfire said, "Won't they see our lights?"

"If they bother to chase us."

"If?"

"We should turn them off," I said. "Just in case. Suit. Extinguish lamps."

Blackness filled the universe.

Not the darkness of an unlit room, or the darkness of midnight. Not even the darkness of an overcast midnight in the wilderness. The human eye evolved to sift light from darkness—not as well as a dog or a cat, sure, but if there's any scrap of light we have a good chance of seeing something.

This darkness was as thick as the stone around us. It filled my universe. I took a breath, and almost felt it flow down my throat. I needed a moment to steady myself. To remind myself that everything was just the same. If anything, turning off the light had made me feel a little less doomed.

Less doomed didn't mean *good*.

Gunfire said, "You all right, Miss Redding?"

"What's with the Miss?"

Gunfire paused. "Sorry, sir. It's how we talk in Texas."

"You might have missed the bulletin, but this isn't Texas. My sex and gender have nothing to do my ability to do my job."

"You're—" Gunfire took a deep breath. "This isn't the time. Sir."

I softened my voice. "Pressure brings out everyone's bad habits. Like this."

"What?"

I made myself chuckle. "When there's trouble, I run towards it."

"We didn't make this trouble."

Despite the pressure suit pushing at my neck and hips, my whole body was sagging. Tired muscles were dissolving to mush, and aching ribs eased themselves with every breath. "We didn't. But we're in it now. If we want to be."

The engulfing darkness made every sound more obvious. Chevy's breath wasn't loud, but I could tell it was deep and thorough. "Your President wants to stop selling tritium to Texas. We need that energy. If I can stop this, I must."

I said, "Even if Soviet Texas did okay without it, Kendall has thirty other countries on this list. Someone's going to react badly."

Gunfire said, "I'm sure Nirvana is on it."

"Them. Seattle Sacred. Fearless." Any nation on Kendall's list might respond with nukes, or bioweapons, or nanotech. Everybody knew how to build dooms-day weapons. Maybe they'd strike Montague facilities across the world, or long-loathed neighbors. Civilization only endures if everyone has equal access to it. We all fly together, or a handful soar until they crash.

I shifted my head to roll another sip of water around my mouth. "We can't sign on. We won't surrender. So let's figure out the mutineers' weaknesses."

"Mutiny," Gunfire said.

"What would you call it?"

Gunfire held his silence for a long moment. "Mutiny works."

I couldn't even guess what he was thinking.

Gunfire continued, "How is it they haven't already run us down like jackrabbits?"

"They've avoided running us down since the mutiny started," I said. "We got plausible orders to go down to level six, then they locked us in—again, for sensible reasons. They totally avoided confrontation until we forced it."

"If they're avoiding confrontation so hard," Gunfire said, "they must have a reason."

"As far as I can see it, either they hope to convince us to support them—"

Gunfire snorted. Was that his laugh?

I continued, "—or they *can't* subdue us by force."

"They tried," Gunfire said.

"They sent five people with stunners. Security has sixty-one people. If I was running a mutiny, I'd need the whole security team with me. And I'd send a dozen to catch a couple strays. Where were they?"

"Busy," Gunfire said. "They're working somewhere else."

I said, "I think they're going to leave us here until we run out of air and come crawling back. We're locked outside. Our supplies are limited. Three fuel containers, plus one in the pack, that's forty-eight hours. Why worry about us?"

"True," Gunfire said. "On the other hand—we're locked outside and have two days of air."

"We're not working construction. The fuel will last longer."

"So we wait forty-nine hours and spring an ambush?"

I gave a little laugh.

In another moment I said, "We know the security people are busy. And I can't believe that Kendall could find nine hundred thirty-six people here who were willing to support a mutiny. I think that means people are raising trouble else-where." A grim smile bent my face. "We aren't alone."

The thought eased a core of hot tension in my spine.

"Good," Gunfire breathed. "Can we reach them?"

"No idea who they are," I said. "I can guess the cooks aren't mutineers."

"Can we be certain Kendall did not find a chef that shared his beliefs?" How could Gunfire sound so professorial when his every word oozed exhaustion?

But he had a point. "No."

"So we act on our own," Gunfire's voice picked up cheer. "Texas style."

It wasn't that funny. I laughed anyway, setting my voice against the darkness.

Gunfire said, "We need axioms. Limits, assumptions."

"Like what?"

"Permanent damage to this facility would inflict more damage to Earth than a prolonged siege."

"Right. No blowing up the tritium extraction plant. And we don't want to hurt people if we can at all avoid it."

"True, true."

"So we don't go after the farms or the air plant." I grimaced. "If only we knew what the mutineers had done."

"In the absence of information, we must meticulously separate assumptions, axioms, and speculation."

I blinked while I processed that. "Daydreaming won't get us anywhere. No, I mean, how are they conducting negotiations with Earth?"

"What do you mean?"

"If the Portal was open as usual, a Disaster Response squad would be here. A mutiny wouldn't last three minutes."

"How often do you folks mutiny?"

I said, "Only this one. DR normally goes in when, say, an earthquake hits, or an expedition suffers unexpected illness, or something like that. But I'm sure Montague has a bunch of wargamers drawing up totally serious plans for every ridiculous contingency they can imagine. You never know what an alien universe will do."

"Sensible." Gunfire's voice hardened. "Yes. If they could be here, they would be here."

"So did Kendall shut down our side of the Portal? Or did we resize it so that only a data card or even a letter could go through? And how is he keeping Montague from opening a new Portal to the facility?" I growled in frustration. "We need information, about the staff and about the Portal."

"Uh…" Gunfire said.

27

Miss Redding didn't notice Chevy's tiny slip.

Or she'd gone silent to contemplate it.

The darkness didn't bother Chevy as much as he feared it might. He'd gone caving more than once. A well-charted cave was a comfortable place to ride out a Texas blizzard. If only the gravity would stop its wax and wane, he might even be able to make himself comfortable in this borrowed suit.

The pressure suit's original owner was a few centimeters bigger than Chevy, in every dimension. He felt like he was wearing a personal bouncy house. If he threw himself at the ground, though, he wouldn't bounce. The bulging suit might puncture.

At least these caves had no stalagmites. They didn't even have pebbles. The machines had carved everything exactly rough enough to offer traction.

None of that mattered. He knew he'd slipped, even if Miss Redding hadn't caught it. She'd probably thought he'd made that noise because he was tired, or confused, or frustrated.

They desperately needed more information, though. And Chevy couldn't imagine any way to gather intelligence on the Montague personnel. That left the Portal.

It's not that Montague protected the Portal math. The math was so complicated and demanded such specialized skill that the company had no trouble luring anyone who understood it into their orbit. Perhaps that's why the Texas datacore had traded Chevy's services to the company—not so much because he understood the math, but because he was capable of it.

He'd had months to ponder the matter.

Indecision churned his stomach.

Chevy burned to go home. He wanted to walk the beach as the Sun rose through the drowned skeleton of Old Houston. Visit family and friends. Hike the mountains. Discover the right woman to achieve one wife, two dogs, and three children.

But every Soviet citizen held responsibility for the safety of the whole. You not only cleaned up your own messes and cared for your own, you contributed to the success of others. You took the datacore's suggestions, knowing they would lead to everyone's greater happiness.

Doing his duty by Texas might cost him his hopes.

And boost the authoritarians.

Miss Redding's sigh sounded half low spirits and half exhaustion.

A tiny hope flared. Maybe he didn't need to surrender himself to this Corporation.

Perhaps he only needed to trust one person.

Chevy reminded himself to speak her language. "What made you join the Montague Corporation, sir?"

"What's this, story time?"

"I'm stumped," Chevy said. "You're stumped. When I'm stumped, I think about something else for a while. Let the problem roll around the back of my brain. Surely you didn't sign on to stand on a shore in a pressure suit?"

Miss Redding chuckled. "If only! You need more experience to work in Surveillance. And you have to like sitting in a chair watching screens. No, I inspected tritium tanks before they got shipped back to Earth."

"I know you have to work hard to get a job with Montague." Weird word, job. Nobody realized how feudal it was. "Why do that to yourself to ship tritium tanks?"

The deep breath sounded like someone getting ready to sleep. "Because it was the only way to see the universes."

"It's nothing like the stories," Chevy said.

"It's not. And it is." He could hear the smile in her tone. "Ever since I was a kid, I wanted to explore infinity. And Montague is how you do that. I don't have the talent for maths or science. My brain just doesn't work that way. But if you get a top-notch criminal science degree, and get the right extracurriculars and other classes, you can get in as security."

"Huh." Chevy couldn't fault her reasoning. "Why not something like mining or cooking? Wouldn't that be easier?"

"Cook for this crowd? With all these different cultures and tastes and restrictions?" Miss Redding's *heh* was less than a laugh. "I don't have near the palate. And jobs like mining, you go to one universe and stay there. I wanted to see all of them."

"Still sounds like a lot of boring work in an underground cave for a few minutes of seeing another universe," Chevy said.

"The work isn't about the work," Miss Redding yawned. "The work… inspecting tritium tanks isn't exciting, but it's needed. And it helps keep Earth safe. It holds civilization together. It puts food on my table, lets me help out my family, *and* it gives back to the human race."

The words eased a tightness in Chevy's chest.

"Listen," Redding yawned. "We're exhausted. We're useless. I know we're in trouble, but we're too tired to think. Let's get a few hours of sleep and figure out a decent plan in the morning."

"I'm good with that." Chevy said. "By the way, I think I know how to find out what they've done to the Portal."

28

At first, I thought my fatigue-loaded brain had dreamed Gunfire's words. "Excuse me?"

Gunfire said, "Before I say anything more, I want your promise."

He was serious. Surprise swept away the soporific darkness. "Wait? What?"

"Your promise," Gunfire said. "You said how you wanted to explore all these universes since you were a child."

"What does that have to do with anything?"

"Just as much as you want that," Gunfire said, "I want to go home."

"Oookay," I said.

"If your company found out that I knew something about Portal math," Gunfire said, "it would never let me go free."

"Oh, they would ne—"

I stopped.

In theory, anyone could build a Portal. Mohammed Montague had built the first Portal out of an old computer and four copper electrodes… plus an understanding of mathematics that bordered on insanity. The modern Montague Corporation maintained its effective monopoly on Portals by sucking in anyone who came close to understanding those maths, making itself indispensable to civilization, and building a tenuous web of international goodwill.

If Gunfire demonstrated that talent, the company would do anything they could to keep him.

It's not that I wanted Gunfire shackled to the company. He didn't want to be here.

But the Montague I cherished worked on openness. Keeping something like that secret went against my nature.

I had faith in Montague. Part of me still hoped that they would open a Portal into Tritium and send a few dozen Disaster Response people through to end this nightmare. I knew the mutineers must have a plan against that, but I still hoped.

Faith was a basis for my decisions. But not other people's.

I swallowed. "If you were to go back to Texas. Back home."

"Yes?"

"What would you do with that knowledge?"

"Pardon me?"

"These Portal maths," I said. "There are reasons Montague holds onto it. Earth has enough trouble keeping random people from building bioweapons or gray goo. The universes are full of wonders, but there's horrible things out there. If just anyone could build a Portal, and could bring those things to Earth—"

"I swear," Gunfire said. "On my honor as a Texan. If I can leave Montague, I will not only bury what I know in the pit of my heart for my entire life, I will devote my research to entirely different areas of mathematics. Nobody will learn it from me."

He sounded sincere.

Was I really thinking of this?

Kendall threatened Earth's stability. Letting Gunfire walk around Earth with Portal maths in his head was a whole different threat.

"None shall learn of it from me," Gunfire said.

I was tired. The gears of my brain cranked slowly. I couldn't be sure I was even rational. Gunfire probably wasn't either. But the choice was simple.

Let Kendall have his way. Or trust someone who had placed his trust in me.

"It's a deal." The words tasted bad.

Gunfire let out a breath. "Thank you."

My voice wanted to shake. I tried to force it steady. It came out flat. "What do you need?"

"I think you have the right idea. Sleep."

Like my conscience would let me sleep now. "All right."

"Tomorrow morning, I'll figure it out."

Despite my trepidation, in a few minutes exhaustion dragged me into my private darkness.

29

I woke up a wreck.

My mouth tasted like the scum beneath Aunt Maria's refrigerator. My left arm trembled with full-on post-stunner shivers. Despite the anti-infection and desensitizing meds, both of the suit's catheters felt bloated.

My bunk featured a plush mattress that let me coast on the gravity waves all night long. The padding in the suit, not so much. I felt like two giant hands had squidged my whole body all night, as if I was the universe's favorite stress ball. Opening my eyes freed lumps of sand without illuminating anything. Blackness pressed on my eyes and ears alike. I groaned and rolled my head, trying to work the kink out of my neck. The pressure of the too-snug collar had escalated into a line of proto-cramps. I itched to massage my neck, my back, my legs, to beat my left arm until the stun shivers passed.

Or at least wipe my eyes.

"Good morning, ma'am."

Gunfire's voice reminded just how much trouble we were in. "Guh."

"I've made coffee. And there's flapjacks on the table. Get on it, we need to saddle up and hit the trail."

Gunfire was a morning person? Ugh. And I'd started to kind of like the guy.

I blinked and ground my eyelids together, trying to clear the sludge. The suit said it was seven forty-three AM. Somehow I'd slept almost six hours.

I sipped water and swished it around my mouth, wishing I could brush my teeth or even scrape my tongue.

Thankfully, Gunfire shut up until I dragged myself to a sitting position and leaned against the wall. I couldn't stretch properly, but reaching towards my outstretched toes pulled my back muscles a little out of their stupor.

"Okay." I coughed to reset my voice. "I'm up. You all right?"

"I'm as okay as I'm gonna be."

I coughed. My throat felt rough. This would be a horrible time to fall ill. I probably just needed more to drink. Real food, not the suit's protein pellets. A bath and a real bed and two months in a warm steamy resort with Olympic-length swimming lanes and a daily massage appointment and a charming but not too friendly young man to bring me fruity drinks. Not someone else's garlic-scented pressure suit that sagged in front and around my legs. I hadn't even noticed the snugness around my neck when I'd put the suit on, but now it chafed.

If we didn't finish this, we'd have no choice but to surrender.

"Right." I coughed again. "You've been up?"

"Oh, we Texans can get by on three hours sleep for a night or two when we have to." I'd never heard the man sound so cheerful. It had to be bravado. I couldn't blame him. "I've had a couple hours to ponder how to pull this trick off."

"You're doing maths in your pressure suit?"

"Hooked my datalink to it."

"You carry—never mind. Of course you carry maths papers in your datalink."

"I was surveying Doctor Sharam's published articles last night. Incredible work."

I sipped more water. "The man the aliens said brought them here."

Gunfire paused. "Right. His transcursive differential operator calculus clearly laid the groundwork for the Portal. By redefining a narrow set—" He coughed. "You probably don't want the details."

Even my tiny smile ached. "Maybe later. Do you still think you can do it?"

"I think I can, with the right equipment."

Trepidation tightened my guts. "What do you need?" Probably *two kilograms of food-grade plutonium* or something equally reasonable.

"Two electrodes. About three meters long each. Any metal will do, so long as they're conductive. Each separately wired into my datalink. That'll let me measure resonance from the Portal here."

I blinked. More crud crumbled from my eyelashes. "That's it?"

"Some time."

"We can probably do that."

"And the closer I can get to the Portal, the better."

Aha. The catch. "The Portal's up on level two."

"Do the tunnels go up that far?"

"They do, but they're a lot smaller. A lot older." I chewed on my cheeks, trying to scrape them clean. Maybe a protein pellet or two would coat my mouth? "But the docs said there's equipment up in there. You've got the electronics kit. If we get you wire, can you knock everything together?"

"Yep."

The pellet didn't taste good, but at least it was fresh. Or, rather, I couldn't tell the difference between stale and fresh. I swallowed it anyway. "Watch your eyes, I'm turning the light on."

After all these hours in the dark, the helmet lamp's lowest setting burst forth like a nova. I blinked away sudden tears. My stunned brain couldn't figure out if the closet's basalt walls were further away than I remembered, or a whole lot closer.

Gunfire sat a meter away, back against the wall, knees bent, feet flat on the floor. The illusion that something inhuman lurked behind that black faceplate returned more strongly than ever. I took a deep breath and forced that fear back into my brain stem where it came from. He was looking at the same thing. That's how the construction suits worked. If bricklayers and pipefitters could acclimate to it, so could I.

The pellet hadn't covered up the taste of my tongue, only added its own special charm to it. Another swallow of water didn't help. "Okay," I said. "How's this. We find our way up to level two, watching out for wire the whole way. If we have to go up to one to find wire, we do. We stay as far away from the brick as possible the whole way."

"That works."

I coughed. "We are mice."

Gunfire paused. "Hug the wall. Steal crumbs. Don't be noticed."

"That's it. Follow me. I've at least seen the map."

By the time I got to my feet, Gunfire was on his. I reached for the voice cable. "Any last words before I unplug us?"

"March on, and remember the Alamo?"

Sigh. Texans. "That works. Let's go."

30

The bots had dug far beyond anything Montague might need in the next hundred years.

We climbed through dusty galleries of blue-gray basalt. The pressure suit's collar chafed enough that I tried to turn my eyes rather than my head. I knew these suits were designed to be worn against bare skin, to wick away sweat and recycle moisture and monitor life signs, but I was wishing I had worn a couple pairs of socks to protect my feet from the centimeter of slop in the boots. The blistered ankle was a constant irritation.

Chevy let me set the pace. We mostly walked heavy left, going to double heavy only on longer corridors. My muscles loosened.

My vague recollections led us to the spiral ramp going up and down. We didn't dare even heavy left up that thirty-degree slope, but the floor was rough enough that we could bear walk up on hands and feet. If I could learn to do double heavy with all four limbs, would that make it count as quadruple heavy?

Keep your mind on the job, Redding.

The spiral went down as well as up. If I tripped, how far would I slide? Level seven? Eight? All the way to the magma?

The shaft took us all the way up to level three, where it leveled out into a corridor. I paused to catch my breath and press my spine against the inside of the suit, hoping it would suck my sweat away. My shoulder blades were beginning to chafe as well. The custom-fitted suit wasn't intended for anyone but the suit's owner.

Maybe it was fatigue, but I was beginning to feel like I knew Simmers even though I'd never met her. I didn't know what she sounded like or where she came from or what she believed, but I knew the exact shape of her body and what she smelled like. I was wearing someone else's clothes, at expert level.

At least this time I wasn't running around naked. No matter what, I was going to keep my clothes.

If it wasn't for the EXIT signs and arrows at every intersection, I would have been completely disoriented. I had no idea of which way was north or south. We could have circled the facility in this unipolar quest. Maybe I'd get assigned to a unipolar universe next?

If there was a "next."

That's why my brain kept veering to anything else. The mutineers might be risking Earth's civilization, but that was abstract. They might have crashed my career. I'd done my best with the alien contact negotiations, and followed the instructions meticulously, but a security third should have been present only as ceremonial decoration; seen, but silent. I'd been following orders, but headquarters might view it differently.

I should have been more suspicious.

Tritium might be the last universe I visited.

It didn't have to be. If Montague fired me, I could join a colony in a universe like ours, either as an employee or a colonist. It would be a new world, at least. An Earth-like world chosen for balmy climate, fecund soil, and compatible biome. No, if I wanted to do that I might as well go out to the human aliens and ask if they were accepting new settlers. The air and water didn't kill people, so long as they never returned to Earth. Anti-Earth probably needed all the bodies it could get. I could become a hunter and protect The Village from the carnivorous elephants and the tree sharks or whatever other menace they'd discovered. Probably Death Fleas. If I wanted to show commitment, I could take my suit off first.

Stop it!

I wasn't going to give up. I wasn't going to quit.

My job description didn't have an open-ended statement of "protect civilization." All the precautionary security checks I performed on tritium tanks bound for Earth sure implied it, though.

Focus on the tunnels, even if they seem endless. Watch for people or signs of people. Warm up your muscles.

Before I expected it, the EXIT arrows led us to a cavern. The moment my helmet lamp picked up a hint of a metallic reflection, I raised a hand and stopped. Gunfire stumbled a couple steps past me, but fell back.

"Suit," I said. "Double magnification."

The world grew closer, but I still had to turn up my helmet lamp before I could make out the shape of a broad airlock door set in a brick wall. The bricks were bigger than those used down on level six, covered with a thick glaze that shimmered in my helmet lights.

Near the wall?

Stacks of replacement brick. Sealed mortar bags. Shovels and picks and trowels. All the equipment suited-up maintenance crews might need on their inspection rounds.

And meter-wide spools of cable and wire.

I'd wanted to avoid the wall, but this close the surveillance cameras must have already seen us. Even if the screens weren't staffed right now, the lousiest motion detection algorithm in history couldn't have failed to notice us. Us taking the wire might even confuse them. I went to tap Gunfire's shoulder, but he was already lumbering forward at heavy left. The gloves made him fumble, but he unspooled several meters of copper wire, snipped them off, and wound them in a tighter spool that hung loose around his arm. He trotted back and offered me a thumbs-up.

I turned back. Near the corridor entrance, skeletal metal stairs ricketed into the ceiling.

Staying off surveillance had been a forlorn hope.

However we fought the mutiny, we'd have to do while the mutineers watched.

31

The metal stairs between levels three and two went on forever. With the unsteady weight of the pressure suits, we could only take them at heavy left. Each tread was marked with the octagonal Montague logo and rang beneath our boots. Far too late, I realized I should have counted the turns to guess the distance. The only reason I could think of to have such a difference between floors was that level two must be above the water, and level three deep enough that it could spread out.

Endless stairs through basalt. I was so sick of blue-gray basalt.

Far too slowly, we reached Portal level.

The cavern ceiling was only about five meters up, shorter than those below. The bricks insulating the facility from Tritium looked even heavier, though. The airlock's fittings made me think of a miser's dream bank vault, all overhung metal and massive gears and sliding bars. The climb had left me short of breath. My legs ached all over again, and the suit was doing a mediocre job of absorbing my sweat. The only part of me that didn't hurt were my hands. The space between the airlock and the cavern wall was a few meters, which meant we couldn't miss the electronic sign.

Surrender and you will be treated well.

I rolled my eyes. Treating me well didn't mean anything if they attacked everyone else.

Gunfire was turning his shoulders to look around. I waved for his attention, then led him to the lone corridor winding into the stone. The mutineers might know we were here, but that didn't mean we had to sit right in front of the obvious camera. We'd at least make them use an invisibly small microdrone.

The corridor floor sloped down. Fifteen curving meters on, the floor turned to sand.

Another bend, and it opened into a natural cavern.

Salt rimed the lumpy walls. The irregular ceiling hung high enough for me to stand, but too close for me to relax. We had five or six meters of floor space before a line of floor-to-ceiling steel bars, each as big around as my thumb and far enough apart for me to put my arm but not my body, blocked the path. A heavy chain held a gate solidly closed.

Beyond the bar, several meters of floor glowed a dim opal blue.

I walked closer and aimed my helmet lamp between the bars.

Water. Several meters of it.

This was a sea cave.

I turned my helmet. Tiny squid-like creatures fled my light, hiding among strands of orange algae. Just like in the lagoon. Fenced off, to keep it from the brick that kept the walls away from the people.

While Tritium has no moon, the gravity waves gave even this isolated pool its own gentle waves. Wait—maybe those waves weren't just from the gravity. Earth had fish that lived in caves, yes, but they evolved. The squiddy fish I'd seen here looked, at first glance, exactly like their cousins in the lagoon, only the size of a fingernail. Hatchlings? Maybe the tunnel we were in continued underwater for a time and came out in the lagoon.

Or three kilometers from shore.

One of those, anyway.

If this was a lava tube, it probably branched a dozen times before it came up anywhere.

This was the end of the line. The pressure suits were waterproof, but untrained underwater spelunking was my idea of a bad plan. The plans I'd conceived and carried out on other assignments had included several variants on "fling myself into a bottomless void," so this had to be the gold standard of Bad Plans.

I heaved an aching breath and turned.

Gunfire had sunk to his knees, right in front of a lump of rock about the right height for him to use as a bench. I trudged over and hooked up the voice line. "Hello?"

Silence. Then Gunfire said, "—hear me?"

"Got you." I peered around. "Is this close enough?"

"It's a fair place to do the building. If we gotta move closer, we can."

"Okay." I crouched to settle on a patch of clear sand. "Before you start, though."

"Yeah?"

"They know we're here."

"And they're uncouth about it. You sure they're not gonna come out?"

"I hope other people are keeping the mutineers busy. A place like this, though? They've got cameras."

Hands on the buckle of his electrical kit tool belt, Gunfire paused. "They'll watch us."

"So we need to be tricky."

Gunfire's hand reached up, thumb and fingers spread in a V, only to bump into his helmet. He'd tried to rub his chin, in a pressure suit. I swallowed a laugh. We were both… not exactly tired, but worn.

To get discussion going I said all that came to mind. "If I can find the cameras, I could block the lens."

"They're pretty small," Gunfire said. "Even these old-fangled ones."

I grimaced. "We'd never be sure I got them all."

"So I need to make my electrodes look like something else," Gunfire said. "Something innocent."

"Yes!" I snapped my fingers, or tried to. You can't snap fingers in a pressure suit any more than you can scratch your chin. "Can you add some parts to make it look like a radio?"

"If we wanted a radio, we could just put our datalinks out of isolation mode."

I leaned forward. "Not if we were so desperate as to try to reach the aliens by radio and enlist their help."

A pause, then Gunfire let out an honest belly laugh. "That is a thing of beauty."

"It's a desperate plan," I said.

"Enlisting the natives to rise up," Gunfire said. "Ma'am, are you sure you're not from Texas?"

I told myself he meant it as a compliment. "The mutineers will happily let us sit here and fiddle with radios until we run out of air. Can you do it?"

"If they're watching, I'll have to build a real radio. Take me… oh, an extra ten minutes or so."

"I'll make some frustrated gestures at you. Like I can't believe you can't make a simple radio."

Gunfire pulled off his tool kit, removed small components, and got to work.

I pulled off the plumbing tool kit I'd uselessly lugged around with me and settled in beside him. I didn't want to go so far as to pull off the life support pack, but I found a half-buried rock of the right height to take some of the weight off.

Up in Surveillance, some mutineer was laughing their head off at our foolishness.

If they wanted foolishness, I was happy to give it to them.

32

Gunfire was a mutterer.

Legs sprawled on the natural cave's sandy floor and life support pack propped on a convenient rock, I watched the man fiddle with parts. His rock was a lousy workbench. He balanced little round mysterious electronic bits like dials and transistors and tubes or whatever in every crevice he could get. When he ran out of space, he tugged a square meter of black drop cloth from the toolkit and claimed part of the sand as well. The whole time he grumbled annoying partial sentences about ohms and watts and frequencies and integrals and differentials and mathematical stuff. He put me in mind of a bad mockery of a witch doctor from the old days when video was black and white, practicing an art the filmmakers considered equal parts mysterious and bizarre.

I'd never heard anyone do calculus out loud before.

Sort of out loud. Even if I could understand the maths, I couldn't have deciphered his fragments.

I fought the urge to scream *did you ever hear of sentences, man!* and let him work.

When he unplugged the voice line to run the electrodes, I welcomed the silence.

If it worked, it could take hours.

Gunfire wound up with a mishmash of parts hooked together into a breadboard. A one-meter cable ran to the datalink clipped to his belt. The stolen copper wire stretched in two parallel lines down into the tunnel to the airlock.

I can only watch other people work for so long before I itch to help. Building a primitive radio was a one-person job, though. All I could do was watch. It made me jumpy. I tried splitting my attention between the corridor entrance and the bioluminescent pond.

Gunfire's fingers twitched. He must have brought the datalink display up in his helmet.

I silently thanked him for disconnecting the voice line.

Don't get me wrong. We need experts. Experts increase our knowledge, and give us tools to build better societies and a better world. Better universes, even. Give experts all the gear they think they need and keep the coffee flowing. But I don't like listening to things I can't understand, and I hate lectures. Give me a task, give me the information to accomplish that, and let me go. Guard a door, inspect a tank, solve a murder, whatever—just don't try to teach me about differential multivariable algebraic calculus linear whatever.

Maybe I could write insulting messages in the sand for the mutineers? No, don't taunt them. That's not even a bad plan, it's flat-out self-sabotage.

For now, the best plan was rest.

I even decided against making private bets on how long it would take Gunfire to remember that he'd unplugged the voice line. If I had, one hour and thirty-eight minutes would have won. He waved, rose from his knees onto one foot, and turned to me.

I tapped the side of my helmet.

Gunfire held still for a breath, then snatched the cable out of the sand and plugged it in. "—haven't heard a single thing I said?"

"I thought you wanted peace and quiet to work," I said cheerfully.

"Yes. Hrm. Well. I have answers."

My relaxation evaporated. "You mean it worked? Already?"

"Sharam had already done most of the work," Gunfire said. "The man deserves more credit than he's given. I just implemented it."

My throat tightened. "What's going on?"

"They have the local Portal dialed down to a one-centimeter square."

My throat loosened enough to squeeze a breath through. "Big enough for a datacard."

"Additionally, they have established an interference pattern that will prevent Earth from opening a new Portal anywhere nearby." Every time Gunfire switched from Texan to Expert Mathematics Professor, my mind gave a tiny lurch. "It's strong. I think they've repurposed an external communications array."

Without an external array, the facility couldn't receive any data from remote monitoring stations or exploration drones. Tritium had two arrays, mounted to cliffs on opposite sides of the island, but the thought of choosing to operate without redundancy chilled me. Like running around in your lingerie, you're only one slip from disaster.

That wasn't the worst part, though. I had never heard of an *interference pattern* in regards to the Portal.

Someone had figured out how to disrupt incoming Portals. It was possible that Montague knew how to do this, that they'd set up something to block aliens from opening Portals on Earth. I couldn't believe that. Aliens invading by opening portals on Earth was a serial staple, and the fear wasn't unfounded. No, someone had invented this. And they'd kept it to themselves.

The mutineers had an ally in the mathematics department back on Earth.

How many more allies did the mutineers have back home?

I couldn't do anything about Earthside mutineers now. Focus on the possible. "How far away could they open a Portal?"

"*Nearby*," Gunfire said, "in astronomical terms."

Oh. "So light years."

"Perhaps geosta… Tritium-stationary?" Gunfire paused. "Several planetary diameters, at a minimum."

My jaw clenched.

Montague wasn't coming to help.

I'd known that, intellectually. But Gunfire had just crushed my faith.

We were on our own.

"Okay," I said. "Let's put this together. The Portal is too small to put a pinky through. Nobody's coming to help us. I'm sure we could open the airlock, but they won't open the inner door until we surrender."

"They'll stun us on sight," Gunfire said.

My hands burned. Memories of the fight in the suit repair lab flashed. I needed two deep breaths before I could speak. "I would." I chewed my lip. "We can't win like this, so we need to change the rules."

Gunfire paused. "You're talking sense."

My mouth was dry, and my heart beating too fast. "Is there anything we could damage that would help? There's the farm, but emergency supplies would carry them for a month no problem. Losing the extraction plant wouldn't do anything but make the embargo permanent." I tried to snap my fingers again. "The array! If we could put it out of order, Earth could get in—no. Kendall would use the other array. He'd have to. It'd blind us."

Gunfire said nothing.

"Air reclaimator? No, that hurts everyone. And the mutineers would be the first to get portable air."

Gunfire's silence stretched.

Uneasiness quivered in my gut. "Can you maybe counter their interference?"

"I would need a bigger antenna than what they have."

I should have expected that. But his silence felt pressured, ready to water-balloon burst at a pinprick. My pulse was still too fast. I couldn't let it leak into my voice. "What aren't you telling me?"

Gunfire sounded ill. "Remember your promise. And my oath."

"I remember."

He still said nothing.

I chose my words carefully. "If this continues, they will hurt your home."

"I know," he whispered.

"Sometimes," I said, "there's no right thing to do. There's only a choice of bad. You want to go home. I want you to have a home to go to."

Gunfire said, "The interesting thing about Sharam's work is that he clearly understood how to redefine mathematics within a limited space."

I wanted him to tell me what he was feeling. Not give me a lecture on obscure historical Portal mathematics.

"He could open other universes, but he had no way to aim those early Portals."

"Okay," I said, to show I was paying attention.

"He must have gone through millions—billions of universes to find Anti-Earth," Gunfire said. "Blindly opening Portals into universes that don't even have congruence to our physics." I let him talk, and his words sped up. "See, when your Montague wanted tritium, they computed the characteristics of a universe where hydrogen would naturally have three neutrons, and where untransformed human beings could go back and forth. Everything else followed from those axioms. They took the results, weeded them down to a handful of candidates, sent a few explorers to each, and selected Tritium as the best choice."

"Right," I said.

"Don't you see?" Gunfire threw his arms down. "With Sharam's work, I have everything I need to open Portals."

"But you just said you can't aim them."

"I can't. But with more computing power, I can establish resonance with the existing Portal." He pointed at the antennas. "Anything one centimeter or less will go through the official Portal. Bigger stuff would come here."

I struggled my reflex to shout.

"Your company can send their rangers right through," Gunfire said. "And they will never let me go."

33

"Wretched" comes in a million flavors.

I wished I could see Gunfire's face. Was he angry? Afraid? How do you support someone an arm's reach away, that you know feels awful, when a featureless mask hides their every feeling? When you can't even touch them? Was he sobbing or livid?

I didn't like the man. He couldn't even perceive the splendor of visiting an alien universe. A machine told him to go to a place he hated, and he did it. Calling me *ma'am* in a professional setting, afraid to so much as glimpse me changing clothes, the way he put his words together, everything about him screamed parochial Soviet Texas.

The man could not banter to save his hide.

I couldn't understand him, but I understood his feelings. He wanted to go home. He had no desire to be anywhere near this sea cave in an alien universe, far from all he loved.

All I could offer him was the comfort of a hand on his shoulder. He was quivering so hard that I felt it through both our suits.

He was too smart to accept lighthearted fluff. "I'm sorry."

No answer. Maybe he nodded inside his helmet.

I licked my lips. "I can't think of any other plan."

He shrugged my hand off. "Do you think I don't know that?" His arms flailed. "I can't let these monsters force Montague to starve my people. And Montague would do it. If it's my people or the whole world, they'll destroy my people." His arms dropped limp. "But I hate it."

"All I can say is, I'll fight as hard as I can for you. If you can figure out how to keep aliens from opening Portals onto Earth, you can name your work conditions. Maybe you can work back in Texas."

"They don't allow that. I already asked."

"If you can protect Earth? It's called *negotiation*. Maybe the mutineers will hand over the secret, but they'll need someone to verify it. Improve it. Besides." I grinned, even though Gunfire couldn't see it. "If you can build a Portal out of a datalink and ten meters of wire, they'll want you. For what it's worth, I'll argue hard for it."

Gunfire let out a deep breath. "A datalink won't do, ma'am. I could precompute about a second's worth of Portal in a day. I need serious real-time number-crunching."

If I asked him why, he'd explain it to me. "How much?"

"A data terminal would work. Or anything compatible."

The data terminals were inside the brick barricade, but Montague made sure all computing equipment in each universe was compatible. "Maybe we could hijack a borer bot."

"And get it up those stairs?" Gunfire's helmet shook side to side.

"I could—no." The borer bots had rockfall-resistant hides covered in rock grinders. I couldn't rip the brains out of one with anything short of a full machine shop.

"Something that does visual processing would be ideal."

The empty caverns were dark. No machine here would do visual processing. Inspiration struck. My heart sank.

"What?" Gunfire said.

I must have made a noise. "What about a tortoise?"

"That would do."

I turned to look through the wall of bars, at the glowing blue-white pool beyond.

Montague might employ me as a Security Third, but temperamentally I am a Bad Plan First.

34

The pipe cutters from the plumbing tool kit made short work of the gate chain, opening the pool to us.

The irregular oval, about six meters by four, went all the way to the far wall. The ceiling curved down to meet it. The water wobbled with the gravity, rising a few centimeters on the light and dropping on the heavy. Bioluminescent algae hugged the rocks and drifted everywhere, giving the water its opalescent glow. My nose insisted that the pool stank of garlic and someone else's sweat, even though I knew I smelled only my stolen suit.

The deep parts of my brain insisted that the water had to be warm. The algae wouldn't be so bright if it was cold, would it? My itchy, aching body begged for a long soak in a hot tub. Never mind that we were in Tritium's lower latitudes, and the water was probably only a few degrees above freezing.

From the shore, though, I could see that the pool was a continuation of our natural tunnel. Perhaps an ancient lava tube, a remnant of the island's volcanic past. The bioluminescence illuminated three or four meters down, until the tunnel curved up and out of sight.

"I go caving on vacations," Gunfire said. "I can go down there."

I almost asked *how's your swimming*, but cut myself off in time. "It's not a matter of skill. It's my job. No matter what, you need to keep working on this Portal thing. Maybe you can figure out a way to do it with the datalink."

"It's not possible."

"Neither is remotely detecting a Portal's behavior. Come on, where's that famous Soviet Texas Alamo spirit?"

Gunfire grumped. "Have you ever caved?"

I tensed, waiting for him to add the *ma'am*. I might have punched him. Not hard. Just hard enough. Without that, it was a fair question. "I can do thirty meters underwater on Earth, in a pool."

"Caves get tight, ma'am." Before I could move he added, "Don't push your luck. If you get stuck, I'll have to come in after you."

Without communications, he'd only know that I had gone into the water and never returned. "The suit still has four hours air left before I have to change fuel cells. If I'm not back in two, I'm dead. Do whatever you think is best."

"Such as?"

"You're the genius. Reinvent the Portal. Something." I paused. "If you get to the end. If you have to surrender." I swallowed. "It's okay."

"I'm not giving in to these monsters," Gunfire replied, quick as his name.

I liked him a little more for it. "Whatever you decide then is the right thing."

"Don't give me that *forgiveness from the dead* cowflop," Gunfire said. "That's old even in Texas."

It wasn't funny, but I laughed anyway.

Gunfire said, "Just grab a tortoise and get back here. Or if you can't, get back here anyway. We'll figure something out."

"Well. Since you asked nice."

"Be safe, ma'am."

I put my smile into my voice. "Where's the fun in that?" With that, I unplugged the voice line and handed Gunfire my end. He stepped back and offered me a thumbs up.

With a wave, I turned my back on him and stepped to the edge of the water.

The pond's edge wasn't a beach. It was barely a shore. Everything within a meter of water was a tangle of rocks, softened by water and obscured by algae, and it only got worse further down. Could any of it puncture the pressure suit? The suit was designed to resist minor accidents, and the manual said they were watertight, but would they endure against the totally different dangers underwater?

Even on Earth, the ocean is a different universe. Identical physical laws have a wholly alien expression. I had to distrust everything.

A laddering section of underwater rocks might serve as a ladder if I was snorkeling in a resort, but I'd never get down it in a suit. Over by one of the walls, though, underwater rocks formed a broad-treaded natural staircase. I could climb down at least as far as my waist. If that fourth rock was as close as I thought, I could even get my helmet underwater. I'd be close enough to the edge to climb back out if the water started eating my suit or the life support pack shorted out or the squiddy things swarmed me to drag me off as a sacrifice to their alien gods.

No, this wasn't a cheesy sorcery serial. This was merely a bad plan.

A short test was the smartest way to start a stupid thing.

Crunching through crusted salt, I got to the edge and eased my boot into the water.

The water pushed back as if unwilling to accept me. It was only air displacement. The boot wasn't heavy enough to sink. I pushed deeper, until the water rose over the top of the boot and squeezed against my suit. Was that extra pressure against my calves? Maybe. Not much if it was.

The foot wanted to float off the rock. At least the algae wasn't as slick as I expected. I eased more weight down, until it seemed stable at the heavy and almost steady at the light.

I almost fell getting the second foot into the water, only to hit my first snag. That first step wasn't big enough for both booted feet. I waited for the light so I could more easily bend and brace my hands against rocks on the shore, then stretched that foot blindly down for the second step.

My toe met the rock. Or something solid. I couldn't look through the helmet's chin.

The base of the life support pack touched water. It didn't burst into sparks. The words LEAVE WATER IMMEDIATELY flashed right next to TOTAL TELEMETRY FAILURE. All systems in trouble? The story of my career. The telemetry warning's slow beep had become mere background noise, but with the second alarm it picked up pitch and acquired an erratic syncopation impossible to ignore.

The life support pack's density more than balanced out the air in my suit. I sank down to that fourth step like I was on the Moon, and the water sloshed up over my helmet.

Bubbles surged past my helmet, air fleeing the suit's folds and crevices.

I held my breath.

Was that water running down my back? No, only sweat. Just like my armpits, and my feet, and… everywhere else. My fingernails were probably sweating.

The bubbles slowed to a trickle.

My helmet light punched through the water, turning the algae from glowing blue to dull brown. The tiny squiddy fish were everywhere, churning around me. They hadn't looked so thick from above. My boots felt loose on the rock, the heavy and the light gravity pressing and easing my guts but ignoring my feet.

Okay, Redding. Make haste slowly. You don't have to swim. You have light. Choose where to put each foot. Pick a rock. Step to it. You have buoyancy, but small steps anyway.

The squiddy fish—squiffish? Squishies? Squiddies, that worked—were getting thicker. I couldn't make out much through them.

I bent at the waist, turning the helmet lamp down below my feet. For a moment I could see the pond's heaped-stone bottom through the lower half of my helmet, then miniature fins and tiny tentacles surged in to fill the space.

Did they somehow sense where I was looking? Were the squiddies telepathic? Were they trying to protect that underwater temple?

No, that was a pretty big jump. Start with the basics.

"Suit. Helmet lamp off."

Everything went dark.

Even on Earth, light attracted certain fish. Assuming that Tritium life followed the same patterns as Earth life was a great way to get killed, but it was a worthwhile and testable hypothesis. If the lack of light made the squiddy critters attack me, I had a chance of getting out of the pool before they ate my suit. I only had to wait until my eyes adjusted to the dimness.

A strand of algae drifted past my helmet, a twisting curve of blue light so pale I could look straight at it. Without perspective, I couldn't tell if it was close enough to touch my helmet or a meter away.

Second by second, the world resolved around me.

The pond looked more alien by algae light. Everything was shades of gray, again like one of those ancient videos. Shadows were deeper and broader, with softer edges. Rocks seemed more tangled, heavier, loaded with menace. My sweat felt colder.

The squiddies had scattered, though. They clustered around the rocks and in the algae. Hiding from their larger kin, perhaps? What ate squiddies? I'd studied every Tritium technical manual and read the basics about land life, but hadn't spent five minutes on the sea life.

Had anyone been eaten by squiddies?

No, I wasn't in my bikini. My construction-grade pressure suit would keep out anything that couldn't puncture the heavy fabric, let alone the armored joints.

Spooky or not, I could see. Time to stop dawdling.

I almost slipped off the first step. My tread was lighter than I thought. Bending my knees helped. I needed to take tiny steps and not rely on the natural buoyancy. If I could drop a couple kilograms somehow, I might float. I wasn't about to try swimming in a pressure suit. Not yet.

Rock by rock, I made my way down the tunnel.

The walls got closer, the squiddies bigger. My sweat began to feel clammy.

Mist coalesced inside my faceplate.

I paused. The water was cold, and the suit was humid. If the faceplate got so clouded that I couldn't see—

The suit clicked. Warm air touched my face.

The Montague engineers had done their usual fine job. My lungs loosened.

I'd gone maybe eight, nine meters, and the tunnel leveled. Ahead, it was bending up. The rocks embedded in the sides looked bigger, brown and gray and the occasional spot of red, all draped with bioluminescent algae.

Wait.

I shouldn't be able to see the colors.

My pulse picked up. If the tunnel rose to the surface again, outside the island, daylight should trickle down. The light could also be anything from live magma to the glare of the sodium torches surrounding the Squiddy Sacrifice Temple.

I studied the shadows.

The light from above wavered in a way that reminded me of the times I'd swum in a mask and snorkel.

I couldn't declare it sunlight. But it was in no way inconsistent with sunlight.

Smothering my excitement, I started forward.

The tunnel grew narrower. Spilled rocks lay everywhere. If the tunnel went to the outside, had storms knocked debris into the tunnel?

The ceiling drew too close for me to stand. I took one clumsy crouching step and almost fell over. Going horizontal, drawing myself forward on my gloved hands, worked much better.

One long straight rock wasn't a rock.

It was a trunk of driftwood.

My heart thrummed.

Rocks scraped the suit's armored shoulders.

I refused to let delight overwhelm my actions. I studied each handhold, checking for stability and robustness before seizing it. My plan had not been so bad after all.

The tunnel bent sharply up at the end. The driftwood log was a good half-meter thick, thrusting down the tunnel and buried in the detritus. Rocks were piled all around it. When the log decayed, everything would spill down. The tunnel might open up wider at the end here but get tighter further up, or it might block off the cave forever.

I would need to bend at the waist to get around that bend, so I rotated to put my belly up and pulled myself along on the ragged ceiling. It meant I couldn't look ahead, so when my head cleared the tunnel and could see up, everything came as a horrible surprise.

Tritium's bruised purple sky gleamed above. Even through the water, three bright stars peered down at me through Tritium's feeble sunlight.

The water's tranquil surface couldn't be more than three meters above me.

Squiddies the size of my palm coursed all around my helmet, darting up to seize mouthfuls of algae or floating bugs before ducking back down.

The tunnel opening was large enough, I could drag a tortoise-bot down.

Even if I ditched the life support pack, the pressure suit was too big to squirm through that narrow gap.

I could swim through it, no problem.

Once I took a breath of Tritium air—or, worse, got a mouthful of that water—a clock started ticking. Twenty minutes later, I could never return to Earth. Even fifteen minutes later, I'd need intensive medical care.

This was cooking my hand all over again, but over my whole body.

And I didn't even know if I was near a part of the island that had tortoise scrubber-bots. Kendall might see me coming and order all the tortoises to withdraw.

I might exile myself to Tritium for nothing.

But if it was a choice between myself and civilization, it wasn't a choice, was it?

My hand twitched against the suit's collar release.

35

Miss Redding's helmet sank below the toxic electric-blue water. Chevy stood vigil until the water stilled and her lamp disappeared.

If you could do nothing else, you bore witness.

Only madmen dived unknown cave lakes. Given that only lunatics chose to visit Tritium, did that mean any Montague employee would jump in? Nope. Miss Redding was a special kind of lunatic. She could almost be Texan.

Trapped in this sea cave, with nothing but his pseudo-radio, Portal-sensing electrodes, and a toxic blue lake, what was he supposed to do? Reinvent Portal math? Chevy might as well draw equations on his back and fly to Mars. From Tritium.

Maybe he should sit down. Prop his life support pack against the wall and lean back. Stretch his feet out. It wouldn't be as cozy as a recliner, but he might rest better that way.

No, he wasn't going to doze.

Building the radio might have convinced the antisocial rebels that Gunfire was harmless.

If Miss Redding stole a tortoise-bot, the rebels would realize they had misunderstood. Even if she was right and something within the facility had them occupied, if Gunfire alarmed them, they might decide to come on out. It would be best if Chevy assumed she would bring a functional tortoise-bot back and he needed to get it to work.

He needed to write a bunch of number crunching code.

He didn't have to compute the targeting for Earth. He hadn't read the right papers to give him the background for reading the papers that would let him develop the math to compute targeting for Earth-like universes, let alone Earth itself. But he needed code to piggyback on the existing Portal's targeting, shift the numbers for the size of the Portal he wanted, and perform all the ongoing computation to hold it open. If he could have the code ready when Miss Redding returned, he could plug his setup into the tortoise's service port and let it ride.

No, he'd need another adapter. A hub, interconnecting datalink, tortoise, and electrodes.

Wiring that up took a whole three minutes. He fretted when he swapped out the existing connector, but the new one worked just fine.

He made himself comfortable. Instead of napping he set to writing a little script to parse out the data, transform it through a touch of basic linear algebra and a whole bucket of downright vicious differential topology, spindle it around his beloved operator algebra, and feed it to the electrodes. The electrodes had to be wider than the Portal between them. This old, pre-boring-machine tunnel looked maybe four meters wide, so call it a three meter sphere. The main Portal here wasn't much bigger than that. He made his helmet translucent, so he could have his work projected on the inside but not lose sight of the room. He didn't have a keyboard, but he could get by with the virtual keyboard in the gloves.

He had his brain well full of math when a muffled but loud voice outside his helmet called, "Chevy? Can you hear me?"

The math spilled away from his brain, leaving him gaping. He needed a moment to refill himself with the world, and scrabbled to place the voice flattened by layers of insulation.

Miss Lucy Kirkland. Montague's maths first.

Montague had cameras out here. They must have speakers as well.

The thought of Miss Kirkland being antisocial disappointed Chevy. She always sounded as enthusiastic as a basket of puppies set free in the hot dog factory. Her relentless cheer had abraded his nerves like ten miles of bad road, but he'd thought she believed in her work. He'd thought she'd been a good person in a warped society.

"I saw your helmet move. I know you can hear me." It wasn't just the insulation that made her sound wrong. Her voice shook. Had she been crying?

Chevy could ignore a punch in the nose more easily than a crying lady. Unsure what else to do, he raised a hand.

A pause. "If you want to answer, say 'Suit, activate external speakers.'"

Chevy saved his work, wiped his helmet display clean, and triggered the speakers. "Miss Kirkland?"

"Yes!"

"Are you all right?"

"We're fine. Most of us. There's a few troublema—" A scraping noise, and her voice cut off. Someone putting a hand over the mic? Was she with the antisocials, or were the antisocials making her talk to him?

Chevy waited. She would return, or she wouldn't.

Miss Redding might have been right. Maybe the antisocials weren't having it all their way. Even an authoritarian corporation had to have good people in it.

"Never mind that," Miss Kirkland said. "Everyone in Maths is fine. They're treating us well."

They? So Miss Kirkland wasn't in with the antisocials? Or was she an antisocial and playing him? "Good."

"Listen. Chevy. President Kendall asked me to talk to you."

"Tell him to come on out and sit a spell."

"I'll pass that on. You know about Kendall's demands—uh, his *reform platform*?"

Someone was with Miss Kirkland. An antisocial, making dang sure she said the right things. The antisocials had picked a familiar person to talk him inside. "He told us, yes."

"He told me to tell you." Another pause. "He doesn't want anyone else—" scuff, buzz, "—*anyone* on Tritium to get hurt. If you'll come inside, you can stay safe with the rest of Maths."

The longer they talked, the better chance he had to learn something. "What about Miss Redding?"

"Redding is welcome to come inside as well."

"We're partners now, you know."

"You should know that Security Third Redding is on yellow."

Chevy scoffed. "That woman's as cowardly as a rabid bull."

"No, no," Miss Kirkland said. "Her employment status. She came here with a yellow flag. If she doesn't straighten up, she'll be released when she gets back to Earth."

"Released?"

"Fired. Let go. Ejected from Montague."

Chevy stiffened. He wanted his freedom, and Miss Redding was going to have it forced on her? How had she not told him this?

Not even that. She'd said she'd do her best to get him sent back to Texas.

Typical authoritarian duplicity. For all her talk about openness, she'd held onto information that might help him make a better decision. She'd been kind, but only to get him moving the way she wanted. She couldn't help it. She'd been raised that way, soaking in that inhuman capitalist culture since birth—

Just like Miss Kirkland.

Chevy yanked his own reins short.

Perhaps Miss Redding hadn't told him everything. He shouldn't forgive her that.

But Miss Kirkland had been raised in that same culture. And the antisocial with her was making sure she said the right things and cutting her off when she wandered.

He couldn't trust either of them.

But of the two, he trusted a freely speaking Miss Redding over an antisocial-supervised Miss Kirkland.

Miss Kirkland said, "You're a unique person on Tritium, Chevy. You're a temporary contractor, not a full-time employee. And you're in a dangerous situation. President Kendall is most concerned that you aren't hurt."

"Very neighborly of him."

"He says that if you come in, if you cooperate? He'll take Soviet Texas off his list."

Chevy's pulse quickened.

"He doesn't like how Texas does things, but it's not one of the really bad ones like Seattle Sacred or France. He'll personally guarantee continued tritium sales to Soviet Texas if you'll come back in and not make any trouble. Not that you could make trouble. They planned this all out, nobody could make trouble for—"

The scraping sound of a covered mic.

Yep, someone was making trouble.

Kendall was an antisocial, given.

Stopping tritium sales to some of Earth's more bizarre nations might destabilize the world. But if he could save his own people, shouldn't he at least consider it?

Chevy had made a deal with Miss Redding, and he hadn't welched on a deal yet. But if she couldn't keep her side of the bargain, if she'd known she couldn't keep her side when she made it, then they didn't have a real bargain.

Miss Kirkland said, "Come on in, Chevy. It's for the best." Her voice sounded even more strained.

If President Kendall was so bent on Chevy surrendering, why hadn't he made that offer himself? Had he gotten Kirkland to talk just because she'd been his boss' boss? Was he relying on reflexive submission to authority? Familiarity?

Or did he think Kirkland could sell his lies better than he could?

But Miss Redding had lied, too.

"I've got to think about this," he said.

Another scrape over the mic. "You know there's people watching you," Kirkland said.

"Just about figured that out, ma'am."

"I'll tell him, but he wants those people on other duties. He'll want an answer soon."

"I got nothing else to do but sit here and think about it until Miss Redding gets back."

"Even if the aliens would help you, there's nothing they can do." Miss Kirkland sounded stiff, like she was reading notes off a screen.

"If nothing else, I had an arrangement with Miss Redding. I'd be a coward to sneak out without telling her."

"Leave her a note." She was absolutely reading someone else's words.

"Your suits don't come with note paper."

"Don't take too long," Miss Kirkland said.

Good manners almost made Chevy say have a good day, but he choked them down. Instead he said, "You be safe now, all right Miss Kirkland?"

"You too, Chevy." Those words were her own. They trembled.

Chevy tried to get comfy again, but couldn't. The Portal math called to him, but his brain felt stuffed with another set of more complicated problems. Miss Redding either wanted to be with Montague, or she was a consummate actress that belonged on a Dallas Broadway stage. Was she on this *yellow* status? What sort of horrible culture blocked people from the labor they so desperately wanted to perform? Or had Kendall whole-hog lied?

If Kendall wanted Chevy dead, all he had to do was lock the airlock and wait two days. Maybe three, if Chevy didn't move much. So his offer to not block tritium sales to Texas might be square.

Only one thing for it. When Miss Redding came back, he'd have to find out the truth.

And if nothing else, him sitting here was wasting antisocial time. That alone made it worthwhile.

36

Returning through the underwater tunnel took not enough time, and forever.

The suit kept up its irritating arhythmic bleeps about damaged telemetry and immersion, but I kept my attention on moving forward. Strands of bioluminescent blue algae gleamed everywhere. Dull dying smears marked where I'd stepped on the trip out. I had survived my feet touching those spots on the way out, so my training insisted I try to step in those same spots on the way back.

Turns out crushed algae is almost frictionless. Only buoyancy and water resistance kept me from landing on my butt.

My suit still smelled of sweat and garlic. But most of all, the bright old-copper taste of fear filled my mouth.

Concentrating on finding different rocks to stand on chained the fear back. Each step demanded I shove the suit through the water. If my attention wandered, I mis-stepped and bounced off the ceiling or the wall instead. The pressure suit was armored, and it had held up well down here, but the last thing I needed was extra exposure to Tritium.

I might have chained the fear, but it kept spitting the words *twenty minutes* at me.

My heart thrummed against my ribs. My jaw clenched so tight my teeth ached in their roots. Yet my legs felt rubbery. My lungs flirted with hyperventilating. And horrible, awful, shameful tears kept seeping into my eyes.

When I burst free from the water and clawed my way up onto the salt-crusted shore, the loss of buoyancy hit me like a life prison sentence.

I knew what I had to do. The only way *to* do it.

The thought made my guts liquid.

Hands and knees on the rocks, palms grinding into salt-saturated dead algae, I fought to control myself.

Someone patted my shoulder. I jerked, raising a defensive arm.

A pressure suited figure. Name tag of NHUNG.

Gunfire.

I swallowed my heart.

His other hand offered me the voice wire.

I needed two tries to grab it, my hands were shaking too bad. Three to get it in the jack.

"—all right, Miss Redding? What happened?"

He sounded almost frantic. Seeing my panic had infected him. "I couldn't get through," I said. "I mean, I can. I can see how to do it. But I couldn't. I couldn't make myself do it."

"Hang on," he said. "Let's at least get you off these rocks and onto the sand."

I fought to swallow my panic down. "Yeah. All right."

Just as with climbing out of a pool on Earth, everything felt heavier. Worse, the water had obscured the gravity waves. Those few minutes underwater had taken my habitual awareness of the heavy and the light. Covering the few meters from the edge of the pool, bending through the gate, and settling onto the sand demanded focused concentration that shoved the panic further back.

"How's that, ma'am?" Gunfire said. "Comfy? Comfy as you're gonna get, I mean?"

I shuddered. The paternalistic *ma'am* had annoyed me, but right now?

I deserved it.

"Comfy," I said in a small voice.

"All right then." He clumsily levered himself down between me and his workbench. The "radio" had grown more connections while I was gone. "Tell me about it."

I took a deep breath, willing my guts to stop twitching. "The tunnel gets narrow."

"All right."

"It curves up. Maybe fifteen meters underwater, then it curves up and you can see the surface."

"That's good."

"The pressure suit was too big, though. There's a great big driftwood log jammed in there. I couldn't get past it. Not even with taking the life support pack off. And the top of the water was maybe three meters further up. Nothing at all."

"All right."

I couldn't see his face, and he couldn't see mine. I still closed my eyes and hung my chin. "All I had to do was get out of the suit and swim up, and I couldn't do it."

Silence.

Then Gunfire said, "Are you *insane*, woman?"

"That's how to get up there!"

Gunfire leaned a few centimeters towards me. I could almost see his eyes, whatever they looked like, burning through the faceplate. "Taking off your suit is nothing but slow suicide. You can't go back to Earth, then you die out here."

"It has to be done," I said. "I couldn't make myself do it."

"You don't have to do it," Gunfire said.

"It's my job!" I snarled. "It's my job to hurt myself, and I couldn't make myself do it again!"

My words shocked me.

I panted into the silence.

Each time I'd needed a hand regrown, I'd been assigned a therapist. Montague employed all sorts of mental health professionals. Some of the universes we visited could have subtle, horrible effects on our minds. People got hurt. I'd admitted to the second therapist that losing my hands on two consecutive assignments had made me a little twitchy. We'd talked about it. She'd given me breathing exercises and worked through mental drills with me.

They'd helped. I'd been ready to go back to work. Ready enough.

Only I wasn't ready.

Gunfire said, "I think this is where I'm supposed to get out a bottle of whiskey and a couple of glasses, pour you a shot, and tell you I want to hear your story."

I coughed something like a laugh.

"I gotta give you a rain check on the bottle. I'll admit easy that I don't like authoritarian capitalists, but I haven't seen anything here that says they employ people to hurt themselves."

I needed to run through one of those breathing exercises before I could say, "It's not like that."

"You just said it is."

"I was upset."

"Seems we aren't going anywhere for a bit. So tell me. What's this about you hurting yourself?"

I willed my heart to slow. My tongue felt heavy.

The therapist had made me tell the story, sure. But she'd already known. I needed a clear mental health report to go back to work. And what else could I do, lying in a hospital bed with my arm a wired-up stump? "You need to work on that Portal stuff."

"Not a thing I can do without more computer."

"Then we need to find more computer."

"Most of all," Gunfire said, "we need you to have a clear head. Or we might as well go in through the airlock with our hands up."

"Anyone ever tell you you're kind of a jerk, Gunfire?"

"A few times, sure. It's why they have me do math, so they can put me in a room all by my lonesome and shove flat food under the door."

My snort wasn't a laugh, but it wasn't not one.

Gunfire said, "We been running crazy for almost a day straight now. Take five minutes and tell me about it. I won't laugh at you."

My chest tightened around my lungs.

But I'd wanted the therapist to like me. I'd wanted my coworkers to like me. I'd assembled a brave face for my parents.

I didn't care if Gunfire liked me or not.

I did care if he *respected* me.

And if I curled around my pain, he'd lose that respect.

And he was right on one thing. This would be easier with a bottle of whiskey.

All I had was a water dispenser.

I took a drink and started to talk.

37

"The universe was called Freefall."

Gunfire made an encouraging noise.

"A man had died weird. It didn't add up. I was investigating."

"That's worthy labor."

Was that Texan for *a job worth doing*? "Turns out one of the scientists had accidentally killed him. I got close. He took one of those diffuse steel knives and stabbed me in the hand."

Gunfire hissed in sympathy.

"I got him, but my left hand?" I raised the hand, then made a slash across it with the other. "I kept the thumb."

"Ouch."

"The next universe didn't have a name. The station was being destroyed. They'd triggered evacuation and everything, but I was pretty sure they couldn't get everyone out in time. Everybody was screaming at everyone. I saw a way to maybe make it stop. Even if we had to evacuate, it wouldn't be total."

"That's a risk people take, working for Montague, isn't it?"

My voice caught. "There were kids. Families."

Chevy coughed. "Right. Go on."

"I had to buy time for this bright kid to save the station. I had an idea. It was a horrible idea. I admit it. Two of them, really. Two thin ideas. Not much chance of success. The first, I had to tell someone else. I did that. The other?" I raised my right hand. "I had to take the glove off my suit." The memory burned bright on my closed eyelids. "The air was full of chemicals. Machines exploding. And it was hot."

"I burned my hand on a grill once," Gunfire said. "Hurt like crazy."

"This wasn't grill hot. Or oven hot." I needed another sip of water. "They said after, more like kiln hot." My pulse had slowed, but still beat so hard in my throat that it felt like twin creatures ready to burst forth from my carotids. "Turned out, the part I shouted to Bear worked. I didn't need the hand plan, at all. So they shipped me back to Earth. They couldn't save any of that hand. Had to amputate and regrow it all."

"And now," I said, "I get here. And we've got a plan to end this stupid mutiny. We've got everything we need," I spat, "and I'm too *afraid* to do my part."

"You've had a real rough time," Gunfire said.

What was I supposed to say to that? *Thank you*?

He gave me time to answer, then said, "I got a couple questions, if it's okay."

My laugh sounded bitter, even to me. "Sure. Why not?"

"When that killer stabbed you. Did you know he was a killer before?"

My chest felt tight. "No. I pretty much ran towards the screams. We'd figured out something wasn't right with him, but then he stabbed the pilot."

"You were sailing?"

"Flying. In a blimp. He cut the rest of us off so we fell."

Gunfire said, "Let me make sure I got this straight. This man had killed before. He pulled the sharpest knife known to man, on a *blimp*, and stabbed the pilot. I'm guessing there warn't no copilot either."

"No. They're not hard to fly."

"Not the point. He stabbed you and dropped y'all out of the sky, and you lived through it."

"Lucy and MacConnor made it too."

"You saved them, I'm guessing?"

"It was more of a team effort." MacConnor had been in the same Montevideo hospital as me. We'd played cards to kill time. I'd bet my cut-off fingers against the lobes of his old liver and his pancreas. We thought it was funny.

But the memory of the week we'd spent together afterwards brought me a smile, even now.

"You didn't go looking to get stabbed, did you?"

This brought an honest laugh. "I was looking to prove myself by investigating something that didn't make sense. It just happened to be a death."

Gunfire had his own laugh. "You did better than me. I tried to prove myself by writing a math paper refuting my undergrad advisor's work."

"Oh, I bet that went well."

"It turned out I was right. It got published, and I needed a new advisor. Took me by surprise."

That drew a deeper laugh. I could just see some professor chewing Gunfire out, and Gunfire looking perplexed. And I'd much rather discuss Gunfire's problems than mine. "Did you learn your lesson?"

"Yes. When you're going to crush someone's life's work, always warn them first." Before I could say anything he continued, "The second time you lost your hand."

My laughter dried up.

"People's lives were endangered. You came up with not one, but two plans to save them."

"Two bad plans. Real thin, both of them."

"And you implemented both of them. Simultaneously."

My discomfort shifted, losing a little of its anger at myself and gaining a little focus on the way Gunfire expressed himself. "It wasn't like that."

"I bet it was. I'll bet you my best boots that the other plan, the plan that worked? It didn't risk you."

"The station was exploding. We were all at risk."

"It didn't *increase* your risk," Gunfire said. "Lots of folks, they would have tried that plan and skipped the one that hurt them."

"Smart people."

"Did you think about that plan first? Or did you just whip off your glove?"

"I thought hard about it. I looked hard for any other way."

"In both of these? Did you take any unnecessary risks? Or did you decide to learn tap-dancing as you fell out of that blimp?"

"Looking back, I could have done other things."

"But right there, at the moment, you thought it through and did your best. With stuff exploding all around you."

"Sure."

Gunfire leaned back, settling on his elbows so he almost rested on his life support pack. "Then that there's why you're so upset right now."

My anger flared. "What are you talking about?"

"You been hurt. You don't want to get hurt again. Whatever we do now, you got a chance of getting hurt. If you don't, other folks are gonna get hurt. Might get hurt anyway."

My throat tightened. "Yeah."

"But see, whipping your suit off down there and swimming up is not a plan. It's not thought out. It's all that fear, coming straight up at you." He shifted to lean on one elbow so he could face me a little more. "Maybe one of us has to go out without a suit. But if we do, we'll do it smart. That twenty-minute limit? We think about it first, I bet with the right plan, we can do it in five. And it starts with taking off our suits *before* getting in the water, so we can get back in them and breathe proper air again."

I stopped.

Gunfire was right.

I'd panicked. I'd stopped thinking. I'd focused on accomplishing the immediate goal and totally forgotten the long term.

I'd leaped straight to doing myself harm.

"Deep breath, ma'am. Let's think this through. You said there was a log in the way. If we get a lever, can we shift it?"

"It has to be me," I said.

"Enough with this noble stuff," Gunfire said. "You're already a hero, you don't need any more."

"It's not that," I said. "The tunnel is so narrow, I barely fit. You won't."

"You could tie a rope to it. We could both pull."

I made myself breathe. I'd realized that he was right, that I wasn't thinking, and even knowing that I *still* hadn't started thinking. "Yes. Yes, you could help. You could go down in your pressure suit and pull on the line. But that log is holding up a bunch of rocks and sand. The whole tunnel might come down. We need a better plan. A solid plan. That doesn't involve anyone trapped here forever." Just like the therapist said, I pulled in air through my nose, filled my lungs, and pushed it out my mouth.

"While the antisocials are watching us," Gunfire said.

"Yep. Or, at least, if we do get trapped here?" I said. "We have to make it worthwhile. We have to win."

38

Quick but thorough, Gunfire and I talked it through.

The computers out in the tunnels had either tiny controllers, like those in the monitoring gear and the screen outside the airlock, or buried somewhere within massive tunneling bots. The moment I went near the tunneling bots, the mutineers would assume I intended to turn the machine against the facility. I felt certain that they wouldn't stand down for *no no folks, I want only the processor cores so we can open up an alternate Portal and let Montague HQ spank you.*

Clearing tunnels required explosives. If we searched, we might find them. They might let us blow a bigger hole at the end of the tunnel. They might also bring the ceiling down on us. And the moment the mutineers saw us open the explosives locker, they'd pull two dozen people off of Project Mutiny and on to Operation Crush Redding And Gunfire With Real Gunfire. The projectile weapons they'd brought out for the aliens would turn us to squiddie bait in two, maybe three seconds.

The mutineers had planned well. I didn't see any way to end this without Gunfire opening that alternate Portal.

That meant he needed a tortoise-bot. No way around it.

That meant someone getting out of their pressure suit and swimming out for it.

I would barely fit through the tunnel opening.

He thought he could squirm through.

But the swimmer might not return. If I was left alone, I'd search for weaknesses outside the brick barricade until I ran out of air. If he was left alone he might figure out how to open the alternate Portal, or force the existing Portal to open wide. Getting him to admit the possibility was like pulling my own molar with a pair of tweezers.

I won, but I got called *ma'am*. A lot.

And if I had to swim, we could make it as safe as possible.

The real question was, how long could someone stay out? Everybody in Tritium knew that twenty minutes was the maximum possible exposure, but one breath meant medical treatment back on Earth. As far as I knew, nobody had ever tried it.

Nobody but our aliens, that is.

When I was working hard, I took about twenty-five breaths a minute. I wouldn't breathe underwater, but I'd certainly gasp coming out. Twenty-five was a usable average.

At two hundred fifty breaths, I would go home only with lengthy medical care.

Five hundred breaths? Exiled.

My sister practices Tai Chi. She says it's all about mastering the breath. I've seen her take three breaths a minute for an hour. I hoped I'd get to tell her how much I regretted turning down her invitations to join her.

Finally, we had the best bad plan we could come up with.

Gunfire needed another half hour to finish his software. I thought it through more as he programmed. The plan had too many gaps, but they all came down to *what if*? What if the squiddies thought I was yummy? What if the tunnel collapsed as I was going through it? What if trace elements in the water made it too acidic or basic for my hide? What if the algae attached itself to my blistered ankles and started eating its way to my brain?

My fear edged back towards panic.

I focused on Gunfire's fractured muttering instead. I preferred annoyance to dread. And these specialist sorts always underestimated how much time they needed to figure things out. There was no point in me playing Great Hunter and returning with a tortoise if he still needed two hours of programming. This had to be ready to go.

To my shock, in about fifteen minutes he said, "Done."

"That's it?" I said.

"I could optimize it further. I'll make a copy while you're gone and do some fine-tuning. But what I have here will probably work."

Probably.

That was one reason why I wasn't dragging the electrodes and adapters out with me. Systems rarely worked on the first try. Gunfire was the only one who could debug this contraption. I felt certain he couldn't squeeze through the tunnel. Gunfire wasn't certain he could get "sufficient Portal resonance," whatever that was, through all those meters of volcanic basalt.

Plus, we didn't know where that tunnel came out. It looked shallow, but those shallows might be behind the sheer southern cliffs as easily as in the northern bay.

No, I had to swim out. See where I was. If I couldn't get a tortoise, I would return and get in my suit. Three minutes of swimming each way, so seven minutes tops. Call it ten, with getting the suit back on and flushing the air.

If I came out of the tunnel and found myself where I couldn't snatch a tortoise and get back to the tunnel inside five minutes, Gunfire wanted me to come back. I'd agreed to prevent the argument. Truth was, if I thought I could return with a tortoise but it would take more than five minutes, I'd fetch it. Even if it terrified me.

But I'd go knowing I'd done everything I could to avoid that fate.

I could deliver the tortoise to Gunfire. Watch to be sure he could open the Portal. Then swim back around to the lagoon to meet my fellow exiles. They'd welcome me. Every colony hungered for more strong backs. And I'd go knowing that I'd been smart. I wouldn't spend the rest of my life whimpering that I'd missed the obvious solution to preserve the life I'd loved.

I shook the possibility away.

I got to my feet. The suit's collar wasn't just chafing my neck, it outright scraped. The blisters on my ankles had transcended spots and become a single mass of pain. Every bit of me itched.

Gunfire got to his knees, but detoured to grab the drop cloth from the electronics kit and a handful of alligator clips.

"What's that for?" I said.

"Do you really want to do this skinny dipping?"

My gut reaction was *sexist Texan*. I bit that back. Then I wanted to snarl something about having walked stark naked, in one and a half gravities, with bare feet, across a sharply textured steel floor.

The truth was, having something—*anything*—to wear would be a tiny bit better than doing this starkers.

If nothing else, forget Gunfire. The mutineers didn't deserve an eyeful.

"Thanks," I said.

"Any Texas gentleman would offer the same." Yes, the word *gentleman* is sexist, but I got the sense Gunfire didn't mean it that way. He'd seen I had a need, and acted.

Gunfire followed me back through the gate, to the pool's rock-laden edge.

What would that blue algae feel like under my bare feet?

I took a deep breath. Garlic. Someone else's old sweat. My own fear-sweat. The distinct aroma of *Redding needs a shower.*

The thick stew tasted delicious.

Water. All the water I could chug. Three protein pellets. More water.

"Okay," I said. "I'm ready."

"Miss Redding," Gunfire said.

I tensed.

"In Soviet Texas, we study organizations. How they inevitably go bad. Especially capitalist ones. And eventually, they all do."

A political lecture? *Now?*

"Come back safe and fast," he said. "Your company needs people like you to hold off their end. Even if they don't recognize it."

I choked up a touch. "I guess Texas can't be that bad, if you came out of there."

"When you're on vacation, come visit. You haven't had barbeque until you've had Texan."

"Okay." I said, shrugging out of the life support pack. "Enough sentiment. Time to save the world."

39

I overrode the suit's screeching alarms, braced myself for a hideous stench, and unfastened the helmet.

Earth air gushed out. Over-neutroned Tritium air flooded over me.

The cave smelled like newly fallen roses. Sweetness with just a hint of decay. My college dorm room often smelled worse. The school cafeteria always did.

Gunfire pulled the helmet from my hands and set it on the sand behind him.

My hands were already moving over the suit seals running down my breastbone. The gloves were not meant for speed, but the closing toggles were sized for the gloves.

Gunfire was already shuffling behind me, to catch the back of the suit.

Shocking cool air washed over my bare skin. The chafed skin around my neck burned and prickled. Was I bleeding? Had I pulled off scabs? No way to answer that, and no time to worry about it. My sweat-damp skin steamed as I exposed it.

The seal ended at the top of my right thigh. I undid it all. No time for even a nod at modesty. A weird tug and *pop* as the automatic catheters retracted. I wasn't going to miss either of those. If—*when*, when!—I got back into the suit, I wouldn't be in long enough to need them.

My head throbbed, and my throat felt tight. Was I already suffocating?

No.

I'd stopped breathing. Precious low-neutron Earth air distended my stomach.

The taut silver-copper fear I'd ignored was back stronger than ever, its taste filling my mouth.

I put both my arms across my stomach and squeezed.

Air gushed out of me.

The smell of Tritium poured into my sinuses, into my mouth, and straight down. Filling me.

Four hundred ninety-nine breaths left.

My soul gibbered.

Gunfire held the back side of my suit, ready for me to climb out.

If I'd been alone, I might have frozen. But there was no way I was going to let a Texan see me freeze up.

What rationality couldn't accomplish, a hint of spite did.

Gunfire lowered the suit's upper half and came to the side, so I could grab hold of him and hoist myself up and out of the right leg. The heavy caught me just as I was coming up, and I had to throw a second arm around Gunfire just to balance myself.

The cool air across my body was a shocking relief after the suit's confines.

I glimpsed lines of blood at the back of my ankles and up the Achilles tendon. The air stung them.

Four hundred ninety-eight left.

No time to be squeamish. I shoved my free foot at the sand like I was kicking at it.

The sand was warmer than the air, but damp. It hugged my foot exactly like Earth's beach sand. How many neutrons did Tritium's silicon atoms have?

No, don't think about that. Breathe slow. Four ninety-seven. Get the other foot out. Four ninety-six.

Waste half a breath grabbing the black plastic drop cloth and clipping it under my armpits and down the side. The stiff plastic crinkled, but it went one and a quarter times and ran halfway down my thigh. I'd had worse beach coverups.

"Don't worry," I said for the benefit of their invisible spies. "I'll come back with help."

Gunfire raised a hand in farewell. "Good luck."

I grinned, just so he could see it. "Wouldn't know what to do with it."

I grabbed the open can of plumber's putty from Gunfire's outstretched hand and dug two fingers in. Slapped a bunch over each ear, blocking the canals. Another wad went over my nostrils.

I trotted fast as I dared for the water.

40

Tritium's water was *cold.*

Just putting my foot in felt like plunging it into an ice bath. Or colder. Below freezing, maybe. Salt water froze at a colder temperature than plain. Maybe Tritium salt water had an even lower freezing point.

I yelped, and almost pulled back.

It wasn't too late. I could pull my foot back and hop into the suit. All it would take was Gunfire seeing that I couldn't do it.

The ruin of blisters around my ankle burned. I could have done without knowing that Tritium salt worked in a wound exactly like Earth salt.

I couldn't ease into this. I couldn't waste the time, the breaths, or the body heat.

I also couldn't throw myself into the water. One careful step at a time.

And water always felt cold when you first got into it. The water here wasn't stagnant, but without tides nothing actively pulled it in and out of the ocean. The far end would be warmer.

The good news was, by the time I got myself in the water, I'd know if the squiddies thought humans were yummy.

Bioluminescent algae that had grown undisturbed for the last century squished underfoot. Some squeezed between my toes. My foot didn't dissolve, so I dragged my next foot into the salt-and-blister torture.

A hooted breath. Stop it. Was that four ninety-two or four ninety-one?

Seconds in, and I'd already lost count.

I shambled down the irregular steps, steadying myself with one hand on a half-submerged rock at the pool's edge, breathing slow and deep as the cold climbed my thighs, my hips, my torso. Countless tiny scrapes and chafes I'd gotten from the pressure suit but hadn't even noticed joined my ankles in burning.

I didn't feel any squiddie teeth or tentacles, though. Peering through my own wake, it looked like they fled my presence. At least they hadn't smelled my blood and realized that I belonged on their sacrificial altar.

The chafing around my neck stung as bad as my ankles.

Now for the next test.

One deep breath. I needed the oxygen, neutron-loaded or not. A second.

I plunged forward into the water.

Nothing reminds you that your body radiates a quarter of its heat from the head like plunging yourself into cold water. The shock stunned me for a beat, plastic swimsuit billowing around me, before I could kick my legs and propel myself back up.

Another shock of cold when my head broke the surface.

The putty felt nasty in my ears and on my lower lip. It stuck, though, and it had kept my ears and nostrils clear. So long as I could keep my mouth shut under water, I would minimize my exposure to the ocean's trace elements.

With my luck, this was an arsenic ocean. Maybe strychnine.

Three strong strokes took me to the far edge of the pool, where the tunnel disappeared under water. I filled my lungs deep as I could, squeezed my mouth shut, and plunged down.

Opening my eyes stung, but I could see.

Streamers of bioluminescent algae ran everywhere, rising from stones and drifting back and forth as the gravity waxed and waned in a constant slow tide. My mouth tasted of dead sweet roses and copper, clashing with the nasty chemical stink of plumber's putty filling my sinuses. The squiddies fled my bare skin, but clustered around my plastic onesie. Figures. I decided to keep it on and kicked my way forward.

My heart pounded against my ribs. Was it fear? Oxygen? The cold?

It didn't matter. I needed to get down the tunnel.

The dive was easy enough. The urge to breathe thrummed in my throat and hammered my temples by the time I hit the few meters of straightaway at the bottom, but I kicked and stroked as fierce as I could.

Could I drag a tortoise back through this cold?

I'd have to get it part way and come back up for air. Might be three or four dives.

The tunnel shrank around me.

Grabbing algae-greased rocks and throwing myself forward was faster than stroking, but I kept my legs working. A toe struck a rock and haloed in pain, but I kept going.

The sharp turn, going up.

My vision was shrinking just like the tunnel. A ring of gray surrounded everything. The urge to breathe joined forces with my fear, demanding I suck everything in that I could.

Sunlight, only two meters up.

The sky looked gray.

I kicked and clawed my way up the driftwood log as fast and hard as I could.

An eternity later, I broke water like a dolphin, gasping for air. Drops of bitter metallic sea water hit my tongue and got sucked in with the precious, sweet, oh so cold air.

Even through the putty blocking my ears, I heard someone bellow "Got her!"

Calloused hands seized my arms.

41

With each slow-poison breath, color flooded back into my vision.

I'd come out in the best and worst possible place.

The tunnel emerged right in the lagoon, not five meters from shore. The tranquil opalescent water looked inviting as a tourist brochure. I could walk to shore from here. A tortoise-bot was working the bottom of the stairs right now, not twenty meters away. Run up. Seize it. Flip it on its back to drop it into maintenance mode. Breathe deep the whole way back to the water, to get my blood going, and plunge back into the tunnel.

The aliens, all eleven of them, stood right there.

When I'd been in my pressure suit, they had seemed large and strong, but reasonable.

Outside my pressure suit? They were *huge*. I'm not a big person, and they were big men.

And they smelled like men who had been on a long sea voyage, in a Viking-style longboat, in cold climates, for weeks. Plugged nose and all, they *stank*.

The brisk air hit me like a glacier, pillaging the heat from my muscles.

I exercised religiously. You never know when you're going to wind up marching two kilometers in two gravities, or throwing yourself into a bottomless pit, or any number of things normal people never get to experience. I'm strong. The men who held my arms were far stronger, and my oxygen-starved tissues wouldn't let me do anything except suck air as they hauled me up out of the water. My putty-plugged nostrils meant my mouth gaped. Salt-bitter water streaming out of my short hair kept trickling in and I kept spitting.

At least I didn't taste arsenic.

They set me on my feet next to one of the fires, right in front of Captain Mason. Heat washed over half of me, while the near-Arctic wind sucked at my other half. Algae-greased pebbles dug at the soles of my feet. My knees wobbled, but I compelled them to support me.

I'd remembered that Caleb Mason was the biggest of his men. His curly beard and hair radiated from his head in every direction in a salted hairy halo, making him even bigger. I hadn't noticed before that he needed to brush his teeth and that his clothes needed a good washing or, preferably, burning. It wasn't fair of me. Old-time explorers didn't carry showers and caterers with them. My first assignment, I'd come home grungy because the universe didn't show the filth. I'm sure when these men got a chance they'd scrub themselves back to brown and beat their clothes on the river rocks until they could bend.

In a year, I might be living like them.

The way I was breathing, more likely than not.

"I didn't believe them," Mason said. The putty squeezed the character from his voice. "But here you are."

I compelled my breath to slow.

The weird thing was? The unexpected capture had shocked my fear away.

I still had a ticking clock. A limited number of breaths. Even if I'd lost count, the limit was there. But the scope of my problem had simplified. I wasn't stuck on the wrong side of the island. I wasn't trying to climb a cliff or fighting implacable current.

Cope with Mason.

Snatch a tortoise.

Get back down the hole.

It didn't matter that eleven huge men who'd been on their own for weeks surrounded me. Or that I wore nothing but fierceness and a square meter of plastic. That alien salt burned the wounds on my ankles and neck, and the tiny scratches all over the rest of my skin.

The job had gotten simple.

I compelled my diaphragm to expand fully, giving me enough breath to speak. "Didn't believe who?" I couldn't quite hear.

Mason said something.

"Can you speak up?" I said. "My ears are real plugged."

"A Mister Kendall said you'd be coming out. Said that if we caught you and turned you over to him, he'd give us a fast ride home."

My spirits plunged, but my brain churned.

"Derek!" Mason said. "Get the lady the spare blanket, she's freezing here."

"Kendall getting people out here will take too long," I said. "You remember about the time limits?"

"You've been out here more than five minutes," Mason said. "You're part of Anti-Earth now."

"Our medicine is better now. I have a few more minutes."

Mason shook his head. "I'm sorry. They've thrown you out."

"You remember me, right? We talked yesterday."

"We sure did. Come on up by the fire."

I barely kept myself from shouting. "There's no time. Look. Do you know why Kendall wants me?"

"Why doesn't matter now," Mason said. "You're committed. My great-uncle Rob tried to blab about the Gateway, way back when. Sharam trussed him up like a piglet and shoved him through. By the time he got free, was too late. He was mad, but settled down. You will too."

"Kendall's trying to start the wars again," I blurted.

Kendall's disembodied voice said, "That's not true."

The mutineers certainly had minidrones plant cameras and mics everywhere around Mason during the night. "It is true. Kendall's said he's busy now, right? That's because half the crew inside is trying to stop him."

"Captain Mason? We'll send up equipment with you," Kendall said. "Just hold her there for another half-hour or so."

Mason's eyes narrowed at me.

"You note he isn't arguing," I said.

"I can't argue with your delusions," Kendall said.

"Look," I said. "If I'm crazy, you'll be stuck with me. If I'm not, though? Why would I be out here? Why would I take this risk?"

"That's a good question," Mason said.

"You've got a choice," I said. "Here's the deal. Let me go. Let me grab what I came for. If I fail? If I'm exiled here? I'll join you wholeheartedly. I will spill my guts. I know a lot about Earth technology."

"Whatever you're doing," Kendall said, "it can't work."

"*When* I pull this off?" I said. "You'll have helped avert war. I'll speak up for you at headquarters. You'll have allies on our side that can help you."

"I could just keep you," Mason said, "get the ride back, and you'd be stuck with us."

"You could," I said. "I'd be on that ride back. And once we're in the village?" I couldn't loom at him. You can't loom over someone forty centimeters taller than you. Especially not while barefoot, dressed only in an alligator-clipped plastic sarong, with near-Arctic wind shooting up underneath it because the promised blanket hadn't yet arrived. But I tried. "Once we're back? I will make it my personal mission to ruin your life."

Mason stared at me, impassive.

"Modern medicine is excellent," I said. "I am in tiptop health. All the things that people die of early? I don't have any of them. All four of my grandparents and seven of my great-grandparents are still alive. I will make myself friendly to everyone in this village, and be an absolute pain in your behind for all the rest of your days."

With that, I stared unflinching into his eyes.

"Plus," I said, "remember who threw you a rope."

Mason blinked.

Then he laughed.

My tension peaked.

"You would, wouldn't you?" Mason chortled. "You would make my days a nightmare and my nights a torment, until I moved to Mount Sharam just to get away from you."

My tension dissolved. "I'd rather be friends." I turned my other side to the fire, trying to warm up. "I'd really rather be friends."

"We have an arrangement," Kendall said.

"We have your promises," Mason called. To me he said, "What do you need?"

I pointed my chin. "A tortoise-bot. One of the scrubbing things."

"Tommish!" Mason shouted. "Grab the lady one of them turtles."

"Are you going to clean us up?" Kendall said.

"That pond is filthy," I said. "No matter how this comes out, it needs tidying."

Tommish, another giant with his hair braided into tight braids that draped to his shoulders, stomped back. The tortoise-bot was cold with dampness, grimy with salt, lighter than it looked, and fit into my arms like it belonged there.

Kendall said, "You'll be sailing back home, Captain."

Mason raised his voice. "I'd rather sail a month home with a friend than fly home with an enemy like her."

I flashed him a smile.

Mason said, "Only seven great-grandparents?"

"Great-grandma Louisa died on her hundredth birthday." I charged back into the water and shouted, "Skydiving."

The last thing I heard was Kendall bellowing, "We're coming for you, Redding!"

42

I should have guessed one detail about the tortoises.

They *float*.

If a tortoise got blown off a wall and into the water, you wanted it to float. And you wanted all the connectors nice and watertight.

Montague didn't want them to get blown into the water, either. That's why they had that low sloping shape. The harder the wind blew, the more air pressure held them down.

That shape sliced through the water.

I broke water in the cave like a breeching whale, shouting "Gunfire!" I was half frozen. My mouth tasted of bitter alien sea water and the putty seemed to have swollen until it filled my sinuses and ear canals. My skin was ice and flame, my muscles only ice, my lungs an inferno.

But I had the tortoise.

I kicked hard as I could for the shore, gulping air and shouting "Gunfire!"

"Miss Redding!" The putty in my ears had wedged deep. "You're alive!"

"Grab it!" I shouted.

I accepted his help climbing out onto the slimy rocks, gasping the precious poison air, stripping away the plastic sarong as I did.

"Here," Gunfire said. "Let's get you in your suit."

"No time," I said.

"You have to!"

"They're coming! Kendall is furious and I'm almost deaf! Grab the bot and get to work. I'll get dressed myself."

Gunfire's blank visor faced me for a beat.

Then he crouched to pick up the inverted tortoise and trotted double-heavy through the gate.

I shook myself as hard as I could, trying to spray as much water off me as I could. The putty came off my nose easy enough, and I could draw part of a breath. I'd need a vacuum hose and a pick to get the putty out of my ears, though, so I didn't bother.

Gunfire had laid my suit on the ground, like I'd asked. I dropped to my butt and squirmed in. The water made the interior cloth stick to me. I had to shove and groan and swear, but I got my legs down. When my skin dried, that salt was going to torture me.

It wouldn't last long, though. We were almost done. Or almost done for. One of those.

And inside the suit was cold. The air wasn't that cold. How could the suit be cold?

Getting my arms into the suit was easier, as was sealing up the front. I thanked Simmers for the extra space up top, pushed out the last of my Tritium air, and snatched the helmet. I'd no more sealed it than every alarm the suit had screamed loud enough for me to hear even through the putty. Atmosphere violations. My right pinky and ring finger, crammed into a single glove finger—oops. Biometrics all wrong, medical intervention needed but no telemetry to complain with. A high pH warning, of all things. Was that an acid, or a base? Base, I thought.

The suit panicked more than I ever did. Life support fuel consumption warnings flared as a torrent of good air flooded into the suit.

I drew a wholesome breath of warm, pure, delicious Earth air.

A humidity warning flashed.

My still tongue tasted of alien salt and metallic ocean. I sucked a mouthful of water, rinsed my mouth as best I could, and dribble-spat. There. That'd give the suit something to complain about.

Childish, yes. But if I'd poisoned myself, I deserved a little bit of childishness.

The suit sucked the water out, exactly as it was supposed to. Every second, the salt on my skin grew scratchier. My blisters and scrapes escalated from scorching to full-on burning. Before it got worse, I got up off my knees and staggered out through the gate, towards Gunfire and Montague and today's debacle.

Gunfire knelt by his tangle of wires. He had the tortoise-bot's belly access hatch open, and one of the adapter cables run into it. Another ran to the datalink on his belt. More wires led to the electrodes, which he'd spread as wide as the tunnel permitted.

If mutineers got down that tunnel before Gunfire finished, we were done. We were probably dead. *I* certainly was.

Gunfire's fingertips twitched and danced on open air. Virtual keyboarding.

I had to buy him time to finish his miracles.

From the open top of his electronics tool kit poked our two captured stunners. I picked them up. My one hand almost fumbled because of the two-fingers-in-one hole problem, but I managed. Wholly focused on his problem, Gunfire didn't even notice.

The electrodes filled the hallway. If our rogue Portal was open, he wouldn't be working so hard.

I took a chance and double-heavied between the electrodes.

I wasn't sucked back to Earth and immediately irradiated by the neutron-heavy atoms in my body, so the Portal wasn't open.

I took two seconds to crank both stunners up to maximum intensity, strong enough to zap through a pressure suit, and ran forward. The tunnel walls turned to finished stone. It wasn't nearly as long as I remembered from when we fled the other way.

I burst out into the cavern just as the big airlock in the brick wall was swinging open.

Four pressure suited people emerging.

All carrying firearms. Aimed straight ahead.

They knew I was right there. Surveillance had told them. But they needed a half second to orient past the opening door, aim, and fire.

I pointed both stunners straight into the airlock, thumbed each trigger half a dozen times, and hurtled myself backwards.

Had I hit anyone? No idea.

But they knew I was willing to shoot.

They had the better guns, but nobody wants to take a stunner to the face. They'd live, but feel awful.

Gunfire, not the man but the real thing, the sharp hurricane of concentrated automatic weapons fire, penetrated my stuffed ears. Maybe my bones had carried the sound, it was that loud.

Bullets pocked against the far wall.

I thrust one hand around the tunnel's curve and fired three times, then yanked back.

The bullets stopped. Had I hit someone?

"Redding!" The word was loud and deep enough for me to hear, conducted more by bone than ears. They'd heard me tell Mason I'd plugged my ears. "Give up, and you'll live!"

Was that supposed to be an improvement over yesterday's "won't be harmed" garbage?

Maybe they wouldn't have hurt me. But people would have died on Earth. That was just another kind of hurt.

The panic and fear were gone, devoured by adrenaline. I didn't know if they would stay gone. I didn't think I'd beaten them forever. But if the choice was let people get hurt, or to abandon my goal for this assignment and set off thirty megatons of misbehavior, I knew I'd picked the right one.

I hugged the wall on the inside of the curve, life support pack pressed into the wall. My right hand faced the airlock, with the stunner in it. It was as small as I could make my profile.

The pH alarm climbed as the humidity alarm quieted. My entire body burned with scratches and salt. Even my armpits burned. My makeshift sarong must have left scratches.

Behind me, Gunfire shouted something. My ears were too plugged, the suit alarms too noisy to understand. I didn't turn around, but kept my attention on my stunner and the tunnel ahead.

He shouted again.

I couldn't help him. He had his job. I had mine.

Do or die, a lot of dying. I'd just be the first.

A rifle barrel appeared around the edge of the tunnel.

I made myself not thumb the trigger.

More rifle barrel appeared.

Then a gloved hand, holding the rifle.

I fired.

Missed.

The man charged forward, rifle coming to bear.

I swung my aching, tired, salt-burning arm, trying to aim.

The blank helmet on the mutineer's construction-grade suit might as well have been a machine. He could have been a robot sent to kill me.

I shot twice more.

He fired, a whole torrent of shots.

I shrieked almost as loud as the rifle. No way I could survive. *Unsurvivable* had nothing on low-velocity rifle rounds. Hopefully I'd bought Gunfire enough time.

No--how was I still thinking that? Why wasn't I full of bullet holes?

The mutineer had shot past me.

I wrenched my head to look.

A different robot stood in the tunnel behind me. A real robot.

Squat and heavy, with caterpillar treads. A prow that looked like it could punch through a steel wall. Whip antennas and big cameras and what might be sensors or might be gun barrels all over it.

With a two-meter transparent shield in front of it.

I could see where the mutineer's bullets had struck the shield. Lines radiated out from the impact points, where the bullets still hung embedded.

Behind the shield?

Two men in Disaster Intervention gear that made the construction suits look like tin foil.

A tight grin cracked the salt crust on my face. My lips burned.

I opened my hands, dropped both my weapons, and stood perfectly still.

They stunned me anyway.

43

People have invented spectacular things. The Portal. Antibiotics. Moon rockets and the Mars colony, music that guts or heals, stories that grant hope and enlightenment, food that mends souls. My favorite, though? The invention that surpasses all others?

Soap.

Yes, all those arts and machines and triumphs are glorious. But when you've been fighting for your life, nothing says civilization and comfort like really good soap in a shower stall roomy enough to scrub without knocking your elbows.

When the soap smells of lavender and sage, your civilization is complete.

Okay, fine, there's also toothpaste, but that's technically a subspecies of soap.

I had the shower room to myself. I had the whole of the so-you've-drunk-the-heavy-water Decontamination Suite to myself. A six-room well-ventilated fifty-person barracks decorated in tile and stainless steel for easy cleaning, and me the only tenant. I'd spent months with a room barely big enough for my bed, and now I had echoing privacy. It wasn't quite the machine-drilled caverns, but close.

And nobody was trying to shoot me.

Disaster Intervention has an "if they're even vaguely suspicious, zap them" policy. My throbbing brain felt detached from its mount in my skull, but the medics had offered me a pain pill and promised I'd recover. Between the headache, the scrapes left by Simmers' ill-fitting pressure suit, the scrapes left by my desperate scramble through the flooded lava tube, and a few random contusions I'd picked up somewhere, I felt ready to flop down on one of the big chairs in the rec room and nap for a few days. I expected the plush Decontamination sweats and slippers to irritate my abused skin, but the medic-prescribed lotion soothed enough that they felt plush and soft.

Maybe I'd go to the kitchen and get some fruit juice. No, they said to drink water. My stomach grumbled. I could grab a meal from the freezer before finding that big chair.

I'd recorded my statement, received medical care, and been dispatched to Decontamination. I'd hear from others, eventually. Disaster Intervention had a whole bunch of mutineers and employees to interrogate. They'd debrief me when they could. The medics would tell me about the results of my exposure when they could. Montague would get to me about my next assignment—if I had one—when they could.

Until then, I waited in echoing solitude.

My hands were scratched and gouged. I'd scrubbed the feeble scabs off my knuckles.

But they were both intact.

Studying my palms, my fingers, I tried to feel triumph. These feeble abrasions would heal in a few days, especially if I kept using the lotion. My hands were just as good as right after they'd been regrown.

I didn't feel victorious. Only shaky.

I'd done better this time, spreading the abuse throughout my body instead of maiming tiny parts. Was that better? It had to be better.

The medics would tell me. If I waited, eventually I'd find out if I could return to Earth or if I was Tritium's newest permanent resident.

I closed my eyes, breathed deeply, and shoved the thoughts away before they got ugly. I'd recovered from those wounds, mostly. Never mind that nicking a finger made me sweat, and that taking a stupid stunner to the elbow drove me to violence. I knew better. I'd get through this.

A meal. A lot of water. Rinsing the dregs of Tritium out of me would take months, if it could be done. Get a snack and settle down in the common room. The couch out there looked comfortable. Grab a blanket, put my feet up, put an old favorite up on the big wall screen. Something without treachery, Texas, or anything beginning with T. Like *trouble*.

When I got to the spacious galley, a woman awaited me. The chair looked far too small for her build and muscles. Faint traceries of veins lurked beneath her translucent skin, and her short-cropped hair was a blond so pale it was almost white. Her liquid brown eyes and the dark green of her Disaster Intervention khakis made her even paler. She sat at the gleaming aluminum table closest to the sink with her datalink, a pad of actual paper, and two pens in front of her.

I stopped in the doorway. "Uh. Hello?"

"Security Third Redding?" She had a tiny voice for such a big person. "I'm DI Third Paktar. How are you feeling?"

My heart tripped. Both of us were Thirds, but we weren't the same level the same way Gunfire and I had been. You had to be crazy good to get into DI, and rumor had it that the *crazy* and the *good* were two separate requirements. "Decent." I swallowed. "I could use a night's sleep before running a double marathon."

Paktar made a note on her paper. "I understand you have been told the initial decontamination protocol."

"Lots of food and water to try to flush high-neutron atoms from my system. Lots of exercise to burn them off. Lots of rest so that I can exercise hard."

Another scratch on her pad. "Get your drink and a snack, and have a seat at the next table over. This won't take long."

Decontamination had felt weird with just me knocking around the cavernous rooms. A second person made it full-on awkward. I felt very aware of my left-heavy stride as I got to the sink, drew a large tumbler of water, and grabbed a pack of walnuts from the cupboard. Every sound, no matter how faint, echoed from the eggshell-white tile walls.

I reflexively moved to Paktar's table. She raised her pen. "Over there, please."

Right. She'd said next table. I was so soiled that she wouldn't get anywhere near me. "Sorry, a bit tired."

"Understandable. You're exhaling trace amounts of heavy CO2, and I don't want to breathe it in. Take your time. I am not in a hurry."

Each metal table was long enough for a dozen people, but the chairs were so far apart that two people couldn't reach out and clasp hands. The theory was that the heavy ventilation would suck away every Tritium particle you exhaled before the next person sucked it in. The table chilled my forearms, and the hard plastic chair exposed leg and lower back aches I hadn't known about. Secondary aches rippled up my spine, across my shoulders and down my shins, until countless tiny aches ebbed and surged with the gravity waves, even down to my feet and my hands.

Hands.

I clamped down on that thought. Panicking in front of a Disaster Intervention interrogator—Paktar had to be an interrogator, who else?—would end my career. I focused on my breath, commanding my fingers to stay loose. They ached, because I'd worked hard. That was all.

She could end my career for any number of reasons, not just panic. Best to say as little as possible.

Paktar studied her pad, flipping up a page already covered with notes.

I drank. The water went down like lead.

"Comfy?" Paktar said.

"Enough."

"Good." Her eyes met mine. "Of the hundreds of people on Tritium, you and Mister Gunfire are the only ones that I can say, categorically and without reservation, are loyal to Montague."

Wait—they'd suspected me?

No, they hadn't. That's what she said. *Calm down, Redding.*

"You clearly had nothing to do with this malfeasance," Paktar said.

Malfeasance? That's what they were calling the mutiny? She seemed to be waiting for something. "Thank you?"

"I've heard your recorded statement." Paktar flipped a page. "Recordings substantially corroborate your account, and Mister Gunfire's statement largely does so."

"Largely?" I said.

Paktar waved a hand. "No two people see the same event the same way. He also has certain opinions on for-profit businesses that color his perceptions."

I snorted. "Okay. Sure."

"Let's start with your medical."

"Medical?" *Oh, that sounds smooth, Redding.*

Paktar raised her eyes. "You do know the effects of breathing Tritium air, do you not? Let alone drinking the water?"

"Yes." I made myself breathe. How much heavy CO2 was I exhaling right now? "I was just expecting to hear it from Medical in a few days."

Paktar frowned. "You can wait for Medical if you wish."

"No, no, that's okay." Was I trapped on Tritium? Could I see my parents again? My family annoys me so much that one visit between assignments is plenty—but that visit is *important*.

Paktar kept her gaze on my eyes. "Initial indications say that forty-six days of decontamination will be enough that you can return to Earth."

One tightness in my chest evaporated.

Paktar gave me a tiny smile. I had the impression she didn't often have the opportunity for that luxury. Disaster Intervention doesn't deal in good news. "You'll be in the hospital for several days upon your return, of course, and your physical exams will include radiation poisoning and cancer checks for the rest of your life. Your little swim should have no negative effect on your Montague employment."

Another tightness faded.

Paktar's smile faded. "You'll need to sweat hard. Do your best to flush out the exercise-induced high-neutron atoms from your body."

A smile split my face. "I can manage that."

"Good!" Paktar flipped a page and held her pen ready. "Now. You've had time to think. Your head should be clearing. Is there anything you want to add to your report?"

"Gunfire," I said.

"What about him."

"I said I'd put in a good word for him. The man wants nothing but to go home—"

Paktar's laugh reminded me of a braying burro. "We didn't even get the facility locked down before he started babbling about interference fields and Portal resonance and all the things he'd give us for free if only we let him work from home."

"We had an agreement," I said. "I'd advocate for him."

"Nothing's official," Paktar said, "but Montague needs that man and we need him productive. That means happy. Gunfire was ready to hand the whole thing over for a ticket home, but that weird Soviet Texas datacore chirped up and raised his rates."

Another knot eased.

Was Paktar trying to relax me? Why?

No, that was sheer paranoia. Kendall's "malfeasance" had made me suspicious.

I took another drink of water. "I think we'll all be happier if he works from home." Better. I was calm. My hands hardly even itched.

Paktar made a notation on her paper. "Let me run through your statement. You sighted the alien sail first—congratulations, by the way, you lucky person— and you volunteered to deliver a raft to the aliens so that they could rescue themselves. You were permitted to stay as part of the first contact team. The next day, you followed the negotiating plan and took point on dealing with the aliens.

When you and Gunfire reasoned that something had gone wrong at a policy level, you both climbed up one level in the elevator, where armed Security intercepted you. When you understood the situation, you chose to fight."

My throat tightened.

I hadn't chosen to fight. I'd said we'd fought, not that I'd chosen to fight. I'd taken a stunner in the arm, and panicked.

No. I'd freaked out.

Paktar went on, oblivious to my thoughts. It all sounded so prosaic. The way she recited how we'd gone into the unfinished tunnels made it sound rational. Even going swimming was sensible. That was the option, I did it.

"And then, you came in for a drink of water and found me here," Paktar said. "Is that an accurate summary of events?"

My stomach was knotted. My perfectly regrown hands burned and burned and burned.

By offering that summary, Paktar had illuminated my problem.

I could say nothing. I could go on another assignment.

But one day, I'd take another wound to my hand and panic.

The people around me wouldn't be mutineers. They'd be teammates.

Maybe I wouldn't attack them the way I had Bakula. But they'd get hurt, and it would be my fault.

I wanted to see all the universes. But I couldn't spend human lives to do it.

My tongue felt heavy as lead. "No."

"Oh?" Paktar put her pen to paper. "Can you tell me what exactly happened differently?"

I couldn't look at her. I couldn't look at my hands. I could only stare at the table, shiny enough to reflect the glare of the overhead lights but not mirrored enough to show my face. "I panicked. They hit me in the arm. I've had—my hands. They're regrown, they're mine. I thought I was okay." My vision was blurring. "They stunned my arm, and I lost it. I didn't choose to attack." I had to force the words around the lump in my throat. "I just attacked."

Paktar set her pen down. "Praise be to the Karni Mata Buddha-Rats. I thought we were going to lose you."

I whipped my head up, breath frozen in my lungs but all my humiliation turned to fury. Had she not heard me? Was she making fun of me?

Paktar spoke with bottomless gentleness. "There's no shame in suffering from wounds. There's no shame in mental wounds outlasting the physical. There's not even in any shame in thinking that you're ready to go back. But when you find out that you're not, you *must* ask for help."

My rage turned back to humiliation. "You knew?"

"I watched the video of the fight in the suit lab." Paktar's face grew sober. "You have been trained in hand-to-hand subdual combat. If you'd tried that, the malefactors could have taken you. What you did instead…" She shook her head. "The important thing is, we can help. People outside the company can help. But you have to admit to yourself that you need it. And then the hard part. You have to ask for it."

I stared at her. "You—you tricked me." My voice barely shook.

Her eyebrows went up. "Tricked?"

"You come in here like a DI interrogator and ask me about my statement. You're from Medical, or something."

"Oh, I'm not Medical. I'm a DI recruiter."

I coughed. "You're—you're a Disaster Intervention recruiter?" Irrational excitement surged. I had nowhere near the qualifications to work in that bleeding-edge team, but even the thought that they knew who I was sent up emotional rockets. "You're recruiting me?"

"Certainly not!" Paktar dismissed that hope with a wave of her hand. "You're not qualified."

I knew I wasn't. But losing that surge of excitement still hurt. It felt like taunting.

"Getting into DI from Security would take a few more Security assignments, then a transfer into, probably, Retrieval. Perhaps more education and then assignments in a few other divisions, to develop breadth of experience."

Rip my secret out. Tease me. Then crush me, and grind me into the dirt. Got it.

"No," Paktar said breezily, "I'm just helping out. Kendall's malfeasance is the biggest structural problem we've suffered in the company's history. Every available body has been pressed into service."

"Oh." That made sense. Disappointment still twinged.

"But facing infinite universes takes a special person. And the work takes a toll on people." Her face grew serious. "Your profile says you read all the manuals and develop competence in every piece of equipment you touch. The human mind is your most important, precious, and irreplaceable equipment. If you can't learn to tell when your mind is running in the red, or if you're too stubborn to admit you're hurting?"

I made myself breathe deeply.

"If you hadn't admitted you had trouble?" Paktar shook her head. "You have potential. I would detest the necessity of terminating your employment."

"You'd fire me for that?"

"Or divert you to a low-stress position, on Earth." Paktar tapped her pen on her pad. "As you're having trouble, let's restart your therapy. Montague is assigning three more counselors to Tritium to start with. You'll get a regular slot, then more counseling when you return to Earth."

I ached to look away. To stare at the floor. Instead, I made myself meet her gaze. "Thank you."

"From there we'll see. After this, you should get a more interesting assignment next time."

"With my record?" I laughed. "I'm lucky if they don't fire me as another troublemaker."

Paktar frowned. "My official duties are concluded. I declare this interview terminated." She tapped her datalink.

My mouth went bone dry. "Did I do something wrong?"

Paktar waved her hand. "No, no. But some things don't need to be on the record. Do you know the hardest part of a job in Disaster Intervention?"

Her sharp gaze made my spine itch. "Going in when everything goes wrong and having to fix it?"

"Not. Even. Close." Paktar put her elbows on the table and leaned a few inches towards me. Even with the distance between us, it seemed intimate. "It's the paperwork."

I snorted. That, I could believe.

"Many years ago," Paktar said, "I was in this numbered universe being considered for exploitation. It had these hedgehog-y things, but with barbed spikes. Cute little critters. The spines didn't come off, so if you got impaled by one the whole critter hung on you. Hurt like mad. Anyway, things went bad. You know."

I nodded.

"And the only way to get my geology team back to the Portal was to make every single scientist strip stark naked, stick half a dozen hedgehogs on everyone, including me, and walk thirty kilometers back to the main camp."

My sympathy erupted into laughter. "That's... Yeah."

"When I got back? The bad reports? The paperwork? The complaints from high-level geologists?" Paktar shook her head. "I thought I'd never get my record clean." She spread her hands. "How do you explain to some Human Resources officer than has never been off Earth that the perfectly insane thing you did was the best option at the time?"

A knot I'd been carrying in my chest for so long I'd forgotten it was there dissolved. "You can't."

Paktar spread her hands. "What I can say is, there are folks all through Montague who look for people with bad reports. Some of them, they need to go. They endanger us all. But a handful of those bad reports make very interesting reading. About interesting people. That wind up in interesting places."

I had to break her gaze then, as if it would keep her from seeing my blush.

"I'm not saying anything you wouldn't figure out sooner or later," Paktar said. "And I'm certainly not promising anything. And you? You might slap some vice president for being a jerk and get fired. You might discover a love of geology and settle in happy." She pushed herself back from the table, gathering up her papers.

"But on an unrelated note, the manuals for the Retrieval equipment are all in every databank. And familiarity with that gear might be an advantage, should you ever choose to move on from Security."

An honest smile crept up my cheeks. "I'll remember that."

"Totally hypothetical, mind you." Paktar started for the door. "In the meantime, flush those Tritium atoms out of your body. I expect to hear you've done the very first double-heavy double marathon. Get on it, Redding."

Sticky Supersaturation

I grew up watching Portal serials on video. *Universe Rangers. Portal Pioneers. Portal Base Alpha. Stranded.* And the movies, like *Return from Madness* and *Unchanged*, stuff my folks wouldn't let me watch, the cheesier and bloodier the better. Adventures of people who went into alien universes for the betterment of mankind, who let the Portal map their bodies into alien physics so they could survive under different physical laws. I don't remember when I didn't want to work for the Montague Corporation, didn't want to cross through the Portals and become the impossible.

My dad mowed lawns for a living until mowerbots became cheap enough, then he found a way to hurt himself to get on disability. Mom taught in a craft store. They liked the name Aidan enough to give it to me, but not enough to find out it was a boy's name first. I couldn't afford the schools, the contacts, the social education I'd need to get a good job at Montague, like bioscience or reverse physicist.

But you only need a bachelor's degree in criminal justice to get a security post. Yes, you'd better have awesome grades, a standout personal record, clubs and achievements, unarmed and armed self-defense, suck-ass high-stress internships at a research firm that survives on Montague dollars, and an attitude that chews steel and spits nails. Especially if you're a woman. But I now had my ID card: Aidan Redding, Security Officer 3rd. A subdural barcode invisibly tattooed on my left shoulder. The uniform, utility belt, the boots. (The boots are pretty sharp: black leather, brass buckles. A good pair of boots leaves you feeling ready to kick down the neighborhood bully and pin her arm behind her back.) Six months of corporate training, and six weeks of actual experience on an actual mission. On an actual world beyond a Portal. Which made Farmer's words sting even more: *We're not sure that Montague is right for you.* Once again, I'd been mouthy in the wrong place. But now it *mattered*

I let the security office door shut behind me and exhaled so hard that my entire torso shuddered.

The camp could have been an Old West mining town, hurriedly thrown together. A single road, worn in the ivy-covered ground. A dozen two-story wood frame buildings on each side: dormitories, laboratories, machine shops. Wooden conduits ran overhead between the buildings, containing network and power cables. The massive windowless cinderblock cube in the center of town held the Portal and its related equipment. The motor vehicle depot at the end was new. They hadn't figured out what to use instead of petrochemicals, but electric vehicles worked. But the gray sunless sky never changed. No clouds. Directionless light came from somewhere, everywhere, constantly, so nobody had a shadow.

Our clock is a mutual fiction. Colors were either too weak or disturbingly vivid. It never rained. And everything stuck together. Even smooth clean surfaces felt like fresh paint. I had to peel my blankets off me in the morning, scrape soap lather off in the shower. I don't know why I bothered, because nobody in this universe had a sense of smell. Or taste. I'd lost fifteen pounds since arriving here, because eating was a pointless chore. And food wanted to stick to my tongue until I chewed it really really thoroughly.

There's no sun. No moon. I'm assured that's because this universe is flat. There's hills and mountains and rivers, but on average, it's a flat surface from here to eternity. Being flat doesn't change anything I can see. The temperature doesn't change much, either.

Montague had thirty people in this universe. Five of us were security. Three of those guarded the Portal against alien incursion. The two of us on staff security had to protect the base against the local chipmunks. Who didn't care about humans. We couldn't even figure out what they ate, but it wasn't human food, or our equipment, or anything we had brought with us.

This was a Grade C universe. Grade D is the worst a human can stand without mental damage. Translating to a grade E drives you mad almost immediately. Just like the guy in *Unsurvivable*.

The peak of my life. Goal of my existence. And I'd told Doctor Davis "romance novels are stupid," the last straw. Apparently Davis cannot tolerate the degree of amount and sarcasm I can cram into four words. (Maybe five. I wasn't sure if I'd dropped the F-bomb somewhere in there.) On its own, that wouldn't have got me in trouble, but four or five petty clashes just like this had alienated her.

I took another breath. This assignment sucked. But Montague would give me other assignments, eventually. If I kept this one.

Doctor Drake slammed the door to the reverse physics lab and stormed across the street towards me. "Security!"

No more screwups, Redding. "Yes, sir?"

"I've been robbed!"

I stopped in surprise. "Robbed? Here?"

He snorted loudly and brushed past me to storm the security office. "Farmer!"

I caught the door before it stuck shut and followed.

Farmer, the security lead, looked up from his console at Drake's entrance. He already looked weary; last night had been his turn to sleep in the security office, in uniform. "What's going on?"

Drake said "One of my samples is missing! And your security guard here thinks I'm crazy!"

Farmer's eyes pivoted to me.

"I was just surprised, sir,." I said. "Wasn't expecting theft."

"I don't expect theft, either." Farmer's frown gave me the rest of the sentence: *but* you *don't get to sound surprised.* He turned back to Drake. "What sample, and where was this?"

"A small chunk of ore from the far side of the river," Drake said. "Taken from my lab."

Farmer nodded. "Redding."

I tried to sound as textbook as the day I graduated. "Sir."

"Handle this," Farmer said.

"Sir." *Well, it's better than being angry.*

"This rates your personal attention," Drake said.

Farmer nodded at me. "Redding is my personal attention. She is perfectly capable of handling this. If she needs my assistance, she *will* ask."

"Yes, sir," I said.

Drake scowled at Farmer and turned his head to look at me.

"The sample was stolen from your office, sir?" I asked.

"That is where I keep all the critical samples," Drake said.

"Could you show me, please, sir?" I said.

Drake spun and stormed right back out of the office. I followed, not even looking at Farmer.

The geoscience lab was a wooden box, studs and rafters exposed, generic frame windows closed. The physics team hasn't worked out how to get wireless working properly here — they get some kind of data pulses, feedback, all sorts of distortion — so all the power and network runs down cables through conduit screwed into the studs. Tables and cabinets filled the space, with occasional screens mounted on the wall and above workstations. Ceiling fans tried to shift the sludgy air. Drake marched over to a broad metal cabinet filled with innumerable drawers too small to hold a can of cola and pulled one open. "See?"

I was proud of myself. I didn't say *It's empty.* Instead I opened my paper notebook and pulled out a pencil. "What did you have in there?"

"A chunk of ore. Drake turned to a screen mounted above the desk. "In a clear bottle. Coded 87-B-12. I traveled a day and a half to get that sample."

I noted the number. "You traveled that far, and only took that much?"

He raised his chin. "Montague rules. Unidentified ore samples must be less than five hundred grams, until they're classified, assessed, and approved."

Scribble. "Yes, sir. Do you have anyone working with you?"

"McKenzie is my lab assistant. He knows better than to misfile my samples. Especially this sample."

"What's special about this sample?"

He peered down his nose at me. "Unusual energy signature. It could be valuable as a power source."

"Very well, sir." I scanned the room. The windows were intact, but I didn't expect any signs of forced entry. We have simple locks on our quarters, but the work spaces were unlocked. With a team this small, you had to trust your co-workers to help you when you needed it and keep out when you didn't. "Any idea when it disappeared?"

"I was working on it last night, before bed. Woke up today, and it was gone."

"Were you working late? Any chance you left it in your workspace?"

Drake narrowed his eyes at me. "You're new here, so you probably haven't realized yet. I do *not* lose things. Montague sends me to universes that nobody else can figure out. My predecessor could not crack the rules of this hellhole. I will. I've done it before. Repeatedly."

"Yes, sir. Your lab looks very clean and orderly. Is anything else missing, or out of place?"

"No. Just the sample."

"Yes, sir." I couldn't see anything else to learn from Drake. "I'll see what I can learn."

"Let me know im*me*diately when you find my sample."

"Of course, sir."

We have video cameras on the outside of every few buildings, feeding their data back to the security office. I nodded at Farmer as I came in, and fast-forwarded through last night's footage. Then headed to the bioscience lab.

I'd avoided Erickson. He seems to be good at his job, but I didn't like the way he looked at me. None of us women did. In a normal universe, Erickson would have bounced out the door years ago. Reverse biologists skilled enough to decode a Grade C universe are rare enough that Montague keeps them on.

The biology lab was built exactly like the geosciences lab. Where Drake's lab had the discipline and order of a military unit, Erickson's looked like a college dorm during finals week. Books and tubing and cables ran everywhere. One wall had a dozen clear ten-gallon tanks, each with one or two of the local chipmunks. The chipmunks were each about the size of the palm of my hand, with short brown fur and a stubby tail. They were chubbier than real chipmunks, and had broad toothlike claws. Once you looked closely, and realized that they had no mouth, no nose, only a half-dozen eyes circling the crown of the skull, they changed from kind of cute to kind of creepy. Erickson's lab assistants, a man and a woman no older than myself, huddled together over a bench. Erickson sat behind his desk, tapping his pencil and staring at a screen.

"Doctor Erickson?" I said. "I need a minute of your time."

"In a moment," he said, still staring at his screen. His pencil tapped more quickly.

"I'm afraid it can't wait," I said. "Security matter."

Erickson looked at me, then seemed to realize who I was. His face lost a little of its color, turning even grayer than this universe made us. "Kelly. Cooper. Get out."

As the back door clanged shut behind them Erickson stood, walking around his desk. "Can I help you?" If my boobs were bigger, his eyes would have moved around more.

"Why were you in the geoscience lab last night?"

He blinked, his eyes finally moving up for a brief glance at my chin before moving back down. "Who says I was?"

"The video cameras."

"There are video cameras in the back?"

"We have to watch the approaches to the camp."

"The only animal in this universe are the chipmunks. And us"

"The only animal we've discovered. So, why were you in the geoscience lab?"

His gaze finally moved up to my face, fixing in my eyes. He stepped closer. His right hand twitched as if he wanted to put it on my shoulder.

I involuntarily took half a step back, just out of his reach.

"I can explain," he said.

"That's why I'm here."

"Are you familiar with Doctor Drake's background?" His eyes didn't blink. He seemed to be trying to pin my eyes to his with his gaze. There was a faint line around his neck, just above the opening of his T-shirt. The skin beneath it was slightly darker.

"He's a highly skilled reverse physicist."

"He's a reverse physicist who gets things done. Usually by breaking the rules." Erickson finally closed his eyes as he mopped his forehead. I suddenly realized that the discoloration under his neck was dirt. We couldn't smell or taste anything here. Erickson had washed his face, and his hands, but hadn't bothered to actually have a proper shower in some time. How long would it take to get that grungy?

"As far as I know, he's in perfect compliance with protocols."

"Now he is." Erickson stared into my eyes again with that distasteful focus. "It hasn't been to his advantage to break the rules here. Yet. I've worked with him before. He's had a couple slip-ups, taken stuff back through the Portal that wasn't cleared yet. But he's good enough he gets away with it. You get good enough, and Montague forgives your… indiscretions. There aren't many people good enough to figure out these Grade C universes."

"So what has he done? What happened that required you to break into the geosciences office and steal a sample?" Studying the work benches was more comfortable than watching the scientist.

"He hasn't done it yet."

"Then I can't act yet." I held out my hand. "Give me the sample."

Erickson sagged, turning. He brought a clear jar out of his desk, its top sealed with a screw cap. I saw a blue-gray rock inside, kind of dusty looking, with tiny pockmarks all over it.

I held out my hand.

He turned his hand over and opened his grip. The bottle clung to his hand for a moment, held by this universe's natural stickiness, then slowly peeled away and fell into my palm. Erickson's eyes returned to my breasts. "Doctor Drake believes that this sample is almost pure antimatter."

I thought I misheard him. "Excuse me?"

"Antimatter. Positrons and antiprotons. It's high-grade antimatter ore."

"Antimatter can't exist with normal matter."

He lifted his eyes long enough to say "That's why we're in another *universe*, miss. The rules are different here. You'll get used to it. After a while."

Your job is already in trouble, Redding. Don't slap him.

Erickson said, "He's smuggled samples back before. Two days in the Portal labs on Earth would tell him more than three months would here. That's how he figured the last two gigs we were on together." He finally turned from me, sweeping his hands towards the cages. "I wouldn't dream of taking a chipmunk back to Earth. I can't dissect one — when I try, it dissolves into goo that eats through the table. And the floor. Proper analytic gear would answer so many questions, but we haven't figured out how to make it work here. And I don't even know how the damn things breed. They've got no genitals. No obvious way to pass out young, or eggs. Even one of the old-fashioned handheld MRI machines would tell me *something*. But until we get some kind of handle on the physics, until we understand how to make the machines to make the machines, we aren't going anywhere. And I still don't even know how they eat! I could drag a chipmunk back to Earth. And nothing bad would happen. I could do it, but I don't because it's against the rules."

He leaned closer, as if trying to bore his eyes into mine. "But this is *antimatter*. *Half* a *gram* of it equals the Hiroshima bomb. Half a kilogram would wipe out South America, and put enough radiation and fallout in the air to kill every living thing on Earth inside a year. You studied the whole global warming fiasco in school, didn't you? They still teach that? This would make the floods look like a happy spring day."

"Can't it be contained? Magnetic bottles, or something?"

"You've been watching too many serials. Detonating all the antimatter we've created on Earth, until we found this, would power a light bulb for an hour. It's about a microgram. Yeah, you could jury-rig something here that might do the trick. If the stuff it was made out of survived Portal translation. If it worked on both sides of the Portal. If the magnetic field didn't flicker, even for a heartbeat." He waved his hands in the air. "Would you bet the entire world on that?"

I took a deep breath. "I'll take your concerns to Farmer. Or you can do it. But I don't want to see this happen again. Understand?"

Erickson reached out, lightly touching my forearm. "I understand. You're just doing your job, aren't you?" His fingers lingered. I couldn't help thinking his fingertips felt more sticky than the universe made everything else.

I turned and left, careful not to run away. I needed another shower.

Drake met me at the geoscience lab door, hand held out. "You got it back from Erickson?"

I froze. "You knew it was him?"

He shook his head impatiently. "He ranted at me for half an hour yesterday."

"Why didn't you say anything?"

"You security types are always happier if you figure it out on your own. Makes you feel like you're doing something."

I gritted my teeth and gave him the sample bottle. As I pulled back, the glass peeled off my hand with a sound like wet plastic. "It would have helped if you'd mentioned it was antimatter."

"I don't know that yet." Drake nodded. "The energy signature matches the curves I would predict for the physical constants here, but that's very different from verification. What about Erickson?"

"I've warned him about this behavior, sir."

"Probably best I can hope for," Drake said. "The bastard is good enough at his job that they overlook this sort of malfeasance."

"Is there anything else I can do for you, sir?"

"Just keep that man out of my lab."

I returned to the security office.

Farmer grunted at my verbal report. "Fine."

Entering the final report left me simultaneously elated and depressed. I'd done my first real piece of security work. And it had been dealing with something foolish. I wanted to roam the universes. Did I really want to do it by settling stupid arguments? I wasn't even roaming the universes. I was stuck in one grade C universe, all the colors squeezed to lifelessness or supersaturation, unable to smell or taste anything. Anything at all. Maybe I really wanted a career as a pizza restaurant critic, something where food had taste and texture.

I awoke the next morning to someone hammering on my dorm room door. "Redding! Wake up, damn you!"

Someone else shouted behind him, but I couldn't make out the words. My room was as well lit as ever; it never gets dark in this universe, even under the covers, and you learn to just sleep through it or you get sent home. Staggering to the door in sweatpants and T-shirt, blinking my eyes to try to make them start up for the day, I flung it open to see Drake and Erickson shoulder-to-shoulder filling my door.

"I didn't touch it!" Erickson said.

"Arrest this man!" Drake said.

"Gentlemen!" I said. "What is going on?"

"I wasn't anywhere near there!" Erickson said.

My stomach plummeted. "Mister Erickson. It does you no good to protest innocence when I'm not aware of what you're being accused of."

Erickson's mouth flapped open, then snapped shut a heartbeat later.

I turned to Drake.

"Another break-in," he said through tightly clamped teeth. "He — pardon me, *the thief* — broke in again. I had left the sample on the test bench. I was slicing it, getting it thin enough to fit in the dynamic spectrometer. I was all ready to make up for the time I lost yesterday, dealing with this silly bastard. Came in early. The bench was trashed, the sample gone."

"I wasn't anywhere near your precious lab!" Erickson said. "I know you. You'd love to write me up on any excuse. I avoided you, and your lab!"

I held up a hand. "Gentlemen, please. Wait just a moment. Let me make a call." I turned before either one could speak again, just like in training. Take charge. Assume that they will obey, and they probably will. I picked up the handset on my dorm wall and pushed a key.

"Security."

"Lomack," I said, "Redding. I have an issue. Can you run the footage and tell me if Doctor Erickson has been anywhere near the geophysics lab after six PM yesterday?"

Drake muttered something behind me. I turned and said "Gentlemen. Please."

Lomack chuckled. "Sure. Give me a minute."

I held the handset as if I was listening closely, but I largely ignored Lomack's distant muttering in favor of staring at the two researchers. Erickson shifted from foot to foot, while Drake's haughty sneer tried to hold mine. I tried to look aloof, as if this was just routine.

"Checked front and back," Lomack said a small eternity later. "I see he went past the geo lab about eight PM. But he crossed the street to avoid it. Drake left, came back this morning. His lab boys left about six last night, haven't been back. That's it."

"Thanks." I hung up the phone. "Doctor Drake, video says that Doctor Erickson did not enter the lab."

Erickson let loose a heavy sigh.

Drake recoiled. "Ridiculous."

"Why don't you show me what happened?" I said. "I can't do anything until I see the scene."

Drake glared at Erickson, glared at me, and whirled.

I shut my door and slipped past Erickson without touching him. I caught up with Drake just before he got to the lab front door. Drake never looked back.

Drake jerked the door handle, and instantly jumped back. Two chipmunks zipped between his feet and the door, scurrying straight at me. I jumped to the side just as they zigged a hard left and disappeared around the building, racing towards the open field. Or just away from the crazy humans.

"Vermin," Drake snapped.

I followed him in.

The lab hadn't changed, still disciplined and orderly. I'd always aspired to have my work area this neat, but homeless clutter always accumulates on my desk.

Drake marched to the back corner. "There!"

On this workbench, the usual order had turned to strew. Clamps, slides, and instruments scattered. Broken glass in small clusters across the pressed-wood surface. The sample jar on its side, cracked open.

"The thief didn't just take the whole jar?" I said to myself.

"Obviously."

I touched a piece of broken glass. It stuck to the pressed board table top for a moment before gingerly sliding along. "Was this a slide?"

"Yes. I had an ore sample in it, very thinly sliced. You put it under a microscope, to observe any crystalline structure."

Does antimatter form crystals? I picked up my hand. The shard of glass tugged against my finger for a moment, then released the table and came up with me. "So they didn't just take the whole thing. The thief broke your equipment to scrape out the ore. Is anything missing?"

"The ore!" Drake said.

"I mean besides the ore. They left the jar, the glass, the clamp things." I tugged the smooth sharp glass with my other hand. The glass resisted for a moment, then came free by slicing down my finger. "Did they take anything?"

Drake scanned the table. "No."

Blood welled from my cut finger. It stuck to my finger more than it should. I wiped off the glass against the table top and pinched the cut closed. Drake scowled at me.

"Is anyone else interested in your samples?"

"My assistants. They know better than to do this sort of vandalism. It has to be Erickson."

I picked up the sample jar. "They didn't bother to open it. They broke the bottom out."

"So the thief is a Neanderthal."

I peered more closely. "Does Doctor Erickson have really tiny teeth?"

"Excuse me?"

"I held up the jar. "You can see the chew marks on the edge. It looks like rat chews."

He scowled. "Rats?"

"I had pet rats, growing up. These are chew marks. If rats could chew glass." I looked at Drake. "There were chipmunks in here."

"Chipmunks don't have teeth."

"They have those claws. They look kind of like this."

Drake's turned dark enough to flood his face with purple. "Are you saying that chipmunks stole my sample?"

I shrugged. "Video showed the only people in here were you and your assistants. All of *you* have opposable thumbs."

Drake swelled even more, and I regretted my words. I'd already angered Drake by not building a gallows and hanging Erickson first thing this morning. I'd just demonstrated that he was wrong, factually wrong, in front of another person. I'd suggested that chipmunks had caused his trouble, and now I'd insulted him. And Farmer already wondered if I was fit for my job.

"You need a chipmunk-proof facility, sir," I said. "We can do that. There is no question that if the little bastards are causing you trouble they've got to be kept out sir."

Drake's jaw worked. "Fine."

His stare could have crucified me. In a different universe. I might have averted an immediate explosion, but that wouldn't last long, even though I had facts on my side. The facts didn't matter. He'd find a way to go nova on me.

It only took an hour to find a section of video that showed one chipmunk slipping in a cracked door in the middle of the night. I couldn't find footage of the second chipmunk. But the footage, plus a comparison of the toothy marks on the bottom of the jar to the chipmunk's claws, convinced Farmer. He gave me a brusque nod and told me to get rid of my sweats and get my real uniform, then called the facilities team to rodentproof the geophysics lab.

Fortunately, Drake disappeared for the rest of the day. I had work I needed to do. Patrolling the perimeter. Inspecting security logs. Triple-checking cargo bound through the Portal to Earth. Cleaning the brass on my belt and boots. Important work. I managed to avoid the geophysics lab for the next couple of days, mainly because the facilities crew was making a racket assembling a wire mesh airlock around the doors and mounting more mesh over all the windows.

I didn't see Drake again until the third day, when one of the heavy trucks came lumbering down the main drag and stopped in front of the security office.

"Start unloading," Drake shouted. Hydraulic pressure hissed, and Drake's shout became frantic. "No, don't dump it! A bucket at a time. Inside. Don't just spill it out!"

Farmer looked at me. I got out of my chair and went outside.

"You can't leave that here," I said.

Drake said "It's in front of my office. For unloading."

I blinked. "What is this, anyway?"

"Ore."

I looked at the truck, riding low on its springs. "I thought you could only bring five hundred grams at a time?"

"The sample is *fine*. I had enough research to show that. It's time for full-scale tests."

"You still can't leave it here, sir. Other people need to use the street. You'll need to unload from behind the building. There's a double door back there, anyway."

"Fine," he spat.

I watched the truck pull around. By the time it reached the end of the street and turned to circle the buildings, springs groaning under the load, Erickson was marching towards the front of the geophysics building.

I grimaced inwardly and moved to intercept him. "Hello, Doctor Erickson!"

"Redding," he said. "Is that maniac doing what I think he's doing?"

"He has a truckload of ore, yes."

He pivoted to me, elbows at his sides but hands up, index finger of each hand stabbing towards my face. "He's not cleared for that!"

"I don't yet know what he's cleared for, but I promise you I will check."

He stepped to the side. I shifted in response, and suddenly he stood within my reach, my back touching the wall of the geophysics building. I wasn't literally pinned, but his presence felt like a physical weight looming over me, pressing my lungs so that I had trouble bringing in air. "That must be a ton of antimatter. Two tons. They're two-ton trucks, aren't they? Can you multiply by that many zeroes, Redding? That's enough antimatter to end all life on Earth. "

"I promise you. Sir. I will check."

"See that you do." Unidentifiable remnants of food grouted the grooves between his teeth. "I'll be taking this up with the Research Director myself. Immediately upon our visit to Earth tomorrow morning for the management meeting."

He loomed a little closer, then spun to hurtle himself off towards his lab. His swinging elbow brushed my breasts, not gently, as he marched off.

I returned to the security office, ignoring the shouts and grunts of the Logistics Team working behind the Geophysics building. According to the security log, Doctor Drake had sent an initial analysis of his sample to Earth, and requested approval for large-scale ore analysis. His request said that he was gathering additional samples.

If a two-ton-truckload is an additional sample, then I'm signing up for an additional pizza when I get home.

When Farmer looked up from his work and seemed open to interruption, I said "Boss, how large is an additional sample? Is there a rule?"

"Why?"

"Doctor Drake's brought back a truckload of that stuff Erickson stole. It's in his research request as an additional sample."

Farmer frowned and called up the request. "There's no regulation. Those things are routinely granted, so long as he's not trying to get any of them back to Earth."

I shrugged. Erickson could be as unhappy as he wanted. I wouldn't have to do anything until he and Drake choked each other, and filling out that paperwork would be a relief. Through the window, I saw Drake and his assistants taking ore samples to other labs, presumably to demand tests. His face displayed the rewards, the awards, the accolades accumulating in his imagination as he dispatched more and more samples.

The next night was my turn to sleep on the cot in the security office. Closing the shades doesn't stop the light; it's everywhere. Shades are for privacy. When you're on night duty, you sleep with the shades open and the monitors on. The first day I opened the office for the morning, I caught Lomack cradling his crotch in one still hand as he snored. I backed out, quietly closed the door, then made a bunch of noise as I returned, giving him an important second. I drool in my sleep. I'm sure everybody knows that by now. But I don't need to know that they know.

I probably had my hands some place I'd rather they weren't when the alarm ripped me from sleep. I rolled to my feet. Fire alarm. Geophysics lab. I grabbed my utility belt and ran for the door.

A river of chipmunks swirled across the road in front of the security office. The only noise they made was the rustle of thousands and thousands of tiny feet scrabbling across hard-packed soil. From across the street, however, I heard the crash of falling furniture and a man screaming high above his normal voice.

I twitched in disbelief.

I couldn't read any expression on the chipmunks, but I didn't want to just step down into them. Fumbling inside the door, I seized the broom and tried to sweep a path clear.

The broom vibrated madly, then the force of the chipmunk current ripped it out of my grasp. I glimpsed it disappearing beneath the creatures, then didn't see it again.

I shut the front door. When in doubt, procedure. I entered my access code and triggered the security alarm to alert my teammates.

Someone screamed again from across the street. I hit the intercom button for the geophysics lab. "Hello?"

Nobody answered.

I didn't see any chipmunks out the back door. I made my way to the side of the building. The chipmunks filled the street between my office and geophysics. While a few staggered out of the main crush into the alley I stood in, it seemed that most of them circled the geophysics building like a school of furry toothless piranha.

Another scream, this one recognizable as Drake.

I looked around, trying to find a gap in the flow that would let me get to the geophysics lab, but the chipmunks moved too quickly. Spaces closed as soon as I saw them.

That left me one daft idea. I took a few steps back, a deep breath, trotted towards the security office, and *jumped*, hurtling myself at the wall.

I hit a few feet off the ground. And I stuck, my cheek hugging the pressed wood, my outstretched hands and arms and legs all providing critical smidgeons of tension. I froze, holding my breath, unsure if the universe's innate stickiness would suffice to hold me.

When I didn't fall off, I pried one arm off and moved it further up the wall. Then the other arm. I hoisted a leg, then used the leverage from those three limbs to pull my torso and remaining leg up. I squeezed my body against the wood, trying to get good contact, then repeated. With five more repetitions, I got close enough to the top to be able to reach up and grab the roof.

Pulling myself completely free of the wall was actually harder than freeing a limb at a time.

Something crashed and splintered across the street. Drake swore, his voice muffled by the walls. I eyed the narrow wooden trench between the security office and the geophysics lab. Power, network, and phone cables filled it almost to the top. If I had my way, I'd go to my hands and knees and crawl across. Instead, I set my gaze on the opposite roof, put one foot on the conduit, and started walking.

If I looked down I'd fall. I set each foot down gently, prepared to lift it back up if I had stepped on a rolling cable. More than once I had to step back and find better footing, but in a surprisingly short time I set foot on the geophysics lab rooftop.

Farmer shouted up at me from street level. "Redding! Situation?"

"You pretty much see it! Someone inside the building, being circled by tiny fuzzy vultures. Angry ones. Sir." My hands felt around the seams. The roof was simple pressed-wood sheets. It never rained here, the roofs were more for the psychological comfort of the employees rather than any environmental need. My hands found a poorly-nailed seam. My bare hands couldn't pull it up. I fumbled in my pocket, found my room key, and used that to pry up an edge. Ruined the key, but I could get my hands beneath the seam with only a few splinters. I wrenched the roof up and stopped, stunned.

The geophysics lab had been trashed. Desks and benches were overturned. Buckets of blue-gray ore lay everywhere, some tipped over, spilling a dusty residue across the floor. Here and there furniture and flooring had dissolved, as if someone had spilled a dozen mugs of acid randomly around the facility. A dozen chipmunks scurried around the floor. Drake stood in the corner with a crowbar. Whenever a chipmunk came too close, he leaned out and whacked at it.

He struck one. It crumpled silently on the floor, twitched twice, then dissolved into a puddle of goo. The floor smoked around the puddle, then in the space of a single breath the entire mess dissolved through the floor, ate through the foundation, and disappeared into the ground.

"Don't kill them, Drake!" I said.

"This is no time for ecofascism!" Drake said.

"They're dissolving your lab!" I said.

"Better the lab than me!" Drake said.

"What's going on?" Farmer shouted.

"Drake's okay. There's chipmunks in here. When he kills them, they turn into a puddle of acid that eats through everything." One chipmunk sat atop a bucket of ore. I had to stare for a minute to be sure of what I saw. "A chipmunk. He's kind of... engulfing it. They seem to be eating the ore." I didn't know where the chipmunk's mouth was, but the ore was disappearing into the front of its head.

"They're not eating my ore," Drake said. "You Security people need to do something. Or Facilities. Someone!" He flailed his club at another chipmunk, and missed.

I looked down into the street. Farmer, Lomack, and the rest of the security team stood outside the circle of swirling furry. A few other people lurked behind them, murmuring quietly to one another. I said, "What would you suggest, Doctor?"

"Shoot them," Drake said. "You've got guns, shoot them!"

"They'll just turn to acid," I said. The chipmunk stuffing himself full of ore suddenly twitched, curled up in a ball, and bonelessly rolled to the floor. He didn't move when he hit. He also didn't turn into acid.

"Cage them, then!"

"They're here for the ore, Doctor."

"They can't have it!" Drake said. "This could solve Earth's energy problems forever. We could give up on this damn fool universe-hopping. This much anti-matter, this cheap, we could go to the stars. In my lifetime."

"We're not equipped for this," I said. "We get the ore out of the camp. Set up a proper facility to keep them out. Let them dance around the pile somewhere out there while we get set up here."

Drake's head swiveled left and right.

"Okay," he finally said. "Damn it, okay."

The chipmunks had swept my broom away, but they couldn't brush off the two-ton truck Farmer drove up to the building. The storage building next to the geophysics lab had an access hatch in the roof. We dropped a ladder between the two buildings so more people could climb across. And then, bucket by painful bucket, we hauled the ore up through the roof and dropped it into the truckbed.

In a way, I was lucky. Drake insisted on remaining, to be sure that the work crew didn't break anything else. He sat on the one remaining table, wedged in the corner. I got the job of protecting him from the chipmunks that found their way in. I had the lab broom, and individual chipmunks sweep away pretty easily. At least this way, I had my back to the good doctor.

And it gave me time to watch the chipmunk who had gorged himself on ore and died. The interesting things happened after he died.

About six in the morning, with the world still well-lit but everyone staggering with fatigue, we got the last of the ore out of the lab. Farmer put the truck in gear, and we all watched as the whirlpool of tiny fuzzy animals followed the truck out of the camp. About a mile out, he tipped the bed and let the ore plunge to the ground.

By the time Farmer got the truck back to the camp, the chipmunks had converged on the mound. Through my binoculars, I watched them lift chunks of ore in front paws and stagger into the woods, the hills, into holes in the ground, bearing it away nugget by nugget. In another hour, the mound of ore was gone and Drake was furiously cursing my name.

I reacted the only sensible way. I took a shower, scraped water and soap and filth off of me, and went back to bed.

My eyes snapped wide open about an hour later. I went by the machine shop. Asked a few questions. Got the answers I feared. And dashed back to the Portal building, my heart rattling like a machine gun on amphetamines.

All four lead scientists – Erickson, Drake, human biologist Davis, and the reverse cosmologist, Jellicoe – stood out front, each with a small bag or satchel for their belongings. The camp leader, Administrator Lopez, had his back to me as I ran up, as did Security Chief Farmer. I got there just as Farmer was entering his code in the Portal building entrance.

I huffed out my breath, trying to catch enough oxygen to speak. "Excuse me – sir."

Farmer said "Yes, Redding?"

"I have some, information that might, affect the meeting," I said. "Sir."

"That's quite enough," said Davis, folding her arms across her chest. "This young lady has been trouble since she showed up. I'm not missing this meeting because of her."

"Absolutely," said Drake. "I plan to make a complaint to human resources after the research meeting. This woman turned a simple sample problem into chaos."

"This better be good," Farmer said.

I raised my hand, displaying a metal cylinder the size of a broad permanent marker. "The machine shop was asked to make a special order. For return to Earth."

"Ridiculous," Drake said.

"What is it?" Farmer said.

"It's a storage flask. With very strong electromagnets. Designed to be hidden inside a portfolio. One was ordered, picked up this morning. But they made two, in case one didn't work."

Farmer turned to the others. "Gentlemen, I'm afraid I have to ask you to open your bags. Again."

"I need to get the library before the meeting," said Jellicoe.

"Then I'll be quick," said Farmer.

He quickly found the flask. Inside Erickson's portfolio.

Erickson turned pale. "That's not mine."

Farmer turned to me. "Who ordered the flask?"

"Doctor Drake. He was insistent it be ready for today."

Drake sputtered. "Preposterous."

Farmer studied the flask he'd taken from Erickson. The top unscrewed. He peered into the opening, stuck a pen inside, and drew out a slender chunk of blue-gray ore.

Everyone turned to look at Drake.

"We understand antimatter containment," Drake said. "It's perfectly safe."

"We understand it on *paper*, you maniac!" said Erickson. "For amounts too small to see!"

"The math is fine," Drake said.

Farmer's lips were a tight horizontal line. "Doctor Drake, I'm afraid you're going to be late for your meeting. No, I don't want to hear it. One more word, and you'll be spending the rest of the day in chains." Drake opened his mouth, and Farmer raised a finger. "Chains, I say. The machine shop can whip up a set of manacles pretty quickly. They can't be as difficult to do as an electromagnetic flask."

Fuming, Drake clenched his lips together.

"I'm sorry," Farmer said, "but I'll have to ask you to excuse *Doctor* Drake and I for a moment. We'll get you on your way shortly. Come along, Doctor." He took Drake's arm and guided him to the security door in the side of the Portal building.

Erickson, grinning widely, watched Drake retreat.

I glanced around the three remaining scientists. "Uh, Doctor Davis. Ma'am." I held up the flask. "This is the second one. It's never had the ore in it. Maybe you could take it with you. See what it does. Just to, you know. Experiment with a blank round."

She eyed me for a moment, then took the flask.

"A reasonable test," she said, her voice carefully level.

Lopez let out a deep sigh.

"Wonderful, miss," said Erickson, turning to face me. Once again, he thought my face was beneath my chin. "I never thought he'd really try to blow us all up. And frame me for it. Like there'd be any evidence left after that."

He put his fingertips on my forearm again. "We owe you our lives."

His fingers didn't move, their tips still just barely brushing my forearm.

"And the way the chipmunks were eating the ore! Amazing. That's going to be a fantastic paper for me. I really appreciate it." His voice carried a completely different undertone.

I moved my hand in a circle beneath his arm, then swept my arm straight across my front. I'd practiced the technique thousands of times in training. If he'd been holding my wrist, if I'd closed my hand around his wrist, if I'd used real force, I'd have started any number of crippling and disabling blows. As it was, I didn't move at all towards him. My arm sweep just guided Erickson's arm back towards him. His arm slapped into his own chest with a surprising amount of force.

His jaw flapped a couple times in astonishment.

"You really think that they were eating that ore?" I said. "Did you actually watch what happened when they ate? They died, Doctor. They curled up in little balls of fur and stopped moving."

Erickson was still staring at me. At my arm at least, the one I'd swept with. That was a nice change.

"And I kept watch on one. You wait a bit, and what happens? The little ball of fur shivers. It splits. It turns into two chipmunks that get up and scamper away. You want to know how they breed? That's how."

"They need to eat to breed," Erickson said distantly. His eyes snapped up to my actual face. "Fabulous."

"You really don't get it, do you, *doctor*? You don't get so upset, so furious, so ready to take on something fifty hundred times your size, when someone steals your *food*." I made my eyes harder. "Maybe it's their food, too. Maybe they're antimatter-propelled chipmunks, who start life with all the food they're ever going to get. But this wasn't about food. You get that upset, that furious when someone steals your *mate*."

Erickson's jaw clenched. "You pushed me. *Shoved* me. I'll have a complaint into HR before our meeting."

I tensed my shoulders. If I was going to get fired, I would take some of Erickson's teeth with me. "In that case, Doctor, might I suggest that, before your meeting, you con*sider* taking a bath. With soap. And maybe even a toothbrush."

"I've been here the whole time," Davis said. "This young lady not only has some interesting ideas, but I'd have to say – under oath, even – that she certainly didn't push you. She moved her arm, but not towards you at all. Not even vaguely. What would you say, Paulo?"

Administrator Lopez blinked. "Oh, I'm sorry. I wasn't really paying attention. Thinking about poor Drake. They might let him keep his job, but he'll never get a chance to do anything with samples again. It's Grade D universes for him for now on, no chance of even a B or a C, and a strip search any time he goes through a Portal." He gave Erickson a thin, bitter smile with no humor in it. "One bad decision. Pushed the wrong issue, just one time. And his whole life is just ruined."

Erickson's face turned bleach white. He looked between Davis, Lopez, and me. His eyes grew wide, and he took a step back from all of us.

We ran light operations the rest of the day, trying to recover from the overnight dirt shuffle. I didn't see Farmer again until the next morning, when I staggered into the security office for a cup of tasteless, odorless coffee.

"Good morning, Redding," Farmer said as I took my first swallow. The heat scalded my tongue, but it's not like my tongue was doing anything except flapping and getting me into trouble.

I took a deep breath. *Show respect.* "Good morning, sir. Any disasters yet today?"

"Not yet, but it's early. We need to talk. Have a seat."

I'd told myself to be respectful. I hadn't made it through ten words before snarking. I sat, but not fast enough to keep up with the sinking sensation in my gut. "What can I do for you?"

"You really need to learn when to keep your mouth shut," Farmer said. "There's times you say sir."

"Yes, sir." I swallowed, but my mouth had gone dry.

"And there are times you keep your cool. And last night, you kept your cool. You were on the roof of the geo lab before any of us could get halfway there. You talked to that idiot Drake. And you prevented an antimatter blast at the Uruguay Portal, and probably the eradication of all life on Earth."

I blinked. "Sir?"

"Davis reported that when she took the high-quality electromagnetic bottle through, it crumbled. Carl and Simon had taken Drake through on the trip. The good doctor damn near pissed himself. They had to drag him off." Farmer smirked. "He couldn't walk any more."

I couldn't help laughing. It wasn't a funny laugh, it was tension audibly escaping from my gut.

"But, while I was there, I had to file a report on your insolence. Your mouthiness."

I stopped laughing. "Yes, sir."

Dang it! I thought Davis and I had started to connect.

"Doctor Erickson is most definite that you're a troublemaker. He ranted to Human Resources about you for almost an hour. We nearly came back here without him."

Erickson? I wouldn't have guessed he had the guts to call me out on standing up to him. Was I expected to take that old-fashioned twenty-first-century crap? "I'll try harder, sir."

"Doctor Davis insisted you had nothing but high adrenaline. Attack of the Chipmunks and all. We were all pretty wired after that. Besides, that gave me time to write up my report."

I couldn't breathe. "Yes, sir."

"Between you and I, you've got to control that mouth. Our job gets boring. Really, really boring. And then everything goes to hell. You kept your head, followed procedure, and calmly went to help someone in trouble, where a lot of greenhorns would have come screaming to me. That's a commendation, from me, already in your personnel file. Right next to Erickson's complaint." Farmer stood and held out his hand. "Good job, Redding."

My knees wobbled, but I managed to get my feet beneath me and take his hand. "Thanks, sir."

Farmer gave me a grin. "If it's just us, call me Steve. And I think you've got a whole lot of universes to see."

No More Lonesome Blue Rings

I'm the only human being in this universe with a blue tattoo ringing my wrist.

It's not a plain band. There's my name in block letters, SHERRY KAREN ROGERS. My birth date, 44 years ago. There's a barcode for my medical records. The fact that it's all in blue flags me as a Gerstmann-Straussler-Scheinker patient. At least it's a nice jewel blue.

The Creutzfeldt-Jakob patients have the same information, but in a red tattoo, also about an inch wide. They're pretty obvious just from their behavior, though. All sorts of things cause dementia, and by the time they rule out Alzheimer's and Huntington's and diabetes and all of the other possibilities, the CJD victim's personality has gone completely out of whack. Red Bands spend sunny days in a fenced park and rainy days inside a lovely room in the care facility. Some walk around freely or play simple games. Others are anchored to wheelchairs with padded straps. The caretakers wear protective gear. If you want to see panic, watch the staff scramble for heavy gloves when a Red Band bleeds.

This universe is close enough to ours to support our kind of life. Going through the Portal from Earth changes your biochemistry so you can survive in a universe with different physical laws, but this universe was similar enough to our own that we don't go mad. But this universe doesn't let prion diseases progress. Nothing can restore our smothered nerves, but we don't get any worse.

I suppose I'm lucky. I used to teach, pacing back and forth before my students. I started stumbling. Then I had trouble speaking. I'd been exposed to GSS twenty years earlier, after they'd identified prion diseases but before they broke the dimensional barrier, so I knew enough to demand the test. I can't speak much, but I'm still in here. I can build sentences, have a coherent conversation, spelling out the words on a touchscreen if the letters are big enough. They let me leave the clinic, walk down the beach or into the woods, so long as I don't go anywhere near the Montague research complex. The sand on the beach is a lot like home, though. The wind forms it into shallow dunes, the gray sea pummels it into hard-packed surface. When the weather changes and the wind rushes down the coast, loose sand skitters over the ground in long ribbons that constantly form and dissolve into each other. If I can ignore the yellow sky and the blue sun, the complete absence of birds and insects and anything else that might fly, and the taint in the air that I would swear is chlorine, I can pretend I'm at home.

I could go home any time. My GSS would pick up right where it left off, its exponential growth suspended but not slowed. I'd decay for another four or five years before dying, losing even more of myself every day. I used to be a woman of substance, a teacher, an author. People knew my name, sought my thoughts. Now I feel hardly human, a Swiss cheese of a person.

The staff in nice enough, but there's always a social and physical barrier between us. I'm a patient. You can't antiseptic away prions. Antivirals and antibacterials are useless. Fifteen minutes in an autoclave at three hundred degrees works, but it's hard on your staff. So is an hour in pure ozone. It's easier to be alone by myself than alone in company. Some days I walk the three miles to the fence.

The Montague Corporation had a long and bloody negotiation with the locals before getting the rights to build here. I'd never seen a local, but had heard that they looked nearly human. The trees looked like trees, the grass like grass, so people that looked like humans. Life had accidentally wandered between universes for millions of years before Montague learned how to do it on purpose. The locals have an official designation in some computerized catalog that nobody pays attention to, but in every universe they call the locals Townies.

I can't practice Tai Chi any longer. My plaqued nerves fire and misfire. I can't even meditate, as my body refuses to stay still. So I walk. If I move slowly and steadily I don't trip even though my muscles twitch and spasm. On my brother Gary's birthday, I'd packed a lunch and walked to the Northeast Stone.

Human territory has four borders, with a great stone at each. Humans were allowed within the rough four-hundred-square-mile quadrangle marked by the borders. They warned me about the townies, how they could do things impossible in our universe, and how they considered any human outside the boundary their property. The staff wouldn't give any patient any specifics, leaving us to create our own myths. I didn't know what Montague made in their plant, taking advantage of the slightly different laws of nature, but it made them enough money to tolerate the risks of that kind of neighbor.

Sitting with my back to the ten foot spire of the Northeast Stone in the robot-trimmed cool grass, equidistant between the perpendicular wire fences stretching out of sight, I carefully unwrapped my sandwich. I usually took some kind of self-warming meal – the canteen pasta isn't bad, and the soy cutlet actually has decent gravy if you can ignore the fact that it's soy. Today's lunch starred a peanut butter sandwich, Gary's favorite.

Gary's in a long-term care facility back on Earth. He was born with Angelman Syndrome. He was always happy, always friendly, but with an IQ around 60 he would never speak, and he'd need seizure medication throughout his life. I was just glad that he'd finally learned to use the toilet. I'd told Mom I would take care of my little brother before she died.

I ate my peanut butter sandwich and thought about my brother, now cared for by strangers. The fact that his smile was a symptom of his disease didn't change how much it had meant to me. I'd avoided marriage because of Gary, taught instead of having my own children. I didn't have Angelman, but my genes carried it.

And now, neither of us could speak. The thought was bitter.

The peanut butter tasted better than I remembered, thick and crunchy between my teeth. I was carefully licking excess off my twitching hand when the Stone vanished.

I almost fell over at the sudden absence. Both fences remained, each ten feet tall wire topped with nanoedged concertina wire. The edges had been anchored within the Stone. The metal mesh sang as it rippled and shuddered with the sudden release of tension. Wire shrieked against wire as the first posts in each line suddenly took up all the pressure.

My breath caught in my throat.

The south pole on the southbound fence screeched and bent, twisted by the tension hauling the wire mesh towards the other end.

My phone bleeped. I wear it strapped to my left forearm, so I don't have to get it out of my pocket. A message blared in large type: CODE FOUR.

The patients were known by colors, so emergencies were numbers. I'd seen a Code One once in the year I'd been here. As prescribed I sat in a chair and watched as the full-body-suit crew came in and bandaged a Red Band's skinned knee. At Code Three I was supposed to go to my room. They'd told me what Code Four was, but I couldn't remember at the moment. I dropped the rest of my lunch and tried to jump to my feet, but a shudder in my legs betrayed me and I fell back to the ground, sprawling on my side atop my banana and chips and cursing myself.

By the time I regained my feet, moving meticulously this time, my phone buzzed anew. TOWNIES INSIDE FENCE. ENGAGE WITH LETHAL FORCE.

In the distance, I heard the sudden rattle of firearms. It sounded too soft after what I'd heard in the movies, but the trees and hills dampened the noise. I took a step towards the medical compound, then stopped. Did I want to walk into a firefight? I'd never seen the guards around the patients carrying anything more than stunguns. The research complex was a mile beyond the dormitory. Did bullets that miss travel that far?

I gritted my teeth and started walking. From the hill closest to the clinic I could see what was happening. Either I stayed here and waited for whatever happened, or I tried to reach safety. I know people who claim that Tai Chi is a martial art, but even if Carry Tiger To Mountain or Needle at Sea Bottom could deflect bullets I shook too much to perform them. I had to reach people who could protect me.

Moments later, my phone buzzed again. I stopped walking so I could read the message.

BORDER STONES HAVE ALL MOVED 10 MILES EAST.

Relief shuddered through me. Until that message came, I wasn't aware of just how afraid I was that I'd hallucinated the Stone vanishing. Prion disease can't advance here, but I don't really know why or how. Or maybe I'd had a stroke. But I believed that a hallucination wouldn't be so coherent. I wouldn't hallucinate a text message confirming my earlier hallucination. The confirmation gave me the energy to pick up my speed just a little.

But the border stones had moved? How? The staff, even the medical agent back on Earth, had all been explicit. The stones are the negotiated border. Don't go past the fence. Human territory was about twenty miles across.

The ground shook and a rumble crept through the air. I thought I heard a very faint scream.

ALL PERSONNEL TO FORTIFIED POSITIONS.

Was the clinic a fortified position? I lurched myself forward, wobbled on my feet, almost fell, and slowed to recover myself and tried to take a deep breath, but the chlorine taste made me cough before I could finish.

As a rule I try not to bemoan my fate, but dammit, I was an invalid. I shouldn't be in a war zone.

I needed almost an hour to get back to the slope overlooking the clinic. If I'd had to stagger through underbrush I never would have made it, but Montague has their mowing robots trim everything except the trees down to an even inch. I approached from the hilly side, staying among the trees to try to conceal myself as I tried to catch sight of the day clinic.

The day clinic was a single story, with an enclosed park on one side, containing spacious recreation rooms for patients and a row of individual treatment rooms. Now the cinderblocks on one side, and the metal roof over them, had run and sagged like warm frosting, exposing interior walls and wiring and lighting. Doors lay on their side, incongruously intact but sunken in molten metal and stone. The gut-high cyclone fence surrounding the play area was gone, leaving holes in the ground where the posts had stood. I smelled hot metal and burnt insulation, but none of the horrible fleshy stinks I expected after a battle. Not that I knew what a battle smelled like. The front door stood barricaded in an untouched wall.

I didn't see any Townies, though. Or any staff. A few patients wandered aimlessly, their gray clothes muddied. I also didn't see any bodies, human or not. Torn between hiding and going down, I watched for a few minutes, then forced my legs to carry me down the hill. None of the Red Bands said anything as I passed between them and entered the day clinic.

Nobody was inside the clinic. The walls and floors bore scattered fire damage, some ten or twenty feet long, but the fires were gone. The overhead fire extinguishers hadn't gone off. I thought some holes in the wall looked like bullet holes, but I didn't see any bodies inside. Or blood.

I came back out to see Richard staring in the gap where I'd entered. Richard is a Red Band, but not too badly deteriorated. I'd played a few simple games with him, kicking a ball back and forth and such. While CJD stripped a lot of people down to angry frustrated assholes or giggling exhibitionists, Richard had retained a vocabulary and a fondness for his family. I think the doctors caught him early, too. One of the staff mentioned that Richard's wife divorced him when he came through the Portal, to protect herself and their kids, but Richard had no memory of that. We'd played cribbage on touchscreens with big friendly buttons instead of cards. I can still add to fifteen. Richard can't, but he'd played before he'd fallen ill and still remembered that a face card and a five equaled good. The computer kept score. Two pathetic shells of human beings, friends in our feeble way.

Richard said "Sherry. What happened?"

Shrugging, I raised my eyebrows.

"Will they be back?"

Had the staff taken the other patients? Or had Townies taken the staff somewhere? Or just swallowed them whole? I gave a tight smile and shrugged again.

"Glen didn't look happy. They had to drag him. He kicked. A lot."

Glen was the staffer who set up our meals. It had to be Townies. I nodded, trying to reassure Richard, then stepped past him. At least they hadn't just killed everyone. Then I shuddered even more than usual as my brain conjured worse possibilities. To distract myself I looked at my phone. No signal. Had the Townies blown the tower?

"Hey, where you going?"

I pointed across the asphalt road. The patient dormitory across the way had deliquesced just as badly as the day clinic, but behind a couple hills stood the Portal, Montague housing, the complex, and all the stuff the Montague Corporation gave a damn about.

"Can I come too?"

I waved my hand for him to follow.

We'd hardly started when the siren sounded.

"That's bad."

Evacuation? Returning to Earth meant a painful slow death, but I had no idea what staying meant. I tried to break into a trot and fell to the road. I gasped as the asphalt skinned my face, and the smell of hot tar blotted out the chlorine stink.

Richard put his hands around my arm. "It's okay. No biggie." His warm hands sent a flush through me. I don't get touched much any more. The staff was all too terrified of prions, and there really wasn't any patient I'd like to get that close too. Richard pulled me gently to my feet and held my quivering arm as we quick-stepped down the road towards the Portal.

The occasional sound of gunfire trickled tendrils of fear down my spine. I hadn't walked this quickly in years. I had to concentrate on every step. Richard just kept walking in a straight line, the poor bastard, so I also had to keep tapping his shoulder and pointing him around each bend of road. We staggered across the campus like damaged dented drunks.

I heard screams and shouts. The distant terror seemed to fill the holes in my mind. I tasted smoke and ash. We moved around buildings marked by fire, by explosions, and every one marred with the melted concrete and slumping metal of the Townie attack.

We passed the ugly blockhouse of the power station, finally bringing the Portal building into view. It was the tallest building in the complex, six windowless floors, and shone in the sunlight. Nobody stood near it, but I still felt warmed by seeing our destination. We'd only taken a few steps when an impossibly loud noise squeezed my entire body, like being engulfed in giant balloons of warm water. I felt my feet involuntarily leave the ground. Between beats of my heart the noise faded to a merely monstrous rumble, then I toppled to the ground atop Richard.

I lay stunned for a moment. What had happened? How was I supposed to deal with whatever this new debacle was? Tears blurred my vision. I'd shredded a strip of skin the size of my hand. Blood seeped around the tiny bits of gravel and dirt embedded in my flesh.

Richard thrashed beneath me, and I rolled to my hands and knees. He sat up. "Ow." Fresh blood welled from his forearm.

I frowned and cocked my head in sympathy. The clinic staff would be scrambling for extra protective clothing right now, face masks and thick gloves, anything to avoid Richard's prion-contaminated blood. I fumbled for his hand and squeezed it, licking my lips, and tried to repeat his words. "No biggie" came out like "Na-ma-na," but at least the tone was soft and gentle. He smiled, blinking away tears.

"Look at the smoke," he said.

I turned to follow his gaze.

A thick column of black and gray smoke rose from where the Portal building had once stood. I stopped, shocked. It wasn't that flames poured from the windows. The walls were *gone*. I could barely see the shape of a mound of rubble beneath the pillar of smoke. The Townies?

No, I realized, the Montague staff had to be responsible. The Townies must have gotten into the Portal building. Montague as a company might be in this universe for the money, but all the Portal staff were ex-military. Dedicated, stubborn, disciplined. Back home I'd seen more than one report on how the Portal teams were dedicated to protecting Earth, how they'd die before letting any natives from any universe come the other way. The Townies must have penetrated the Portal building, so someone hit the big red button.

The only way back to Earth, gone.

Beside me, Richard said "That's a biggie."

I shifted back to my knees, so frustrated and angry that I couldn't help pounding on my thighs and shouting obscenities that came out in a long string of meaningless sound, which only made me more angry, until finally I devolved into pure incoherent screaming, eyes clamped so shut that tears couldn't bubble between the lids, my shoulders shaking, tasting copper and chlorine in the tightness of my throat, shuddering and quivering.

Then I had to take a breath or faint, and sagged, staring at the ground, suddenly aware that my knees ached from kneeling. My chest burned. I smelled ash and smoke and dust from the explosion, even though the wind from the ocean carried the cloud inland away from us.

I forced myself to take a deep breath, then another. My mind turned back towards Tai Chi, and I made myself visualize the beginning of the First Loop. By the time I reached the first Ward Off, my eyes had stopped watering and my breath came with no more tremor than usual.

Richard nudged my shoulder. "Biggie. Biggie now. Biggie."

The light stung my eyes. My breath wobbled, then steadied, as I took in my surroundings again. Asphalt road. Smoking ruins. Trees that looked just wrong enough to remind me I wasn't on Earth, was in a subtly different universe.

And a Townie.

He came from the direction of the Portal building, walking in a loose-jointed jaunty gait. From a hundred yards off he looked human, but his joints moved too widely, his head too large, his shoulders too broad. He ignored the curve of the path in favor of walking straight at us.

I pushed myself up, one hand on Richard's shoulder for leverage. I tried to tell him we had to run, but only grunts came out.

Richard started to get up, then cried out, crumpling down. "Foot! Biggie!"

The Townie was getting closer. I glanced between Richard and the Townie, then worked my way around to Richard's injured side. With gestures, I got him upright, his arm over my shoulder, my arm around his back. The smells of institutional disinfectant and cheap soap filled my nose, and I could almost taste his sweat. We shambled back the way we came. The scabs on my hand tore open, and I felt sticky blood stain the back of his shirt.

I didn't dare look back. Was the Townie gaining on us? I couldn't imagine outrunning him, after the Townies overpowered the staff, but maybe he didn't care about us patients, or maybe his work shift was over, or maybe we looked too grotesque to bother.

The air blurred in front of me.

The Townie stood before us, only ten feet away. I hadn't seen him run around us. I hadn't seen one approach from the front. He just appeared, as if by magic.

From this close, he looked like a genetic experiment gone horribly wrong. His nose was the most obvious change, tri-lobed and black. The lobes shifted as he looked at us, almost prehensile like a cow or a rat. His fingers were too long and too jointed. He wore no clothes. His penis was incongruously human, more hairy than any I'd seen but shockingly familiar. If he'd been erect, I think I would have completely lost it.

Gasping, I pulled Richard to a stop. Richard pushed me back and shouted "Sherry! Run!"

I staggered backwards, windmilling my arms to catch my balance, twitching and shaking and just about collapsing. My feet left asphalt and went to grass.

Richard leaped at the Townie, driving forward with his good foot, arms outstretched, hands hooking for its face. They collided. The impact knocked the Townie back.

I wavered where I stood. Then the Townie seized Richard's shoulders.

I turned.

I ran.

I ran too fast, my feet unable to keep up, but somehow I held my balance through the involuntary tics and shivers. My hands oscillated out of control, nervous impulses running amok through my plaqued nerves, my brain's messages disappearing into ravaged nerves.

Richard screamed. His terror and panic bled through my skin, and while my heart begged me to go back I kept my feet staggering forward.

The screaming stopped like it had been severed with a knife.

I didn't have time to cry. I didn't have time to wipe away the water in the edges of my vision. I ran and scuttled and did everything I could to carry myself back towards the smoking ruins of the Portal building, towards the invaders who had destroyed what little life I still had.

Then Richard said "Sherry."

The timbre of his voice had changed. The childlike lilt had vanished. He sounded firm and commanding and capable, like I imagined he sounded back on Earth, before CJD ripped out the top of his brain. He sounded like a man I would have had to turn down a date with, because I would have wanted it to be serious and my genes wouldn't permit that.

"Sherry, stop. It's all right. You don't have to be like this."

The air quivered before me, and the Townie stood there. His hands were now upraised to protect his face. I saw scratches from Richard's jagged bitten nails.

I heard even footsteps behind me.

The Townie reached for me.

I kicked him in the crotch.

The Townie's eye's bugged out, and when his air blew out I smelled chlorine even more strongly. The impact threw me back, and I landed hard on my rump, toppling backwards, striking my head against the road. My vision turned gray, with a halo of black around the edges.

Richard said "We trespassed. But they're here to help us."

The gray wobbled like gelatin, and the spinning in my brain started to ebb. I tore my fingers scrabbling at the ground, trying to regain my balance, trying anything to just get to my feet, my legs thrashing to just *find* my feet.

Then the Townie walked over and plunged down at me.

His hands on my wrists were clammy and damp, and his breath stank of bleach with an undertone of fish. I screamed, thrashing. He didn't resist, content to just hold my wrists as I flung myself back and forth. My hand slapped against the side of his head. I'd like to say I tried to hit him. Blood from my injured hand smeared across the scratches Richard had left on the Townie's cheek. I screamed.

The Townie let me go, falling back to his knees.

Somewhere, Richard made a stuttering inhuman sound, like an engine belt catching on something each spin.

I scrabbled backwards, feet kicking, arms flailing, my wrists still damp where the Townie's clammy paws had seized me.

The Townie shuddered. His back arched. His head tilted back. I saw unfamiliar muscles ripple beneath taut skin and teeth clatter against each other. He let out an unearthly shriek that I imagined to be pain. Agony.

Sudden silence. He sagged forward. His chin dropped to his chest. His hands twitched on his thighs.

I rolled over, getting to my own knees, my hands fumbling at the ground to push me up. My breath shook in and out.

The Townie smiled at me. The first human expression I'd seen on that face. And I'd seen that particular smile before. On my little brother. The classic over-stretched grin of Angelman's Syndrome. He gave a laugh, his voice thick, as if he hadn't practiced it before, and clapped his hands together joyfully.

Revulsion twisted my stomach at the sight. I knew Gary's smile was a symptom of his disease. I'd seen other Angels, and they all had that happy grin to one degree or another. But that precise smile belonged to my brother. To see it on this alien's face kindled the marrow in my bones. I let out a harsh snarl and steadied my feet, ready to walk forward and bludgeon his face until his broken teeth shredded his smile.

Richard said "Sherry." His voice had lost its new firm confidence, but he still had the timbre. "They're coming."

The Townie laughed again. I heard childish glee behind the alien tones.

I grabbed Richard's arm and tugged. He rocked on his feet, but didn't otherwise move.

I turned to stare at Richard's face. He shook his head, eyes sad. "I can't go with you. I can feel them. They can feel me, too. They know something happened to one of theirs." He pointed at the hideous, smiling Townie. "They're shocked. Horrified." He closed his eyes, putting his hands over his face. "I'll tell them I didn't see which way you went."

I shook my head. "No." The word came out almost recognizable.

"The human territory now begins about three miles east of here. Once you get through the border, you'll be safe. You've been a good friend. When I didn't have any. I think. I think. I think I loved you. But I think – no. I have new friends now." His voice caught. "I'm sorry."

I sobbed, whirled, and like broken clockwork, let my ratcheting twitching steps carry me away.

#

I hid in a ruined cafeteria, smothering my exhausted cries amidst a mound of freshly laundered towels. I popped open a self-heating soy cutlet and made myself choke it down. I drank. I cried some more. I've had my share of furtive noises in the dark, shared my body but never my soul. I'd never expected to hear those words. Especially not now. Not at the end of my life, in a clinic for those condemned to a painful demeaning death but living under a suspended sentence.

The day passed in silence. I slept, when I could. Once the light sifting down the stairwell faded, I crawled upstairs to watch the twilight through a cracked door. When the last sunlight disappeared, leaving a black sky scattered with sapphire blue stars, I quietly swung the door open and tiptoed out.

A few solar lamps still lit sections of the road. Buildings were only visible by how they blocked out the sky. The chlorine smell had faded with the day, leaving a loamy smell that seemed almost tangible. No insect song stirred the night, no bats cut the air. Nothing flies here. I've never seen a plane or a helicopter, actually. We're all nailed to the ground.

I'd lose my way in the dark. I couldn't help it. I looked around and picked out a cluster of six stars in the eastern sky. They'd move as the night passed, but at least they'd lead me eastish as I crept towards other people. If there were other people. If the Townies hadn't eradicated everyone except the Red Bands and I.

Moving cross-country, I shuffled around the concrete flowerbeds along the roadways. I came across more than one of the electric carts the staff uses to get around, tipped over or run into a tree. Trying to hold my breath steady, moving slowly so as to not trip in the dark. I hadn't had my medication in hours, and my tremors were growing more persistent and more violent. My hands quivered so badly that I couldn't have lifted a pill to my mouth if I tried.

I stumbled on for hours, beyond the main buildings, through parts of the complex I'd never visited, through warehouses and loading docks and silent machines, past tubes wider than I am tall and canisters taller than my old house, into machine-groomed woods. The night blurred around me, one featureless moment turning into the next in a long stumbling hallucination.

Then I heard the unmistakable metallic click-click of a weapon cocking. A gruff voice said "Hold it, townie."

I stopped. *I surrender!* "Ah urdo!"

A flashlight illuminated my side. A different voice said "A Red Band?" His tone changed to incredulous. "How the hell did *you* make it out?"

I held out my right wrist, to show the blue tattoo, but he didn't notice. "You're two miles inside our line. The Townies ate half our people, but *you* made it?"

I wanted to slap him, but tried to hold still. As still as possible. Not actively flail around.

"That's enough, Stevens," said a second voice. "Jimmy, you can take her back to HQ."

"Yessir." The third voice didn't bother to hide his reluctance. "Come on, you."

The headquarters had been some sort of industrial complex amidst the forest. Half a dozen buildings no larger than mid-range private homes stood in a rough circle. Lights shone in the windows, showing people gathered and talking and arguing. Men and women in Montague uniforms lay exhausted on the grass, sleeping. A row of figures along one building were wounded, injuries bandaged and splinted and cleaned, and then drugged into unconsciousness. I didn't have the strength to argue as a couple of office managers read my name off my tattoo, entered some stuff in a handheld, and bickered like I wasn't even there, debating if I could be trusted to not wander off and hurt myself. Eventually I looked around for an open patch of grass out of the way, sat down, and, safely surrounded by people, immediately fell asleep.

I was awakened by someone shouting "Sherry Rogers!"

I blinked. Crud filled my eyes. My tongue tasted like a dead skunk. Muscles I hadn't used in years complained. My back had cramped from sleeping in the ground, and a spasm made me gasp as I tried to sit. The sun must have risen above the horizon, but I couldn't see it through the smoke-shrouded buildings of the main complex.

"Sherry Karen Rogers!"

The shouter was a soldier. Montague isn't supposed to have their own military, using only security guards. But he wore body armor. He carried a nasty-looking rifle with telescopic sight and this and that. He had a helmet with computerized goggles covering his upper face. The name PETERSON was embroidered above his pocket. As security guards went, he was a soldier.

I used the tree beside me to claw my way up. The tremors had receded with rest, but if I didn't get my medication soon I wouldn't be able to walk. The prions can't advance, but my nerves don't work so well any more. When he shouted my name a third time, I raised my hand and walked towards him.

Peterson blinked. "A Red Band?"

I thrust my wrist out at him. "Ooo!"

"Blue band? What the hell is a blue band?"

I wanted to slap him. We'd all had a hard night, though, and my emotions had spent the last day scraping over the cheese grater. Instead I held out my hands, palm-up.

"You're needed at the border," he said.

He must have seen the look on my face through the shivering. "I don't make up the orders, lady. I just follow them. Come on."

Peterson had to help me climb into the golf cart. I'd hardly sat when he put the vehicle into gear. I slid across the vinyl as he spun the wheel, almost tumbling out, but he grabbed my arm just in time. Muttering to himself, he stopped the cart and walked around to buckle me in. He cinched the belt and asked if I was okay.

The sudden rush of adrenaline had made my spasms worse. I had to exaggerate my nod to differentiate it from my uncontrolled tremors. I clenched my jaw, trying to hold my face still, and wound up only clanging my teeth together. I had to consciously relax, let my jawbone hang loose, to avoid injuring myself further.

Peterson didn't care about things like gullies or rocks, barely swerving to avoid trees. I rocked bonelessly against the shoulder belt with every bounce and rattle.

We pulled up next to a line of other vehicles in an open grassy space. Peterson unbuckled me. I tried to walk, but the maniacal ride had shaken my nerves too badly to keep my balance. I trembled with frustration until he slipped an arm around my midriff and quick-stepped me towards a cluster of people standing on the other side of the vehicles. Most of the people wore military uniforms, but a few wore business suits. The crowd parted as we approached.

A few yards beyond them stood Richard. Between two Townies.

I stopped dead on my feet. Peterson staggered and grunted, staggering under my dead weight. He tugged, and I allowed myself to be urged forward, to stand near the front, beside a table littered with papers, writing implements, palmtops, and remnants of breakfast.

The woman closest to the Townies said "Here she is." She wore a severe blue pantsuit that probably cost several hundred dollars before it got dragged through a war zone. "As you can see, she's fine. *We* didn't hurt her."

Richard looked at me. "I was worried about you."

I tried to shake myself free of Peterson's grasp. He released my waist. I wavered on my feet, and he put a steadying hand between my shoulderblades. Resenting his touch, but unable to stand without it, I looked at Richard and held my hands open.

"The Townies wouldn't have hurt you. They can't kill anyone. But you might have gotten hurt walking here."

The woman said "He demanded you be brought here before we talked. So talk, Miss Rogers."

I glared at her and tried to say *I'd love to.*

She recoiled as if slapped. "You made all this fuss over a tard?"

I'm still in here, you fucker. In that moment I wished I could walk even more than I wished I could speak, just so I could kick her as hard as I'd kicked yesterday's Townie.

"Seeing her was my condition," Richard said. "Not theirs. Sherry can understand everything you say. If you give her her medication, she'll even stand on her own. And she will break you at cribbage."

"Your condition for what?" demanded the woman.

"Translating." Richard nodded to the woman. "Alice Redwood, vice-president of Montague Corporation for this universe, permit me to introduce Spring and Sand, two representatives of the Townies. Their own word for themselves translates as 'human,' of course. I've taken the liberty of explaining the origin of the word Townie to them. They wish to return the sentiment, and believe it is appropriate to refer to the people from Earth as 'Carnies.'"

"Now you want to talk," Redwood said. "When the Corporation gets the Portal back, they'll bring the Army with them. We will destroy you."

"Carnies have been on this world for ten years," Richard said, hands folded calmly over his stomach. The two Townies stood even more still. A sudden wind ruffled the trees behind them, and carried the ocean's bitter scent to me. "In all those years, you have only managed to injure one Townie."

"We filled you people with bullets!" said Redwood.

"Injured Townies disappear," Richard said. "They heal almost immediately. They come back. Townies don't die. That's how this universe works. Carnies have death. You brought it with you. They really don't understand it."

"We'll figure out how to export it. We have nucleonic bombs. We have designer plagues, superstring viruses, dimensional vortexes." Redwood thrust up a finger with each name, enumerating doomsdays. "Maybe we can't kill the Townies, but we will eat the planet away from under them. Leave them eating vacuum, forever, or burning inside the Sun. We made a trade. You broke the agreement."

"The agreement was that the Carnies could use the space between the Stones," said Richard. "Townies have not, and will not, enter the space between the markers."

"You stormed into our compound!" Redwood said. The soldiers shifted, tension rippling through them like a wave.

"Your compound was outside the markers," Richard said.

Redwood's face swelled and reddened until she looked ready to explode. "You moved the stones!"

"The Townies never said they wouldn't," said Richard. "They saved their resources for quite a time to be able to work that change." Richard still didn't move anything beyond his mouth. He could have been cast from bronze.

"You've taken two-thirds of my people," said Redwood. "What do they want?"

"Initially, they wanted to learn what you did," said Richard. "They wanted to learn about the Portal. About the machines. The Townies have nothing like Carnie technology. Their civilization uses utterly different sciences."

I breathed deeply and slowly, trying to calm the fire spattering along my nerves, willing my muscles to relax, trying to recover some modicum of self-control. No meds, no food, no sleep, and Richard. This wasn't the Richard I had known. The Richard I had known was damaged, incomplete. This Richard might have moved into his shell, might have taken some of his personality, but he wasn't really Richard. He couldn't be. Richard couldn't talk this well, couldn't think this well, couldn't hold his own in an argument.

"Not going to happen," said Redwood.

"They knew that," said Richard. "So they moved the border stones. Everything outside the border stones is their property. Including people"

"What have you done with my people?" Redwood said through clenched teeth.

"They've been healed of their mortality."

Every soldier in the line froze.

"Regrettably, mortality is hard-wired into the Carnie mind. By removing mortality, they've become more Townie than Carnie. They can no longer speak Carnie."

"Then how can you?" said one of the soldiers next to Redwood.

"My brain was already damaged. I'd lost enough of my sense of mortality that the Townies had a blank slate for filling in the missing parts. I am a bridge."

"I want my people back," Redwood said, visibly restraining herself from leaping across the invisible line.

"And we can give them back," said Richard

"As humans, damn it," said Redwood

"Townie human, or Carnie human?" Richard smiled. "I understand you. What has been done can be undone. Your people can be returned to you, as the Carnies they were when they were found roaming free outside the border. The stones can be restored. The agreement can be amended so that the stones can never be moved again. I'm still Carnie enough to know how you think. So long as no Carnie crosses the fence into Townie land, they will still be Carnie property. They will even expand the land an extra ten miles in each direction along the shore, and another twenty miles inland."

Redwood raised her chin, eyes narrowed.

"What do they want?"

Richard raised a hand and pointed. "Sherry."

I staggered. Peterson caught me.

Redwood was staring at me. The soldiers around her were staring at me. The men further along the line shifted, their weapons more closely focused on the Townies and Richard.

"There are other things to negotiate," Richard said. "The poor Red Bands. The Carnie Corporation runs the clinic for public relations. You give prion disease victims a place where they can live, where they cannot get any worse. The Carnie part of me guesses that there's no money put into actually treating the disease, and that it's one hell of a tax write-off."

"What does that have to do with anything?"

Richard shook his head sadly and raised his hands, a very Human Richard gesture amidst his inhuman stillness. "Mortality is human. Your human. You suspend them forever. The Townies would offer them healing. A future. Give them the choice. Or their families. Don't condemn them to live like this."

Did he have tears in his eyes?

Redwood was trembling with rage, on the verge of boiling over everything. "Let me see if I understand. You give us our people back? With their minds and bodies intact?"

"Yes."

"You quadruple our territory, and you won't move the border again?"

"Yes."

"And in exchange, you want –" Redwood swiveled to point at me " – this one Red Band?"

My shaking wasn't nervous plaque any longer. It was fear. Sweat soaked my armpits and trickled down my back. My bowels felt loose.

"Yes," Richard said.

"Why?" asked Redwood.

"My condition for translating. She is a good person locked inside bad flesh. She will be healed."

Redwood stared at me.

I couldn't run. I couldn't get five steps before Peterson or one of his friends brought me down, hogtied me, and flung me across the line.

"I'm sorry," Redwood said, her eyes still on me. She turned to look at Richard. "Listen carefully. Go to hell."

I blinked in surprise. I felt tension ratcheting through the soldiers around me. A weird combination of relief and excitement rippled through me.

"You took my people by force. You destroyed my facility. By force. I want my people back. But there's something else here," Redwood said, stepping forward. "Something evil. You have a secret. I will get that out of you. A real human would never dream of trading one of our own. I don't care if she is a Red Band, a tard, whatever. We will figure out your game." She stepped forward again. "We will figure you out, and we. Will. Break. You."

Maybe Redwood wasn't such a jerk after all.

One of the suited men jumped forward and seized Redwood's arm. She whirled in fury. He softly said "The line. You're on the line."

Redwood's glare could have cut steel. She stormed back. "Montague is coming. Earth is coming. And we will burn your world to ash and stone."

"That's your last word?" Richard said.

"I have a counteroffer. Give my people back. Get out of our territory. Never come again. And maybe we won't genetically engineer something that turns all you Townies into sponges."

Richard shook his head. "The Townies have experience in moving the stones. They can do it before Earth can reestablish the Portal. This time, they will move the stones into the ocean. Force you to march into the sea. Earth will reestablish the Portal on Townie land now. We'll be waiting for them."

"And they'll come in force." Redwood's lips twisted. "You have no idea of the weapons we have these days. And the kind of people aching for an excuse to use them."

"And once they fail, the Townies will heal Earth. The Portal will be on Townie land, after all." Richard had reassumed his inhuman stillness, but his eyes still flickered at me every few seconds. I could see something in them. Maybe I was lying to myself.

I didn't know who would win in a battle between humanity and Townies. Humanity had horrific weapons, but Townies could teleport and heal themselves. Whatever happened would appall everyone.

And both Richard and I would lose.

Peterson supported me with one hand on my back. He didn't worry when I put a hand on the table, as if trying to support myself. By the time I grabbed the dinner knife and leaped forward, it was too late for him to react.

If it had been a flat-out foot race, I couldn't have gotten away. But nobody expected me to stagger towards the Townie line. I shook. I quavered. Tremors rippled down my limbs. But I swung my rippling legs forward, demanding just a few seconds of performance from them, knife in my hand.

I'd grabbed the knife by the blade. Grease-encrusted metal sliced my palm. That was okay. If I was right, I needed to bleed. If I was wrong, they'd heal me anyway.

I don't know if Richard or Redwood were more shocked as I shambled four steps across the dividing line and plunged at the nearest Townie.

I heard rifles snapping into place. Someone shouted "Hold your fire! Hold your fire, dammit!"

The nearest Townie turned to look at me. Its prehensile nose wiggled at me. I imagined that it was in confusion. I savored every sense: the chlorine stink, my own fear-sweat, the coppery scent of my own blood slipping down my hand.

"Sherry!" Richard screamed. "No!"

I raised the hand holding the knife, a trickle of blood dripping down my wrist, and clenched the edge of the blade to the Townie's naked chest.

A line of pain ripped across my palm. I cried out, surprised at just how badly the blade *hurt*. My tremors were a constant ache, but this felt like I'd pressed my hand onto a hot wire. I felt the Townie's skin part, the knife edge digging into his flesh as it sliced mine. Our blood ran down his chest, streaming and separating and coalescing around the black hair on his stomach.

For a long moment, nobody moved.

Then the tremors claimed me. I fell back from the Townie with a shudder. My left hand tried to clasp my bleeding right, but I couldn't move well enough. A spasm rippled down my back, then I toppled to the grass. I choked back a shriek.

The Townie gave his own shriek. He starfished on his feet, limbs spasming, and toppled backwards.

I hardly dared breathe.

The Townie screeched, thrashed, and lay still.

Richard said "Sherry?"

Then the injured Townie sat up, with an overstretched smile on his face, and gave a distorted chuckle.

Shock rippled through the human ranks, then Redwood said "Get Sherry!"

Men dashed forward, seized me, and wrenched me backwards. Someone stood on my hand as someone else pulled my body, and I cried out as my shoulder lit with its own agony. Then I was almost thrown back into human territory.

The Townie I'd assaulted didn't react, only holding his smile. The other Townie had stepped back. I chose to think it was in surprise.

Redwood studied me. "Did you do that to one of them before?"

I managed to nod.

She set her jaw and turned back to Richard. "Here's the deal. We know how to hurt you. You've been human. You know we'll use it. We nuked our own species just to make a war shorter. You still know that, don't you? You're still human enough?"

"Yes," Richard said quietly.

"So, you're going to return all our people. You're going to expand our territory as you suggested. You're going to stay the hell away from us. I don't understand what she did, but I know you don't like it. And that's all I need to know. Sherry is a weapon, a living weapon, and we will use her at any excuse. Any excuse. Do you understand?"

Richard nodded and turned to the Townie. They communed in silence for a moment, then Richard turned back to Redwood. "It will be as you say. Your Townies will be restored to mortal Carnies within the next hour and returned to the place where they were taken from. Or the nearest open space, for the buildings you destroyed trying to stop us."

The Townie vanished. Richard looked at me, then back at Redwood. "Please," he said quietly. "Please care for her as I would."

Redwood studied Richard's face. "You have my word," she said quietly.

Richard looked at me one last time, turned, and walked away.

Redwood watched him go for a breath, then turned to me. "You, ma'am," she said quietly, "have nukes in your guts." She raised her voice. "Get this woman to medical. And for God's sake, get her the medicine she needs so she can stand!"

They've never used me since.

The rules are different here. Prions can't reproduce. Some genetic diseases are communicable to the Townies. I carry a genetic disease. The Townies have no experience with disease, let alone one that scrambles their genes.

I'm well-treated. The Red Bands get better treatment too, with more caretakers and more recreation activities and better facilities. Specialists come through the new Portal to examine my genes, and other specialists come to examine prion disorders. It's one of *my* conditions for negotiating.

I get what I want. And some days, I want to go to the border. Beyond the stones is Townie space. Within, Carnie. But in the space the stones themselves stand, that six-foot or so ribbon that represents the width of the stones themselves, the inside of the boundary...

That's where Richard and I play cribbage. Or we kick a ball back and forth across the line. There's a twenty-foot gap in the fence, just for my ball. I'm probably the only person in any universe who plays kickball supervised by two machine-gun nests and with two dozen armored soldiers as escorts.

I make myself expensive. Expensive enough that they'll want to replace me. And they're trying. One day, one of the prion researchers will uncover a cure and reverse my damage. Or, one other day, I won't be so important. They'll have other living weapons.

One day, I will no longer need my tattoo.

About the Author

https://mwl.io

Never miss another new release!
Sign up for Michael Warren Lucas' mailing list at
http://mwl.io.

Novels:
Immortal Clay
Kipuka Blues
Butterfly Stomp Waltz
Terrapin Sky Tango
Hydrogen Sleets
Drinking Heavy Water
git commit murder

Nonfiction (as Michael W Lucas):
Cash Flow for Creators – Relayd and Httpd Mastery – PAM Mastery
FreeBSD Mastery: Advanced ZFS – FreeBSD Mastery: Specialty Filesystems
FreeBSD Mastery: ZFS – Tarsnap Mastery – Networking for Systems Administrators
FreeBSD Mastery: Storage Essentials – Sudo Mastery – DNSSEC Mastery
Absolute OpenBSD – SSH Mastery – Network Flow Analysis – Absolute FreeBSD
Cisco Routers for the Desperate – PGP & GPG –FreeBSD Mastery: Jails – Ed Mastery
SNMP Mastery – TLS Mastery

The Networknomicon

See your favorite bookstore for more!

www.ingramcontent.com/pod-product-compliance
Lightning Source LLC
Chambersburg PA
CBHW051604100726
47898CB00001B/224